MARTIN'S EYES

'Written with the flourish of a storyteller and the eye for detail and accuracy of a historian, Martin's Eyes is an engrossing thriller, a searing blend of war, crime, psychology and history.

'Iain Ballantyne perfectly captures the mood, chaos and ambiguity of the immediate post-war period on the Continent, taking the reader into a dark - and often forgotten - world where the line between justice for victims of Nazi crimes and revenge are frequently blurred.'

— RICHARD HARGREAVES'S, AUTHOR OF *OPENING THE GATES OF HELL: OPERATION BARBAROSSA, JUNE - JULY 1941.*

'Martin's Eyes is a terrifically gripping WW2 novel. Beautifully written and wonderfully atmospheric it tells a compelling tale of wartime life in all its aspects. Masterly!'

— MARK ELLIS, AUTHOR OF THE AWARD-WINNING *FRANK MERLIN* WW2 LONDON DETECTIVE SERIES.

'Powerful and gripping - move over Len Deighton!'

— ROBERT LYMAN, HISTORIAN

'This is an ambitious and atmospheric novel of wartime intrigue and adventure. Although it spans many theatres of war - and numerous gritty war stories - it hinges on a small number of characters you come to care about, and who consistently surprise right up to the final pages'

— PHIL CRAIG, AUTHOR OF *1945 THE RECKONING*

'An unforgettable saga of converging destiny of captive and captor, set in the ruins of vengeance-torn Europe at war's end'

— JULIAN STOCKWIN, NOVELIST, BEST-SELLING AUTHOR OF THE *KYDD* SERIES AND OTHER BOOKS

'Iain Ballantyne has written a gripping novel of love, betrayal and espionage spanning the years of the Second World. *Martin's Eyes* is John Le Carré meets Alistair MacLean.'

— GAVIN MORTIMER, AUTHOR OF *STIRLING'S MEN* & *THE PHONEY MAJOR*

'An impressive and highly ambitious debut. The detail is superb, the characters are compelling and the action is relentless.'

— ALEXANDER NORMAN, AUTHOR OF *CAPTAIN DE HAVILLAND'S MOTH*

Iain Ballantyne is an award-winning, widely travelled journalist, magazine editor and author of acclaimed non-fiction books including *Killing the Bismarck*, *Hunter Killers*, *The Deadly Trade* and *Arnhem: Ten Days in the Cauldron*.

Inspired in part by interviews with a real-life Nazi hunter and victims of war crimes in the Second World War, *Martin's Eyes* is his debut as a novelist. It is his first book for Chiselbury.

Ballantyne's assignments in Berlin, Prague, the Balkans, Russia and Austria provided further inspiration for its epic story, as did teenage travels down the Rhine, from Switzerland to the Netherlands. A UK Maritime Foundation Fellow, Ballantyne is the founding and current Editor of *Warships IFR* magazine.

For more information about him, his books, blogs and other stuff visit iainballantyne.com and bismarckbattle.com

instagram.com/iballantyn

x.com/IBallantyn

bsky.app/profile/iainballantyne.bsky.social

youtube.com/@iainballantyne2886

facebook.com/IBallantyneBooks

MARTIN'S EYES

A NOVEL BY

IAIN BALLANTYNE

Chiselbury

Published by Chiselbury Publishing, a division of Woodstock Leasor Limited 14 Devonia Road, London N1 8JH, United Kingdom

www.chiselbury.com

ISBN: 978-1-917837-40-8 (hardback)

ISBN: 978-1-917837-46-0 (ebook)

A CIP catalogue record for this book is available from the British Library

Cover by Indra Murugiah

Printed and bound by CPI (UK) Ltd, Croydon CR0 4YY, United Kingdom

FSC
www.fsc.org
MIX
Paper | Supporting responsible forestry
FSC® C013604

PART I

1

Southern Austria, May 1946

THE HUNTSMAN STALKED his prey through the woods with absolute stealth, very slowly placing each boot-clad foot on the forest floor to avoid cracking dry twigs.

He cocked his head to determine from exactly which direction raucous laughter was echoing through the trees – it was to his right.

The huntsman sniffed the cool alpine air – polluted with wood smoke and the fatty, oily smell of roasting poultry, carried to him on the soft breeze. His stomach rumbled, for he hadn't eaten all day.

In a glade, now no more than 100 yards away, he spotted a fire crackling under chickens on a spit around which sat four cut-throat ruffians - deserters from various armies; a vagabond band of murderers and black marketeers. They turned their hand to anything that produced ill-gotten gains, not least hijacking food relief convoys and pillaging local villages, with no care for those they killed, raped or maimed.

Tied to a tree behind them were the despoiled corpses of two British military policemen they had captured and used for sport, but now the bandits were being careless. Their weapons were not near at hand as they swigged beer from small stoneware flagons and tore at chicken legs and hunks of bread.

Enjoying their al fresco banquet, the bandits were oblivious to their nemesis sliding in behind a nearby fir. With very deliberate, noiseless movement, the huntsman slipped off his knapsack and pulled his G43 short-barrelled, semi-automatic rifle across his chest.

He'd picked the G43 that morning because he fancied a change from the K98k bolt-action rifle with a telescopic sight that he usually favoured. At such close range there was no need for it anyway. It was true that a bolt action rifle offered more consistent accuracy and, over greater distance, delivering harder recoil into the shoulder which could, however, be absorbed and controlled. A more sophisticated, gas-operated mechanism (with more working parts), such as the G43's, introduced variations in aim - a recoil that was harder to control as it went about its business - but, at ranges this close, it was ideal and speed was imperative. To miss in this instance - due to a lack of skill or, more likely, a jammed round - could spell the huntsman's demise, for the bandit gang was four-strong and he was just an army of one.

If the bandits had time to take cover and fire back it would be a hell of a job to eliminate them all – and they might even kill him instead.

Crouching, the huntsman carefully stretched out on his back, head pointed towards the targets. Clutching the rifle to his chest, he rolled to the left, towards a tree felled by a storm, lying forlorn and dead - just food for bark beetles. He stopped after about two yards, staying very still on his back.

In their fireside bonhomie the bandits remained oblivious to him. One of them was roaring with laughter as they swapped war stories, bellowing in great admiration for something a comrade in crime said or just did, the words echoing loudly through the trees.

'Du verdammtes tier!'

'You damn animal!'

As the bandits indulged in nostalgia, their prospects for a future grew bleaker by the second, the huntsman tuning out the cacophony of their revelry to focus on the job at hand.

After rolling onto his front, and holding the rifle tight across the crooks of both his arms, with the deliberate, agonisingly slow speed of a sloth the huntsman leopard crawled the final few feet to the felled tree.

Hidden from sight, he laid the rifle gently on the ground and, carefully rolling onto his back again, loosened the hessian scarf around his neck.

This was all preparatory to kneeling behind the tree, its remaining rather withered foliage helping to hide him and hopefully obscure the gun flash. His beard and longish dark hair would help to reduce the white of his face, and the old brown leather hunting jacket was perfect camouflage too.

The huntsman took a few moments to relax both mind and body, gently inhaling then exhaling, listening to the wind caressing the trees, his blue eyes made translucent in the soft light filtering down.

A red-breasted Barn Swallow settled momentarily on a branch directly overhead, its forked tail twitching nervously. Keeping perfectly still, the huntsman looked up at it as the bird stared down, uncertain of what exactly lay below.

Wasn't it a Swallow that stole fire from Satan and gave it to mankind?

The huntsman's pastor father had told him that tale when he was a child - the fire he was about to rain down on the bandits was cleansing *and surely God's work?* He smiled at that thought, imagining the furious debate with the Old Man it would kindle.

Disturbed by the harsh laughter of a bandit, the bird flew away.

Returned to the task at hand, Martin sighed. Maybe some men would have been filled with righteous anger - curses whirring around their heads and hearts swollen with rage but the huntsman needed to keep a lid on that. This 'God's work' was a mechanistic process.

The united nations of European thugs enjoying their fireside bonhomie outraged him, but, for the sake of his role as the avenging angel of the woods, the huntsman expunged those fiery feelings.

They mustn't intrude into the business of killing – of attaining maximum speed and efficiency in the act of execution – and above all he must ensure his aim was true.

Local villagers were surely grateful for his work - for he was the deliverer of justice in their lawless land. He lived by his own chivalric code and, in those woods, he was, as far as he was concerned, a champion of what was right and good in the struggle against Evil. Nonetheless, he sensed the villagers feared him, too.

On those occasions when he visited on supply runs – to buy eggs, bread, milk and so on - they never asked exactly who he was, or where he had come from. They hardly dare utter a word even in private - except maybe the occasional whispered speculation about what he might have done in the recent conflict. *A soldier, for sure, but exactly what kind…well, it was better not to know.* They just thanked the Lord when they heard the rifle shots resounding through the trees - grateful there would be no survivors, to reap revenge by raiding their homes…or worse.

* * *

How many people had the huntsman killed altogether?

Not even he knew the exact total. He recalled only some of those whose lives he had ended during the war: in 1940 an English tank commander in France foolishly sticking his head out of the turret hatch – a burst of MP40 fire blew apart the man's skull; then there was a couple of Croat terrorists at Split in 1941, shredded by a grenade lobbed into the living room of a villa; there were two or three Russians, in hand-to-hand fighting at Kharkov in 1943, with more of them later sent to their moustachioed maker in Hungary. There were other deaths, and one incident in particular he preferred not to even think about.

Today these bandits in the lawless woods would join the amorphous mass of miscreant scum nobody would mourn, or so he told himself. That even they might have loving mothers or sweethearts he preferred to ignore.

Having as a teenager surrendered to a twisted ideology that

turned everything right and wrong in the world on its head, the huntsman's crusade against crime was, he suspected, an attempt at redemption.

There had been a time, a place and a person who stirred a feeling of love that threatened to redeem him, but it had all faded into the shadows - and now he sought to live by the Book of Leviticus.

'Fracture for fracture, eye for eye, tooth for tooth…'

Though the huntsman was sure his father would condemn him for interpreting such things to suit his aim - feeding his fury and sorrow rather than starving it. The huntsman felt he was delivering a small measure of natural justice - an attempt to hold back the tide of anarchy by way of atonement. It was maybe a futile effort, but it filled the time while he waited for the final pages of his own tale to be written by fate.

* * *

Kneeling behind the felled tree, the huntsman pulled the weapon up into his right shoulder, the beechwood stock warm against his cheek, the smell of gun oil reassuringly familiar.

Calming his breathing, he put his trust in its semi-automatic mechanism and ten-round box magazine enabling swift elimination. The bandits would never reach their own weapons. The first one killed would not even complete his last breath.

The line of sight was clean and the range, for a skilled marksman, point blank. Since receiving wounds during the war, the huntsman's long vision had actually achieved enhanced acuity.

He could pick out even small details from further away than most people. The bandits' gargoyle-like features were shockingly clear: yellowed, brown decaying teeth in gaping maws; hideously bulging eyes wildly flickering from side to side as they relived murderous deeds.

One of the drunken gang – a scrawny fellow, wearing what looked like the moth-eaten remnant of a Red Army fur hat - was holding a flagon of beer above his head and pouring it into his mouth. Some of it spilled onto his clothes, which his comrades found hilarious.

The huntsman slowly swept the rifle barrel from left to right – finally sighting on a ruffian wearing a green woollen beanie cap, a US Army deserter, the one nearest the bandit group's stacked weapons - an assortment in a chaotic tangle, reflecting their owners: a British Sten, an American grease gun, a Russian PPSh-41 submachine gun with its drum magazine, and a German G41 rifle.

The huntsman inhaled, slowly exhaled and when satisfied his aim was true gently squeezed the trigger.

Crack!

The man's head exploded.

Crack!

The scrawny Russian went down – the bullet ripping a ragged hole in his gullet, toppling him off the log to drown in his own blood, the flagon rolling away.

Crack!

Another target, in a frayed and much-patched, broad pinstripe suit, threw himself to the ground, trying to seek cover behind a large log. As he unwisely popped up to see where the assailant lurked a bullet drilled into his forehead.

With machine-engineered efficiency and speed, the rifle's mechanism brought another bullet up into the chamber. Squeezing the trigger again, the huntsman claimed the last remaining bandit – who appeared to be dressed in a charcoal grey trachten jacket – as he tried to escape through the trees. Punched in the back by the bullet, his legs folded like a concertina, the lifeless body dropping with a dull, flour sack thud onto the soft forest floor.

In the deathly silence draped over the woods – animals having flown or scampered away, others frozen in mute silence - his hearing was affected slightly. Not like the crashing cymbal effect of cannon fire, but rather a buzzing.

The huntsman got to his feet and slung the rifle behind his back.

He pulled a Walther PPK pistol from the holster on his left hip, which was attached to a broad, brown leather belt.

Hoisting the knapsack onto a shoulder, keeping an eye on the, hopefully, slain - wary for signs of life - he slowly walked over to the birds still roasting on the fire. The huntsman pulled off a chicken leg. Teeth stripping it, he stared at the dead British soldiers tied to the tree. Their faces were all mashed up – one of them had an eye hanging out. Not even a flicker of emotion passed across the huntsman's face. He had seen far worse in the charnel house of the Eastern Front.

Casting away the chicken bone, wiping the grease off his lips with the back of his left hand, the huntsman inspected the corpses of the bandits.

All well and truly dead. The huntsman holstered his pistol.

Curious about the one with the pinstripe suit, the huntsman opened the jacket, pulling a wallet from a pocket.

In it he found only a single British Armed Forces ten shilling note, occupation currency, and a well-worn photo - possibly the suit-wearer, but in some kind of infantry battle dress uniform, posing unsmilingly for the camera with a similarly sombre young woman.

A sweetheart, or even his wife?

The huntsman discarded the wallet, some of its contents, including the snapshot, falling out to be scattered by the breeze.

Taking the bandits' ammunition pouches, slinging them over a shoulder, he smashed their weapons with great force one-by-one against tree trunks to make them useless.

The ammunition and a small flagon of beer were placed in his knapsack while at the same time he retrieved a cotton pillowcase from it. The huntsman kicked dry soil over the fire, removed a roasted chicken from the spit, putting it into the pillowcase.

Satisfied he had taken whatever was useful, the huntsman went over to the fallen tree and gathered up his still-warm bullet casings, or as many as he could spot.

Raising one of them to a nostril, the huntsman inhaled the acrid metallic rotten-eggs-with-a-hint-of-nail-polish tang emanating from its burned propellant.

It took him right back to a room in a Ukrainian tenement, the flames of a burning T34 tank outside in the street making the scene brighter than day. The stink of cordite and body odour was in the air. A tear trickled down the cheek of a young woman whose hand he held in his own as she died in a pool of blood on the floor. The glimmering tear track shone wet even after her eyes had lost their spark.

Frowning and blinking to erase the flashback, the huntsman slipped the casing into the same pocket as the others, then tightened the hessian scarf around his neck. Adjusting the knapsack straps and picking up the pillow case containing the roast chicken, the huntsman melted into the woods, leaving behind the corpses for animals and insects to dispose of.

* * *

Backtracking twice, the huntsman waited patiently each time with his rifle at the ready, making sure nobody was trailing him as he made for the abandoned lodge that was his base. Set back in the woods, out of sight from the main road, it was serviced by a spur track just wide enough to take a single, small vehicle - its access was therefore limited and easy to monitor.

Keeping himself in the shadows of some trees, the huntsman paused for precautionary observation of the lodge's exterior and its surroundings.

He tensed at the unfamiliar sound of a combustion engine.

An olive green-painted jeep with a lone occupant came along the track, pulling up by the front door of the lodge. The Allied soldier climbed out and knocked on the front door, disturbing Jackdaws ground-feeding nearby. They rose screeching and squawking into the air while the Allied soldier disappeared from view, around the rear.

Leaving the pillowcase containing the roast chicken by a tree, the huntsman sprinted over, knapsack banging heavily on his back, beer in the flagon sloshing around. Edging his way down the side of the lodge, the huntsman found the Allied soldier peering in the kitchen window. The visitor wore a light green beret, shoved back off his forehead, both hands cupped over his eyes, face pressed against the glass. There were three pips on the epaulettes of his khaki battle dress, indicating an officer. The huntsman raised his rifle to waist height, finger caressing the trigger very lightly.

'What do you want?' he asked softly, in almost accent-less English. They were the first words the huntsman had spoken to another human in some days. The Allied officer tensed and slowly turned his head, his grey-blue eyes widening for a second.

'Go in, please,' the huntsman instructed, 'it isn't locked.'

Once they were in the kitchen, the huntsman told the Allied officer to sit down at its large wooden table.

'Very carefully pull your pistol from its holster and place it in front of you.' The Allied officer meekly complied with this instruction.

Sitting down in the chair opposite, the huntsman laid his rifle and the knapsack on the table, pulling out the Walther and pointing it straight at the other man.

With cold eyes and a mirthless smile, the huntsman enquired lightly: 'Beer?' The Allied officer frowned at this incongruous idea.

'A small one perhaps?' the huntsman suggested. 'Please, get up and take the jug and two glasses from the cupboard behind you.'

The huntsman laid down his own pistol beside the Allied officer's Browning Hi-Power and pulled the small flagon from his knapsack, placing it on the table with a thump. 'Sit back down,' he ordered, 'take the stopper out and pour some beer into the jug.'

As the Allied officer did this, the huntsman studied him: tall, reasonably well built, an open face and with what looked like the letters S.G. mounted in silver on his battle dress blouse collar. The man's dark green woollen tie was snug at the collar of his khaki drill shirt. His beret sported a rose emblem badge. By the look of him, this was definitely an officer in the British Army. Having finished pouring some beer into the jug, the Allied officer sat down and took his beret off, revealing a full head of fair hair. He put it down next to the Browning, eyes fixing momentarily on the pistol - tempted to make a grab for it - something that did not go unnoticed by the huntsman.

After picking up the glass and gulping some beer down, the

huntsman made small talk to relieve the tension, all the while ready to kill the Allied officer.

'What brings you here?'

'Passing through.'

The huntsman pursed his lips in doubt.

'It's a long way off the beaten track,' he ventured and then asked: 'What's your name?' He gestured for his empty glass to be filled again and, as beer glugged in, the other man revealed: 'Captain Eric Wise of the British Army…and you are?'

'A simple huntsman – my name is irrelevant.'

Eric refilled his own glass, thinking it very interesting that this so-called 'simple huntsman's' weapon was a semi-automatic rifle.

Despite his beard and untidy mass of dark hair, the other man, so Eric judged, was the product of Teutonic militarism.

'It was stupid of you to drive around on your own, if I may say so captain,' the huntsman observed, 'these are dangerous times and the woods are filled with savagery.'

'True,' admitted Eric, 'but my men are busy elsewhere.'

'Oh, with what?'

Eric decided to make a big revelation in the hope of provoking a reaction. 'I am investigating a war crime – they are busy digging up the evidence in the woods nearby.'

The huntsman's expression was deadpan as he offered:

'I cannot help you. I am a newcomer – since the war was over.'

Eric prodded again.

'What unit were you in?'

The huntsman turned the half empty glass in his right hand, studying the glowing amber liquid and then looked straight at Eric, claiming with a broad, confessional grin: '5th Gebirgsjäger Division.'

'A mountain division?'

The huntsman smiled and nodded, seemingly impressed with the Englander's knowledge of the German military.

'You were taken prisoner and released?'

'No,' admitted the huntsman. 'I made sure I got as far to the West as possible and discharged myself.'

The huntsman reached for the jug and, as he did so, Eric lunged for the Browning, but the other man was quicker. Leaping to his feet he karate-chopped Eric on the right-hand side of his neck, just as the British officer's fingers were closing around the pistol butt.

Eric toppled from the chair onto the floor with a groan, curling up in agony. The huntsman helped him back into the chair, taking the Browning and putting it in a drawer on his side of the table.

With Eric still stunned, the huntsman smartly fetched a bottle of pear schnapps and two shot glasses from a cupboard above the sink.

'You are lucky I did not use my full force, or you'd be dead,' the huntsman remarked equably, placing the glasses on the table alongside the flagon. Sitting down again, he poured some schnapps, pushing a glass towards Eric, who was still slumped in the chair rubbing his neck and groaning from the pain.

'Drink,' the huntsman suggested, 'it will help – please don't try any more funny business.'

Eric felt his gut tighten – this huntsman surely had the better of him - but even so, he enquired defiantly: 'Will *you* at least tell me *your* name?'

The German glanced away for a second, evaluating whether or not to comply, then returning his eyes to Eric, volunteered: 'I am Martin Walder.'

Gently hammering the stopper back into the schnapps bottle, he added: 'Actually, I am a former officer in the Waffen SS.'

Eric frowned, puzzled by the other man's easy admission. He might have known this hard case was from the Waffen SS, the shock troops of the recently deceased Third Reich. Eric knocked his schnapps back, its burn kindling his resolve to somehow prevail, while Martin banged his empty shot glass back on the table and growled: 'Pour me another, Englander.'

With a grimace at his throbbing neck, Eric did the honours.

Martin raised the glass and exclaimed: 'Zum Wohl!'

Cheers!

After knocking the schnapps back, and putting the glass down, Martin picked up the Walther and waggled the gun barrel towards the bottle.

'Before I settle on what to do with you, let's have a few more drinks. Let's tell our stories - and if I like yours…' The German paused to grin arrogantly and then added: 'Maybe I'll let you live.'

As he reached for the bottle Eric thought this was one Nazi he would enjoy sending to the gallows, but he needed time to recover before making another move. He decided to play along with the pantomime of swapping yarns and toasting each other's good health…

2

Plymouth, England, Night of 28 May 1941

DUST.

It had lain on the buildings for decades, in some cases centuries - composed of coal powder, particles of dirt, fragments of dried horse dung, car tyre slivers or the debris of heel-scoured pavement slabs; not least tiny flakes of human skin and sand from the Sahara.

It had been in eaves, on the sills, in the nooks and crannies of the buildings. Now it was in the air, thrown up by the impact of the bombs, disturbed by the thunderous disintegration of buildings. The dust was in his eyes making them sting and water; it was in his throat, forcing him to retch and cough. It penetrated deep into his lungs, triggering wheezes.

And it was all over him, covering his dark blue uniform with a thin, light grey film. As another bomb shrieked in, Constable Eric Wise of the City of Plymouth Police stumbled for cover. He skidded on something soft and squelchy amid the brick fragments and shattered glass.

A link of sausages from the butcher's shop?

The tip of his boot was covered in blood.

No... it was some kind of raw offal, probably human in origin.

Eric leaned against a wall, stared down at his boot, no longer seeing the hellfire around him or hearing the groaning, creaking snap, crackle and pop of structures teetering on the edge of collapse.

The sight of whatever was smeared across his boot made him retch, though nothing came up. He dug in a trouser pocket for a handkerchief.

There was another deep, earth-trembling roar as a nearby building - weakened by fire ravenously consuming its heart – collapsed into the street.

A fragment of brick bounced across to glance off his steel helmet, making Eric start and blink. Looking down again at his boot he saw it was covered in dust already.

Eric peered around the corner of the building. Looking across the square - known locally as 'the Octagon' - he saw a fire crew wrestling in fury and frustration with a fire main their hoses could not connect to. They had been called in from all over the county and beyond, nearly 800 firemen and dozens of policemen like himself, all trying their best to save the heart of Plymouth from destruction at the hands of the Luftwaffe's incendiaries and high explosive bombs.

* * *

Earlier that evening an imminent air raid had been signalled by sirens wailing across the darkened city, followed by the drone of several aircraft and strings of parachute flares blossoming in the black sky – from south to north, all the way from the Narrows, gateway to the Hamoaze, and over the dockyard and naval base, to Brunel's famous railway bridge.

It was a bewitching display of evil beauty – hot, white flares serenely floating down, starkly revealing ships at anchor in the river or berthed at wharves, along with the giraffe-like massive cranes; the railway bridge's broad, rounded curves; angular pale stone barracks buildings tightly-packed; red brick residential streets of terraced houses huddling next to the great dockyard wall. More pearls of doom were sewn across the sky west to east, leaving the city naked and at the mercy of bombers whose engines could be heard throbbing as they came in across the Channel from their bases in France.

Eric had been chatting with the Army crew of an anti-aircraft gun on the broad, flat Hoe parade ground by the towering Naval War Memorial, whose bleached Portland stone shone in the light of the flares like a navigation beacon for the enemy.

He and the gunners fell into grim silence as they waited for the aerial assault – there had been no firing at the pathfinder aircraft dropping the flares, for their targets would be spindly Dornier bombers whose bellies contained fiery death and destruction.

With the gunners checking their weapon was loaded and ready, Eric turned away from the emplacement and headed across the Hoe towards the spectacular Victorian row of mansions that dominated its western end. Number three was Lord Mayor Nancy Astor's residence and he wanted to check she had gone to the nearest shelter.

As he approached the front entrance, warships anchored out in the Sound by the Breakwater opened up at the first wave of enemy bombers, a nerve-jangling ripple of sharp cracks that saw Eric jump in his skin. He rang the front doorbell, not that anybody would hear it now. Eric hammered on the door and waited, despite a voice screaming inside his head to take cover. He had done his duty and there was apparently nobody at home, so he could move on.

Swiftly rising in intensity and volume, the anti-aircraft fire became so loud Eric no longer heard anything except a background roar – unable to pick out the barking guns filling the air with glowing shells, nor the thrumming engines of the enemy aircraft as they began to disgorge incendiaries and bombs. The hellish, air-wobbling explosions - *Satan playing his timpani!* - made Eric's entire body vibrate.

Now, barely half-an-hour later and turning his face away from the heat of the flames consuming the Octagon, Eric leaned back against the warm brick wall. He felt strangely calm – not like the first night of really bad bombing he had endured, when he was scared witless for most of the time. He'd drawn on every ounce of mental and physical strength he possessed to even take a step as the bombs screamed down. After several nights of it, he had become fatalistic.

In secret moments of self-pity and sobbing fear when off duty - in the privacy of his bedroom - Eric let go of his future, resigned himself to a lifespan lasting days, or weeks…if he was lucky.

'Where's the fucking Royal Air Force!?' exclaimed a gruff voice, interrupting Eric's thoughts.

Eric turned his head to the left, finding a naval fireman, also covered in dust - from tin hat to steel-toed steaming boots; another grey ghost, who grinned and remarked: 'Sorry shipmate, didn't mean to shock you.'

To show his disgust, the sailor spat out a dirty great globule of phlegm.

'I heard them fly boys is nicely tucked up in bed, like they was last night and the night before. Sideways-walking crab bastards, sipping their bleedin' pink gins while we burns.'

Eric said nothing – he knew for a fact that the ancient Gladiator biplanes based at an airfield on the city's outskirts were not fast enough to catch the German bombers. Their own side's anti-aircraft guns might have shot them down anyway. Eric unbuttoned his tunic pocket and pulled out a packet of Senior Service cigarettes, offering it to the naval fireman who declined. 'No thanks, I'm dry enough as it is.' Eric smiled and nodded, putting the packet back in his pocket without extracting a ciggie.

A loud explosion reverberated between the buildings, another of the delayed-fuse bombs the Germans liked to throw into the mix. Eric turned his head to the wall, hunched his back against the shockwave and debris, and lifted a hand to press his steel helmet down.

When it was over and he looked around, the naval fireman was no longer there. *Vanished. Had Eric imagined him?*

Looking back across the square, Eric saw the fire crews had also disappeared. Probably given up and left the Octagon to burn.

He was all alone in Hell.

Still, he had to maintain his patrol against looters. *Those sods were always active during the bombing.* Sure enough, as he carefully picked his way across the square - stepping over burning timbers and the occasional singed body part - he saw a dark shape flitting about amid the blown-in shop front of a haberdashery. Running, Eric bellowed: 'You there!'

It was lost amid the roar of the flames, so he yanked on the chain of his whistle, pulling it from its tunic pocket. Putting it to his lips, he blew but it issued no sound – *clogged with dust.* Eric shook it and, with a disgusted grunt, let the whistle drop to swing on the end of its chain against his chest. As he burst in through the front window – glass blown in earlier by an explosion – Eric almost tumbled over the sill.

The dark shape bolted, crashing through what remained of a door into a side street. A roll of cloth appeared to be tucked under one of its arms.

Plunging into darkness in the shop interior, Eric fought his way through a jungle of torn curtains, spilled rolls of silk and fluttering reels of ribbons. Cursing, leaning against the door frame to cough up some dust, he glanced up an alleyway opposite and saw a dark huddle of something no longer alive.

Much though it filled him with dread, as a policeman he had to investigate. Whatever it was would need clearing up with the rest of the awful debris. Crossing the road to take a look, for the second time that evening the inferno around Eric faded to nothing, his focus narrowing to a vision of chilling horror.

They must have been making love when the shrapnel cut them down; a sailor in his best going ashore rig and a pretty young girl. She was clearly not one of the prostitutes that frequented nearby Union Street.

Her face was familiar, though – untouched, as if she was asleep, still perfectly made up. Just the lipstick was smudged slightly, from kissing in the moment of death. Her long dark hair was in disarray, but it had been pinned up in that popular piled-high style.

Then he twigged.

Fucking hell.

It was alderman whatshisname's little girl. He was a good bloke; bit of a drinker, but one of the better civic leaders in Wise's book - a firm supporter of law and order.

Why hadn't they gone to a shelter?

Boy meets girl, seeking urgent release amid the terror of war. Or so he deduced. There was a small hole in the sailor's neck, at the base of the skull. On lifting the lad's body slightly, Eric found blood soaking the girl's flank, turning the white polka dots on her navy blue dress crimson.

Crouching by the entwined lovers, Eric pondered what to do.

Moving his gas mask box and helmet satchel around to the front, digging out a lighter and pulling the cigarette packet out of his right breast pocket. He lit up and pondered the delicate situation, actually glad of the momentary break from his beat amid the inferno.

If he left them here like this, there would be a scandal.

She didn't deserve it.

Nor did her dad.

Nor did *her* reputation.

Screw the sailor's...

Jolly Jack was doing what sailors did. His shipmates would, no doubt, toast his memory with a tot of rum and crudely remark that at least Jack went out - as he would have wanted – by dipping his wick.

But, the alderman's daughter?

She wasn't the first to be caught doing something foolish down a back alley with a smooth-talking sailor. With the blood rush of youth amid sweet talk about Jack not wanting to die a virgin on his next Atlantic patrol, and her wanting to live life to the full - *what with the bloody bombing* - and the sheer excitement of the war.

Even so, what was she doing out on a night like this?

Couldn't even be 20-years-old.

Eric glanced up, watching the searchlights criss-cross the sky just as a German bomber strayed into the beam of one. Two or three zoned in on the enemy aircraft, fixing it for destruction.

All over Plymouth, and aboard warships in the dockyard and anchored in the Sound, anti-aircraft gunners fixed the Nazi plane with a baleful stare through their gun sights.

A symphony of revenge was written across the heavens, climaxing in a crescendo of hate, the metallic thump and crack of the weapons spitting fiery death into the night.

Eric drew himself under his helmet, making as small a ball as possible – not easy for a man who was 6ft tall. The steel protection his headgear offered was meagre and hot shrapnel from the exploding British shells pattered down around him. He yelped as the still lit cigarette cupped in his palm burned his skin. It dropped to the ground, the ash tip glowing but soon fizzling out on a damp alley paving stone.

After the rain of metal stopped Eric peeked out from under the brim of his helmet. The glowing sky was empty of enemy aircraft, with searchlight beams silently switching back and forth, finding no victims to hold in their glare. Returning to his dilemma, Eric looked at the corpses of the lovers, noticing the sailor's back was smoking where tiny shell fragments had penetrated the thin uniform jacket. Couldn't hurt now, though.

The solution was obvious.

Eric stood up and got to work. First of all, he pulled the sailor off her, glad to see intercourse had not actually begun, that they were merely necking at the moment of death. Eric closed the boy's eyes, to lessen the lad's surprised look, which was unsettling. He dragged him down the alleyway, away from the haberdashery shop end. It wasn't easy, 'but', he reflected, 'lugging a corpse was hardly likely to be so.' As he grunted and sweated, he recalled all the times he had helped puny ambulance men get the bodies of murder victims onto stretchers.

The sailor's head bumped along, which would be a give away if a coroner properly examined him, but the likelihood was he would swiftly be sent for burial in the naval section of a city cemetery.

After fetching the boy's hat, he placed it nearby, rolling him over onto his side against a wall of the alley. Those who came to collect him might otherwise wonder how the matelot got shrapnel in his back. 'Sorry lad,' Eric said to the corpse, patting Jack on the shoulder.

He decided to leave the girl where she was, gently rearranging her legs and pulling down the petticoat and dress to preserve her modesty.

Eric was glad her eyes were closed. He pulled a strand of hair away from where it had become glued to her lipstick.

'Bloody Germans,' he sighed, feeling an upwelling of grief not just for this poor dead girl, but his home city - so sorely abused by the nightly blitz.

Going back down the alley, adjusting the chinstrap of his helmet - recomposing himself - Eric stepped out, looking around to see if there was anybody else in sight. Luckily, no, so he walked over to the haberdashery, carefully climbing in again through the shattered front window.

Searching amid billowing rolls of material, he found some white chiffon and sprang the roll of material from its holder. He dragged it across the shop to the main counter. Opening a drawer Eric pulled out a pair of large, serrated-edge scissors and cut some off.

Gathering material in the crook of his right arm he climbed back out through the window and ran across to the alleyway.

Eric draped it over the girl's head and shoulders, a veil for her poor, lost beauty and shroud for a future stolen by jagged death. He weighted it down at the corners with some lumps of shattered brick. She would never be married, but she deserved some grace in her passing. Or as much as could be afforded.

After a farewell glance at her pretty face - faintly visible, seemingly asleep, not yet eaten away by the cold corruption of death - he walked quickly down the alleyway, stepping over the sailor's corpse, apologising. 'Sorry, no shroud for you Jack.'

Striding out into the street, Eric found the city centre was now comparatively quiet. The remnants of nearby buildings continued to burn with a roar, but the anti-aircraft guns remained silent.

Walking down the street towards Millbay Docks, glass crunching under his hobnailed boots, Eric felt very weary. The adrenalin surge having seeped away, he was now exhausted and on edge all at once.

He passed the smoking ruins of Millbay railway station, its sign dangling at a comical angle from a platform awning. Before the war he'd stood outside it, on crowd control duties when the transatlantic liners came in carrying Hollywood royalty. The likes of Charlie Chaplin, Errol Flynn and Bette Davis used to disembark straight onto a fast train for London. Now look at it: all torn and ragged, beaten about and distinctly unglamorous.

Beyond the shambles, a white band of light in the east - over the roof tops and tall chimneys of the miraculously untouched Duke of Cornwall Hotel - heralded curtain up on another day in the drama of war.

Eric spotted a couple of middle-aged Air Raid Precautions wardens sitting on a railway trolley, smoking cigarettes and leaning back against empty metal milk churns, others of which were scattered on the ground around them. The ARPs didn't notice the young policeman until he was standing right in front of them, Eric giving a polite cough to attract their attention. Tired, glazed eyes in blackened faces took in the dusty wraith before them without any sign of comprehending who or what he was.

'There's a couple of bodies down the alleyway opposite the Octagon Haberdashery,' Eric told them. No reaction at all, except to carry on puffing their ciggies.

'I want you to get some of your pals and go and get them so they can be dealt with properly.'

The ARPs still gave no affirmative response.

What did it have to do with them?

They were all in. They'd had a hell of a night.

Eric was all out of patience.

'Snap out of it you two and go and get on with it or I'll arrest you.' This got their attention. Helping each other off the trolley, the ARPs brushed past him, Eric turning to watch them go.

While his companion carried on, one of the ARPs swung

around, eyes blazing with anger. 'You think I didn't have a belly full of this in the last buggerin' war sonny?'

'Get on with it,' Eric urged him gently.

But the man wasn't finished yet.

'If you wants to order people around why don't you go and join the bloody army and see how you like it when Fritz is trying to blow your brains out?' Eric teetered on the edge of punching him or laughing hysterically in his face. It was all too ludicrous. Adopting a pseudo-posh voice, Eric remarked:

'I don't think it was Saturday night at the Palladium, do you old boy?'

The other man was stunned by this unexpected response; finally registering Eric's own dust covered, smoke blackened appearance.

He broke into roaring laughter. Still shaking with mirth, he turned away to follow his mate, saying over his shoulder: 'Alright son, go home, we'll do the rest.'

Eric watched the ARPs for a few moments, amazed by the ability of the British Bulldog to laugh in the face of disaster; *the old bastards*. He smiled.

As rays of sun kissed the edge of the railway platform, or what remained of it, Eric headed down the road towards the police station to clock off.

* * *

An hour or so later, as he made his way home, Eric's boot steps echoed on the cobbles of New Street, a shady way on his route from the wide-open green of the Hoe to Sutton Harbour.

The tight cluster of houses, pubs and bonded warehouses around the ancient anchorage had once been the heart of Plymouth's, if not England's, renown and prosperity – a bustling piratical haven into which the stolen treasures of the world were sometimes brought.

In British propaganda literature, invoking the nation to gird up its loins against the Nazi menace, the spirit of the seadogs who took on the Spanish Armada - setting sail from *this very place* in 1588 - was often invoked.

Helmet back in its bag and bouncing jauntily on his hip - uniform still greyish and with a slight breeze ruffling his hair - Eric could rightly feel that he'd shown some of that Elizabethan defiance.

It was a pleasure just to still be alive.

At the bottom of the hill, a postman whirred by on his bike, heading up around the seafront, waving and yelling out a cheery 'good morning constable!' Eric waved back, then lifted his face to bathe in the sun's warm glow as it climbed higher in the east above Jennycliff.

Avian screeching drew Eric's attention to the ornate, iron-framed covered fish market to his left, where trawlermen were off-loading the early morning catch. Seagulls were hovering over the quay with frantically beating wings, swooping every now and then to pick up scraps. It was a reassuringly familiar scene. No matter what, the fishermen put to sea to make their harvest - the centuries old rhythm of their trade could not be halted by the Nazis or anyone else.

Walking across the road, Eric headed for the free-standing portico with its Doric columns atop the old seawall by the so-called Mayflower Steps. He was pleased to find a small wooden ferryboat nestled at the bottom. It would not be high tide for another six hours, so Eric clattered all the way down. 'Good morning Fred,' he said to the grizzled old seadog sitting in the stern. One elbow on the outboard motor, the other bent under the pipe upon which he sucked impassively, the ferryman murmured in a haze of smoke: 'Mornin' Constable Wise.'

Climbing aboard with elaborate care due to his fatigue, Eric slid along to sit in the bow, looking expectantly at the ferryman. Fred shoved his ancient, rather greasy Breton fisherman's cap back off his brow and got up. 'What a bloody mess they German buggers must have made last night,' Fred observed, legs apart in the bottom of the boat to keep his balance, as he pulled on the starter cable for the motor.

Fred slumped back down in the stern, while Eric pushed off from the steps with a boathook retrieved from the bottom of the boat, which turned around, emerging from the shadow of the harbour wall.

'A right old shambles,' Fred mumbled, his pipe assuming a defiant upwards tilt as he clamped hard on its stem.

Eric was too tired to comment and just nodded, gazing across the water towards the far horizon beyond the Breakwater, a dark, thin scar across the Sound. In the foreground, a Royal Navy cruiser - drab grey and rust streaked - was following the deep channel around, headed for the Narrows to go up river to the dockyard.

Its high-angle guns were still pointing into the sky, now glinting where the paint had been burned off the barrels by furious barrages hurled at enemy bombers. The sound of a bugle as a Royal Marine played the call to hands over the public address system drifted across the water. The warship's screws churned harder as the vessel turned tightly, sliding past the foot of the Hoe and out of sight.

The turbulence caused by the cruiser's passing reached the small ferry boat, rocking it violently, making Eric reflexively grip the side and Fred grind his pipe's mouthpiece with a growl.

An image of the dead girl's face under her chiffon shroud flashed into Eric's mind. *Asleep. Not dead.*

The gentle bump as they reached the seawall steps at Turnchapel Wharf brought Eric back to the present. He reached into his trouser pocket for some coins but when he held out his hand, Fred shook his head. 'You keep 'em and buy yourself a pint on me,' the ferryman suggested, puffing out smoke and giving a wink.

Eric smiled, put the coins back in his pocket and, grabbing the coaming, clambered over the side. He pushed the boat back off, gave Fred a wave as the ferryboat headed back across to the Barbican.

Feeling a spurt of energy as he bounded up the steps, Eric paused to gaze at Plymouth over the water. The sun was turning the smoke and dust cloud hanging overhead into a kaleidoscope of golden, purple and brown hued greys, all shifting slowly in the wind. The surface of the Cattewater twinkled and the Royal Citadel - a fortress built back in the late 1600s by order of King Charles II, to repress the people of the town after their support for Parliament in the civil war - towered over the Barbican on its rocky mount. The limestone-dressed Citadel walls gleamed wetly; three barrage balloons bobbed and dipped high above, bucking gently in the wind against steel cables tethering them to trailers parked on the edges of an enclosed parade ground. A Union flag on a pole affixed to the Citadel battlements defiantly lifted itself in the strengthening breeze off the Sound.

3

Bacon.

His dream of it was so vivid, that Eric's mouth was watering even as he slept, the enticing aroma all too real. It even made his stomach growl.

Opening his eyes, he found himself looking at a tiny model biplane he made when he was ten-years-old. Suspended in a cradle of cotton thread hanging from the ceiling, it twisted gently in the warm air coming through his bedroom door, which was slightly ajar.

What was she up to? Mother didn't normally make him anything to eat until he had first been awakened with a mug of tea and a digestive biscuit – but today there had been no morning shake.

Yawning, he wondered what time it was. Turning around the alarm clock on his bedside table, he saw it was one o'clock in the afternoon.

Time to get up.

Throwing the covers off, Eric swung his legs out, scratching his torso through his pyjama jacket. *Was that a man's laugh he heard downstairs?*

Exiting his bedroom onto the landing, Eric paused by a large photographic portrait of his father, George Edward Wise, which was hung at the top of the stairs. Dressed in the best number one uniform of a naval Warrant Officer, Dad's eyes twinkled - his pencil moustache flecked with silver made him look as handsome as a movie star. *How old was he there?* About 45, taken just after he was called back into the Navy in 1938, one of the so-called Naval Service pensioners off to war a year later.

And one of hundreds killed when a U-boat sank the elderly aircraft carrier HMS *Courageous* off Ireland on 17 September 1939. The city's first serious blow of the war – so many families lost fathers, brothers and sons. A date stained in Plymothian blood.

Hauling on and tightening his dressing gown with its chord, Eric thundered down the stairs, eager to find out who this male visitor was.

Entering the kitchen, initially he saw only his mother, Gladys, in her apron hunched over a frying pan. She gave him a strange smile as he came over and kissed her on the brow.

'Morning, mother.'

'Feeling better?'

There was that smile again. Turning around Eric was stunned to find a whole ham taking up pride of place on the kitchen table, and – *my goodness* – even some egg boxes, not to mention a couple of packets of tea.

Picking them up and turning them over in his hands, Eric asked suspiciously: 'What's going on?' And then he understood everything. For there - framed in the open back door - was his little brother, Albert, in his sailor suit, wearing a broad grin, cigarette between the fingers of his right hand. Where Eric was tall and solidly built, Bert was short and wiry, with curly black hair. 'Good morning my sleeping beauty!' Bert exclaimed.

Sticking the cigarette in his mouth, he stepped forward, hand outstretched. Laughing, Eric observed: 'Home is the sailor, home from the sea!' They shook hands, arms pumping vigorously, their mother laughing with delight at her two boys reunited.

'Where did you spring from?' Eric asked, still a little bemused as his mum pushed him into a chair at the kitchen table. Sitting down opposite and stubbing his cigarette out in a petite brown glass ashtray, Bert revealed breezily: 'The *Aztec* got in this morning.'

This was HMS *Aztec*, one of the Tribal Class destroyers, fast and heavily armed – and, like Bert, invariably in a scrap.

'We've been in a fight brother, like you've never seen, so we need some big repairs – plenty going on out there at sea while you lot ashore are loafing.'

Eric did not rise to the bait, for fear of spoiling his mother's joy.

She was fussing around, moving the goodies off the table - to the larder - coming back to slap Bert's left shoulder with a tea towel. 'Don't be cheeky to your older brother! He was out in the middle of it all last night.'

Bert suddenly looked sheepish.

'We saw the smoke for miles as we came in - was it really bad?'

Eric nodded, reaching for the steaming cup of tea his mother had just placed in front of him. Two plates, each piled high with eggs and bacon and fried bread soon appeared before them. 'You going to sit down then Glad?' enquired Bert through mouthful of grub.

She gave her youngest son another slap with the tea towel.

'Don't speak with your mouth full.'

'And don't call our mother "Glad",' Eric suggested, genuinely offended by his brother's lack of respect.

'Sorry,' Bert grinned back, while Eric ventured: 'It's all those Londoners he's mixing with in the *Aztec* – she's a Chatham ship.'

Bert carved into a rasher and speared it on his fork, before adding a piece of egg white, correcting his landlubber brother's lingo:

'*On* Eric, us lot serve *on* a ship, only the officers are posh enough to serve *in* it.'

Grinning cheekily, Bert popped the fork-full into his mouth while Eric's own knife and fork hovered over the eggs and bacon. There must be weeks and weeks of rations on his plate alone and so he felt dubious about digging in. He sighed, finally giving in and fell on it with gusto.

Cup of tea in hand, Bert asked his mother: 'Aren't you going to eat with us?' She shook her head.

'Later. I shall just enjoy watching my boys if you don't mind.'

Eric knew she would hoard the treasure Bert had brought home. He gave his brother a hard stare, putting his knife and fork down. Bert looked at him quizzically. 'Lost your appetite?'

'Where's it all from?'

Bert, very nonchalantly – *too nonchalantly* for Eric's liking - reached for his cigarette packet. 'Nothing to worry about here.'

Their mother frowned, turned away and went to the sink with Bert's empty plate and cutlery.

Bert grinned defiantly, eyes flashing with irritation.

'Always the policeman, eh Eric?'

This was like old times – the younger brother doing something suspicious that could land them all in the dung and the older one seeking answers to avoid trouble.

'Don't fret. German shells took out the ship's refrigerator machinery and most of the galley, so they said we could take what we wanted. I was lucky. I got in there first.'

Eric maintained his hard stare.

Their mother had stopped washing the dishes and turned to observe, an anxious look on her face.

'Bert, tell me you haven't been up to any tricks?' she pleaded.

He made an X on his chest. 'Cross my heart; it was a hell of a fight you know, that *Bismarck* business.'

Bert did not appear to be lying, but there again he was always very convincing. Eric capitulated and shrugged.

'Haven't seen a paper for days, nor heard the radio.'

He began eating again, satisfied - for now - that Bert had come about this bounty by fair means. Bert pushed his chair back and stood up, remarking: 'You lot might be starving ashore, but at sea we are all very well fed indeed.'

'I'd heard there were no starving sailors,' Eric observed drily.

'Come on then old man,' said Bert, picking up his cigarette packet and matches and lifting his cap off a hook by the back door. 'Let's pay a visit to the Boringdon Arms.'

Eric looked at the kitchen clock.

Just past opening time.

Slowly folding the remnants of his last rasher onto the prongs of his fork, he dipped it into egg yolk. 'Blimey, I've only just got up' he mumbled as he chewed but Bert didn't want to hang around.

'I'll see you in there.'

Gladys wore a troubled expression on her face as she came over to pick up the cups and saucers. Looking up at her, Eric realised his mother's thoughts would be of her sailor husband's final cheery farewell, as he too disappeared out that back door - never to return. Eric placed a reassuring hand on her forearm.

'Don't you worry about Bert.'

'It's just good to see the two of you together,' she sniffed, eyes moist.

He pushed his chair back and got up, stretching his arms out for a yawn. 'I better follow up and see he doesn't get into mischief.'

'I'm glad I've still got you at home,' she observed, turning back to the sink. Eric paused on the threshold. 'Even with the bombing?'

She turned and smiled.

'At least I know where you are.'

He nodded and laughed: 'Yes, mother, indeed you do.'

As he went back upstairs to get washed and dressed Eric frowned, wondering if he could endure being blitzed in Plymouth without any chance of hitting back at the Germans. The urge to do something, to take some kind of action against the enemy burned within him.

* * *

Pausing on the terrace outside the Boringdon Arms, Eric peered through a dirty pane of glass in the saloon door. He could tell from the beguiled smile of the buxom barmaid that Bert was working his magic, or trying to. He wondered what jewels from the *Aztec*'s knocked-out refrigerator he had promised her. Perhaps some pork chops, or sausages - *whatever would work?* Hearing the door open and the noise of a passing truck spilling in, Bert turned around and flashed his brother a knowing grin.

The young, impressionable barmaid gave him a warm smile, calling out: 'Good afternoon Constable Wise!'

Eric joined Bert at the bar, surveying his surroundings, which were adorned with various familiar items of naval bric-a-brac on the wall – smoke yellowed engravings of ancient sea battles, with line of battle ships belching huge clouds of smoke as they fired broadsides, holes ripped in their limp sails; ship's crests belonging to vessels long since gone to the breakers yard or sunk in war, including *Caesar* and *Indefatigable* - the former boasting the head of old Julius himself and the motto *veni vidi vici*, the latter a lion rampant above *Deo Adjuvante*. Directly behind the bar, above the spirits optics was a stuffed seagull with a cap ribbon from HMS *Royal Sovereign* hung around its neck while a grubby, crumpled Petty Officer's hat hung from the antlers of a cobwebbed stag's head. An age-dulled silver trophy for *'Devonport Division tug -o- war' 1928'* given to the Royal Marines of HMS *Rodney* even had its own little shelf.

Within all this faded glory, the pub was host only to Eric and Bert along with a couple of tables with elderly male domino players locked in combat, their pipes and cigarettes creating more fumes than a dreadnought.

'Another pint of your best bitter for my brother please Lizzie,' beamed Bert. Blushing a little, the barmaid bent to her task. Bert winked and put some pennies on the bar top. Taking his pint, Eric nudged his brother to draw his attention away from the target of his dubious charm.

'Let's sit down,' he suggested.

Bert could tell Eric wanted a serious word and was tempted to stand his ground at the bar. There was, though, something in Eric's stare, even in civilian clothes, that made him submit and adjourn to a table in a dark corner at the back.

'See you tonight at seven then,' Bert told the barmaid as he departed. Lizzie gave his brother a shy smile that in Eric stirred up the urge to issue a protective caution on her behalf to his brother.

'You're on a promise then?' Eric asked, as they sat down at a small table towards the back of the pub.

He wore a troubled frown as the image of the sailor and the girl lying dead in each other's arms had flashed through his head. Bert supped his pint, before remarking, with a line of white foam on his upper lip: 'Hopefully.'

'Don't get yourself into trouble,' Eric warned.

Bert wiped the foam away, taking his cap off and laying it on the table. The 'H.M.S.' in gold lettering on its ribbon shone as it caught the light coming through a window in the door leading to the toilets out the back.

'No romances yourself then brother?' Bert asked pointedly.

'Not since I broke it off with Eleanor.'

'Good old Ellie,' Bert remarked with a chuckle, recalling the girl's constant suspicion whenever the two brothers socialized. Bert pulled a cigarette out, offering the packet to Eric who shook his head.

'It's crazy you know,' ventured Bert, expelling smoke with a soulful sigh. 'What is?' asked Eric.

'This bloody war.'

'On that point we can agree.'

'Two nights past we were out there in a storm, ship going all over the shop, the *Bismarck* firing dirty great big shells at us, dousing us in spray and shrapnel.'

'Seems like quite a business,' Eric conceded, genuinely impressed.

'Likely, we never hit her with any of our torpedoes, but there I was in the radar shack watching as we tracked German shells - bloody big blobs coming in. I was a bit worried, I don't mind telling you.'

Eric nodded, recalling his own fear the night before, but giving nothing away. Bert leaned forward, grabbed his arm. 'I shouldn't have told you anything about that scrap, so do me a favour and keep mum.'

For added emphasis, he pointed to a framed poster on the wall above them. 'Like it says, "Loose Lips Sinks Ships".'

Eric glanced up at it and bit: 'First of all, I don't know what the hell you're talking about and second, you should know me better than that.'

Bert sat back, grinning cockily.

'Lighten up.'

In retaliation Eric decided to press home the point he made earlier.

'I might do that when I am absolutely certain how you came by all that food - fair means not foul.'

Bert made a show of looking shocked and hurt.

'I was telling the truth. No point in the old *Aztec* keeping all that stuff as it will only go to waste while she's in dock at Devonport.'

Eric couldn't help but smile at Bert's irrepressible cheek, leaning forward to ruffle his brother's unruly hair.

'You never change.'

Annoyed, Bert brushed Eric's arm away, trying to smooth his hair back down again. 'Anyway Eric, I'm glad Jerry didn't put a load of hot metal into you last night.'

Eric shrugged, determined to play it down.

'A policeman's lot.'

Silence fell as they supped their beers, Bert catching the eye of the barmaid and firing a few smiles and winks her way.

Breaking in on his brother's flirting, Eric announced: 'I'm thinking of joining up anyway.' Flashing up, Bert asked him: 'Why would you do that!? It'll break our mother's heart.'

'To hit back.'

'Yes, but after she lost Dad and then I got called up...'

'What do you think I am? Some kind of babysitter?'

'No, but…'

'But nothing; she'll understand. I might be safer anyway than being here.' Bert shook his head and sighed. 'It's not like the pictures you know – most of the time you don't see the enemy and it's bloody boring, but terrifying every now and then.'

'Even so.'

Bert grabbed Eric's forearm and fixed his brother with his own version of a hard stare. Eric almost laughed at this attempt to intimidate, but instead revealed: 'I was thinking of the Army.'

Bert let go of his arm, observing sarcastically:

'That'll make mum feel *much* better.'

Eric shrugged.

'Will they let you, though? You know, as a policeman?'

Bert waited for the answer, but Eric didn't reply, just looked out the pub's picture window at Plymouth still smouldering across the water.

Knowing his luck, they probably wouldn't let him go.

* * *

Just as suddenly as he'd breezed into their lives again, Bert departed, barely a week later. Wartime naval vessels and the men who sailed in them liked to make a big entrance on their return, but hesitated to create much of a fuss when departing.

The enemy must not know where a vessel was going – in order to lie in wait – but also there was something innate in the character of sailors; a love-you-leave-you attitude.

Bert had made a sudden announcement of *Aztec*'s work being completed at Devonport Dockyard in an amazingly fast turn around – *so much for Bert's claim of big repairs in dock*. There was a firm handshake for Eric and a kiss and a hug for his dear old mum. Then Bert was away, kitbag on shoulder, sailor hat at a jaunty angle, whistling tunelessly as he strode down the garden path. Mother was anxious, but she put on a brave face. Eric, meanwhile, was glad of the peace and quiet – free from worrying about what Bert might get up to next.

4

In mid-June Eric was asked by the station's long-serving desk officer, Sergeant George Benson, to go out to Devonport where there had been a burglary at Browns' Haberdashery in Marlborough Street. Booking out a bicycle, Eric set off for a pleasant afternoon's ride across the city.

There were just a few white fluffy clouds drifting in an otherwise blue sky, though smoke and dust from the previous night's raid lingered in the air. The Germans endeavoured to hit the Devonport docks themselves, but often took out terraced houses clustered around the yard or unloaded their deadly cargos on the city centre. The tightly packed Victorian shops of Marlborough Street had taken their share of bomb damage - especially at the end nearest the dockyard.

Eric had made a mental note to stop off at Russell's grocers', to see if he could pick up one of the bags of the home-made broken biscuits they gave away sometimes – doing their bit to cheer people up.

Rationing meant they were seldom as sweet or refined as they used to be, while the current fad for carrot biscuits was the fault of the Government's insistence their carotene helped people see in the blackout (and night fighter pilots shoot down enemy bombers). And also, because if there was one thing the nation had plenty of at the moment it was carrots – there might be no bananas or oranges, but root vegetables thrived in British soil.

Eric knew from the number of people run over each week in darkened streets by cars using headlamps - covered except for a narrow slits of light - that it was likely no matter how many carrot biscuits someone wolfed down, it would not give them owl vision.

* * *

Pushing open the pebble-glass paned door of the shop, it took a few seconds for Eric's eyes to adjust to the dark interior. It was lit only by a single feeble bulb overhead, which revealed rolls of fabric stacked up to the ceiling and below them racks and drawers of ribbons and buttons.

Pulled by a wire attached to the door, a bell tinkled somewhere out the back. This summoned Mr Brown himself, who was small and squat, rubbing delicate little hands on a navy blue apron. Eric noticed a few crumbs on the man's ginger moustache.

The haberdasher smoothed his sparse hair back nervously, enquiring: 'I suppose you've come about the burglary?'

Eric nodded, taking his helmet off, placing it carefully on the dark, highly polished wooden counter. 'That I have Mr Brown.'

The shopkeeper twirled around, his shiny black leather shoes squeaking. 'This way Constable.'

Noticing he still had his bicycle clips on, Eric stooped down to ease them off, placing them carefully on the counter beside the helmet before following on.

He discovered the back door had been smashed in and Mr Brown – who lived in a flat above the shop – reckoned it had happened during the bombing raid, when he'd taken refuge in a nearby communal shelter.

The frame was splintered, with shards of glass on the floor – all left by the shopkeeper where he'd discovered it. This was, he announced proudly, 'to assist investigations.' The door didn't look like it would have put up much resistance and Mr Brown speculated it had been done by outsiders, 'from the slums in the Barbican most likely.' *People in Devonport apparently never burgled each other*, Eric thought, a tinge sarcastically. *Mr Brown was talking cobblers, or whatever haberdashers spouted.* The shopkeeper stared at Eric's pencil as it moved across his notebook, frowning when he saw the policeman smile at some silent joke. Following Mr Brown back into the shop itself, Eric enquired what had been taken.

'White linen - which is very difficult to get these days,' sighed the shopkeeper. Eric nodded sympathetically.

'How much of it?'

'Single roll, which would be about as much as a man could carry…though he'd have to be *very* strong.'

Suddenly an image of dark figure making off through the inferno of the Octagon haberdashery during the blitz flashed into Eric's mind.

A bombing raid burglary.

Roll of fabric under arm.

A big bugger, too.

Eric felt his pulse quicken – *this was a pattern of events. A black marketeer pilfering?* He loathed those who profiteered from the misery of the war, the beggars who robbed and burgled. He thought little of the so-called Dunkirk spirit. *We are not all in it together - some of us are in it for ourselves.*

The shopkeeper coughed and Eric realised he'd been rudely lost in thought, pencil still poised over his notebook

'Is there anything else Constable?' the man enquired rather too eagerly. Eric shook his head, putting the pocketbook away.

'I would get that back door replaced,' Eric suggested, 'and with something more substantial.'

Mr Brown glared at the young policeman as he bent over to put on his bicycle clips. 'What about catching the burglar?'

Putting his helmet back on, pulling down its chinstrap, Eric smiled apologetically. 'Sorry, not much hope of catching him unless he tries to sell it on.' The shopkeeper turned away dismissively, calling over his shoulder as he disappeared into the back office: 'I'll let you see yourself out.'

Feeling embarrassed, Eric exited and all the way back to the station on his bike burned with anger, not so much at the prissy little shopkeeper, but at whoever was sneaking around in air raids getting away with burglarising honest folk.

Sgt Benson told him to log it and then get over to North Road at the top of town. A soldier home on leave had been run over by a coal lorry. On his way up the hill, this time on foot, Eric passed the Plymouth Co-operative Society Drapery and a bright idea came to him.

How about he kept an eye on it next time he was on duty at night?

Returning from taking details of how the coal lorry casualty met his end – kitbag on wrong shoulder, blocking the lad's view of the oncoming traffic - Eric found Sgt Benson dubious about the worth of the proposed night watch. He did, though, recognise that Eric was an eager young copper with a sincere dislike of bad 'uns, *so why not?* 'Only for one night, mind you,' he said, 'as it isn't worth any more than that.'

Deciding not to trouble with going back home across the Cattewater, Eric visited a local café for his dinner, such as it was. As he sat down to a mug of dark brown tea and a fish paste sandwich, he realised that he'd forgotten to pick up a bag of the carrot biscuits from the Marlborough Street grocers. *Munching a few of them might have relieved his night watch boredom and even improved his night vision… or not.*

* * *

Eric's plan was to lodge himself in the Town House pub. It had a window overlooking a street on which the Co-op Drapery sat, in fact almost directly opposite. There was only one way in and out of the shop, too - even for deliveries - and that was the front door.

The landlord was retired Chief Petty Officer Cedric Barlow who'd served with Eric's dad during the Great War. Fortunately for him, Cedric had been just that little bit too old to be called up again or he'd have been killed in *Courageous* too.

Settling himself on a bar stool by a sash cord window – blackout curtains open for just this one night, but lights off - Eric sipped a glass of water. 'Are you sure I can't pull you a proper pint?' enquired Cedric, crinkly-eyed smile lighting up his broad, weather-beaten face. Eric declined. 'No thanks, Cedric, but appreciate the offer.' Eyes firmly fixed on the shop front, Eric added, 'best to keep a clear head on duty.'

Cedric chuckled.

'Not every copper thinks like that.'

'I'm different,' Eric observed quietly.

Cedric squeezed his shoulder and remarked regretfully: 'So was your dad, God bless 'im.' Cedric left Eric to it, locking the doors except for the main one at the front. Eric needed it unlocked should he have to make a swift exit to arrest his burglar. Cedric returned momentarily to deposit a plate of cheese sandwiches and pickled onions on the broad windowsill. Just before he descended into the cellar to join his wife, Cedric suggested to Eric that if the bombers came along he would be very welcome to take cover with them.

Eric smiled and nodded.

'Goodnight son,' the landlord said softly, the cellar door clicking shut, leaving Eric alone in the darkness with only a ticking clock for company.

* * *

No Nazi incendiary bomb firestorm was unleashed that night.

Having finished the sandwiches - but avoiding the onions - not long after midnight, and keen for a break from the wooden bar stool, Eric decided to take a wander over the road. Leaving his blue steel lid and gas mask satchel on the bar in the pub, he gently closed the front door behind him.

The sound of smashing glass shattered the silence and - freezing on the pub's front step - Eric swept his eyes from left to right, hoping to catch movement with his peripheral vision.

Just then a break in the clouds allowed moonlight through. There, caught in a silvery beam, was a shadowy figure hesitating in the doorway of the drapery, roll of white cloth under an arm.

Heart thumping in his ears, Eric did not dare move a muscle. He was sure whoever it was must have seen him. Eric feared the burglar might even hear his pulse, it was beating that hard.

With a crunch of glass, the burglar staggered forward, no longer able to keep still, especially with that heavy roll of cloth.

Eric could just make out a pale face scanning back and forth, along with a white coat – which seemed an absurd choice of clothing for a nocturnal raider.

The miscreant hadn't seen Eric yet, so carried on easing himself over the glass, faint crackling underfoot; then, without any urgency, started to walk up the street, towards North Road railway station.

Eric decided if he waited any longer the burglar might get away.

This time he did not blow his whistle and call out, but stalked the man from the opposite side of the street, parallel to him, but just behind.

The burglar was not casting any glances astern – so confident was he by now of getting away with his stolen goods.

Eric decided to risk crossing the road.

There was a crunch as his right boot crushed a snail's shell.

It had been raining and thousands of them were on the move in the dead of night - a phenomenon that always made Eric nauseous walking home from a late shift. It was very difficult to avoid treading on them.

The burglar snapped his head around and now saw Eric. Both men froze, eyeballing each other – each in a quandary about what to do next.

More snail shells popping underfoot, Eric began to run, fumbling for the truncheon at his belt. The burglar made off at a fast pace, after a few yards dropping the cloth, which rolled down the hill, almost tripping his pursuer up. 'Stop!' Eric yelled hoarsely.

His entreaty was ignored, but the policeman's long legs and adrenalin began to gain the edge. The other man was big, almost as tall as Eric, but he carried more weight and was gasping.

With a loud groan, Eric hurled himself the last couple of feet, lead-lined truncheon raised in his right hand, left hand fingers outstretched to grab the burglar's collar.

He got a hold of the man's coat but in the grapple that followed succeeded only in knocking himself on his right cheekbone with the flailing truncheon. Like some latter-day Houdini, the burglar somehow slipped Eric's grip and got to his feet.

Eric was by now on his knees, still holding the jacket, his truncheon swinging from its wrist strap - confused at where the burglar had gone.

He solved that mystery by delivering a kick to Eric's ribs, the policeman moaning in agony, dropping the jacket and making one last attempt to halt the burglar, by lashing out with the truncheon.

It hit the man's right calf as he began to run away, provoking him to bellow loudly: 'Das tut weh!'

The burglar limped off into the dark while, losing his balance, Eric sprawled in the gutter, moaning.

'Are you alright, son?'

It was Cedric from the pub, peering anxiously down at him, bald pate shining in the moonlight.

* * *

At the police station Eric was eased into an armchair in the office behind the front desk while the police surgeon, Dr Sam Villiers, was summoned to treat his injuries. As the doctor bound his ribs, Eric watched Sgt Benson inspecting what had turned out to be a Plymouth City Corporation bus driver's summer jacket.

With a twinkle in his eye, Benson joked: 'Good collar Constable Wise.'

Eric did not laugh – for fear of it hurting too much. He would be sore for several days, with an ugly looking weal on his face and bruised ribs.

Benson stepped forward and showed Eric a nametag inside the jacket's collar, which read in neatly stitched letters: 'Charles Koehl.'

Benson revealed he'd been on the phone to the bus depot and

Mr Koehl was indeed one of their drivers, a Frenchie who had come over to Devonport in the submarine *Surcouf*. That large craft had managed to escape capture by the Nazis in the summer of 1940, but when the Royal Navy told the French submariners they had to fight on under British command, some of the *Surcouf*'s crew mutinied.

Not many people were aware of the affair - there had been a news blackout at the time - but Sgt Benson saw no harm in letting on now. He told Eric and Dr Villiers - already looking suitably amazed - that British and French sailors had died in a shoot-out aboard the vessel, though Koehl did not take part and was assessed a good sort.

Subsequently declared unfit physically for service in the British fleet, Koehl decided to do his bit for the war effort by getting behind the wheel of a corporation bus. Eric suddenly recalled the man's exclamation during their fight in the street: 'Well, he did say something foreign when I whacked him with the truncheon.'

'You can pull your shirt on now,' Dr Villiers suggested, changing tack to offer an opinion: 'It does sound like a German name.'

Frowning, Sgt Benson sat on the edge of the desk, watching the doctor putting rolls of bandages away in his bag. 'A bloody German? What would he be doing driving one of our buses? They said he was French, I am sure of it, Doc, not a Fritz. How else would he be in their navy?'

The doctor, who was not a young man, groaned as he straightened up, snapping his bag shut and venturing: 'Not necessarily German, but perhaps with sympathies, due to his place of birth?'

The police surgeon's wild thatch of eyebrows flew up, looking from blank face to blank face. 'Possibly from Alsace-Loraine,' he elaborated, 'the provinces Germany took off France in the Franco-Prussian War and then had to give back when they lost the last time?' As he pulled on his overcoat, the doctor asked Eric: 'Can you recall what he said exactly?'

Eric suggested it sounded like 'dash that way?'

Doc Villiers had picked up some German during the previous

war and, after ruminating for a few seconds, suddenly blurted out in a loud voice, as if in pain: 'Das tut weh!'

It was clear to see why the police surgeon was a leading light in the local amateur theatricals. Chuckling, Villiers explained: 'Your miscreant said "that hurt" – it's German, but a lot of the Alsace-Lorainners probably speak it, or a variant, as fluently as French. I tended to a lot of Huns at a field hospital in the Great War. When my ministrations were not as gentle as they should be that's what they said.'

Sgt Benson gave a vexed sigh, twisting the garment in his hands: 'But imagine wearing your own jacket, with your own name in it to do a bloody burglary.' The stupidity of it depressed him but war apparently made burglars dumb and lazy.

'Well, I'll be off,' the doctor announced, sliding past the sergeant, who bade him farewell before returning his attention to Eric as he gingerly pulled his uniform jacket on.

'Shall we pop up to our suspect's lodgings in Milehouse Road and see if we can apprehend him, Eric? Or do you want to head home?'

'No fear – I'd like to get him, if he's daft enough to still be there.'

But of course, Koehl wasn't there and his landlady said she hadn't seen him since the previous afternoon before he went to work. Perhaps he'd gone over to visit his girlfriend. She was a Land Girl on Brook Farm over by Cawsand, the one with the fishing lake. For Sgt Benson that was the end of it – anything over the Tamar was something for the Cornwall County Constabulary to investigate.

As a victim of the burglar's kicks, Eric disagreed. He burned with indignation that a foreigner they had given refuge to was using bombing raids to steal from Plymouth shops.

Benson suggested he would sign Eric off for a couple of days, that he should just go home and forget about it. Eric resolved privately to do some investigations himself and knew just the man to help him and make sure the Frenchie did not get away with it: his old pal Ted Bodman, featherweight boxing champion of the Plymouth Division of the Royal Marines.

At the Stonehouse barracks the duty Non-Commissioned Officer sent a runner across the parade ground to fetch Ted from his block.

He arrived a few minutes later, at the double, most intrigued on why his mate was calling on him in the middle of the night. Eric drew Ted into the shadows of the stone arches that formed the barracks' main entrance. He asked if Ted was off duty the following evening for a little trip into Cornwall.

Short but fiery, Ted had been Eric's back-up in a few playground scraps – and that was what he needed again, only this time to catch a crook. They decided to meet at the Cremyll Ferry slipway.

'Does your cousin still farm over by Millbrook?' Eric asked.

'He does,' Ted confirmed, 'delivers milk and greens for the barracks to the ferry.'

'How does he do that?'

'By lorry – he's allowed petrol to run it.'

'I was hoping that would be the answer.'

'Can he meet us over at Cremyll?'

'I'll phone the local post office and ask them to take him a message.'

'Is he handy in a fight?'

'I should say so.'

Eric grinned broadly.

'Good.'

'Did whoever we're after give you that bashed up face?'

'And some sore ribs.'

A mad gleam entered Ted's eyes, visible even in the shadows.

'Then we must return the favour.'

5

IT CONVEYED the heartbreaking news with brutal, clipped efficiency – a closely typed telegram delivered that morning to the house in Turnchapel.

> From: Commodore,
> Naval Barracks, Chatham.
> To: Mrs Gladys Wise, Catchgate Cottage, St. John's Rd, Turnchapel, Nr Plymouth.
> REGRET TO REPORT THAT YOUR SON ALBERT H WISE, ABLE SEAMAN DP/DRK 10072 IS MISSING PRESUMED KILLED ON WAR SERVICE.

Numb with shock, unable to believe his eyes, Eric turned the piece of paper over. The other side was blank. He now burned with anger:

Was that all they could give by way of an explanation? No location, no cause of death – yes, the fucking Germans did it, but how exactly? – or even a date when his brother had lost his life. He turned it over and read the message again.

And what was this 'missing presumed killed'?

The air of uncertainty offered by 'presumed' was appalling.

Eric sat down at the kitchen table, where he'd found the telegram, staring at the piece of paper while the sound of a dripping tap started to niggle him intensely. *So, Bert was gone, just like their dad – sailed off never to return and no body to bury. Vanished like some kind of cruel magic act.* Intruding on his morose thoughts was *that bloody dripping tap.*

Looking around, Eric glared at the culprit, cursing under his breath as his bruised ribs protested, getting up and going to the sink. With all the force at his disposal, he tightened it, feeling the thread begin to grind. Through the kitchen window, beyond the back garden he could see the dark waters of the Cattewater. The sound of the door into the hallway opening startled Eric. On turning around, he was astonished to find his mother dressed in hat and coat, ready to go out.

'Hello Eric, didn't know you were still at home,' she remarked with mock brightness, her face ashen, eyes red-rimmed from crying.

'I've got a couple of days off. Where are you going?'

'To do some cleaning for one of my old ladies.'

Slumping back against the sink, Eric watched with dismay as she opened a cupboard and pulled out a small wicker basket of polishes and rags.

'But, mother…'

She gave him a defiant glare.

'No, Eric – she needs me, has nobody in the world.'

He sighed.

'I think today of all days, she'd understand.'

His mother shook her head. Firmly grasping the basket in her left hand and walking to the back door, she turned to him with tears in her eyes:

'I've still got you Eric, haven't I?'

He nodded, smiled and, after she'd gone, went back to the table, picking up the telegram to read it again. With an angry growl, he screwed it up into a ball and threw it across the kitchen, but instantly regretted it. Fetching it back he smoothed it out and left it in the centre of the kitchen table, weighed down with a pepper pot. It was, after all, possibly the only acknowledgement his mother would ever get of Bert's sacrifice and she could keep it in the same dressing table drawer as her husband's telegram.

With dark resolve he knew that he had to get out of the police force, to go and kill some Germans. First, he needed to get a few hours' sleep so he could catch a French black marketeer and bring him back across the River Tamar to face justice in Plymouth.

* * *

After meeting Ted at the barracks, both of them wearing their uniforms under raincoats - to give them some authority in their endeavour, but still subtle - they walked the short distance down to the ferry.

On the way Eric told him about Bert's death. Not having known Eric's brother well, Ted was gruffly sympathetic and most concerned for Mrs Wise. He'd enjoyed a few of her bacon and egg breakfasts in his time.

'She's keeping busy,' Eric reassured him.

The Cremyll Ferry was a one-time steam-powered naval picket boat converted to carry passengers, boasting a long cabin forward lined with bench seats. Eric and Ted were the only passengers for the five-minute crossing to Cornwall. Once they were settled in, Eric enquired: 'What's in the gas mask bag, Ted, surely not a gas mask?' Grinning, Ted hoisted it onto his lap and unbuckled it, offering Eric a look inside. He saw a metal thermos flask and what looked like two packages of sandwiches wrapped in greaseproof paper.

'Essential provisions,' the Royal Marine remarked proudly.

Turning on the bench so his back covered the view from the cabin where the helmsman and his crewman were, Ted pulled one of the packages out and partially opened it. It was a snub-nosed Browning Hi-Power pistol, of a kind Eric had heard about and seen in photographs but never for real. The sight of it twisted his gut and he asked angrily: 'Why did you bring *that*?'

Taken aback, Ted offered lamely: 'I thought we'd need a bit of firepower.' As an embarrassed Ted buckled up the gas mask bag, Eric explained: 'We're going to arrest this blighter, not kill him. Couldn't you get into trouble taking that out of barracks?'

To hide his annoyance at his friend's reaction Ted looked over the side of the boat at the foamy water rushing past the hull.

'I thought we were hunting Nazi saboteurs,' he suggested sullenly, 'and they won't give no quarter if they're cornered will they?'

Eric snapped back: 'No, we're after a black marketeer and he's a Frenchie from a German speaking part of France.'

Ted snorted.

'Bollocks. If he speaks German then he's a fucking German.'

This made Eric wonder if he should have brought a police service Webley revolver but, aside from having no idea how to get it out of the station, the only time he'd used one on the range it misfired.

He was a rotten shot, anyway.

The boat nudged the short concrete slipway on the other side and they stepped off onto Cornish territory. Eric conceded by way of mollifying his friend: 'Maybe the gun is worth bringing along, but let's be very careful.'

That seemed to cheer Ted up.

Waiting for them on the other side of the road was cousin Denzil in his milk and veg lorry, a red Morris C11/40 two tonner. A ruddy-faced county rugby player, Denzil was as broad as he was tall and with no neck. He waved at them, but before they crossed over to climb in, Ted grabbed Eric's forearm for a quick word in private.

'Whatever happens Eric, take it from someone who has seen a bit of bloodshed - we must not hesitate to dish it out if things turn nasty.'

Eric had never seen that killer's look on his friend's face before but, oddly enough, it was now calming rather than worrying.

* * *

Crammed into the small cabin of the lorry – Ted next to Denzil and Eric by the passenger door - they bounced and swerved along narrow country lanes empty of all other traffic. It was still warm and the smell of dung and other farmyard filth, mingling with stale cigarette odour and motion of the vehicle, made Eric feel sick.

Denzil knew the way to Brook Farm like the back of his hand as he'd often been up there to do some fishing. The family there were, according to Denzil, good honest folk and they'd be as horrified as anyone to think of dodgy things going on.

He volunteered with dark relish: 'If there be any need for sortin' someone out, I've got a couple o' twelve bores in the back, I 'ave.'

Ted chuckled while Eric sighed.

Denzil gave them a quizzical look.

'That's very good of you,' Ted explained with a glance at the bilious looking Eric, 'but our job is to try and arrest the blighters not kill 'em.'

The lorry juddered as it hit a pothole and Eric's head glanced off something hard clipped on the back of the cab. Rubbing the crown of his skull, he glanced around to find a lamp of some kind.

'Rabbit light,' Denzil explained, 'goes in a socket doo-dah on the outside o' either door connected to the battery– for fixin' the rabbits wi' – so they just freeze an' gets all bewitched by it. Then ye gives 'em a blast.'

'Might come in handy,' Ted observed as he reached into a coat pocket for a packet of cigarettes. Eric grabbed it and scrunched it up, letting the remains fall into the footwell, causing Denzil to frown, but the lorry was already a bit of a tip so he said nothing. Not so Ted, who protested.

'What did you do that for!?'

Noticing Eric's pallor, he suddenly understood, reaching past him to try and open the window.

'I tried that,' Eric moaned.

The handle still didn't budge, so Ted turned to his cousin.

'Next time we're on straight bit can you open that window of yours?'

Denzil gave him a puzzled look.

'It stinks in here and my friend is used neither to the confines of a battleship messdesk or a stinking farmer's lorry.'

'Bluddy Plymothians,' Denzil sighed.

6

THE ELDERLY FARMER was deeply suspicious, having spotted the police number on Eric's collar and the globe and laurel badge on Ted's.

'What's a copper and a Royal Marine want with our Ethel and her gentleman, anyway?'

Eric explained that their sister Sadie had been knocked up and they needed to have a word with Ethel's young man. This shocked the old boy, who closed the front door of the farmhouse behind him so his wife couldn't hear. 'Well I never,' he gasped, 'I knows he be a Frog but I thought 'e was sweet on our Ethel, not chasin' other girls.'

Brook Farm had four young women from the Land Army to help the old farmer and his wife out. Two of them lodged in the farmhouse itself and the other pair were accommodated in a converted barn that incorporated a kitchen and a bunkhouse.

One of its residents was the aforementioned Ethel, a posh young lady from London. It was a weekend and so the two young ladies that stayed in the farmhouse were out with their boyfriends, who were sailors under training over at Torpoint. As for the other two, the old boy had seen an oil lamp on in the barn just a short while ago, indicating somebody was there. The farmer generally kept himself to himself, preferring to give them privacy at the weekends. 'I reckon I remember the Land Girl what Ethel shared the barn with bein' away due to a family bereavement,' he revealed.

Neither the farmer nor his wife had *actually* seen Ethel or her young man that weekend. He often came over at weekends on his bicycle, with a suitcase tied to the back, which was an intriguing detail for the farmer because, he never stayed over.

That wouldn't be proper, you see so he'd often puzzled over what the lad brought with him in that suitcase, *but didn't like to pry*.

As he listened to the farmer's prattle, Eric wondered if perhaps a few goodies, such as alcohol or chocolate, or the odd bit of fabric had also come the farmer's way. Eric thanked him for the information but declined his offer of accompanying them to the barn. The farmer admitted it was never usually locked anyway, so they could let themselves in, Eric and Ted going over to investigate while Denzil waited in the Morris.

* * *

The oil lamp in the kitchen was still warm, as was the kettle. Plates and cutlery were tidily left to dry on the draining board of the sink. Next door they found the two single beds neatly made, with no obvious sign of a male presence. Eric noticed a loft hatch in the ceiling and against one wall a suitable ladder. Acting on instinct, very carefully and gently he and Ted picked it up, laying the top of it against the hatch frame.

With Ted steadying it at the bottom, Eric began to climb up, only to be halted by the marine touching his left leg and whispering urgently: 'What if someone's *really* up there?' He was right. The Frenchman could very well be waiting with something to hit him on the head, or worse.

Ted had slipped the bag off his left shoulder to help with the ladder and now crept over to where he'd deposited it on the floor, retrieving the greaseproof paper package containing the Browning. With consummate care, he unwrapped it, then, silent as he could, pulled the slide back, simultaneously chambering a bullet and cocking the hammer. Finally, he took the safety catch off.

Eric waited anxiously, hardly daring to breathe.

Ted tapped his chest with his left hand and pointed up, suggesting he should go up into the loft. Eric shook his head. With a disappointed sigh Ted handed over the Browning.

Going up the last few rungs, Eric tightened his grip on the pistol butt, careful not to put too much pressure on the trigger. With his left hand he shoved the loft hatch with all his might. His logic was that it would fly up with such violence that anyone waiting on the other side would be well and truly brained. It shot into the loft, clacking on the plank floor. Eric lunged up, finding only a musty, empty space. He discovered it was playing host to large straw-filled sacks covered with rumpled blankets and a pillow in a sweat-stained, striped case.

'Nobody here,' Eric called down, 'but there is a bed of sorts.'

Then he looked up. There, hanging from one of the rafters, was a wire, with something small and rectangular on the end of it.

Climbing all the way through the hatch and getting to his feet, Eric reached up and twirled it around with his fingertips. In the gloom of the loft - lit only by a single, dirty skylight – he couldn't quite make it out. Then, he suddenly realised what it was: a Morse signal key. He tugged it gently but it was attached securely to something heavy hidden on top of the rafter. Spotting a wicker stool, Eric decided to use it for some elevation and a closer look.

* * *

A few minutes later, leaving the radio where it was and after retrieving the hatch, Eric climbed back down, putting it in place again.

He handed the Browning over to Ted who put the safety catch back on, wrapped it up again and secreted it in his bag.

They came out of the barn, crossed the small bridge over a stream to the lorry where Denzil waited expectantly behind the wheel. The old farmer sat in the passenger seat next to him puffing on his pipe.

'Well?' Denzil enquired.

'Ain't nobody at 'ome?' the farmer asked, blowing smoke out the open window. Eric shook his head and asked the old man: 'Where do you think they might be now?'

Furrowing his brow, the farmer pondered things for a moment. 'They was fond o' long walks down by the coast', he revealed, 'usin' that path up o'er the hill 'n beyond towards Tregantle. There's a lovers' seat over by the road, got a lovely view o' the shore 'n down the coast, it has. Easy enough to spot by the disused golf course.'

'I knows where 'tis,' Denzil confirmed.

The old farmer climbed down from the Morris, taking a long suck on his pipe as he stood aside for Ted and Eric to climb up into the cab. He ventured suspiciously: 'I reckon you're spinnin' me a bloody yarn an' there's more to this than meets the eye.' Eric glared at the old man and proposed harshly: 'I should keep such thoughts to yourself.'

The old boy smiled slyly.

'Cause, y'know, them two really are lovebirds an' I can't believe he'd do the dirty.'

'Know him *that* well do you?'

The farmer shook his head.

'Nah, not really, but I got a hunch.'

'Alright, here's the true story,' Eric told him. 'I'm a copper and he's a dirty black marketeer who gave me some bruised ribs and nasty knock to my face – and I aim to give him some justice.'

The old farmer peered through the gathering gloom at Eric's face, finding it both battered and baleful. He was short-sighted and hadn't taken much notice earlier. Eric added, to further deter the old boy: 'And anybody who accepted stolen goods from him runs the risk of being just as guilty as he is.' The pipe drooped and the farmer looked very worried. Eric slammed the door shut, which provoked a glare from Denzil as they pulled away. 'Mind my bloody truck,' he muttered.

In the wing mirror as the vehicle swung away, Eric saw the old man scurry back into his farmhouse.

'Is there more to this than meets the eye?' Denzil enquired.

Eric sighed, aggrieved at all the questions when he hardly knew where it would lead himself.

'Possibly. In fact, I would say yes.'

'In wha' way might I be askin'?' Denzil enquired as they came to a halt at the top of the lane and turned right onto the coast road.

Eric finally revealed what else he'd discovered:

'I found a radio in the loft.'

Ted frowned, while Denzil looked puzzled, asking:

'That's not illegal, be it?'

Eric shook his head.

'Not a normal radio - equipment for sending and receiving messages via Morse.' Ted gasped, while Denzil still didn't twig. He was too busy with navigating along the road in failing light.

'You mean they're spies, Eric?' ventured Ted.

'The dials were marked in German.'

Finally, Denzil understood.

'You mean them saboteurs!? Fuckin' filthy fifth columnists!?'

'That's about it,' Eric confirmed.

'Jus' as well I brought me shotguns!' Denzil declared.

Ted reached inside the bag on his lap to pull out the Browning pistol and unwrap it. Pondering the wisdom of what they had embarked on, Eric decided he was doubtful spies or saboteurs would be hanging around having a lover's tryst. They must be miles away by now, but the thefts of the white cloth seemed to indicate a definite purpose, which he had still not figured out. That was undoubtedly what was in the Frenchman's suitcase along with other ill-gotten goods. Eric asked Denzil: 'How far to this lover's seat by Tregantle?'

'bout a mile.'

'Give it half a mile and then kill your lights.'

'Good job I know this 'ere road.'

'Then what?' Ted asked.

Eric replied: 'We park just down from the lover's seat...'

Denzil observed, with a nostalgic tone: 'I used to romance the wife there when we were courtin'.'

'And then, once we're there, do we go hunting?' enquired Ted eagerly.

Eric nodded.

'With the guns?' asked Denzil.

'Yes,' Eric agreed reluctantly, 'but the idea is to take them alive.'

7

Leaving the Morris in a lay-by hidden from the shore by a stone wall topped with a hedge, Eric and the other two made a crouching run for the lovers' seat, which was really just a glorified park bench.

Throwing themselves to the ground behind it - Eric grimacing as his bruised ribs griped - they peered out, trying to spot the Frenchman and his girl. 'Can you see them?' Ted asked, his voice quavering with adrenalin.

There wasn't a great deal of light left – just a few orange daubs on the sea, the fiery orb of the sun flashing from behind the jagged outline of Tregantle Fort, an old Victorian sea defence a quarter of a mile down the coast to the west.

There was a grassy slope immediately below the lover's seat, which dropped away to rocks and then a broad expanse of sandy beach. Eric could just make out two figures flitting back and forth on the grass.

'What are they up to?' Denzil whispered.

It looked like they were creating a large white X, or cross. 'So, that's what the cloth's for,' Eric gasped.

'Huh?' enquired Ted.

'What!?' bellowed Denzil.

'Shut up,' Ted hissed.

Fortunately, the breeze off the sea together with the crash of the waves breaking on the shore obscured any give-away sounds.

'The cloth that was stolen,' Eric explained, 'is what they've used to make that bloody big white cross below us.'

'Bugger me,' observed Denzil, 'but why?'

Eric had no idea and then Ted pointed out to sea.

'Look, there's a thing that wasn't out there a minute ago.'

Raising his eyes, Eric picked up a low, black shape floating not far offshore. *A U-boat!?* There was something smaller and lighter in colour crawling towards the beach. The figures below moved off the grass and made their way down through the rocks, and across the sand to wait by the water's edge.

'They *are* bloody spies!' Ted declared triumphantly.

'I think it's some form of dinghy,' said Eric, then suggested to Denzil: 'Come on, let's push your lorry along here and make use of that rabbit light.'

Ted climbed behind the wheel, let the handbrake off and steered, while Eric and Denzil pushed the vehicle from out of cover to just by the bench. Denzil then unclipped the rabbit light from the back of the cab and plugged it into the socket on the outside of the passenger door. 'Only problem is,' Denzil explained, 'we needs to get the engine goin' to give it power, to avoid runnin' battery down.'

'They won't hear it,' Eric reassured him.

Denzil's eyes bulged with anger.

'Then why did we huff an' puff to push the blasted thing an' not just drive it up 'ere?'

Now he thought about it, Eric was at a loss as to why they had done that. He smiled apologetically. Climbing back into the cab and winding the passenger door window down, Denzil grumbled about there 'being no need to tell him off fer shoutin' earlier, neither.'

As he was about to turn the ignition key, Eric leaned in the window and said urgently: 'But don't actually switch the light on until I say so.'

'I'm not thick y'know,' Denzil complained.

'Are you sure they can't already see us?' Ted asked.

'They'll be too busy getting their friends ashore,' Eric said with the confidence of someone who trusted in luck rather than any scientific fact. He went on to outline the plan: 'Right, Denzil stays here and switches the light on once we are a bit nearer to them – my suggestion is that you signal him by firing a single shot in the air Ted. If he can't hear it, he'll see the flash.'

'Then I can give coverin' fire with a shotgun, eh?' Denzil proposed.

Eric grimaced and shook his head.

'Better not, or you might hit us by mistake.'

Denzil sighed heavily.

Ted and Eric set off in a crouching run down the grassy slope, dodging around the large white cloth cross and coming to a halt in the rocks to get their bearings. Shivering in the damp night chill, his light raincoat and uniform jacket not giving much protection, Eric peered down at the beach.

It was almost completely dark, but he was able to pick out the Frenchman and Ethel still waiting patiently at the water's edge.

Beside him Ted slipped the Browning from a coat pocket and asked anxiously: 'What if there's loads of Germans in that boat?'

Eric hadn't thought of that.

Ted added rather unhelpfully: 'I mean we're here to arrest the Frenchie and his girl, not see off a Nazi invasion.'

This could turn very nasty but then Eric had a bright idea.

'What if we fire the shot, Denzil lights them up – they think a whole army's waiting to see them off and, in the panic, we nab Ethel and Frenchie?'

There was no response from Ted, so Eric tugged his sleeve and added: 'Go on then…'

But before he could add 'tell me what you think?' Ted raised the Browning and squeezed the trigger. A second later Denzil's powerful rabbit lamp lit up the beach, revealing the Frenchman and Ethel frozen wide-eyed in horror as they looked back up at the road. Just beyond them a dinghy-load of Germans was about to make landfall. Out to sea there was a series of flashes and cannon shells tumbled overhead, followed by the percussive crack and thump of the U-boat's 20mm anti-aircraft gun letting rip.

'Why did you do that!?' Eric screamed.

'You told me to go on!' Ted shouted back.

The first half dozen shells missed the lorry, some digging up turf while others shattered rocks, sending tiny razor-sharp fragments everywhere. Eric scrambled back up towards the grassy slope, leaving Ted to take cover below.

'Turn the light off!' Eric screamed, tripping and becoming entangled in the white cloth cross. Instead of turning the lamp off Denzil raised its beam to his assailant, revealing the cannon mounted on a platform aft of the conning tower, with several figures clustered around it gesticulating wildly.

It fired again.

Cursing like a lunatic, and grabbing one of his shotguns from the back Denzil tumbled out of the lorry's cab as shrapnel flew around, and futilely gave the U-boat both barrels.

Untangling himself, Eric got up and lurched forward, screaming: 'Turn the fucking light off!'

A shell thunked into the vehicle's engine. Another shattered the driver's cab and along with it the rabbit lamp. Realising the folly of his defiance, Denzil chucked the useless shotgun away, hurling himself down and rolling under the bench. A cannon shell pierced the lorry's fuel tank, making it explode in a roar of flames. Hands over the back of his head, Eric rolled himself up into a small ball as bits of wood, metal and glass rained down.

Opening his eyes and uncurling, he saw Denzil wedged under the bench, quivering with fear.

And then the night lit up as bright as day - searchlights mounted on the walls of Tregantle Fort illuminated the shore and the beam of one caught the U-boat cold.

With a very loud *crack!* that made Eric jump, an artillery gun opened fired from by the fort. He covered his ears with his hands and curled up again, this time even tighter.

Crack!

The gun fired again and again, each time making Eric twitch

involuntarily. Shell after shell tore through sky, landing around the U-boat, which was now recovering its dinghy and men.

With desperate screams for them to get a move on from those exposed to fire on the outer casing of the submarine, the occupants of the dinghy were hauled aboard and bundled down through hatches.

With fountains of spray and hot shrapnel leaping into the sky around the U-boat, the dinghy was cast adrift.

Despite this bombardment the sinister dark craft managed to disappear safely under the sea. The only remaining indication of its presence was a patch of blue-white phosphorescence and the yellow dinghy bobbing on the surface. The latter soon suffered a direct hit and was ripped asunder.

A metallic squeal sounded out from speakers on the fort's battlements, a voice booming in harsh, guttural German: 'Bleiben, wo Sie sind! Sich nicht bewegen, oder Sie werden erschossen werden!'

This was followed in less strident tones by the same instructions in English: 'Stay where you are! Do not move or you will be shot!'

Eric remained curled up, eyes tight shut against the glare. There was the swish of undergrowth being shoved aside and he felt something hard poked into his sore ribs. A gravelly Scottish voice ordered: 'Stand up laddie!'

Getting unsteadily to his feet, Eric found himself surrounded by fierce-looking commandos.

Distinctive green woollen comforters clamped on their heads, their webbing was festooned with grenades and they held evil looking submachine guns, menacing muzzles pointed right at him.

One with three stripes on his sleeves - the owner of the Scottish accent - bellowed: 'Hands on heed, Pal!'

Doing as ordered, Eric watched Denzil being grabbed roughly by his overalls and hauled out from under the lover's seat. Unceremoniously dumped onto his feet, he was similarly instructed to put his hands on his head.

Down below Eric saw Ted also surrounded by commandos, one of them taking the Browning pistol from his right hand. Then he was ushered towards the grass slope to join Eric and Denzil.

On the way Ted passed by a body slumped on a patch of sand between rocks – it was the girl, Ethel, victim of the German U-boat cannon. Even though as a Royal Marine he'd seen a few dead bodies, the sight of the girl with the top of her head sliced off made Ted feel sick.

Bending over, he vomited.

'Are you done?' one of his escorts, a Scouser, asked impatiently.

Vomit glistening on his chin, Ted nodded and the commando shoved him forward. With all three gathered by the remains of the linen cross, out of the darkness waddled a portly officer in khaki battle dress. Webbing waist belt straining against a considerable tummy, his bespectacled eyes regarded the trio malevolently from under the peak of a cap displaying the Military Intelligence Corps badge. Cheeks red with anger, he enquired of Denzil: '*What* are you?'

Having recovered some of his composure, Denzil was infuriated at the rough handling he'd been subjected to.

'I am, Sir, a farmer o' this parish,' he replied haughtily.

Looking Denzil's dirty overalls up and down, with his nose wrinkling, the officer remarked with heavy sarcasm: 'Yes, I can see that.'

This further annoyed Denzil and he enquired with unwise fury: 'What about my *bludy* lorry? That's my livin' gone up in flames!? Who's goona pay for a noo wan!?'

Turning away disdainfully, the officer remarked with menacing calm to one of the commandos: 'If he doesn't shut up, shoot him.'

Denzil decided to say nothing more. Eric was next for inspection. The portly officer surveyed his grubby raincoat, noticing the police uniform collar poking out. 'Unbutton his mac,' the officer ordered. The Scots commando stepped forward and undid the belt and buttons, so it fell open to reveal the full uniform jacket, the portly officer enquiring:

'Are you a policeman?'

Eric nodded and confirmed: 'City of Plymouth Police, Sir.'

Raising his eyebrows and sighing, the officer turned away and walked over to Ted, instructing one of the commandos there to undo his raincoat too. 'And *what* are you?'

'Royal Marine, Sir. Plymouth Division.'

Noticing Ted's wet chin, the portly officer enquired:

'Is that vomit?'

Embarrassed, Ted merely nodded.

Digging in a trouser pocket the portly officer offered him a hankie. With the guns still pointed at him, Ted didn't know whether or not he should lower his hands and accept it.

'Oh,' said the officer, realising Ted's quandary and shouting to his men: 'They can lower their hands and you can lower your guns. I want a sweep of the shoreline to find the Frenchman and any German stragglers.'

The commandos departed, leaving the portly officer, standing in the centre of the rumpled and torn cloth cross.

A radio operator stood to one side of him, the set on his back crackling with static and voice traffic. On the officer's other flank was a lanky commando cradling a Sten gun with wary cool.

The portly officer scrutinised Eric and his companions with the kind of amused contempt professionals reserve for amateurs. Eric, Ted, and Denzil were, meanwhile, feeling extremely tired, cold and confused.

'Well, all-in-all this is a bit of a thunder-fucking cock-up,' the portly officer remarked acidly. Turning to the radio operator he told him to contact the fort and get the searchlight turned off. This duly happened, restoring darkness and for a moment the only noise was the gently breaking waves, until the sound of a far-off explosion rolled in on the wind.

'Jolly good show,' came the officer's richly satisfied voice out of the black. 'Got the swine – shall we retire indoors gentlemen?'

8

'WHAT WILL HAPPEN TO THE GIRL?' Eric asked.

Captain St. John Spendlove looked up from reading a sheet of paper in an open foolscap folder resting on the desk's blotter. He had asked Eric to sit in silence for a few minutes while he scribbled some notes about the evening's events. Spendlove looked at Eric over the top of his glasses, as if not understanding the question.

'Well, she's dead, so not a lot,' he observed with a chilly smile.

'No, Sir, I mean will they send her body back to her family?'

Spendlove leaned forward to uncork a bottle of J&B Scotch sat next to the blotter, topping up Eric's glass and also his own.

'We'll create some cock and bull story about her being mangled in farm machinery. The body will be sent to her ancestral home, for interment in the family mausoleum alongside the national so-called heroes, lunatics and charlatans among her ancestors.' Eric nodded, not really understanding what had happened that evening but relieved to know the dead girl, traitor or not, would be disposed of with decorum.

Spendlove had brought them back to Tregantle Fort, which these days was a Royal Artillery gunnery school. While Ted and Denzil went off to get some hot food in the Gunners' canteen, Eric was asked to accompany the captain to a vaulted, red brick-lined office deep below ground. He was to be debriefed, for Spendlove had earlier judged Eric was leader of the motley crew discovered on the shore.

'So, Sir,' Eric asked, 'can you explain to me what happened tonight?'

Spendlove signed and dated his notes, then closed the file. 'Before I do Constable Wise, could you explain what you were doing there?'

Eric told him the story of the May blitz, the robbery at the haberdashery – leaving out his escapade with the corpses of the councillor's daughter and the sailor – then the burglary at Marlborough Street and how a copper's instinct led to his observation post in a Plymouth pub.

Then there was the subsequent fight outside the Co-op Drapery with the German-speaking Frenchman who left his jacket behind and turned out to be a bus driver. Which all led to some off-duty investigations in Cornwall and the beach by Tregantle Fort.

'Well, your Frenchman is still alive,' revealed Spendlove.

'We found him with a broken leg. Must have slipped on rocks while trying to flee…' Eric gave a satisfied smile on hearing this, while Spendlove added: 'He is from Alsace, of German ethnicity and loyalty, a paid-up enemy agent who infiltrated the Marine Nationale - the French Navy - before coming over here.'

Spendlove pulled out a box of matches from a desk drawer.

He offered Eric a cigarette from a red NAAFI tin of Benson and Hedges that he'd produced from the breast pocket of his battle dress blouse. Eric declined, while Spendlove lit up before continuing.

'The Land Girl was Lady Ethel Bullrush…'

The surname name rang a bell with Eric but he didn't know why.

'…the sister of Lord Charles Bullrush, a notorious leading light in the British Union of Fascists before the war…'

That was it.

Eric had read about Bullrush and Moseley and his mob in the papers.

'...and after he was sent to the Tower of London as a traitor on the outbreak of hostilities we did think it peculiar that she never went to see him. Instead she turned into a fanatical British patriot who wanted to help us dig for victory.'

Leaning down to stub out his cigarette by pressing it against the inside of a metal waste paper bin by the chair, Spendlove straightened up and took a sip of Scotch before continuing.

'But she was writing confidentially to a friend from her Union of Fascist days who had all along been an informer for us. Lady Ethel was being dreadfully indiscreet about her true motivations and goings on.'

Eric interrupted: 'And you are, Sir, if you don't mind me asking?'

Spendlove took his glasses off and rubbed the lenses gently with a thumb. 'Part of the apparatus of national security.'

Blinking furiously, he resumed the story. 'Anyway, this informer kept us appraised of what was going on down here in Cornwall. We realised something big was going to happen, so some careful reconnaissance - and Lady Ethel's incautious blethering in her letters to someone she thought was a fellow fascist - enabled us to pinpoint with fair accuracy the likely scenario, and its location.'

'Did you know what the white cloth was about...I mean did you know he was stealing it?'

Spendlove smiled, put his glasses back on.

'No, we didn't – but once my commando scouts saw them making the cross I realised instantly what it was for. They were making a sign for a U-boat dropping a visitor off – another agent, coming here to cause trouble via some sabotage. Anyway, we'd also picked up the U-boat's rather incautious radio signals to its masters across the Channel.'

Spendlove smiled at Eric's single-minded tenacity.

'... and well done on spotting all that business with the stolen haberdashery. The U-boat will have popped its periscope up to take a look at the approximate location of the landing spot and - even in the gathering dusk - found the large, white X. So, in summary, you and your merry band blundered into the middle of an agent being dropped off with the assistance of the Frenchman and the late, departed Lady Ethel. We had a nice little reception committee waiting for them, as you found out, of course.'

Spendlove paused briefly for a self-satisfied smile, then carried on.

'Our enemy may be frightfully efficient and precise at many things, but in the game of espionage they are shockingly incompetent – I can think of no worse a landing site than the one they chose, right next door to a coastal artillery fort. No matter, for despite our firepower - and we had some anti-submarine ships loitering at sea - it was our aim to capture everything intact – U-boat, certain key pieces of equipment aboard it, spies and traitors. Sadly, the submarine got blown to bits when our warships pounced. But, no mind, we have the Frenchman in a cell here, awaiting a naval surgeon to fix his leg and then our interrogators will get to work.'

Eric enquired: 'Was the explosion that we heard out to sea the U-boat meeting its end?'

Spendlove nodded.

'So, Sir,' Eric coughing nervously, the dampness in the underground office aggravating his chest, 'what happens to us?'

Spendlove gave a dry laugh.

'Well, you did rather cock it up, but in the end, it was not a bad result, just not the best. In fact, I quite admire your initiative and willingness to take risks – foolish perhaps, but brave. We shan't drop you in it with your superiors, either you or the Royal Marine – but we will sign you up to secrecy in this matter.'

Eric let out a sigh of relief.

'Appreciated, Sir.'

Spendlove had a funny look in his eye and enquired:

'Ever been in the Army?'

'No, Sir and not likely to be,' Eric revealed angrily, 'as being a policeman is a reserved occupation. I am to be kept on the home front.'

Spendlove waved his hands, dismissing the notion.

'I could fix that – get you released.'

Eric leaned forward, eyes burning eagerly, energised just by the mere thought of it, but Spendlove's face suddenly clouded over.

'There's just one problem.'

Eric sensed looming deflation.

'Which is, Sir?'

'That I cannot recruit directly into my gang – you have to be in the Army already and also be a seasoned soldier; you are neither of those things.' Eric coughed in embarrassment; well aware he lacked field training, weapons skills or anything else that made a soldier.

Spendlove provided a reassuring smile for he liked the cut of the copper's jib. 'But, I could one day see you performing admirably on my team, so let's say I get you out of the police?'

Eric still looked a little crestfallen, which irritated Spendlove, who asked sharply: 'Is that not good enough?'

'I think I've had enough of police work and but I fancy something more aggressive than just catching spies. The Fritzes killed my dad and my brother, so I'd like to get them back.'

Spendlove sympathised.

'I'm sorry to hear all that. Revenge, though, in my opinion is a dish best served cold – not in the heat of combat – but I understand.'

Spendlove got up and held out a hand, signalling the interview was over. 'Go and get yourself something to eat and we'll take proper statements from you and your fellows shortly.'

Eric shook his hand and, as he was shutting the door, Spendlove added, with what seemed like genuine concern: 'And, whatever transpires, try not to get yourself killed.'

9

Stonehouse Hospital, Morning of 3 May 1942

RED FROTHY BUBBLES formed on the man's lips and then he coughed, shoulders heaving. A pink mist filled the air. Eric with dread lifted a hand to wipe his own left cheek, which suddenly felt damp. He looked at the scarlet smear on his fingertips with horror, which he suppressed, showing only a thin smile.

In the bed, propped up by pillows was Leading Seaman Geordie Hallewell who lifted a ragged, blood-spotted handkerchief to his mouth. A concerned nurse came over, with a small stainless steel bedpan – the same middle-aged ward sister who earlier shot a glare at Eric for bothering the patient.

As the fatally ill sailor coughed his lungs into the silver pan, Eric looked away, out the window, through the colonnade columns. The soft morning light was bathing the buildings opposite in a golden glow, their 18th Century stonework still wet from passing showers. The ward sister whispered something in Geordie's ear.

'Naa, naa, ah've gotta telt him,' Geordie wheezed.

'Well, don't you overdo it, Constable,' she urged Eric resentfully.

Eric smiled and told her, he hoped reassuringly: 'I won't.'

The ward sister glowered suspiciously at Eric as she reluctantly withdrew. Once the nurse was gone, Geordie croaked: 'She means reet, but divvun't get how important it is tha' I tell ya what happened.'

Geordie dabbed his lips with the handkerchief and spluttered:

'Bring your chair closer man!'

Eric hesitated, not keen on more red mist.

Geordie waved him in. Eric got up, with the toe of a boot poking his helmet bag under the bed, while moving the chair closer to Geordie.

'Whey, whar wor I?' the sailor whispered.

'You said the *Aztec* had left Gibraltar to meet a convoy coming up from Sierra Leone.' Geordie nodded and resumed his story of how the destroyer was sunk eleven months earlier, honour-bound to tell how Able Seaman Bert Wise met his end.

* * *

The night was black as pitch.

Some sailors, including Bert, were huddled around the Asdic repeater on the bridge, as the Aztec *tried to pin down an echo that might be a German submarine moving in for the kill against a merchant ship lagging behind.*

Geordie was acting as lookout, peering out into the dark, straining his eyes to spot anything out of the ordinary, while also being ready to run errands - such as fetching hot cocoa for his fellow watch-keepers or taking messages from the captain to other parts of the ship.

Down below other sailors were frowning with concentration as they twiddled knobs and wheels and things, or whatever it was they did to turn the thing on the bottom of the ship that shot out the noise pulses to try and get a decent echo off the U-boat.

About ten minutes later Bert and Geordie came off watch, to go and get their heads down. While Bert climbed straight into his hammock on the ratings' mess-deck, Geordie just couldn't sleep.

He decided to get some fresh air and went topside to visit a rating he knew on one of the twin 4.7-inch guns. Coming out onto the upper deck, Geordie paused, going to the guardrail around its edge and looked over the side. He marvelled at the bioluminescence created by the ship's wake – a ghostly glow trailing away from Aztec*'s sharp bow due to disturbance of plankton in the sea. He watched it gradually fizzling out, but then something cut through it - a few feet below the surface, heading diagonally past where he stood.*

Geordie paused in his account to cough some more blood into his handkerchief, suppressing the violence and noise as much as he could, so as not to bring the nurse over again. With the paroxysm past, Geordie wheezed with venom: 'It wiz a fookin' U-boat torpedo, man!'

Hearing the curse, the ward sister looked up from the table nearby where she was writing a report, shooting a glare in their direction.

Smiling sheepishly, Geordie wheezed 'soorree!' and resumed his tale, Eric feeling his heart beat faster, sick to his stomach at what he was about to discover. Conveying even a fraction of what he was about to hear to his mother would not be a great job. She had been devastated by Bert's loss but was getting better now. Perhaps he wouldn't tell her anything. He'd kept his meeting with Geordie a secret anyway. The sailor was, meanwhile, explaining how he'd yelled 'Torpedo!'...

...but his shout was lost in the deafening roar of an explosion, after the magnetic pistol detonated the warhead. Hurled to the deck and banging his head, Geordie reckoned he must have blacked out. When he came to, the night was bathed in an evil red and orange glow from the flames.

Eric swallowed, unbuttoning the top button of his police tunic.

He knew what it was like, to be surrounded by the fires of Hell.

It seemed the entire front of the ship had disappeared, the ammunition in the forward shell magazine going off and vaporising everyone and everything for'ard. Could have been Geordie and Bert gone in an instant, if they hadn't been sent off watch. Somehow what remained of Aztec *was still afloat, so Geordie went below decks, clambering down ladders in the blackness to the ratings messdeck. It was a shambles, with lockers tumbled over, hammocks all of a tangle...clothes and bits of paper floating around on water swilling all over the deck.*

He shouted out for anyone still alive, provoking a chorus of curses and groans. Bert's voice came out of the darkness: 'Don't just stand there you Tyneside twit, come and get me out of this hammock!'

Geordie laughed hoarsely, his shoulders shuddering with the black humour of it all but he calmed himself down and went on with the story.

That was just like Bert, always ready to laugh in the face of disaster. So, Geordie released him from the hammock, Bert tipping onto the floor with a volley of curses. Climbing back up topside, they grabbed a hose and helped fight some of the fires, but the ammunition for anti-aircraft guns - which was stored in lockers on the upper deck - was detonating as flames reached it. Try as they might to stop this - directing their hose jet at the lockers - it was simply too bloody dangerous, especially when whizz-bangs started going off everywhere.

Quite sensibly the order was given to abandon ship, which Bert and Geordie heartily agreed with. They shook hands before climbing over the rail and leaping off into the cold, dark heaving sea. They both managed to swim to the same Carley float, where some others helped haul them aboard. And so they sat there, in the Atlantic off Iberia, watching their old ship burn.

Geordie's voice died away as he was lost to the moment. He stared into his lap, seeing not the bedclothes but the night of horror all those months ago and *Aztec*'s remains ablaze.

Geordie settled his teary eyes on Eric, struggled to keep down a wave of emotion that threatened to overwhelm him. Eric felt the pain in his own heart, imagining his brother in the midst of that horror - remembering his nights amid the bombs of the blitz. Geordie explained almost in a whisper:

'She'd been our hoose y'see. Brought Bert an' me all the way through the Battle of Narvik - where we gave them Jerries a right pastin', but lost loads of good lads we tipped o'er the side. Then there was *Bismarck* – even she couldn't get us - but one bloody U-boat…hidin' oot there did for our home-from-home…our canny *Aztec*.'

Geordie fell silent, shook his head, then picked the yarn up again.

So, there they were, sitting on the Carley float, soaking, shivering with the cold, the nerves and excitement and relief at not being dead. They looked at

Aztec, *her outline revealed by raging fires. Bert remarked that a lot of their shipmates must have died in the ship and never got off.*

Then they saw a dark figure flitting about amid the flames and they shouted for him to jump off but he disappeared. They wondered if they were hallucinating. Now the survivors on the float got a bit of luck, for the first time.

A British corvette, the Carnation, *loomed out of the night and picked them up. Her sailors cursed cheerfully as they helped everybody up scrambling nets and over the side. There was rum and hot steaming cocoa to revive the* Aztecs *and change of clothes, even if it was difficult to get anything that fitted. Geordie was not feeling too good, as he had ingested some oil, so they took him down to the sickbay. That was where his part of the story ended, at least so far as* Aztec *was concerned.*

Geordie stopped talking, playing with the blood-speckled handkerchief in his lap. Eric frowned, waiting for him to go on with the story.

Was that it?

He had expected to hear more about his brother.

'What happened with Bert?' Eric asked, barely able to conceal his impatience. Geordie smiled, dabbed at his lips.

'He wor a canny lad, yer brother.'

Eric didn't like the sound of that.

Geordie explained: 'We mighta abandoned *Aztec*, but she hadn't abandoned us, like. She didn't sink, so they sent some damage control teams, includin' Bert back aboard her in the mornin', like.'

At one point, so Geordie later heard, Bert knocked up a breakfast of bacon and eggs on a galley stove.

It cheered everyone up as they tried to shore up collapsing bulkheads, pump out water and damp down the last fires.

Eric smiled at this, remembering that morning when he'd been awoken by the aroma of bacon acquired by fair means or foul from *Aztec*. Geordie explained that he'd heard about the bacon being cooked up for the damage control team from Bert himself, when they all came back aboard *Carnation* that evening.

Bert sat by Geordie's cot in the sick berth and gave all the details.

Geordie smiled at the memory, then resumed the story.

Bert and the others went back aboard early the following morning, but the sea and wind was rising and the situation was hopeless. When he heard Aztec *was being abandoned again, Geordie hauled himself out of his cot, much against the orders of the sickbay attendant, went up to* Carnation*'s upper deck to say goodbye to his ship.*

He saw the damage control team men, including what must have been Bert, climbing over the side Aztec *into a whaler. Blanket draped around his shoulders, steadying himself on the guardrail, Geordie watched as* Aztec *slipped beneath the waves. She threw her stern high in the air, the White Ensign still flying.*

Geordie felt a lump the size of a rock in his throat, tears running down not just his cheeks but also those of other Aztecs to either side of him. It was a very sad experience as she had been 'their Ship' and took many messmates with her down into deep forever. The whaler had paused, hove to at a respectful distance to watch Aztec *go. An officer standing up in the whaler's stern saluted the ship's passing while the men rested on the oars. Then there was an air raid alert, and Geordie was bundled back down below decks as the* Carnation *upped steam and turned swiftly towards the north, her anti-aircraft guns banging away.*

Geordie fell silent again.

He was submerged in thoughts of the *Aztec* and the men she took with her. Eric leaned forward and touched the sailor's pyjama sleeve to bring him back. With tears running down his cheeks, Geordie regarded Eric with uncomprehending eyes, lost in the past.

'What happened to the whaler?' Eric enquired eagerly, 'to Bert and the others?' Geordie looked out the window at the trees on the edge of the green, their branches swaying gently in the wind. He dabbed his tears away, leaving a pink patch on his cheek.

'They were picked up by a Dutch merchant ship, like.'

'A merchant vessel? I imagined from what I was told by someone at the naval barracks that it was a warship.'

Geordie looked at him, exhaled a sarcastic, wheezy chuckle.

'They're always a bit light on the facts, like. Nah, she was a Dutch tramp steamer, part of the convoy, might've been the one left behind that we thowt the U-boat was after. The *Carnation* intercepted a signal ter the Admiralty sayin' they'd picked up a bunch o' sailors in a whaler, close ter where *Aztec* went doon. This ship got attacked a day or two later by a U-boat as she made for Gibraltar, might've even been the bastard that sunk us. *Carnation* intercepted the signal sayin' she was gannin' doon, but by the time we'd steamed back south, aal that was left was a few bits o' wood an' oil patches.'

Geordie stared out the window again, not wanting to look at Eric as he said: 'There was nae survivors.'

Eric opened his mouth, intending to ask if that was for certain when Geordie started coughing violently. The nurse came running over, bowl in hand, towel draped over a forearm, giving Eric another one of her glares.

'Finished?' she asked, angrily.

Eric nodded, retrieving his helmet bag from beneath the bed and placed the chair back against the wall as Geordie, bent double over the metal bowl, coughed the remnants of his life away. Eric thought that it was better to have been taken in a cold sea - sliding swiftly and numbly into the afterlife – rather than linger in this world to drown in your own blood as your lungs dissolved. *Perhaps Bert had been the lucky one?*

He walked down the covered way towards the hospital exit, between the columns, with sparrows flitting through them. They hopped out of his path and then winged low across the lawns. Eric forgot about the war for a second. Stopping to lean against a column, he looked back at the hospital's isolation wards. They were just yards away from the destroyed Octagon, where he'd first spotted the drapery shop raider, and yet the firestorm had not claimed these ancient buildings. Built at Stonehouse Creek two hundred years earlier, their original purpose was to take the diseased survivors of Britain's empire-founding naval wars straight into hospital from the old wooden fighting ships.

Tipped into a rowing boat, not unlike the one that had brought Bert away from *Aztec*, those sailing navy men were delivered up the Creek and straight into a hospital bed. It wasn't long before the phrase 'up the creek' became common currency to describe anyone who was unlikely to be able to extricate themselves from their predicament.

Not alive anyway, and Stonehouse Hospital was still a place where sailors without a hope of surviving were eased from this world into the next. Today, away from Geordie's coughs, with the sun on his face and the birds cheeping - the stone of the column warm on his cheek - Eric felt at peace. There were no sirens, no screaming bombs, roaring flames or the rumble and crack of buildings collapsing.

'Are you alright?' a woman's voice asked.

Opening his eyes, Eric turned to see who it belonged to, finding a pretty young nurse, one of the Red Cross volunteers. With her dark hair tucked up under her hat – a few strands having escaped - she wore a light grey ward dress and a crisp, white apron. Rosy-cheeked and clear eyed, she was the picture of health and vitality compared to poor dying Geordie.

Eric nodded and the nurse gave him a relieved smile.

'I thought perhaps you were ill.'

Eric's reaction did little to dispel that notion - though he shook his head, Eric shivered and looked down at his boots. Putting thumb and forefinger to the bridge of his nose he closed his eyes and squeezed. He was suddenly overcome with weariness and sadness, as if her simple, objective concern had broken a dam of emotion. She stepped forward, placing a hand on his arm, looking up with concern into his face. 'Why don't you come in and have a cup of tea?' she suggested.

'I must get back to the station,' he replied.

The nurse stood back as he pushed himself away from the column, buttoning up his collar.

He looked straight into her eyes for second and smiled, then away in case she saw how much he was all mixed up with emotion.

For her part, the nurse was suddenly scared of something powerful and strong she felt pass between them – a link, an understanding that she could not define. Later she would reflect that in this war they all shared heightened emotions, at least when the barriers were unexpectedly broken. Whether policeman or nurse, the requirements of the job usually demanded a professional demeanour.

'If you are sure that you are alright,' she enquired, resetting her formal nursing persona, 'then I'll say good day.'

Eric laughed, finding the sudden change to a stern nursing tone in one so young and lovely rather incongruous. He gave her a twinkly-eyed grin and nodded. 'Yes nurse, I'm fine.'

She blushed and quickly turned away.

He watched her walk off down the covered way, the sun between the columns lighting her up, a dazzling angel of mercy on her way to salve the pain of the dying. 'What a job,' he thought, 'and what a beautiful girl.'

Before entering the ward, she turned and looked back, giving him a smile and a little wave just before vanishing inside. In that moment, thanks to that look and gesture, Eric fell a little bit in love with her, something that would normally have appalled him.

A copper couldn't be so soppy.

Exiting the gates of the hospital, Eric turned left to walk down Clarence Place and, as he crossed the road to head down onto Union Street, found his attention grabbed by a poster on the wall of the Clarence pub on the corner opposite.

Under the screaming header 'HELP BRITAIN FINISH THE JOB' was a vivid piece of art showing helmeted, khaki-clad Royal Artillery gunners, sleeves of their shirts rolled up and hard at work. They were serving a big gun firing out to sea, with one of them putting a shell into its breech, while another waited to close it. Eric thought he'd like to be loading that gun. *Heck, he'd like to close the breech and fire it too, if it meant killing Nazis.*

Eric vowed to go along to an Army recruiting meeting. He'd heard about another one being held on the other side of the city at Prince Rock. Turning away from the poster he frowned at the thought of breaking the news to Mum, that he was joining up and there was no hope for Bert.

Perhaps he would not tell her the details of Bert's end at all? Probably best.

Eric had, though, decided after months of prevarication that he could stand it no longer and must go and fight the Germans.

Mum would understand. He'd wanted to join up since the blitz and recalled that meeting with that Army officer at Tregantle Fort. It had also fired him up, though only for a short while. Now, almost a year on, with Plymouth slowly rising from its knees, he felt it was time to cut the apron strings. Both his mum and the city were tougher than they looked, or so he hoped.

10

The Road to Monte Cassino, February 1944

THERE IT WAS AGAIN.

Scratch...scratch...scratch.

It is never a great idea to take a hand off the steering wheel of a vehicle on a narrow Italian mountain road. And so it was that Bombardier Eric Wise of the Royal Artillery watched with mounting fury as the driver, Lance Bombardier Hywel Jenkins, plunged his right hand into his nether regions yet again.

Jenkins' left hand, while thankfully remaining on the wheel, jerked in time to his right's frantic scratching. Eric leaned over, grabbing the wheel to steady it and ensure they didn't veer off the road and plunge to their deaths.

'Fucking cut it out!' he snarled.

Jenkins shot him a resentful glare and put his right hand back on wheel, which was just as well, as they were entering a hairpin bend.

Eric unbuttoned the flap of his pistol holster.

Jenkins saw this out the corner of his eye and was genuinely alarmed, and even more so when Eric shouted: 'If you scratch your balls again, I'll shoot you!'

Exiting the bend, the jeep hurtled down a long straight into a broad valley. Eric could tell by the pained look on Jenkins' face that he was finding it really hard not to scratch, but the threat of being shot was - *for now* - sufficient deterrent.

For men like Eric, who had seen enough of women selling their bodies along his home city's Union Street and in its back alleys, the fleshpots of Naples had not been appealing. For Jenkins - a simple lad from a God-fearing village in Pembrokeshire - the bordellos of Naples were a *Sodom and Gomorrah* to be plunged into with eager abandon. And why not, for he might be dead tomorrow? Eric knew why not, because an itch in the crotch could lead to disaster on the road to Monte Cassino.

Eric could have decided to get behind the wheel after receiving orders to go north, where he and Jenkins were needed temporarily to join the 2nd New Zealand Division as forward artillery observers. However, that would have seen Jenkins in the passenger seat scratching his groin to shreds. Eric would have been forced to push him out of the jeep, tumbling to his death down a vertiginous slope.

* * *

Depending on your point of view, the monastery was either a comforting, watchful representation of God on Earth, protecting his flock below, or an ominous presence, casting evil over the land. To Italian civilians hunkered down in the towns and villages, not least in the town of Cassino itself - at the foot of the mountain on which the monastery sat - its shining white walls offered permanence in a world of savagery and chaos. Within it were courtyards and cloisters of peace and tranquillity with meditative silence broken only by tinkling fountains and the occasional high-pitched scream of swooping swifts feeding on the wing. Several hundred people had even taken refuge within the monastery's precincts, camping out in the corridors and monks' cells around St Benedict's Tomb.

Founded more than a thousand years earlier the monastery had somehow endured in the past - despite being attacked and turned into ruins three times already in previous wars.

It had always risen again, just as Italy surely would from the current darkness. These were more civilised times though, weren't they? Nobody would dare bring the walls down again, or so the fearful civilians prayed.

The Vatican had urged the armies to leave the monastery intact, along with its treasures, which included priceless medieval books, fragile scrolls, golden-framed paintings of the Madonna and Child and carvings in stone and wood depicting the crucifixion.

Now, amid the rumble and thunder of heavy artillery its bells tolled - straining to establish sonic supremacy - accusing the world of failing to hear the word of God. In the headquarters of Allied forces, the generals were desperate to find a way to break through the Gustav-Cassino Line, a bitterly defended barrier of fortifications thrown across Italy from the Mediterranean to Adriatic, taking advantage of the formidable natural barrier of the Apennine mountains and various rivers. Once the Gustav-Cassino Line was punctured the Allies could push on to capture Rome itself - *the Eternal City*. A bauble of victory that certain ambitious top brass wanted to hang from their belts.

The Italians may have surrendered in September the previous year, but the Germans were determined to make the foe pay a stiff price for every accursed mile of territory taken.

It was a struggle that had already drenched surrounding valleys and mountains in the blood of thousands – while the rotting corpses of humans and animals, the rivers of faeces and muddy quagmires in the valleys below the infernal slopes, created a stench that assailed the nostrils of those approaching the battlefield for miles before they even set eyes on it.

Churchill's so-called soft under belly of Europe - through which Allied armies could supposedly slice before making a thrust deep into the Reich itself - truly was a tough old gut. Hitler's Wehrmacht, including its mountain troops, the Luftwaffe's paratroopers and Waffen SS fanatics fought as fiercely as wolves, contesting every barren foot on the road to Rome. To Allied troops crawling along the old Via Casilina in early 1944, Monte Cassino was a hateful thing and they loathed it with all the dark bitterness in their war weary hearts. *Why should it stand up there, invi-*

olate on its mountaintop, resplendent and impregnable? The Vatican could go screw itself.

Was a single Allied soldier's life worth sacrificing to save that monastery?

It was host to German artillery observers whose binoculars glinted at its windows, calling down death on the poor bloody Allied infantry writhing in the hell below. Their sacrifice was made in the stinking, sucking mud and amid jagged rocks that chewed boots to pieces. Shivering in the hard, freezing rain, tortured souls leached out by the torrential mountain streams, they were all the while under a merciless fire that was sheer butchery.

This was their Calvary, in the cause of democracy against Fascism that no elderly man in his ornate Roman palace could endure for even a moment before fleeing.

Yet the Allies had an ace card.

They had air power.

And the generals decided that after London, Warsaw, Rotterdam, Plymouth and Coventry, along with other towns and cities, had suffered vast swathes of their history and culture destroyed - along with thousands of people killed - due to German bombing, they could not in all conscience let preservation of the Pope's treasures cost more lives. They would eradicate the monastery and rip a hole in the damned Gustav-Cassino Line.

* * *

By the time Jenkins and Eric reached the positions of the 2nd New Zealand Division, the first wave of bombers had already begun the job of destroying the monastery. Now, in the afternoon of the same day, the second assault was eagerly awaited.

Parking their jeep by the radio tent of a heavy artillery battery, whose guns were silent - their crews absent to watch the spectacular unfold - Eric and Jenkins climbed up a path through the trees.

On the way, Eric noticed pieces of paper littering the ground or hung up in the trees like some form of Christmas decoration.

Before the high explosives were disgorged from the bellies of bombers pregnant with doom, there had been artillery bombardments using shells adapted to dump a blizzard of leaflets on the monastery, the town and surrounding landscape.

It was one of these that Eric paused on the path to read, plucking it from where it had been speared by a low branch. Finding one side printed in Italian and the other in English, it was addressed to 'Italian friends' and warned them to 'BEWARE!' It advised that special efforts had been made to avoid shelling the monastery but the Germans had 'known how to benefit from this' and now, with the fighting having 'swept closer and closer to its sacred precincts' the time had come when guns would be trained on the monastery. There was no specific mention of the aerial storm to come.

The leaflet concluded by explaining that it was giving them a 'warning so that you may save yourselves!' It concluded by telling the monks and those who had sought sanctuary with them: 'Leave the Monastery. Leave it at once. Respect this warning. It is for your benefit.'

Jenkins, who had come back down the path to stand alongside Eric, read the leaflet over his shoulder, and remarked: 'That's bloody decent of them isn't it? Letting them know they can save themselves before the shit is bombed out of them. More notice than the bloody Jerries ever give us!'

They joined a group of artillerymen above a precipitous slope of scrub and rocks that fell away to a road where various military vehicles had halted. Their occupants were like picnickers on a day trip, drinking red wine, eating bread and cheese, digging into ration cans, or simply brewing up some tea – all while sitting on vehicle bonnets, perched on tailgates or vehicle bumpers. *Waiting for the big show.*

Eric borrowed a pair of binoculars, bringing into focus the peak of a hill in the middle distance - Monte Cassino itself. It was still wreathed in smoke, a filthy smudge against the white of the much higher Monte Cairo beyond. As the smoke and dust from the first aerial bombardment finally cleared, the monastery was revealed, looking battered, its walls smashed in several places, chapel domes collapsed in on themselves.

Eric thought that the rubble would now make excellent cover for the Germans who would be sure to make it even harder to subdue the monastery and punch through to Rome. Below, the town of Cassino itself had been ground into dust by the hammer blows of the bombers' payloads, with only a few buildings seemingly left untouched.

The sky was bright and cloud-free, though the light was waning, its sharp, cold blue turning softer but a storm now approached - massed formations of bombers, casting a dark shadow over the ravines and mountain slopes, flitting faster than any cloud.

An eagle circling over Monte Cairo wheeled away, powerful wings carrying it back towards the sanctuary of its eyrie. On the slopes directly below where he stood Eric saw a wild cat dart for cover.

He looked up at the roaring mass of aircraft - aluminium angels of death, heralding a hard rain on Monte Cassino like no other before. Dropping the binoculars, to swing from the strap around this neck, Eric cupped a hand over his brow to shade his eyes. Hundreds of eruptions all combined into one massive cloud of dust, billowing flame and smoke. Eric wondered if this is what Plymouth would have looked like had raids taken place during the day when he was able to watch from home in Turnchapel. Fortunately, the bomb capacity of German bombers was much less than that of the Allied aircraft and, whereas in his home city's case the citadel watching over its residents escaped harm, here it was the principal target.

As the throb and roar of the bomber engines began to fade it was replaced by a tsunami of exultation sweeping along the valleys. Tens of thousands of Allied troops cheered themselves hoarse. No sound issued from Eric – he felt overwhelmed with sadness – another act of vandalism had seen human endeavour and history wiped out.

The bombing of Plymouth had not broken the city's will to resist. It only made its people more determined not to give in and he feared that was the case here with the Germans. Eric raised the binos again and watched the dust and smoke dissipate, the even more reduced jagged remnants of monastery walls gradually becoming distinct. He pulled the binoculars down again and stared miserably at a tuft of grass between his boots, shivering in the breeze. Eric knew today's jubilation would turn into mothers' tears.

* * *

Carefully picking his way down the muddy path through the trees to the artillery battery, Eric halted on some wooden steps somebody had banged into the ground. Trying to light a cigarette, he was astonished to see a bear. With trees either side of the path closing in, the animal was framed tightly. Standing upright holding a shell, its big brown eyes looking straight at him.

The bear snorted, breath hanging in the air, then shuffled away out of Eric's line of sight. Tucking the unlit cigarette in a breast pocket, Eric bounded down the steps to see where the beast had gone. Coming out into the open, he found it handing the shell to a soldier stacking them by a howitzer. The bear slumped down onto all fours and ambled back past Eric to a nearby truck. 'Hello, how can we help?' a lightly-accented, foreign voice enquired in English. When Eric turned around he found it was a short, stocky Polish Army officer – the crowned eagle badge on his beret glimmering in the sun. Eric saluted and asked: 'Where on earth did you get him, Sir?'

The Pole laughed.

'Ah, Wojtek…In Iran, when he was a cub.'

The bear was now standing by the back of the truck, a Polish soldier gently laying a shell from a crate across his giant, outstretched paws.

'He is our good luck symbol,' the Polish officer explained.

'Your mascot?'

The bear lumbered past with the shell.

'Yes, that's correct.'

'He's quite some beast.'

Two soldiers took the shell off Wojtek.

'Does he ever drop them?'

'No fear!'

Wojtek headed over to them on all fours, Eric tensing as the creature got nearer. Sensing his unease, the Polish officer put a steadying hand on Eric's forearm. 'He won't harm you - only Germans.'

The bear rolled onto his back, squirming into mud and giving the Polish officer a beseeching look, letting out a pleading yowl.

'I get his reward.'

On the Polish officer's return, Wojtek immediately sat up, eyes shining. There was the hiss of a beer bottle being opened and, much to Eric's astonishment, the bear grasped it between his paws and greedily sucked the liquid down. Dropping the empty bottle, Wojtek chugged another beer down.

'I trust he doesn't handle shells after this?' Eric enquired.

The Pole grinned proudly.

'Why, of course - in fact he works faster.'

Eric couldn't tell if the man was serious or not. Hurling away the second empty bottle, the bear downed a third beer and then got up onto his hind legs, yawned and headed over to the truck. Instead of a shell being handed down, a couple of Polish soldiers pushed Wojtek up into the back. With a loud laugh the Pole revealed: 'We are going now bombardier, back to get more shells, always more shells.' Holding out his hand, he added: 'Good luck.' As they shook, the Polish officer suddenly looking concerned.

'You go against Cassino?'

Eric nodded.

'With the New Zealanders.'

'Then may God be with you.'

Eric frowned, watching the Pole walk over to a jeep. It started up and followed the truck along a narrow road through the trees, both soon disappearing around a bend. Eric was not a religious man, but if a few prayers would see him through, *then perhaps he could try?*

But God's protection had been as nothing against the bombs that destroyed the monastery, so what armour would prayers provide for him?

11

Captain Matarehua 'Monty' Wikiriwhi, the Officer Commanding the 28th Battalion's B Company, gathered his officers and NCOs together in the kitchen of a ruined farmhouse, water dripping from the scorched rafters onto a plastic covered battlefield map. Moving a small oil lamp over its surface, Wikiriwhi explained the brutal simplicity of what lay ahead during Operation Avenger, in which B Company would play a key role alongside A Company.

The key objective for B Company would be the station itself.

The assault by the battle-hardened Maori warriors would use cover of the night to reach the railway station on the edge of the Cassino town. With the valley flooded by the waters of the Rapido the only way to reach their objective was across a causeway formed by a railway line and its embankment. The Germans, lurking in the town's ruined buildings and dug into slopes above, would know the precise range; they would have it all mined and covered by intersecting machine gun fire.

Intelligence said the Maoris' opponents were not just paratroopers, whom they had met before on the battlefield, at Crete in 1941, but also elite mountain troops withdrawn from Russia and sent to defend Cassino.

This caused a murmur of satisfaction around the table – the Maoris would enjoy fighting the best the enemy had to offer *and give them a good hiding*. However, the only defence the Maoris would enjoy during the initial assault was the cloak of darkness - and speed after the current artillery bombardment ceased.

Wikiriwhi paused to scan the circle of faces, most of whom were his fellow Maoris but a few were white New Zealanders.

Two of them were strangers - Eric and Jenkins, loitering at the back listening intently, waiting to hear about their part in the forthcoming attack.

Eric noted with alarm that other people's eyes were filled with fire and couldn't help but express his misgivings. 'Fuck.'

Hearing Eric's curse, the captain enquired:

'What was that bombardier?'

The Kiwis parted to let the captain get a good look at him.

Jenkins tugged at his sleeve to urge caution, but Eric shook him off.

'I said "fuck", Sir.'

Wikiriwhi gave him a grim smile and nodded.

'Indeed, bombardier,' he agreed, 'but we Maoris can handle it. They give us the impossible and we pull it off because we fight not necessarily for King or Empire but for each other, and for our tribes.'

Eric returned the captain's gaze equally steadily, but a muscle twitch in his temple gave away the anxiety he felt. The Maori officer added, his eyes softening: 'And you too must fight for your kith and kin even though they be far away.'

Finished with Eric, Wikiriwhi moved his lamp across the map again, the circle of officers and NCOs closing up around the table.

Feeling an urge not to appear too much a mere quailing Englishman, Eric interjected: 'Well, begging your pardon, Sir, but…'

The captain stopped, looked up his jaw taut with fury, the circle parting once again.

'The Luftwaffe bombed the hell out of my home city…'

Anger dissipating, Wikiriwhi suggested softly: 'Go on.'

'And after they killed my father and my brother,' Eric explained, 'if I can help your lot kill a few of them tonight it will even the score.' Nodding, Wikiriwhi boomed: 'Alright, that's the spirit!'

Resuming his briefing, the captain explained the idea was to treat the night attack a bit like a beach landing – except launched across the causeway of the railway track against the station beach-head. They would seize and hold the buildings, calling down heavy artillery fire when needed. This would be the job of their two Royal Artillery friends - another glance in the direction of Eric and Jenkins - providing a distraction, so Kiwi engineers could throw a bridge across the water from Allied lines to the nearest suitable road into the town. This would enable 2nd New Zealand Division tanks and troops in half-tracks to storm into action.

The captain suggested it would probably be a bitter battle getting across to the station and they would face a hard fight hanging onto to it, but they must - for the pride of New Zealand, and - more importantly - for the honour of the Maori people. There were nodding heads and grimly determined smiles all around the table. It would be no tentative thrust, for the Maoris would go all the way, even if it was through the Gates of Damnation. The briefing broke up, with Eric and Jenkins - each lost in contemplating the high likelihood of an imminent death - walking slowly back to their jeep, which was parked behind the farmhouse. 'This is a bloody suicide mission, isn't it?' Jenkins ventured morosely, his voice heavy with Welsh doom.

Eric made no comment.

The two artillerymen climbed into the open-topped vehicle, Eric reaching down for a sack in the footwell on the passenger's side and pulling out a small bottle of raw, southern Italian grappa. Unscrewing the top, he took a very big gulp, which set fire to his gullet, then handed it to Jenkins.

'Drink,' he urged.

Jenkins regarded the clear liquid with suspicion.

'Go on, man,' Eric growled.

Jenkins consumed the rest of the bottle's contents, grimacing.

Eric climbed out and went around to the back of the jeep to check the small backpack he would be taking with him, sorting essentials from the non-essentials – retaining the former (half a loaf of bread, another small bottle of grappa, a compact cleaning kit for his machine gun) and putting the latter (sewing kit, spare pair of socks, small shaving mirror) inside a kitbag in the back of the vehicle. He stooped down behind the driver's seat where Jenkins was sprawled and flipped open a metal ammunition box. Squinting in the dark, but mainly using his sense of touch, Eric retrieved spare magazines for his Thompson submachine gun. These he shoved into his back-pack along with a couple of grenades, also putting a couple of magazines and grenades in ammunition pouches hung from the webbing fastened over his leather jerkin along with a waist belt.

Noticing that his hands had a slight tremor, to steady them Eric grabbed the rim of the jeep chassis and squeezed. 'Come on,' he told Jenkins, who was again lost in morose thoughts.

'Check your stuff.'

As Jenkins climbed out, Eric came around to the driver's side of the jeep, reaching into the sack in the foot well and extracting a rectangular tin containing soot. Prising the lid off and putting it on the bonnet, he streaked his face and neck with the soot, then the backs of his hands - the objective being to reduce the chances of his pale face giving him away during the coming night battle. Occasionally he replenished the tin's contents from some recently burned down Italian building, using a knife to laboriously scrape it off a wall or some such - Eric hoped to do so one day in Germany itself. The smell of the ad hoc skin camouflage as he applied it made Eric think of Plymouth – the burned out buildings of his home city, left in ashes by the Luftwaffe. Using the soot was a suitable act of remembrance and revenge.

Jenkins was meanwhile checking the lightweight WS38 back-pack radio, using a voltmeter to ensure its valves were in working order. 'Put some camo on,' Eric told him, offering the tin. The other man was still busy with the radio, so Eric nudged him, provoking an irritated exclamation. 'Yes, in a minute!' Eric left the tin on the bonnet of the jeep, reaching into the back again, this time to pick up his helmet and pull it on. Finally, in a reflexive good luck gesture he'd picked up along the way, Eric thrice patted the holster on his right hip that carried his 9mm Browning pistol.

* * *

They were currently well out of danger from enemy fire, tucked away in a wooded spot about half a mile from the start line of the attack, the night sky lit up by the occasional explosion and tumbling arc of tracer fire as a machine gun chattered. Then out of the darkness, came the most blood-curdling sound - dozens of voices reciting the ancient war cry of the Maoris, intended to send a spasm of fear through the bowels of the foe they were about to meet. Investigating, Eric and Jenkins found New Zealand troops arrayed in rows in a clearing, moving in unison as they performed the war dance of their people, a haka. The chant reverberated through the trees.

Ka mate, ka mate! Ka ora, ka ora!

It is death, it is death, it is life, it is life!

Despite the darkness, Eric could make out the maniacal grins and the quivering tongues, clenched fists, arms and legs moving in unison – beating chests and slapping thighs, gesticulating towards the foe. The chatter of small arms fire and explosions seemed to die away in fear as the haka continued, culminating with

A, upane! Ka upane!

Up the ladder, up the ladder!

A, upane! Ka upane!

Up to the top

Whiti te ra!

Into the sunlight

The sound of the haka faded, swallowed up by the mist and the trees, the men dispersing to sort out their kit. 'That's brilliant isn't it?' Jenkins hissed. 'Now every German in the valley will know we're coming.'

'Come on Taff, that's the point of a war dance, to let the bastards know their end is nigh – and put the shits up them.'

This did not impress the dour Welshman.

'Oh, that's alright then, makes me feel a lot better.'

They walked back to the jeep, awaiting the order to move off on foot to the start line, which was a railway siding that bisected a grove of olive trees. The track emerged into the open on the other side and ran for 100ft before joining the main line to form 'the causeway' to the railway station.

Eric and Jenkins walked down with the headquarters platoon, directly behind Captain Wikiriwhi and his radio operator. The sky overhead was clear and, as Eric looked up, between the branches of olive trees, he could see stars twinkling.

He shivered and sighed, strangely feeling almost happy. In accepting that whether he lived or died came down to events beyond his control, Eric had cast off all his worries and cares. There was only the here and now. They would soon be living very fast indeed – *acting and not thinking.*

Of course, that could all change in a second and he might go insane and collapse into a terrified heap or, worse still, lose his life. For now, the pack bobbing between his shoulder blades and machine gun slung across his chest felt very light indeed.

The battlefield had become unusually quiet – but it was a momentary lull before the tumult of a preparatory artillery barrage against the Germans - as if both sides were waiting for the curtain to go up. There was the occasional bang and fizz as a mortar-launched star shell from the German side of the valley curved into the sky, popping open its parachute and drifting down slowly to bathe the tops of trees in an eerie blue light.

After struggling across a stretch of water-logged land, having to jump a few streams, the start line was reached.

Captain Wikiriwhi was among his troops, occasionally pausing to have a word with soldiers adjusting their kit and busy making sure their weapons were loaded. There were clicks of mechanisms being slid home – a bullet snugly up the spout – grunts here and there as strap buckles were tightened with a hard tug. Careful not to fall into a shell hole, Eric followed close behind the captain as the latter continued providing encouragement to his men and shaking hands.

At the starting line, the captain entered into conversation with the lieutenant in charge of the spearhead platoon. After a strong handshake with his subordinate, Captain Wikiriwhi turned to walk back down the track to where the headquarters platoon waited in the centre of the battle formation.

He took Eric and Jenkins to one side and told them in a low voice: 'You men are bloody important to me, because if we need the big guns I've been told you can call in fire right on top of us to dig us out of the shit.'

'We won't let you down, Sir,' Eric assured him.

'Good,' said Wikiriwhi. 'Because of your importance bombardier I am giving you over to Private Armstrong and Private Green here.'

Two enormous Maori soldiers loomed out of the night, one holding a Sten gun, the other a Bren. Even in the dark, the weapons looked like toys in their hands. The captain elaborated: 'They were both in the All Blacks team of 1937 that destroyed England and Wales, and are more than equal to handing off any German who tries to kill you. If they have to they will haul you by the scruffs of your necks, screaming and shouting to where I need you.' Armstrong and Green grinned broadly, deeply gratified by such high praise. Eric nodded, but calm acceptance of his situation flew away – his fate would be in the hands of these two hulking brutes and now he felt gnawing fear in the pit of his stomach. It was not helped by Jenkins whispering: 'That's us fucked then.'

Hearing this, Private Armstrong remarked with an evil chuckle:

'Don't worry mate, *we're all fucked*.'

Captain Wikiriwhi went over to the nearest of his NCOs and ordered:

'Alright, tell the boys to fix bayonets.'

The instruction was passed on in a loud whisper. Up and down the line cold steel was withdrawn from dozens of scabbards followed by clunks and clicks as bayonets were fitted to rifle muzzles, and Stens. Right on queue the Allied artillery began its bombardment of Cassino to, hopefully, make the enemy keep their heads down.

* * *

The Germans had expertly sited their MG34 machine guns – air-cooled weapons capable of spewing out 900 rounds a minute – to create withering fields of fire. Their mortars were, as expected, zeroed in on the railway line and embankment along which the brave Maoris charged.

Barbed wire was artfully, if inefficiently, arranged here and there across their anticipated path too, with exploding mines underfoot soon taking their toll. Assault troops slipped through what few gaps were offered, though some were entangled momentarily - not a pleasant predicament with shrapnel and bullets flying around - while others, unable to beat the prickly steel thickets, called for wire cutters to be brought forward.

With the enemy deluge of fire intensifying it became a cavalcade of horror, for the attackers had no other way across the flooded valley floor - the darkness actually gave little protection amid the flashes of exploding mortar bombs and mines. The first platoon was thinned out within seconds, men jerking like marionettes in the flickering light of tracers and parachute flares before thudding to the ground as if their strings had been cut, limbs jumbled at unnatural angles.

Yet the Maoris did not falter as they charged…firing and moving…firing and moving…even as the storm of hot lead and shrapnel eroded their numbers like a cruel sea eating away sand and shingle on a beach. It was both pitiful and magnificent and - true to their mission - in the centre of this maelstrom Armstrong and Green safeguarded their precious charges. Several times they shoved Eric and Jenkins to the ground, providing suppressing fire before picking them up and pushing them along.

With the half-demolished station in sight, Eric broke free, dragging Jenkins with him and cursing in the foulest language. He had become a demon, too. Tumbling to the ground, face slamming into crushed stones, ribs hurting keenly, Eric pushed Jenkins away. Moaning, he also couldn't help but laugh at the awful pain and the insanity of the situation. Determined not to be manhandled by the Maoris again, Eric popped his head above the railway track, instantly withdrawing when several bullets clanged off it. 'Come on

Jenkins, move your fucking arse!' Eric yelled, gathering up his courage and throwing himself across to the other side.

He began leopard-crawling towards a railway platform, a process that was extremely hard and painful on the knees and elbows. The Welshman, still cursing for all he was worth, followed on, shoving the radio along in front of him. Reaching the shelter of the platform lip, they collapsed into a wheezing heap, only to be immediately disturbed by Captain Wikiriwhi who had crawled along to see them. Trying in vain to make himself heard above the explosions, he screamed something unintelligible. Eric stared blankly at the man's flapping mouth until the captain grabbed him by the collar and yelled in his ear: 'Call for fire on the street opposite the station, so we can get inside these bloody buildings.'

'Yes, Sir!' Eric bellowed back.

Looking around for shelter, Eric dragged Jenkins over to a pillar supporting the remains of the shredded platform canopy and behind it they set up the radio.

Pulling a map from inside his jerkin, Eric also dug out a small torch, flicking it on and scrutinising the map, orientating it so he could call artillery fire right on top of the enemy. Resting the map on his knees, Eric extracted a notebook, pulled out a pencil tucked into its spine and scribbled down fire co-ordinates. A massive explosion shook the platform violently, making Eric bang his helmet on the pillar and drop the flashlight while Jenkins collapsed on top of him. Growling with frustration, Eric pushed the Welshman off, screaming: 'Are you hit!?'

Shaking himself, Jenkins blurted sheepishly: 'Don't think so.'

Fumbling around on the concrete platform Eric found the flashlight, picked it up, using it to try and locate the notebook. 'Where are you!' he screamed in frustration and fury as another explosion shook the platform and...*thank Christ, there it was by his feet.* He grabbed the notebook, turned the flashlight off, slipped it into a pocket and pulled the slightly dazed Jenkins back behind the pillar again, pressing the notebook into one of his hands.

'Get a grip!' Eric yelled. 'Radio in the co-ordinates.'

Nodding and wincing as more shells slammed in nearby, Jenkins coughed nervously and adjusted the headset and microphone, the exploding shells making it difficult to make himself heard over the radio – but he persevered. Eric braced himself for a back full of shrapnel or a bullet at any second.

Captain Wikiriwhi appeared out of the dark, crouching down beside Eric and yelling: 'Where's the bloody artillery!?' Looking over his shoulder, Eric shouted: 'On… its way, Sir, to give the bastards the pasting they deserve.'

The captain grinned and punched him gently in the arm, shouting:

'Praise the Lord and pass the ammunition, eh?'

He disappeared somewhere else to rally his troops, leaving Eric awestruck at the man's indestructible courage under fire.

'Well!?' Eric yelled at Jenkins, who flinched as a bullet ricocheted off the lip of the platform. Brow covered in sweat, eyes flickering from side to side wildly, the Welshman flashed a devilish grin and bellowed: 'Oh yes boyo, them bloody Fritzes are going to regret tangling with Mother Jenkins' boy.' He handed the notebook back to Eric and they hunkered down behind the pillar. Within seconds the air was torn open by incoming heavy shells. Gigantic explosions turned night into day as the remains of houses opposite the station vanished.

An unearthly silence descended, soon broken by the war cry of the Maoris as they rose up from shelter below platform lip and all along the railway line. The Maoris charged – the scene starkly lit by the burning buildings - still yelling their blood curdling ear cry as one voice, one man, one fearsome organism.

'Whakatangata kia kaha!'

Acquit yourselves like men, be strong!

* * *

Having made it safely into the wrecked, but somehow still standing, vestibule of the station, Eric and Jenkins headed into the shattered remains of the ticket office to set up their radio and prepare for calling in more artillery fire. Their Maori guardians followed them, smashing out what remained of the windows and making firing positions.

It took the Germans an hour or so to get their senses back and then the counter-attacks began, Eric and Jenkins calling in two further bombardments, wiping out enemy assaults before they could get in among the railway station ruins. But then a third enemy counter-attack came in almost immediately, the two sides soon locked in a desperate close quarters struggle.

Eric and Jenkins played their part at the windows, firing bursts of machine gun fire whenever they saw something move in the shadows.

Eric stepped back from a window, to go over and grab a grenade from one of his webbing pouches, which he had put on a high back chair by a table on which the backpack radio had been deposited.

As he did so, the Welshman cried out, sent flying by a MP40's metal stock in the face, his Sten gun skidding across the tiled floor. A German was climbing in through the window where Jenkins had been while Armstrong and Green were otherwise occupied at their own firing positions.

Pulling his Browning pistol from its holster with his right hand, Eric leapt forward, grappling with the enemy, who wore the distinctive cap of mountain troops. Snarling in each other's faces - spittle flying - they were evenly matched opponents.

The other man's MP40 submachine gun could not be brought to bear. With his left hand, Eric shoved the German's weapon flat against his chest. The man screamed in agony as his right thigh came down on the windowsill, in which shards of glass were still embedded. Eric used the rim of his own helmet to bang the bridge of his opponent's nose, shoving the muzzle of his pistol under the German's chin. He froze, arms dropping, as if accepting his end, light blue eyes locking with Eric's, seemingly calm and without fear. Eric could even feel the man's breath on his face and noticed the German bore a nasty scar down his left cheek.

With a loud groan, Eric shoved him back against the left-hand side of the window frame but instead of blowing the man's brains out, pressed the pistol against his right leg and pulled the trigger.

With a scream of agony, the German fell out the window and onto a pile of rubble in the street, where, as he writhed in agony, two comrades grabbed his shoulder straps and dragged him off into the dark. Eric fired a couple of desultory shots after them, then staggered back and collapsed onto the chair after shoving the webbing off it, groaning from the sheer effort of the struggle. Jenkins, who had by now recovered - after lying momentarily in a dazed heap gawping as the struggle unfolded - grabbed his weapon, leapt forward to the window and emptied a magazine's worth of Sten gun fire after the fleeing Germans. Turning to look at Eric he shouted in disbelief: 'Why didn't you blow his bloody brains out!?' Giving him a stunned smile, Eric could only manage a supercilious response, which seemed perfectly in keeping with the situation. 'It just didn't seem very sporting old chap!'

* * *

After daylight the Maoris tried valiantly to hold on at the railway station, but it was impossible – the Germans just kept on coming, while New Zealand divisional engineers failed in their bid to put the bridge across. Reinforcements were not arriving any time soon.

The company's PIAT anti-tank weapons were soon expended - no matter how many oncoming panzers the Kiwis destroyed the enemy pushed ever harder. Captain Wikiriwhi radioed battalion headquarters for instructions and was told to hang on at all costs.

'To hell with that,' Wikiriwhi muttered.

He was soon allowed to stage a fighting withdrawal – it was that or cease to exist in a hopeless last stand. What was left of the company would attempt to get across the railway track causeway, hoping to benefit from a smokescreen laid down by Allied tanks firing from the edge of some olive groves.

The artillerymen smashed their radio – something Eric knew would get him into deep trouble later with his parent unit's quartermaster, but humping the unwieldy thing back to friendly lines under fire – *and it seemed a lot heavier now than on the way in* - would most likely be fatal. After doing that Eric and Jenkins were to join

Armstrong and Green already waiting under cover of the station platform lip.

Eric did not make it far, a bullet slamming into his right thigh as he exited the ticket office, sending him arse over tit. Jenkins and the two Maoris pulled him over and under the platform edge and once he was on the ground a bayonet was used to rip open his trouser leg and a field dressing applied to the gaping wound. Armstrong used a syrette to stick a dose of morphine into him for good measure. Green fished a rolled up puttee out of his back-pack, which he used to make a tourniquet, Eric groaning in agony until the drug kicked in.

The New Zealand tank guns began barking, attempting to lay down their smoke on the German side of the railway causeway, but too many of the shells landed in the water and were damp squibs.

Captain Wikiriwhi gave the order to withdraw, but, as he made to lead the way, a burst of enemy machine gun fire caught him in the legs. Yelling at his men to press on without him, three of them refused to leave, dragging Wikiriwhi down the embankment to get out of the line of fire.

Sticking to their task with grim purpose, the two Maori privates picked Eric up, one taking his legs - making him scream despite the morphine - the other grabbing him under the arms while Jenkins carried the weapons.

Green and Armstrong did amazingly well for a few hundred yards, especially with Eric effing and blinding at them – dashing for the touch line like the star rugby players they were. But, when the Germans landed a string of shells smack on the railway line it all went to shit amid a shower of stones, hot shrapnel and smoke, with Armstrong and Green felled, Eric slamming to the ground. Dragging himself along the railway track, within a few feet he was too exhausted to go on. Pressing himself as flat as he could, with bullets coming in thick and fast, the only thing that stood between Eric and death was some rusty old metal a few inches thick and not much higher. Overcome with a wave of pain, he blacked out.

When he came to a while later, Eric very slowly turned his head to try and see if anyone else was alive nearby. He stared into the dead eyes of Private Armstrong for a moment and then, looking down between his feet and past blood-soaked trousers, found what was likely to be the corpse of his other guardian, Private Green. It was hard to tell. The top of the man's head had been sliced off, as if by a giant knife cutting open a boiled egg.

German snipers were still trying to hit Eric, hoping for a miracle but each time their bullets ricocheted off a rail.

Occasionally there was a flash of fire from the Allied side and sometimes *the stupid bastards* almost hit him by mistake. It was only a matter of a few hundred yards across the flooded ground to the nearest trees, but, of course, nobody was going to dash across to get him in daylight. *If they even knew he was alive*? Looking on the bright side, it also stopped the Germans from chancing a charge, and bayoneting him as they went by.

Sleep beckoned, *and boy was he tired.*

With sunset the chill came on, creeping up his legs and arms from the increasingly damp, cold ground, seeping into his back through his leather jerkin. Eric tried to flex his limbs so that, after dark, he could try and push himself back to Allied lines, but the pain was immense. Eric doubted he would have the strength. His teeth began to chatter and he started mumbling incoherently about all manner of random things: railing against God; raging at the enemy for shooting him; the Maoris for getting killed and dropping him – a thought about which he instantly felt guilty. And what had happened to the fearless Wikiriwhi? Such men! Such courage, all for nothing; due to a surge of pain, he cursed his mother for having given birth to him in the first place. Then, with hot tears streaming down his cheeks, he just gave up and stared at the stars. They were *very beautiful and it wouldn't be long now until he was up there too*, or, and this made him cackle, *maybe down there in the fiery flames of hell.*

A dark shape flitted past to his left, a footstep crunching on the embankment ballast. Grimacing at the pain, Eric reached into the holster for his pistol, but it wasn't there. There was nothing to lose, so he shouted: 'Friend or foe?'

A gun fired a single shot and then a storm of fire from the German lines swept the tracks, provoking plenty of cursing as other dark shapes nearby threw themselves flat. 'Bloody hell!' came a distinctive Welsh voice he knew so well. Eric croaked: 'Jenkins, is that you?'

A bullet hit the rail by his head, making an absurd *wheeeeyow* noise as it zinged away into the dark. Then some figures were crouched around him, rolling him onto a stretcher, making him grind his teeth in pain, but not crying out - in case it attracted more enemy lead.

They carried him down to the bottom of the embankment and somebody pressed a canteen to his cracked lips, a Kiwi voice gently whispering: 'Drink, mate.'

He downed it greedily and began coughing. *Brandy.*

As the warmth burned through his cold body, the canteen was taken away and the New Zealander told him: 'Right, now this is going to hurt, but we can't do anything else.' Eric wheezed: 'Get on with it.'

The Kiwi squeezed his shoulder then took one of the stretcher handles. 'Right boys…one…two…three…' They hoisted him up and began to run, keeping their heads below the top of the embankment as bullets kicked up stones along its top. The pain was excruciating and Eric felt so ashamed to cause them such trouble – he could hear their laboured breath and their curses while he ground his teeth to stop from screaming out in agony.

A shambling dark shape appeared by the side of the stretcher, whispering loudly: 'I didn't think we'd find you alive.'

It was Jenkins, voice laden fear and exertion as he ran to keep up. Despite his pain, Eric smiled and joked: 'Worse luck for you, eh?'

12

Stonehouse Naval Hospital, July 1944

It was burrowing away at the core of his brain - the need for alcoholic release. His mind's eye was fixed on a glass of relief, condensation running down its side, bubbles rising in lazy streams – that latter revealed as he ran a finger down it - the sunlight creating a bewitching honey glow…a pale Italian lager; cool, fizzing on the tongue, sliding down smoothly. He could knock a few of them back and slip into a hazy, mellow intoxication. *Or maybe Scotch on the rocks, the ice cubes clinking as he swirled it around in the glass?* In his mind's eye he marvelled at the deep caramel colour. Then there was the hard-edged sting on the tongue and burn as it blazed a path down his throat, straight to the nub of the problem.

Eric sighed, screwed his eyes shut.

It would pass; this yearning for oblivion in a bottle.

The easy way out.

The click clack of a nurse's shoes echoed down the corridor.

Opening his eyes, he looked towards the sound, seeing a slim, shapely silhouette advancing, wondering if it was the nurse who had taken his fancy during a past visit to the hospital.

As she got closer he could see this one had peroxide blonde hair - and she was smiling at him, her deep, dark brown eyes utterly magnetic. Eric wondered if perhaps a fuck would be a better release for his pent-up fury.

Once upon a time he would have felt ashamed at having such crude thoughts. *The old Eric would have been.*

Bloody upright Constable Wise.

Well, he wasn't here, now was he?

'Sergeant Wise?' the nurse asked, her soft American accent incredibly sexy. He nodded and she led the way back down the corridor, his admiring eyes fixed on her nice little behind. Fortunately, he was looking up when she glanced over her shoulder and so was able to return her smile. The nurse opened the door with an unabashed grin and suggested he should just shout when it was time to leave. She promised to make sure he got to the gate safely.

Eric reckoned he would ask her out.

* * *

Dust motes twirled and pirouetted in a beam of light that penetrated the sash cord window of the doctor's office, settling on the bare wooden boards and faded Persian rug between Eric's feet and the front edge of the desk. Behind it sat Surgeon Lieutenant Commander Samuel 'Doc' Darrow, US Navy who was smooth in every way – tanned, slicked back dark hair, perfect white teeth and all.

Eric was feeling jaded, as the pick-me-up of the nurse's flirting had soon faded. On his return from Italy, after time in a field hospital and evacuation by Red Cross ship to Southampton, he'd been sent back to the South West, finding Americans had flooded Plymouth.

Making it the biggest of their naval bases in Europe, their warships dominated the Sound while Yank soldiers poured into local barracks to replace British troops away fighting in Italy or Burma.

It seemed there were also tented cities and hut villages wherever there was a patch of green. The Americans had even taken over the old naval hospital at Stonehouse.

To some locals their accents, their tans and their jitterbug ways all seemed incongruous in Devon. They were *overfed, overpaid , over-sexed and over here*, as the resentful saying went.

Newly promoted to Sergeant, Eric was staying at Raglan Barracks, just down the road from Stonehouse, one of the few remaining islands of British Army presence in the city. He had put in several requests for a return to the front line and was growing increasingly frustrated about the delay as fighting in Normandy raged.

At least once a week he had to come across to the hospital for psychological assessment, which was *a right load of Yank balderdash.*

A cough brought Eric out of his grumpy musings. The doctor was staring at him with an encouraging smile that invited him to open proceedings. *Alright then, he would…*

'Why am I here *again*, Doc?'

'Talking to me?' Darrow asked, leaning forward to pick up a packet of *Players Navy Cut* cigarettes from the blotter on his desk

'Yes.'

Darrow waved the cigarette packet invitingly at Eric, who shook his head. 'Because orders is orders. To decide if you are fit to be sent back to the front line.'

Eric sighed heavily.

Darrow flicked open his Zippo lighter and thumbed the igniter to make the flame leap as he touched it to his cigarette. Thoroughly irritated at being in front of the Doc at all, Eric asked: 'To determine if my nerves have had it…if I'm a coward now?'

The naval surgeon snapped shut his Zippo emphatically and said: 'No. In the American services we understand that sometimes people have had enough.'

Darrow let the lighter tumble onto the blotter, Eric leaning forward to pick it up. He studied the worn ha'penny with the Elizabethan galleon Golden Hind engraving that was affixed to it. The year of the coin was 1937 - back when his dad and brother were alive, when the heart hadn't been burned out of Plymouth. Eric was tempted to ask Darrow why exactly he'd put the English coin on his Zippo, but then decided not to. He placed the lighter on the blotter and leaned back in the chair. The American pressed on.

'Let's discuss the fight in the railway station at Cassino.'

'What for?'

Darrow placed his cigarette on the edge of a metal ashtray and blew smoke out of the corner of his mouth.

'Just humour me,' he suggested. 'Specifically, I'd like to discuss the officer you shot; the German climbing through the window. Why didn't you shoot him in the face?'

'Who told you about it?'

'I talked to your old Italy buddy, Jenkins, on the phone, yesterday.'

'Never could keep his mouth shut.'

'So?'

'Why didn't I shoot the German in the face?'

Darrow nodded.

'The truth?'

'Yes.'

'Well, as he was trying to climb through the window and his leg was right next to my gun muzzle, I pressed the trigger and he screamed and fell out.' Darrow decided to see how Eric would respond to an accusation of timidity: 'Not because you didn't have the guts to kill him?'

Eric suppressed his annoyance at the implication.

'A shot in the leg can kill, if it severs the femoral artery.'

'Here you were face to face with the enemy, at last - the enemy who had killed your father, your brother and wiped out your home city - but you chose not to kill this guy.'

'Maybe the German died later?' Eric proposed.

'Let's just go with the flow and have him living. You could have made certain – put a bullet right through his head and you didn't.'

Eric shrugged.

'Perhaps for you the war had been about remote killing – the bombing of your city, your father's ship being hit by a torpedo and your brother killed after a U-boat sank his ship. It's a fact that in modern warfare we rarely see the enemy face-to-face, hardly ever see the human beings trying to kill us from such a distance. When we are under fire, merciless fire, like bombing, the fact that we can't hit back threatens to destroy our minds.'

Eric laughed harshly and asked:

'And you would know, how?'

'I was at Pearl Harbor,' responded Darrow with equanimity, 'one of the doctors in the battleship *Arizona* and we got the crap bombed out of us. Sunk without being able to do a lot to stop it.'

That shot Eric down, and he felt a little ashamed of himself.

Darrow sprang out of his chair and went across to a table by the window, where there was a pot of coffee on a hotplate.

Picking it up, he enquired: 'Want some?'

Eric shook his head.

Why couldn't the Yanks drink tea?

As he poured himself a mug, the doctor carried on with his story: 'I was plenty angry after that. Then I was in the cruiser *Quincy* when the Japs murdered us in the night at Guadalcanal, and nobody saw that coming…' He stopped, turned around and shrugged.

'…but we're not here to discuss my history.'

Taking a gulp of coffee, the Doc remarked:

'Wonderful cup of Joe.'

'Are you sure I cannot tempt you Sergeant?' Darrow asked, waving the mug in Eric's direction, some of the coffee slopping over the rim and onto the floorboards. 'No thanks,' replied Eric.

Digging in a trouser pocket, he offered the Doc a neatly folded white handkerchief. Taking it and kneeling down to mop up the spillage, Darrow observed: 'I am *such* a messy pup.'

He went around behind the desk, letting the handkerchief fall to the blotter. 'I'll get that laundered for you,' he promised Eric who nodded. Bringing things back to their discussion, Eric conceded wearily: 'Alright then, maybe I didn't want to shoot another man in the face because when it came to it I didn't have the guts.'

Darrow shook his head, retrieving his cigarette from the ashtray.

'Don't believe it. You were given a King's medal for your actions in the blitz here and the Military Medal for the Cassino railway station fight.'

He blew smoke into the air, where it caught a sunbeam, reminding Eric for a moment of the plume over Plymouth the night after the bombing raid that burned down the Octagon.

'You're not a coward Eric, but you think war is wrong?'

Eric's eyes flashed. 'That's a stupid question! Nobody thinks war is right, except maybe the Nazis and Japanese, but we can't let the bastards get away with it, so we fight fire with fire.'

Darrow, cigarette clamped between his lips, smiled apologetically and held up both hands. He balanced the cigarette back on the ashtray. 'Sure … but you wanted to hit back at those who had inflicted so much pain on your family and your city?'

'Something like that.'

But then Darrow went and spoiled it.

'You wanted a moral crusade?'

Eric snorted and looked out the window to hide his annoyance with this devil's advocate game – like he was some criminal in for questioning.

'Well, anyway, you didn't just want to sit on your ass,' suggested the psychiatrist. 'You wanted action, but you joined the artillery, not the infantry.'

Eric shook his head and sighed.

'I didn't join the infantry because they wanted people in the artillery. I said that would be fine by me. Nothing deep – I just went where I was needed.'

'And sent death to the enemy by remote control, from a distance, like they did to you and yours?'

This was daft, thought Eric.

'Look, I was a policeman and it would have been pure murder to just shoot that German in the face.'

Darrow nodded. 'Alright then, we'll agree on that point.'

Eric shrugged, as if to admit defeat, though he wasn't sure what use any of this to and fro discussion was.

'It was my bad luck to be sent as a forward gunnery observer, into a hopeless fight in which a lot of people died. I had to give a hand and at least shoot a German. It was only polite.'

The American cut to the chase, giving an encouraging smile.

'Yet you were grievously wounded, so why do you want to go back?'

Eric laughed and decided to be equally forthright.

'To finish the job, to not "sit on my ass", as you Yanks say.'

'Not to get away from your mother?'

'What?'

Eric's eyes blazed, but the doctor avoided his angry stare by opening a drawer in his desk and pulling out a notebook, which he flicked through as he continued. 'You said in an earlier discussion that one of the reasons you joined up was your mother was very frightened during the Plymouth bombing raids of you not coming home from duty one night. She'd lost your dad and brother, so perhaps her anxiety was suffocating?'

Eric smouldered, staring at the cigarette slowly burning down to ash.

'Wanted to do my bit, not to let the family down.'

'I believe you haven't told her you're here.'

'How do you know these bloody things?'

Darrow smiled, but did not explain.

'Alright, yes, I can't face telling her about what happened to me… I can't bear to see her suffer more. It's just better not to go home.'

Darrow decided to give him a poke.

'Did you cry out *for* your mother when you lay wounded by the railway track at Cassino.'

That really was a contemptible ploy – *did this American think he was some kind of an idiot?*

'Excuse *me* sir,' he protested indignantly, 'but fuck off.'

The doctor's eyes twinkled, his grin flashed its brilliant white and he waved off the insult. Darrow chuckled, made a note in his book, informing Eric as he wrote: 'I know you want to go back, but I'm not going to send you.'

Eric flashed up again.

'Why the blazes not?'

The American remained cool under fire.

'Because I'll be doing my bit by keeping you alive.'

Eric groaned.

'What makes me special? Thousands of others go back…'

Darrow nodded.

'Yes, but they don't pass through my hands.'

Eric growled but the psychiatrist was unapologetic.

'You've done your bit Eric - here and in Africa and Italy - and you've paid the price. Your mother has, too, and I don't think she should suffer that telegram telling her that her only surviving son is never coming back.'

So, this medical pen pusher really could keep him at home…

'That's a medical decision?'

Darrow nodded.

'To be blunt, I think you are not fit for it – not mentally or physically, not yet anyway.'

Eric stared out the window, angry but he couldn't be blamed for some doctor stopping him going back. 'Given that I am recommending you don't go to France, where would you like to be?'

Eric shrugged.

'Not in this office, with you right now.'

He would just have to accept what the Yank decided was best for him.

'Why don't I send you across the water?'

'I thought you said no to France?'

'No, Eric, the Tamar – to Cornwall.'

Eric frowned, looked extremely puzzled.

'To dig up potatoes with our coloured troops, Eric, because my country in its wisdom won't let them fight, even though they are mentally and physically fit for it. Maybe they will benefit from hearing what it's like from someone like you?'

'Are you joking?'

'You can bitch about not being allowed to fight and it will see you out of the war.'

The doctor had seen enough dead heroes amid the smoke and

flames of Pearl and floating in the treacle black waters off Guadalcanal. If he could preserve one life from being pointlessly thrown away that would be something.

Eric snorted.

'You'll excuse me if I don't thank you, but this war will never be over.'

'You may be right Eric. There will be casualties even after the guns are silent, of that I am sure, but I think you will recover. You know, if I was a Limey doctor, one of your army surgeons, I'd tell you to keep that stiff upper lip buttoned tight and send you back to get killed. We Yanks treat things differently. Your death wouldn't make any difference and your mother, well she'd be all alone for eternity.'

Eric could only sigh at the inevitability of the doctor's logic.

'So, you can do your bit now, for the ongoing war effort by digging up spuds old bean.'

This provoked a resigned insult:

'Hope you don't mind me saying so, but sod off, Sir.'

Darrow grinned back.

'Not at all Sergeant.'

13

Cornwall, 20 July 1944

GOD'S COUNTRY, truly it was.

Eric was looking across the wetly shining mudflats of the Lynher, to a Norman church tower peeking over leafy trees against the rolling green hills. He sighed and inhaled deeply. This view must have been the same for centuries. The only 20th Century sound was the distant putter of a motorboat, which accompanied the swish of tall grasses as he pushed through them, down to the pebble beach, his boots crunching as they displaced stones.

He smiled and sighed contentedly, closing his eyes.

Opening them, shading his brow with a hand, he scanned sky for clouds, finding none, seeing only a drifting gull.

Eric tramped back up the beach, the old leg wound griping, easing himself down onto a patch of grass.

He unbuttoned his battle dress blouse, took it off and carefully folded it on his lap. The Military Medal ribbon above his left breast pocket was uppermost, while three stripes of his new rank were still freshly white on its sleeves, though unevenly sewn by his unskilled hand. It was incredibly hot – too hot for headgear - and his beret was tucked into the left epaulette. Using his battle dress jacket as a pillow, he lay back, at ease and peace after all the tumult of recent months.

That bloody Yank doctor had been right.

This was the right rest cure, digging up potatoes in the fields with his American chums. He hadn't thought about a drink, except when he had one in front of him in a local pub, for weeks.

The American nurse had been an exciting, uninhibited lover.

She had not reached his soul, or heart. This had surprised him, for he had thought of himself a bit of a sentimentalist when it came to women. He had enjoyed her and she him, but they parted on good terms knowing it had been what it was, and nothing more.

Picking off a grass stalk, Eric chewed it, eyes following its head as it switched back and forth against the blue sky.

He slipped into a nap, one of those in which you dive into the pool of sleep, pulling down with a few strokes to swim around at the bottom and then, a few minutes later, rise to the surface refreshed.

Waking up and spitting the stalk out of his mouth, he watched a falcon drift by overhead, wings twitching as its eyes searched out prey.

He looked at his wristwatch. It was nearly 2.00pm and time to get back to work.

As he sat up Eric heard a voice cry out in indignant frustration.

Looking around, he spotted somebody on the track that ran along the top of the beach bending over a cycle. Getting to his feet and putting his battle dress blouse on, Eric saw that it was a young woman, dressed in dark blue culottes and a yellow blouse, her dark auburn hair in a pony tail. She did not notice his approach, so absorbed was she in fiddling with the bicycle chain and muttering under her breath.

'Hello!' he called out as he got near. 'Got trouble!?'

She cast an angry glare in his direction.

'Want some help?' he asked.

'No thanks,' she finally responded with an uninviting tone.

He turned away and headed off down the path, back towards the farmhouse where his workmates would be waiting. 'Excuse me!'

she cried out, this time less hostile. Eric turned around and found her with hands held out to either side, covered in bicycle chain grease.

She asked with a conciliatory smile: 'Do you have a handkerchief?'

Walking back to her and digging in his pocket, before handing it over Eric noticed to his embarrassment that - despite being laundered and sent back by Doc Darrow - his handkerchief had a permanent brown coffee stain. Their fingers brushed as she took it from him, the contact causing Eric's pulse to quicken. She used the hankie to try and wipe the filth off her hands, then stopped, a horrified look exerting itself as she saw the mess she'd made of it.

'Oh, how terrible – do you mind?'

He smiled, shook his head.

She laughed and his heart beat a little faster at the sound, so he leaned over the bicycle and inspected it, his mind racing, trying to think of something to say.

'Well?' she asked as he straightened up.

'Your chain has had it,' he ventured, which was not much of a line, but it was all he could think of. Their eyes met for a moment and she shyly looked down, continued cleaning her hands on the handkerchief.

He picked her bicycle up, turned it around.

'We could take this down to the farm if you like and try to fix it.'

She grinned, nodded.

'That would be great.'

He was suddenly overcome with a desire to kiss her there and then, but he suppressed it and began pushing the bicycle down the path.

'What shall I do with your handkerchief?' she asked, walking alongside him. 'You're welcome to it,' he suggested with a laugh.

'I shall treasure it.'

He glanced at her, their eyes meeting again.

'Good.'

Picking up the emotion in his voice, she was shocked but also excited.

He ventured: 'Didn't knights of old give ladies handkerchiefs?'

She laughed and shook her head.

'No, it was the ladies who gave the knights scarves to tie on their lances before they went into battle, I'm sure it was.'

Keen to keep the conversation going, he told her:

'Well that hankie has been from North Africa to Italy and back.'

As soon as he uttered that sentence, he felt it was a stupid thing to say, but she didn't seem to find it crass and merely smiled.

They stopped at a stile, and he went over first, bicycle on his shoulder, turning to take her hand and help her down.

'How were you going to manage to get the bike over this?' he asked.

'I'm stronger than I look,' she said with a challenging look.

Feeling foolish he lapsed into silence as they neared the end of the path, the farmhouse in sight.

'We've met before,' she announced.

'Really?' he couldn't recall it at all and wondered how he failed to remember such a lovely girl.

'At the hospital. I was a naval nurse at Stonehouse.'

He smiled, leaning on the handlebars but said nothing, so she went on. 'You were upset by something and I asked if you were alright. I think you came in to visit someone at the hospital, a sailor who was very poorly.'

He smiled, now finally recalling the incident and her, which made his heart beat faster. 'Why, yes, of course - that was a shipmate of my brother's ...I was looking for information about how Bert, that's my brother, came to lose his life.'

She frowned, and asked cautiously: 'Was he able to help?'

He nodded.

'Sort of.'

'It won't surprise you to hear he died not long after,' she revealed.

Eric nodded but made no comment, an awkward silence disturbed only by the mewing of seagulls overhead and to fill it he enquired: 'Where are you now?'

'Oh, a naval hospital in Torpoint.'

She stared at him with growing curiosity as he pulled his beret from his epaulette, her bike resting against him. He had a twinkle in his eye that she liked, but there was something deeper and complex.

She wondered if it was a good or bad thing to have met on that path? *Another soldier to break her heart?*

Yet, there was something different about him, and she felt like she'd known him for years in the space of a few minutes. Now he was looking straight into her eyes and she didn't look away.

'By the way, I'm Eric,' he revealed.

'Katherine,' she replied.

'Come on,' he said, taking the bike's handlebars, and they pushed it down the slope towards a farmhouse, which was nestled in a dip.

14

Cremyll Boatyard

THIS TIME it wasn't the smell of bacon that woke Eric, but loud, tuneless whistling by whoever was shoving it around the frying pan below.

Throwing back the single sheet, springs inside the sagging single bed mattress squealed, one even twanging loudly as Eric sat on the edge of the bed, staring at the whitewashed door of the attic room. It looked like it had been put together by a drunk - hung lopsided in the frame, light streaming through gaps in its panels.

He half expected his mum to walk in with a cup of tea and a cheery hello, to open the curtains and fuss around picking lint off his battle dress blouse hanging on the corner of a wardrobe door.

After running a hand through sleep-jumbled hair, yawning and stretching, Eric ventured across the bare floorboards.

Taking the serge battle dress trousers from the back of a chair - the room's only other piece of furniture – Eric climbed into them then pulled on his working shirt, sinking back onto the bed to grab his boots and pull them on. Getting up again, Eric ducked to avoid the roof timbers, reaching for his battle dress blouse and hauling it on.

'Good morning you noisy bastard!' Eric exclaimed as he plunged down some stairs into the small kitchen, taking a diversion into the lavatory just next door.

A spindly, weather-beaten form in faded blue naval boiler suit hunched over the frying pan gave a smoky chortle, eyes crinkled up in his sea salt-blasted face. 'Morning Eric!' he called out. Shivering as he unleashed a torrent of urine, into the pan, Eric yelled back: 'Morning Jan!'

By the time Eric emerged, there was a white enamel plate with an egg and bacon doorstep sandwich nestling up to a blue enamel War Office mug full to the brim with dark brown, steaming tea both sitting the centre of the crooked kitchen table.

Jan's ability to whistle up hearty breakfasts was impressive and testament to the fact that those with connections among the local farming community could get whatever they needed - rationing be hanged.

Flinging the frying pan with into the half-filled sink - provoking a splash and a cloud of steam - Jan grabbed his own bacon sandwich and mug of tea, making his way out of the kitchen, down a short corridor and into the adjoining covered slipway.

Its sole occupant, filling the small dock almost completely - revealed by shafts of sunlight breaking down through an ill-assembled roof - was a naval attack craft. Cables snaked all over its upper works, the paintwork chipped away in many places to bare wood or metal, the whole vessel having an air of purposeful disarray so typical of refits.

Eric brought his breakfast out to join Jan and they surveyed the chaos. The river lapped against the slipway at the bottom end of the dock where special doors let the water in and out, but hid what was inside from any curious waterborne passers-by. Jan reached up to balance his plateful of bacon and egg sandwich on the boat's upper deck. One rough, calloused hand reached into a boiler suit pocket for a packet of cigarettes while the other picked up the mug of tea for a sip.

'Still a bloody mess Jan,' Eric observed, before taking a bite out of his own sandwich. Jan coughed as he shook his head and spat some phlegm into the dust and wood shavings on the dockside. 'What d'ye know?' the sailor suggested, 'you're just a footslogger.'

Flicking his cigarette into the damp dock, placing his mug next to the plate on the vessel's upper deck, Jan reached up to grab hold of a guardrail stanchion. Pulling himself up onto the craft with a strength and agility that belied his age, the veteran chief petty officer then disappeared below deck.

Chewing on his sandwich, Eric put the plate on the upper deck alongside Jan's, retained the mug of tea and walked up around the side of the vessel to inspect its back end. Something draped over the stern of the craft had attracted his attention, which - in all the time he'd lodged at the boatyard - was an end of the vessel he'd never laid eyes on. It turned out to be quite a shocking discovery and Eric blurted out: 'Jan, what on earth's going on!?'

Now covered in an oily, battered old senior rating's peaked cap, Jan's head appeared from a hatch that gave access to the engineering spaces at the stern.

'What's wrong young 'un?'

A bemused Eric gestured up at the Ensign hanging from the stern with the mug, some tea slopping over its lip.

'That's a German flag, Jan.'

The old sailor grinned, climbing out of the hatch and walked along the upper deck to the stern, hauling down the Kriegsmarine ensign and unhooking it. 'Well, that's because this is a captured E-boat.'

Eric's eye widened, his mouth dropped open.

A German motor torpedo boat.

'No?'

Jan laughed hoarsely, gathering the flag into his arms.

'Why do you think they cleared all the civilians out of the boatyard and neighbouring houses. By order of Mr Spendlove who has designs for this beauty, or so I believe.' Eric frowned deeply – *Mr Spendlove?*

'Would that be *Captain* Spendlove?'

'Don't let on I let the cat out of the bag,' said Jan, a little sheepish as he stuffed the flag into dirty old kitbag. 'I gets my orders from on high and I goes where told with my mob.'

This being a weekend, Jan was on his own, just titivating the boat, while his 'mob' – a rough and ready group of naval artificers and chippies – were at home or in the barracks, where no doubt a few hangovers were being nursed.

'I thought it was a British boat,' Eric remarked distractedly, for it had suddenly dawned on him that his strange billet and potato picking assignment were likely no accident. *Courtesy of the mysterious Army intelligence officer from the Tregantle Fort incident? And with Doc Darrow's collusion?* 'He's been keeping an eye on me,' thought Eric, 'like a fairy godfather, and Jan here is my baby-sitter?'

Jan opened a bridge locker and stuffed the kitbag containing the flag into it, carefully latching the lid so it was all tucked away from prying eyes. Swinging himself back over the side to stand beside Eric, Jan remarked: 'She looks a real sight at the moment, but give us a few weeks and she'll be ready for whatever may come her way.'

Eric nodded, walking back down the side of the boat to gather up the plates and mugs.

'Do you know this Spendlove then?' Jan enquired hesitantly, digging another cigarette out and lighting up - regardless of the strong aroma of diesel fumes in the air - and sitting down on the upper deck, letting his legs dangle over the side. Eric sighed heavily, admitting: 'I did meet him a few years ago, but only briefly.' Jan cocked his head on one side, exhaled smoke, frowned and observed: 'Maybe he's got plans for you?'

* * *

Learning of the Spendlove connection did not exactly kindle joy in Eric's heart for he had come to love his stripped-down life, reduced to a Spartan existence in the loft above the Cremyll Boatyard slipway.

Who would recognise him as *Constable* Eric Wise? Clothed in an eagerness to conform, to enforce the norms of society and always –

yes, always - smartly turned out. War in the heat and sand of the desert and Italy taught everyone to become a scruff, dressed for comfort - for fighting not parading.

He was living out of his kitbag, with a few hangers for drying a change of shirt and battle dress, doing his own laundry in the kitchen sink downstairs. Eric lived off the potatoes and other produce he dug out of the fields, supplemented occasionally by an egg and bacon breakfast with Jan - and whatever else he could forage or charm out of someone.

On weekend days in that hot summer of 1944, stretched out on his creaky, knackered bed, staring at the rafters, his mind drifted back to the emptiness of the Tunisian desert where there were no horizons, though Eric preferred not to dwell on the cold, wet, bloody misery of Cassino.

Occasionally he'd visit his mum, but Eric couldn't bear to stay long in the Turnchapel house of ghosts. She'd taken in lodgers anyway and that kept her busy. It was far better for Eric in his current frame of mind not to be there.

Some afternoons when he wasn't out in the fields, he sank into a pleasant, somnolent emptiness, laying on the bed in the loft – lulled by the cheeping of the birds in the eaves, the low whisper of the water washing onto the shore just a few yards away. Only now, the girl with the bicycle occupied his thoughts. Eric had asked her out as his pals on the potato digging team helped him repair the bike at the farm. Ignoring their sniggers and digs in each other's ribs, Eric had ploughed on. She had smiled indulgently, keeping a straight face. *There was a Benny Goodman concert in Plymouth, would she like to accompany him?*

* * *

Walking to work along the shore by the pub, to Eric's left across the broad, fast running waters of the Narrows were the tightly packed houses of Stonehouse crouching under a steel blue, cloudless sky.

Squinting against the sun, he scanned the waterfront of the neighbouring Royal William Yard - a marvel of Georgian naval architecture, its bakeries, malthouses and slaughterhouses now given over to stores for naval uniforms, engineering spare parts and small arms.

Eric passed between the gateposts of Mount Edgcumbe Park, where its tree-lined avenues were still populated by the tents of American troops waiting to go across to Europe or held back in England for other duties.

Plunging through some woods, following a snaking track, Eric emerged into the sunlight again, finally reaching his objective - the gently shelving Barn Pool beach. It was here that he usually found his potato-picking comrades enjoying a smoke before heading for fields over by Torpoint in their lorry. They weren't yet there today, so Eric picked up a flat stone and skipped it across the water.

'It is a lovely morning,' a mellifluous voice observed.

Turning around, Eric found Sgt Cyrus Fleetwood who was, as usual, immaculate in neatly ironed working fatigues, making his way through the rocks and down onto the beach, careful not to spill any coffee from the canteen cup in his left hand.

They fell into an easy, contemplative silence, enjoying the moment of calm and peace at the water's edge - the cool before the heat of the day.

Cyrus and Eric had a lot in common, as they were both involved in law enforcement on Civvy Street. Cyrus had graduated from Lincoln University, Pennsylvania, became a lawyer - a good one who was a member of the National Bar Association.

Prior to the war he'd joined the New York City Prosecutor's Office to pursue America's Nazis – the German American Bund. He took great pleasure in putting some Bund leaders behind bars following a notorious rally at Madison Square Gardens of early 1939 where thugs dressed like Hitler's stormtroopers beat a Jewish protestor who had stormed the stage. 'Those sonsofbitches did not like being sent to Rikers Island prison by the likes of me, not one bit,' he once told Eric with relish.

Eric heard the story as they sat on logs around a fire late one night out in the fields, roasting potatoes on the ends of sticks, like

Boy Scouts on a jamboree. There was plenty of laughter and Cornish cider.

The men Cyrus had charge of were all keen and fit to fight, but crushed by being told due to the colour of their skin they could not. They had listened awestruck as Eric described his exploits and those of the Maoris at Cassino - only elaborating his heroics a little bit while playing down his agonies.

'But, you know, there's no glory in war,' he told them, 'look what it's done to Plymouth and I saw that, too.'

They nodded in agreement, but still had the desire to fight burning in their eyes by the firelight. Cyrus clapped Eric on the knee, offering him the flagon of cider.

'But you see sport,' Cyrus said, his speech slightly slurred, 'if my men fight they finally get that piece of respect they lack and show they are every bit the equal to anyone else. After all, nearly 200,000 Black soldiers fought in the Union Army to win their freedom from slavery in the Civil War - so why not fight today to liberate us all from the fascists?'

Eric smiled and nodded – he couldn't argue with that and understood their frustration only too well. It was what had propelled him from city copper to artillery soldier. Cyrus shook his head and took the cider flask back. 'No insult to you, as you are an Englishman, but there are plenty of people in the States and likely over here in your green and very pleasant land who think that we are simply morally and spiritually unfit to fight. When they stopped you from going as a policeman it was because your service was already highly prize my friend, whereas we ain't fit for nothing except potato harvesting.'

A chorus of mutterings and curses circulated around the fire.

Now, on this morning, a new day in the fields beckoned.

'I do hope this war will last long enough for us to win the right to kill Nazis,' Cyrus reflected, as he gazed out across the water.

Cyrus swallowed the last of his coffee and shook the canteen to get rid of the dregs. Skipping one final flat stone across the water, Eric replied: 'You and me both.'

15

A FEW DAYS later Eric met Katherine outside the Odeon Cinema, which was one of the few buildings in Plymouth city centre that remained untouched by the blitz. On one side of it were vast areas of rubble-strewn wasteland where streets once stood, while buildings clustered around the cinema had fared better - most with minor damage, except for one that had been cleanly cleaved in two. A rather grand fireplace defiantly, if somewhat absurdly, clung on half way up an exposed interior (now very exterior) wall.

Slap bang in the middle of the cinema's towering art deco façade was an old advertising hoarding that in huge bold capitals urged: 'GO TO IT!' This referred to the war effort, but for those waiting impatiently in line outside on this night it could apply to many things, not least satisfying their urge to blow off some steam.

Katherine was pretty as a picture in her floral summer dress, hair teased into big bouncy curls and wearing a smile so bright it kindled a glow in Eric. They mingled happily in the long queue with Cyrus, his men and their English girlfriends.

Benny Goodman and his band had that afternoon flown into the military airfield at Harrowbeer on Dartmoor, to give the biggest concert Plymouth had seen for some years. But the carnival atmosphere was rather spoiled by the menace emanating from a gang of white American soldiers.

They barged their way along the line until a group of Royal Marines commandos dared them to come any further, jaws jutting out, fists clenched. Deterred, the Yanks backed off, for now – a pack of hungry wolves, huffing, puffing, pawing the ground, but they didn't dare blow the marines down. The proximity of joint patrols of British and American military policemen sitting in their wagons nearby also kept a lid on things.

The MPs were soon joined by naval shore patrols - pairs of Royal Navy and US Navy sailors prowling up and down the line, the latter batons in hand, giving likely ruffians the evil eye.

'Crushers,' Eric muttered, smiling at a bull-necked British naval policeman who did not return the cordiality.

'What?' Katherine asked, her arm tightening around his as she gave him an anxious look. 'Naval policemen - they're called Crushers, which speaks for itself.'

'Those Southern boys better wind their necks in,' Cyrus growled, staring hard at a tall crew cut meathead glaring at him over the heads of the Royal Marines. Tall and muscle-bound, a star football player in his youth, Cyrus had the beef to back up any threat.

'Southern boys?' enquired the American Sgt's date, a tightly packaged Devonian blonde hanging off his right arm.

Adjusting his tie with his free hand, Cyrus flashed her the broadest of confidence-building grins and purred: 'Don't you worry honey, everything's gonna be alright.'

The queue started to move into the cinema, Crewcut Meathead calling out: 'We'll see you inside!'

Clemons, a wiry pocket rocket of a Private in the potato picking crew, turned and shot back a defiant: 'Oh yeah!?'

An American naval shore patrolman stopped pacing up and down the line and touched Clemons on the shoulder with his baton.

'Keep it down soldier,' he advised sternly.

Clemons glowered but nodded.

Ignoring the taunts was the better part of valour…*for now.*

* * *

There was applause, wolf whistles and cheers as Goodman's outfit came out onto the stage. Smiling and bowing was Benny himself – *the King of Swing* - alto sax dangling from his neck, a big grin on his face. After he gave his spectacles a quick polish with his tie, he put them back on and turned to the band, counting them in.

Some of the Yanks danced in the aisles as the jaunty *Frenesi* started up and stayed on their feet for a frenetic *Swingtime in the Rockies.* A few couples immediately went to dance in the open space in front of the stage. Cyrus and his boys, with their girls went down to join them though Eric and Katherine settled into seats a few rows back and watched the show.

The band slowed things down with *Moonglow*, a smoochy number. Katherine decided to be bold, taking Eric by the hand and leading him down to the front. Eric was careful not to hold her too tight, frowning with concentration as he tried not to step on her feet. She laughed at his lack of finesse, but really didn't seem to mind that much.

Becoming flustered, Eric wanted to retreat but she must have sensed his embarrassment, pulling his head down to apologise, her breath hot on his neck: 'Sorry, I shouldn't laugh.'

Eric looked around, finding Cyrus and his partner gliding effortlessly. He couldn't help laughing at himself now, shrugging as he admitted: 'I'm a terrible dancer.'

The band took things up a notch, leaping off onto the swingin' escalator of *Down South Camp Meeting*. The Americans, including Cyrus and his crew, started really hurling their girls around, *dangerously so* in Eric's opinion. 'Oh, my goodness!' Katherine exclaimed in shock, hand to mouth as they ducked to avoid being hit by flying limbs. Grabbing Eric's hand, she drew him out of harm's way, shouting:

'No way am I letting *you* try that.'

Grinning at each other, hot from their exertions, flushed from the heat in the increasingly stuffy cinema, they dropped into seats. She leaned forward, her fingers unbuttoning his shirt collar.

'You must be hot!'

They looked into each other's eyes, high on the sheer exhilaration of the evening. Her cheeks were bright red, her lips glistening, and on impulse he kissed her. She pushed him away, shocked at his brazen move, making him wonder if he'd blown it. Then she smiled, reached up, cupping her hand behind his neck and pulling his mouth down to hers.

It was just as well, for at that precise moment a seat, which had been ripped off its mountings, skimmed low overhead, wiping out several couples as it carved a path across the dance floor.

There was a blood-curdling rebel yell, as a score of white American soldiers charged, vaulting over seats or pushing people out the way to charge down the aisle.

Shielding Katherine with his body, Eric took in a scene of utter chaos. The big drum rolls of *Sing, Sing, Sing (with a Swing)* kicked in as the perfect soundtrack for a brawl. Even as fists flew, shoulders barged and boots lashed out, couples were still recklessly swinging themselves around. The musicians leapt up from behind their music stands as the various trumpet and saxophone parts came in while, below the stage, it was primarily a case of white Southern troops against Cyrus and his group. The motivation had to be nothing less than a violent objection to black soldiers dancing with English girls. Eric knew what he had to do.

Turning to Katherine, the surging drums of the band growing ever louder and more insistent, he yelled: 'Keep down...I'll be back in a minute.'

She grabbed his hand, tried to tug him down beside her.

'Don't go!'

He grinned recklessly, adrenalin surging through his veins, kissed her and vaulted over the chairs, while she peeped over the top, scared and thrilled all at once to be in the heart of such an amazing and terrible drama.

More and more people were barging down the aisle. It appeared the Royal Marines were coming to the aid of Cyrus and his beleaguered group – surrounded as they were like Custer at the Little Big

Horn. The dancers, meanwhile, had made space for the scrappers and, incredibly, danced as the band played on.

Katherine spotted Eric skidding into the middle of the melee, landing a punch on Crewcut Meathead, preventing him from socking Clemons in the gut. She gasped as Eric set about the Southerners, literally banging heads – skills of riot control learned pre-war as a copper coming to the fore, like muscle memory. Katherine winced and cried out when Eric landed in a heap on the floor, but somebody helped him to his feet.

Dazed, Eric pulled his fist back and was about to mash it into the face of whoever had grabbed him, when he realized it was someone he had not seen since their little spy-catching adventure in Cornwall.

'Great Scott – it's Ted Bodman, as I live and breathe!'

Ted grinned, taking his Royal Marines Commando green beret off and tucking it into the back pocket of his trousers.

'Well, I couldn't let my old mucker down.'

'Shouldn't you be fighting the Germans?' Eric shouted, as they ducked to avoid another flying seat, which landed on the stage, making a couple of trumpet players scuttle out the way, while a percussionist was sent tumbling amid a loud clash of cymbals.

'My wife has been knocking off a Yank soldier, so they let me come home to sort out family matters,' Ted yelled, as they crouched down. Straightening up, Eric gestured towards the tangled mass of fighting men: 'Well, fill your boots – there's plenty of Americans here.'

Ted grinned, nodded as he rolled up his battle dress blouse sleeves. 'Don't you worry,' he promised, rather ominously.

Eric grabbed him by the arm and cautioned: 'Don't hit the black ones – they're alright.' Ted, nodded, broke from Eric's grip, a wild look in his eye, hurling himself into the chaos.

Seeing Cyrus needed help, Eric plunged back in too, landing a hit square on the left ear of a Southerner.

'What took you so long!?' Cyrus roared, twirling around, fists raised and poised to be unleashed.

The sound of the band suddenly died away - like the air being let out of a party balloon - Benny Goodman and his musicians fleeing the stage as grappling soldiers tumbled onto it. Standing back to back with Cyrus as they fended off lunges from Southerners, Eric laughed with abandon. 'Bloody hell, this is fun!'

'You must be kidding!?' Cyrus shot over his shoulder in disbelief.

Eric roared: 'Just like breaking up a riot on Union Street in the old days!' Cyrus groaned as a stocky Southerner laid into him, landing a hit in the guts while Clemons leapt on top of his attacker.

Eric would have turned to help, but he was fending off a lanky red-haired American sailor who jabbed inexpertly towards his jaw. Eric parried him and kicked the man's feet from under him.

Katherine looked on from cover, wishing she could get in there and help Eric, while also appalled at the sheer stupidity of it all. Whistles shrieked above the bedlam of the brawl and storming down the aisle came a battalion of military police and Crushers. They broke like a tidal wave over the fighters, sweeping Eric and the others out of sight, amid thrashing batons.

Katherine, meanwhile, was seized by an American naval patrolman and bundled away up the aisle, protesting: 'Leave me alone!'

16

DOOR HINGES in need of some oil squealed loudly in the Plymouth police station corridor. Boot-shod feet rang out on the flagstones - each footstep like a hammer blow inside Eric's throbbing head - but they passed by and faded away.

Later on, the custody sergeant, whom Eric had known since before the war, took pity on him and came into the cell with a pint glass of water. His hangover receding a little, Eric swung his feet off the mattress and sat up, just as the cellblock door down the corridor opened to admit two new pairs of boots – one of them had hobnails, the full shooting match. They clicked and snapped extra loud.

This was somebody who liked to make a big impression - liked to intimidate people before they even saw him.

The clickety-clack stopped outside the cell and, despite feeling grumpily defiant, Eric's stomach clenched with anxiety.

A set of keys jingled as someone sorted through them for the correct one. Soiled and crumpled though it may be, Eric decided to put his battle dress blouse on and, with a groan, got to his feet to greet the mystery visitor. The key turned in the lock as Eric slipped into his boots and bent over to tie the laces. Feeling dizzy, cursing the still disorderly laces, with a defeated sigh, Eric sank back onto the mattress.

The door swung back and a stentorian voice boomed:

'Pardon this intrusion, Sergeant Wise!'

Sighing heavily, Eric squinted up at whoever was standing in the door, glad to see it was at least not his old mentor Sgt Benson come to shame him.

It was a short, portly bespectacled major in service dress uniform, Sam Browne belt struggling to restrain a bulging tummy. Eric thought he looked familiar but could not quite place him.

'Perhaps you dimly recall our meeting a few years ago?' the major suggested. 'I would like to have a fresh chat with you.'

Surveying Eric's unshaven cheeks - the bloodshot, baggy eyes and generally dishevelled state from head to toe - the visitor observed caustically: 'You're an absolute thunder-fucking mess. Get your backside off that thing and follow me!'

Eric swallowed nervously and nodded, putting down a trembling hand to lever himself up.

Then it all came flooding back – the episode of the spies and the U-boat in Cornwall and he realised that this was *that* Intelligence Corps officer. None other than the mysterious, formerly Captain Spendlove, whom Eric wouldn't be surprised to learn had played a role in finding his lodgings at Cremyll.

* * *

Spendlove took him along to a shabby interview room, which was not promising but a pair of steaming hot mugs of sweet tea were soon delivered.

'Here's the deal Wise,' Spendlove boomed, 'you're in the pooh and I can dig you out of it!'

Eric said nothing, merely took a sullen sip as Spendlove show-boated. 'You should by rights lose your stripes, even be stripped of your Military Medal y'know. Bally stupid thing bare knuckle brawling with our American friends – they are over here, over sexed and over paid but they are also our salvation. Concert hall punch-ups with our colonial cousins are frowned on and so you earn no gold stars. '

Eric still did not respond, merely slurping down some more tea, Spendlove gazing intently at him from behind the thick glazing of his glasses.

'I've been keeping an eye on you,' the major continued, 'since you won that gong for foolish bravery at Cassino.'

'Is there any other kind?' thought Eric, though admittedly his own bravery was more accidental than anything else.

Spendlove dabbed his lips with a handkerchief, coughed, and then extracted a manila folder from a briefcase that until then Eric had not even noticed.

Opening it, Spendlove reeled off a summary of Eric's fighting career since joining the Army in late 1941.

'With the Royal Artillery – here, at the Royal Citadel – and after training as a forward observer you were sent to North Africa where you soon got assigned to a special reconnaissance unit for the push on Tunis…'

Spendlove looked over the top of his glasses at Eric, who affected an air of total boredom. 'This was followed by the usual progress one would expect for one of Monty's Desert Rats, from Sicily, into Italy itself and then up through the so-called soft underbelly of Europe.'

Spendlove paused for a bitterly amused 'ha!' – sharing the joke with Eric by explaining: 'Wasn't very soft though, was it?'

'No, Sir, it was very tough.'

Spendlove nodded and took a sip of his own tea.

'Yes, another of Winston's mad ideas to end the war quickly.'

Before he could carry on Eric asked:

'Do you *actually* know the Prime Minister?'

Spendlove gave him a wary look.

'A little, but what we're interested in here is *your* pedigree isn't it?'

Eric sighed and, as Spendlove looked down to carry on reading, he stared up at the blue sky visible through the barred window of the room.

'Then there was helping our New Zealand friends trying to take Monte Cassino railway station – wounded badly and that's when you won that medal.' His voice trailed away, prompting Eric to look down, finding Spendlove regarding him with intense curiosity.

'Where Sgt Wise?'

'Pardon, Sir?'

'Where were you wounded?'

'Cassino, Sir, like it says.'

Spendlove sighed.

'No, no Sgt, I mean where on your body?'

Eric reflexively caressed the outside of his right thigh where the scar tissue was still sensitive.

'Hit in the leg,' he told Spendlove, with a hard stare that suggested the intelligence officer knew nothing about combat.

Spendlove dropped his gaze to the paperwork, turning over a sheet.

'It says here you recovered reasonably quickly physically but they sent you along to an American naval psychiatrist at the Stonehouse naval hospital whose job is to deal with their battle fatigue cases.' Eric tensed, uncomfortable with being reminded of all that.

Spendlove enquired mildly: 'What was the Yank's verdict?'

'He decided after a few weeks of chit chat in his office that I was fine,' Eric revealed.

Spendlove harrumphed and went on: 'We don't have battle fatigue in my mob – I am surprised they subjected you to the indignity.' Eric smiled as that had been his view too and suggested: 'I rather thought maybe someone was mucking me about deliberately.'

'Anyway, forget about that nonsense,' Spendlove suggested, rather too casually, returning to his recitation of Eric's career: 'So, this American sawbones decides to send you to pick potatoes with a group of black soldiers over the river in Cornwall. What was that like?'

Eric shrugged, but then admitted: 'Actually, it turned out to be a rest cure – fresh air and good honest work in the fields - and they are a great bunch. I was given some lodgings in a boatyard with a rather curious craft on its slipway.'

Spendlove closed the folder.

'Slipway… "curious craft"… "boatyard"?' he ventured, working a little too hard at being mystified. 'What are you on about? It just says in your report that you have digs in Cornwall.'

Then, with a look of deep disapproval on his face, Spendlove suggested: 'Anyway, wasn't it your association with your potato-picking pals that got you arrested and where you are today?'

Eric felt anger rising and a need to justify his actions.

'I don't like anyone abusing my friends, least of all a bunch of bastards telling them that they are unfit to fight for their country.'

'All very embarrassing, though.'

'There are plenty of brawls in Plymouth of an evening,' observed Eric, 'this one was just a bit bigger.'

'Yes, but in the past it was you who used to break the fights up and do the arresting,' proposed Spendlove, with more than a hint of sarcasm, which made Eric want to bop him on the nose.

The major reached into his left breast pocket for a silver lighter and a packet of cigarettes. He lit one up without offering Eric, raising his eyebrows, to suggest the sergeant should carry on with his mitigation.

'So, Sir,' Eric growled, 'when they started hurling insults and punches at my friends during the concert I decided where my loyalty lay.'

'Yes, Sgt Wise, as did our old friend from the Cornwall escapade, Ted Bodman, who is – by the way – still dead to the world in the cell next door to yours. Does he always get involved in your extra-curricular exploits?'

'Of course not – he's been away and was only home because some Yank screwed his wife.'

Spendlove dropped his cigarette on the floor and ground it out under a boot, drumming the fingers of his right hand on the paperwork.

'I gather the safety of your lady was also at stake.'

Eric blushed and stared at his boots.

'I had asked a girl out to the concert and when a few chairs came flying our way got her under cover and decided to wade in.'

Spendlove grinned, as if this was something he could admire. He leaned forward, hands gripping each side of the small table.

'Alright Eric – I've heard enough, so let's cut to the chase. I'm here to suggest you scrawl on the dotted line and join my merry band – rank, medal, freedom, unsullied service record, all in my gift d'you see? You will recall at Tregantle three years ago I said I would keep an eye on you and sign you up if you made the grade?'

Eric gave Spendlove a sceptical stare.

'That would be nice, Sir, but what do I have to do in return – I mean what would my duties be?'

Spendlove maintained a poker face – he had a prize pike on the hook and hopefully could pull it in without it snapping his line, or taking a chunk out of his hand.

The man in front of Spendlove was clearly a long way removed from the eager, even naïve, young police constable of 1941.

This Eric was battle hardened, cynical and right now on a short fuse, as evidenced by his part in the aforementioned brawl and ease with which he angered.

'My unit is small,' Spendlove explained, 'and a little unconventional. Not purely Military Intelligence anymore, more with a brief to master all sorts of dark arts and crafts. We need chaps who are tough, resourceful, brave and pin sharp in the noggin.'

For emphasis, Spendlove tapped his right temple with a couple of fingers and with a sly smile added: 'Oh, and with a propensity for calculated, precise violence if needs be.'

'That's quite a shopping list,' Eric suggested.

Spendlove rested his forearms on the table, laced his fingers together and elucidated further.

'We are quite a bag of tools – suitable for all sorts of covert jobs other folks don't want to do. There are also plans once the war is over for us to attach ourselves to troops occupying Germany…'

Eric interrupted with a harsh laugh, observing acidly: 'The war is long way from over and Adolf may yet have a few surprises up his sleeve.'

This provoked a flash of anger in Spendlove's eyes that made Eric instantly regret it, for, actually, he didn't want to stay in jail and lose his medal.

'I didn't ask for your opinion on higher Allied strategy sergeant,' Spendlove said coldly, giving Eric the fish eye from behind his glasses. 'The point is that we will win sooner or later. Then our job will be help to subjugate the Nazis, indeed eradicate their evil, noxious presence from the face of the planet. Some of us, Sgt, have ambition - an aim in life.'

'You sound like Adolf talking about the Bolsheviks, if you don't mind me saying, Sir,' Eric suggested glumly.

Spendlove laughed and protested: 'Not at all! Of course, we will act well within international law to bring certain naughty boys to book.'

'I still don't get it,' Eric sighed. 'Why do you want me?'

'You now fit the bill, Eric. We can evolve your current situation away from this slight unpleasantness. Your police background and instinct for huntin' out bad 'uns may prove useful, too. I suggest you say yes, or you'll be off to the glasshouse. When they release you, there will be no career as a jolly copper in Plymouth to come back to.'

Eric inwardly baulked – that was a cold bath alright and so he took the plunge, remarking sarcastically: 'Well, if you put it like that, how can I resist signing up for your lot?'

Spendlove grinned broadly and patted him on the forearm, then got up, walked over to the interview room door and rapped on it with his knuckles.

He turned around and told Eric:

'Welcome, aboard Wise.'

'I suppose I should say thanks.'

'Yes, you should. Return to the Cremyll boatyard and I'll pop over and see you later this week and take a look at the E-boat. In the meantime, carry on as normal with the potato picking and keep your nose clean.'

And then Spendlove was gone, boots clicking away down the corridor, cell block door clanging shut behind him.

Eric's racing mind tried to grasp what had just happened, suddenly wondering if all had not been as it seemed, for months or even years?

17

The Netherlands, January 1945

THE WINTER HAD, so far, been dreadful - freezing and wet, which was deeply depressing all of itself, never mind the war and its devastation.

Eric was hunched miserably over a small primus stove in the front parlour of a wrecked townhouse in Nijmegen. The Spendlove Group – some 50 men of all ranks - had for some time been lodged in the Dutch city on the River Waal, which was almost at the tip of a tongue of territory seized from the Germans during the ill-fated Operation Market Garden thrust of September 1944.

The idea had been to launch Allied troops across the Lower Rhine, deep into the Nazi heartland and so they had raced up the narrow causeway through the polder - securing a succession of bridges - only to fail in taking the final (and most important) one, at Arnhem, just 15 miles away from Nijmegen.

Arnhem and the northern bank of the Rhine were still in German hands, a zone from which the entire Dutch population had been forcibly evicted after the British 1st Airborne Division was defeated, its remnants evacuated across the river. An air of doom and gloom pervaded on the Allied side now in Holland, contrasting so starkly with the exhilarating dash from Normandy to Brussels after the breakout from the D-Day beachhead.

Now, into the ruined townhouse came Spendlove to disrupt Eric's melancholy pondering of this war seemingly without end, brimming with glee for some reason, plonking his backside on Eric's camp bed – *nearly breaking the bloody thing.*

Major Spendlove by early 1945 regarded Eric fondly as his right-hand man – but showed a bit of steel, as and when needed, to keep him in his place. Having been sprung from his Plymouth jail cell, and returned to potato picking for a few days, Eric was shortly thereafter sent off for a rushed fortnight of training to be an officer and commissioned 'toute de suite', as Spendlove put it.

Holding the rank of 2nd Lieutenant, Eric acquired important skills such as knowing which piece of cutlery was used for what course during a mess dinner. *Work your way in from the outside gentlemen!* Eric also learned the precise angle at which to tilt the soup plate away, which, he thought, sarcastically, would be *very useful* under fire in a foxhole.

He was then catapulted into Spendlove's japes in the last week of August 1944, the major's merry band racing ahead and alongside the main British force as it swept through from France and into Belgium.

It had been intoxicating – as was the wine the men of the Spendlove Group drank and easy romantic liaisons made amid the joy of liberation.

The exit stage left of the bad guys was celebrated wildly, Allied liberators bombarded with kisses and flowers by grateful civilians, along with offers of booze and sex.

They seized Nazis of interest - such as bureaucrats who knew where the incriminating occupation secrets were buried and even a fine art expert who had been pilfering museums; all that while trying to stop vital paperwork held by the ultra-bureaucratic Nazis being ruined by the enthusiastically plundering Allied troops. If you wanted to know when exactly X executed townsfolk Y for sins of aiding and abetting Allied agent Z behind enemy lines, all you had to do was investigate the filing cabinets at some HQ. Often everybody left in too much of a hurry to make bonfires of all secrets. And they were catalogued by the Fritzes – including photographs of the slain citizenry – with typical Teutonic efficiency.

Happiness for Spendlove was neat, well-ordered German files that had not been violated, but this intelligence could occasionally be scattered to the four winds, thanks to Allied troops and local civilians celebrating by throwing it out of windows like so much outsize confetti; or persons unknown urinating joyously into drawers or even defecating in them – how they arranged themselves to achieve such gymnastic feats was a mystery. Then there were the looters upsetting the filing systems while rifling through looking for gold, souvenir Luger pistols and other Nazi booty. Some cabinets and their contents were set on fire by people gripped with ecstasy at seeing hated occupiers fleeing – though in several cases, no doubt, the perpetrators were making evidence of their own misdeeds (as collaborators) disappear in smoke.

After the party came the Market Garden hangover – the villains of the piece had not quit the stage after all and refused to be evicted entirely from the Netherlands.

And so it was that Eric found himself shivering over an inadequate little stove, stirring the contents of an aluminium mess tin on a sputtering flame: water, fatty bits of ham and peas - boiling it all down to a lumpy green puree – the staple diet of the Dutch, but only if they were lucky, for otherwise it seemed to consist of pickled legumes with a dessert of apples.

'We have a mission at last!' Spendlove cried in delight, shifting his weight alarmingly on Eric's fragile camp bed. The premise of the adventure was this: they must retrieve a Dutchman - a civil servant working for the headquarters of Organisation Todt, which ran a major part of the Nazi military industrial complex.

The Dutchman had indicated via an underground resistance communications net that the Germans had implemented a heinous scheme that would, potentially, enable them to prolong the war for months if not years. It might even give the Nazis a last-minute winning edge.

'In what way?' Eric enquired, using a spoon to taste the ham and pea mush. It was, not surprisingly, *very* salty.

'Well, he won't tell us exactly, but says he has material that he wants to hand over,' Spendlove explained. 'Not a splendid filing cabinet, but a tidily gift-wrapped package, apparently.'

Spendlove pulled a stainless-steel table spoon from a breast pocket of his battle dress blouse and dipped it into Eric's mess tin soup. Spendlove cheerfully ignored Eric's displeasure.

'Bit bland,' Spendlove decided, 'needs a pinch of pepper.'

Licking the spoon clean before popping it back in his pocket, Spendlove cast an eye around for something else to eat, but could not even spot a mouldy old crust of bread.

'And the Dutchman,' Eric enquired, 'what's the plan?'

'You have to go and pick him up from a farmhouse on the German side of the Lower Rhine along with the package.'

Seemingly unfazed by this news, Eric turned off the stove, wrapped a piece of rag around the mess tin's handle and picked it up to spoon soup into his mouth.

'When, Sir?'

'Ten days. You'll be going with that friend of yours I got out of jail for you after the punch-up…'

'You mean Sergeant Bodman?'

'He did well when we snatched those Luftwaffe rocket fellows from the Brussels brothel didn't he?'

Eric smiled at the memory – it was a hell of a job, though he had personally declined to accept special thanks from the brothel ladies for their liberation. Ted, he suspected, had obliged them.

'He's a useful sort,' Eric agreed, wasting no more time spooning the soupy mush down before it got cold, or Spendlove dipped his spoon again.

'And you'll get another Royal Marines Commando NCO,' said Spendlove, keeping his spoon in its pocket. 'Corporal Tom Pilbeam, whom I have just recruited – two tough nuts, which is what you'll need behind enemy lines. Besides you are going across in canoes and I don't know if you are much good at paddling; they will do the hard work while you sit back and enjoy the ride.'

'Hardly,' thought Eric, his mood darkening as he pondered the high-risk potential of the mission. In fact, he decided, it was most unappetising: across a very wide river under German guns on a freezing cold night, to fetch back a Dutchman who was nothing more than a traitor who'd decided to change sides when he realized the Nazis were going to lose. Eric realized that sometimes you had to get into bed with the enemy, as Spendlove once put it, but he still didn't like the idea of risking his neck for such a person.

In the meantime, to give his loyal assistant some release from Dutch misery before the mission, Spendlove provided a pass for seven days leave at home. After all Eric might get killed and it was only fair for his loyal right-hand man to see home again before he went off to risk his neck for King and Country. It might turn out to be a suicide mission.

'You've really stepped up to the crease,' Spendlove suggested to Eric, 'so you deserve a break in the pavilion.'

It lifted Eric's mood, for he had written to Katherine regularly and she had already suggested that, if he could get home, *it could be rather fantastic*.

He *must* come and visit her for a few days at Drake Cottage, not far from Torpoint, which she shared with some other nurse chums.

The others were often away and she'd be all alone and in need of company. This was a most wonderful and *very* inviting prospect, so Eric wrote to her immediately.

It took two days to reach the coast, hitching a series of lifts in jeeps and lorries, and then it was onto a tank landing ship from Calais to Dover.

Finally, Eric set foot on British soil and jumped straight onto a train for London then caught an equally crowded, smelly hot one from Paddington to Plymouth, arriving in the early afternoon. Beret clamped on his head, gathering his frayed greatcoat about him and hoisting the kitbag on his shoulder, he trudged through the shattered cityscape from the North Road station down to the Torpoint Ferry. It was a long walk and he was grateful for the break during the short trip across the Hamoaze.

Stepping off onto the slipway on the other side, Eric suddenly wondered how he might get to Drake Cottage. He had been so intent on just getting to England from the Continent – and so pleased with conquering that challenge - he'd not thought about this rather important detail.

He knew it was somewhere off the road to Antony. About four miles in all he reckoned - maybe two to Antony on a main road and then somewhere south. He'd knock on some doors, or pause at the village pub, to ask for directions.

Unfortunately, it was sleeting with a cold, knifing wind, forcing him to bend into it, grunting irritably at various items in the kitbag digging into his shoulders and back.

Eric grumpily contemplated the miserable trek that lay ahead – already exhausted from all the travelling – but it was amazing the things a man would do for love, and in hope of sex. A booming voice interrupted these musings, enquiring: 'Would you like a lift?'

Eric turned around to find a black Morris Ten with the passenger door open. Leaning across from the driver's seat was a distinguished looking, grey haired gent.

'This isn't the weather to be walking anywhere,' he suggested to Eric who grimaced at a knife-sharp gust of wind.

'Well, if you don't mind?'

'Come on then,' the man said with a note of impatience, 'put your kitbag on the back seat.'

Eric did so and climbed in, taking his beret off and unbuttoning his coat, telling the driver: 'It's very good of you – I'm heading to Antony, or thereabouts.'

'That's on my way,' the driver observed. 'But where, exactly?'

'Drake Cottage,' Eric said, frowning as he tried to be more precise by recalling the exact address, 'St John's Lake.'

The driver nodded, 'by the big house…I know it.'

Eric noticed the driver's charcoal pin stripe suit and navy polka dot silk tie – their quality – and, sneaking a look at the man's face, realised he'd seen him before. As the car began to snake up through Torpoint, Eric revealed: 'I think I know you, Sir.'

Grimacing as he peered through the windscreen, which the ineffectual wipers were hardly keeping clear, the driver responded with a distracted 'Oh, yes?' Eric suggested: 'Judge Smith-Glosson?'

The driver glanced at him for a second and there was a flicker of recognition. 'Yes, you do seem familiar.'

He eased the car to a halt at a junction and then turned left.

'These wipers are useless,' complained the Judge and then, glancing at Eric again, enquired: 'Constable Wise, is that right?'

Eric beamed.

'Blimey, Sir you must have a photographic memory.'

The Judge laughed.

'Not all of us are asleep under those wigs you know.'

'You presided over that murder trial in summer 1939, the sailor who strangled his wife. I gave evidence.'

'A tragic case.'

They lapsed into silence, Eric not wanting to interrupt the Judge's concentration in such filthy driving conditions.

'I don't know how you were expecting to walk there Constable Wise,' the Judge eventually observed.

Eric laughed nervously.

'Actually, I'm a soldier now, Sir.'

'So you are,' the Judge remarked in surprise, finally taking in Eric's khaki coat. 'They let you out of a reserved occupation like the Police to risk getting your head shot off, eh?'

'Leg in my case.'

The Judge's eyebrows shot up in surprise.

'Are you trying to get to St John's Lake with a wooden leg?'

Eric coughed, embarrassed.

'No, Sir, not shot off, just badly punctured.'

'What is?' the Judge enquired, reaching down for a cloth nestling in a door pocket. He handed it to Eric, instructing: 'Wipe the inside of the windscreen would you?'

'My leg,' Eric explained as he complied, 'not shot off, just wounded.'

'Glad to hear it,' the Judge laughed.

Eric handed the cloth back, the Judge stuffing it back into the door pocket.

After ten minutes of silence, except for the squeaky wipers scraping back and forth, the Judge announced: 'Here we are.'

'Just pull over and I'll jump out,' Eric suggested, 'I don't want to delay you.' The Judge shook his head. 'I can do better than that,' he suggested, 'especially in this foul weather.'

He turned the car into the driveway and about a hundred yards ahead, in the centre of substantial grounds, was a rather imposing Georgian manor house – all shuttered up and seemingly lifeless. The Judge frowned, muttering something that Eric couldn't make out. There was a pretty sizeable single storey cottage to one side, encircled by what would normally be a luxuriant green hedge. It was encrusted with a topping of dirty old snow. Smoke curling from the cottage's chimney was violently whisked away by a gust of wind.

'Do you think Drake Cottage is that building next to the posh house?' Eric asked. The Judge nodded, concentrating on not losing his grip on the steering wheel, as the drive was quite bumpy.

'Here we are,' he announced swinging the car around in front of the portico of the main house. This embarrassed Eric, as he felt if anyone were around they would be wondering who on earth had the audacity to just brazenly pull up like that.

'Thanks very much,' Eric said, quickly opening the door, grabbing his beret and pulling it on.

'Not at all,' the Judge said.

As Eric reached into the back seat to get his kitbag, he saw Katherine - hair encased by a scarf and bundled in a long coat - emerging as if by magic through a gap in the cottage hedge. With his heart racing in anticipation, Eric bent down to look through the passenger door window to thank the Judge again, so he could depart. But there was nobody behind the wheel. Eric found Judge Smith-Glosson standing on the other side of the car, staring in the direction of the cottage.

Confused, Eric became even more befuddled when Katherine called out: 'Oh, hello! I wasn't expecting you.'

He felt anger surge in his veins – *hadn't his last letter reached her?*

'Oh, a last-minute thing,' the Judge was saying.

It was then that Katherine noticed Eric for the first time and started laughing - a mix of embarrassment and hilarity. The Judge and Eric exchanged puzzled looks over the roof of the car. 'Whatever is the matter with you Katherine?' the Judge asked testily.

'I gave this young man a lift, and I presume he's come to see Mrs Bancroft's daughter.' This seemed to make Katherine even more amused. 'What's so funny?' Eric enquired, beginning to laugh himself but not knowing why. The Judge launched a furious look at Eric, thundering: 'You've come here to see *my* daughter – *not* our housekeeper's!?'

Eric felt his bowels turned to water.

'*Your* daughter!?'

Katherine subdued herself and came forward, grabbing Eric by the arm, his kitbag falling with a loud crunch on the gravel. She pulled him around the other side of the car.

'Daddy, I'd like you to meet Eric Wise, *my* young man.'

The Judge's mouth dropped open, while Eric was equally amazed at being referred to as such so publicly. He extended his hand, which the Judge regarded most suspiciously before shaking it.

'Come on you two,' Katherine suggested, shivering as they reluctantly shook hands. 'It's too cold to be out here.'

Eric hoisted his kitbag while the Judge pulled a suitcase from the boot of the car, asking his daughter: 'Why aren't you in the big house?'

'Oh, it's bloody freezing in there!' she cried out running back into Drake Cottage. 'Mrs Bancroft and her daughter are lodging with relatives in Antony.' With a sigh the Judge gestured with his left arm that Eric should go ahead and follow Katherine. Not daring to look the Judge in the eye, Eric mumbled 'thanks' and did as ordered. He suddenly felt depressed. *With the Judge around his hopes of carnal pleasure were surely sunk.*

* * *

'I had no idea you were Judge Smith-Glosson's daughter,' he said later, between passionate kisses during a moment alone on the back porch of the cottage. 'I should have guessed you might have encountered him during your days as a policeman,' she conceded.

'But you said you were Katherine Smith.'

'I do that to avoid people going on about me being the Judge's daughter.'

He gave a dirty laugh and exclaimed:

'She was *only* the Judge's daughter!'

Katherine pushed him away.

'Well you did wear your disreputable old coat Eric, and just a beret, so he had no idea you were more respectable than you appear.'

'Hey, that coat's been everywhere with me.'

'Yes, but now you are an officer you must smarten up.'

'Not much point in being smart in the muck and bullets, even for an officer.'

'You poor love – what can I do to make you feel better?'

'How about another kiss?'

* * *

That evening after dinner, which was accompanied by a rather decent bottle of claret from the cellars of the big house, they sat admiring the crackling fire in the lounge. The Judge saw how easy and happy his daughter was in Eric's company and thawed a little. While Katherine saw to the washing up, they chatted about other pre-war cases brought before him and he asked Eric about his ambitions for after the war.

'I hadn't really thought about such things,' Eric admitted.

'You ought to – and perhaps something other than the policeman's lot?' Eric smiled, thinking this was another indication that an ordinary copper was not quite who he wanted his daughter to be consorting with.

When Katherine returned she made a point of stating that she had made up a bed in each of the other bedrooms.

'I'm sorry gentlemen,' she warned, 'it's all rather feminine, but it can't be helped.' The Judge snorted into his wine glass, remarking:

'I suppose I can tolerate one night in a boudoir.'

Eric had to suppress a smile and dared not look at Katherine.

He resigned himself to a lonely time, not in Katherine's room *as he'd hoped*. He pulled on a pair of pyjamas that had belonged to her brother, and which had also been retrieved from the big house. Finally emptying his mind of all thoughts, Eric turned over and drifted off. He was dimly aware of the door opening and then Katherine's shivering form wrapped itself around him, absorbing his warmth.

'Can't let the soldier miss out on a belated Christmas present before he goes back to the front,' she whispered in his ear.

* * *

The following morning Katherine slipped back to her room before the Judge was awake. After breakfast she took Eric for a walk around the big house. Peering in a large window and finding dust-sheets over the furniture, he remarked: 'Closed for the duration of hostilities eh?'

'Yes, finally, and quite right,' she responded, also peering in.

'What's this pile called anyway?'

She prodded him playfully, laughingly observing: 'St John's House is hardly a pile.'

He pursed his lips and conceded: 'I suppose not.' A bemused smile asserted itself on his face as she grabbed his hand, pulling him away from the window.

'Strange that's it's called St John's House,' Eric reflected coming to a halt as he pondered it. She shot him a puzzled look.

'You know, what with my boss being called *St. John* Spendlove.'

'Never met him,' she said, eager to resume the walk, 'except via amusing pen portraits in your letters.'

'Just one of those coincidences I suppose,' he conceded.

'Yes, well,' she said, bored with the dead end trivia of it. Tugging him along, she resumed the walk and her story of how the house came to be mothballed.

'My father works in London now, and I don't know how or why

he expects me to keep this running for him when I have to help the war effort. He hangs on to the past with tenacity, but all this entire sprawling place does is remind me of my dear, lovely departed mother and happier times.'

She gave a little embarrassed laugh.

'You must think me silly,' she confessed.

He gave her hand a reassuring squeeze, but with a shiver as if troubled by ghosts, she broke his grip and walked on.

Eric stepped back, to hide his embarrassment, looking up at the moss covered tiles on the roof of the big house, thinking just how little he knew of Katherine's world beyond their brief romantic liaisons, their letters.

Her upbringing was a galaxy removed from his own and the upper class world she had circulated in before the war was alien to a policeman-turned-warrior from humble Turnchapel. He wondered if he would always feel like a weekend guest, which was fine for now, of course, as that was indeed what he was. She turned around on realising he had not followed her and strode back to pull him along. 'Come on, slowcoach.'

They walked arm-in-arm around to the back where he was stunned by the view from a broad, balustraded terrace.

'We used to have lovely parties on this very terrace,' she revealed, wearing a nostalgic smile as they stood there taking it all in.

Under gossamer ribbons of mist, a deer park stretched all the way down to St John's Lake and beyond it was the Tamar. Across the broad, circumfluous river was the dark mass of the dockyard with its miles of wharves, huge basins, dry docks and workshops, all sprawling beneath a pale blue sky.

'But it's all vanished now…our lives in limbo,' Katherine went on, turning her head away from the view to search his face for a reaction as she continued. 'Do you think it will ever return as it was?'

Eric shook his head and observed: 'Well, my life across there was not quite like yours, but for all of us, I think it will be very different after the war.' Katherine smiled, pulled him into an embrace, which she then broke with a self-conscious grin, walking over to lean on the balustrade's weathered stonework top, gazing out across the park and river as she talked.

'Do you ever feel afraid, Eric?'

He walked over to lean on the balustrade next to her.

'Of course - during the blitz.'

She nodded. 'Yes, it was a bit scary…but did you…do you imagine you won't survive.'

He frowned, knowing that his own survival in Europe was a matter living from day-to-day, wondering what she was trying to tease out of him and why. When he said nothing, she pressed on: 'It's strange, isn't it Eric, how sometimes even normal things, become a calculated risk - like crossing the road in the blackout along Union Street, what with all those cars blundering around with slits for lights that could very easily run you over.'

He nodded.

'Yes, it was quite shocking how many people got run over.'

'Or, deciding which way to go in an air raid. Do you recall the night that bomb killed all those people in the Portland Square shelter just up from the city museum?'

Eric shuddered inwardly, as he vividly recalled staring down into the black maw of the massive crater after he and others on duty ran up the hill to see who could be saved – the answer was no one. Eric had turned away from it but was confronted with something truly horrific – limbs and other body parts dangling from surrounding trees. But, this wasn't about him, so he kept quiet about the details of what he saw, observing only: 'Yes, I do recall it.'

'Well, I had been out with some of the other nurses at a pub nearby and when I heard the air raid alarm decided to call it a night, pleaded with my friend Elsie to come with me. But she was too smitten by an RAF pilot, so I couldn't drag her away. She said I should stay, but, not wanting to play gooseberry, I went back to our lodgings just up the hill, took cover under the stairs. And, anyway, the Portland Square shelter was always packed with people during a raid, and too clammy for my liking and only hard wooden benches to sit on. It seems that when the bombs started dropping she and the RAF chap went to the nearest shelter…'

'The Portland one?'

'Yes,' Katherine whispered, wiping a tear away, then gave a bitter laugh and added: 'So, she and the pilot went down into it, which got a direct hit from a ruddy big bomb. She was killed with all those other people, while I got away with it in my digs with only a leaky slate roof for protection…'

Deciding to lighten the mood, Eric said, gazing around at the landscape: 'It is a lovely view.'

With her fingertips she turned his face back to her and gave him a kiss on the lips, then moved away, walking to the end of the terrace.

Shielding her eyes against the glare, Katherine observed:

'Yes, it's amazing.'

'Amazing,' he felt moved to agree as he looked at her.

As they walked back to the cottage, despite his private misgivings Eric tentatively broached the subject of them 'going steady'. She looked shocked and said: 'I should bloody well hope so – you don't have a judge's daughter and *not* go steady!'

18

Back in the Netherlands, it seemed to Eric as if the Cornwall interlude had never happened. Sent up the line, he and the two commando NCOs Bodman and Pilbeam whiled away their time before the night raid across the Rhine by hunkering down in a small tent beside the ruins of an old windmill just south of the river.

Largely shot to bits by German artillery, it hosted the Headquarters of a Cornish infantry battalion in the 43rd Wessex Division but had a deep, very safe cellar filled with large wheels and cogs and other long neglected machinery. Crowded in among all the gubbins were the staff officers, their map tables, camp beds, radios and other paraphernalia of military command.

Eric and his Royal Marines companions decided it was also rather too crowded, so instead chose to go under canvas. Ordinarily the tent was occupied by the battalion's head chaplain who had a slit trench dug next to it for use in emergencies.

Considering what little protection he had, either above or below ground - the waterlogged slit trench wasn't very deep – Eric felt the Padre must also be trusting in the Lord's shield. He was currently away visiting the poor bloody infantry on the river bank itself, ensuring their spiritual needs were being met.

Eric and the Royal Marines passed around a bottle of gin to try and warm themselves up, sat on two camp beds inside the tent – the marines precariously balanced on one and Eric on the other. Being a bit pissed might help to ignore the fact that they could soon be blown to pieces as they tried to sneak past sharp-eyed Nazi gunners.

The Cornish infantry battalion second-in-command had suggested covering fire - a short intensive artillery barrage and hosing down the opposite bank with heavy machine guns. Eric declined the offer as he was concerned it would not only warn the Germans something was up but might also claim them, through so-called friendly fire.

A pair of Folboats – special two-man collapsible canoes developed for the Commando forces – already waited by the river, concealed under some foliage. When midnight came, Eric would lead the way up a ditch to the battalion's position on the river bank. They would then crawl to the boats. After being carefully uncovered, the Folboats would be pushed into the water, Eric and Ted Bodman in one, with Tom Pilbeam taking the other. Eric had never mastered paddling to any great proficiency, so he would rely on his old mate to lead the way.

* * *

'I suppose I'm meant to call you "Sir" these days?' enquired Ted.

'Yes, you should,' Eric observed with a tight smile as he took the gin bottle. Accepting the bottle from Eric, Pilbeam observed: 'Hard to think of you as a copper on the beat, Sir. Not that I'd 'ave wanted to meet you as I was probably out burglarising some toff's house at the time.'

'Don't' worry Tom,' said Ted, taking the bottle, back 'he'll get *you* after the war.' The Royal Marines NCOs chuckled satanically.

Ted wiped the opening on the sleeve of his grubby combat jacket to get rid of germs.

Looking at them in the lamplight, faces all crinkled up under their green berets, smashed teeth showing and their bent noses, Eric thought they could have been twins.

'Did cousin Denzil ever get his truck replaced?' Eric asked Ted, guardedly, for he wasn't keen on giving away too much about the Cornwall escapade in front of Pilbeam. Ted grinned. 'They were very generous and bought a shiny new one, which shut him up. But, Eric, I mean *Sir*,' he grinned cheekily, 'that was a helluva punch up at the concert back home, wasn't it?'

Eric didn't like to be reminded, restricting himself to merely nodding as he took another sip of gin.

Pilbeam shoved Bodman and remarked: 'I hear old Ted here gave some Americans a hiding for fucking his wife?''

'Oi,' said Ted, shoving him back, 'it was only one American that fucked my wife and I never got to him.'

'No,' Eric observed drily, 'but you did *get* to a fair few others with your fists?'

Ted regarded him with mock outrage.

'And so did you,' he pointed out, adding: 'Sir here gave some of them Yanks a right bashing.'

Pilbeam regarded Eric with more respect. He liked the sound of an officer who could cut up rough when required. It gave him confidence tonight's little jaunt would go alright.

19

THEIR LAUNCH POINT was from the cover of a ramshackle old houseboat where a British infantry section of eight men occasionally lurked hoping to catch Jerries trying to sneak across the Rhine. It was never occupied during the day for it was a very obvious and tempting target. There wasn't much left of it anyway, except a shrapnel punctured steel hull, with most of the superstructure and fittings torn away by months of enemy gunfire.

Eric was told that, on his group's return down river, the infantry would help them get themselves and their boats out the water and across the mud - but this depended on them doing it before dawn.

'If you lot run into trouble up stream,' the Sergeant in command of the houseboat section told them with a gruff Cornish burr, 'I'll be buggered if I'll expose my lads for Fritz to rip to shreds as he pleases.'

If they could get to the houseboat ahead of sunrise, the sergeant assured them, 'you will get all you need - covering fire along with a helping hand onto friendly shores.'

* * *

As Eric feared, he did not paddle well and it was upstream on the way out - about a mile of thrashing about. He failed utterly to keep rhythm with Ted in the front while Pilbeam raced ahead in his Folboat.

Finally making it to the landing point - Eric had no idea how Ted found it – but three owl hoots guided them in. Hauled up on shore, the Folboats were covered in camouflage netting pulled from storage wells in their sterns and then slid into some bushes.

There was about a mile to cover on land, too, skirting a road that ran parallel to the river and then went arrow straight at a right angle to it, across polder to the farmhouse.

They silently leopard crawled up the grassy bank above the beach, their condensed breath hanging in the air, the only give-away. Halting at the top Eric scanned all around for a few minutes – ears and eyes straining for any sign of the enemy. The Dutch Resistance had claimed the Germans regularly mounted road patrols along this stretch of the Rhine, to match those by the Allies along the southern bank, a sort of unspoken live and let live agreement for there was not much combat going on at all. When there was, however, it soon became pretty brutal.

Clutching his Thompson submachine gun close to his chest, Eric sprinted across the road, dropped down and surveyed both directions. He could not see anything to worry about.

'All clear,' he pronounced in a loud whisper.

After about 40 minutes of careful movement, every now and then stopping to listen and scan up and down, they were almost at the objective. There was a nasty moment when something moved in some pasture below them. Immediately freezing - guns raised - a gap in the cloud allowed enough moonlight through to make out a patchy black and white blob. It snorted and snuffled.

A cow.

* * *

They lay on the wet grass, looking over the top of the road at what Eric's rudimentary map reading skills – aided by a carefully shielded torch – told them was the destination – a two-storey farmhouse. It was bloody damp and cold with their teeth chattering, but this time there was no warming alcohol passed around. Clear heads were required.

The thing about night vision is not to look directly at the target, or so Eric had learned during field craft courses. Picking something out requires at least a little moonlight but there wasn't much of it, which made seeing the rendezvous farmhouse not entirely easy.

To help things along the Dutchman had promised to switch a light on and off at precisely 02.00 and then do it again at 02.05. According to a briefing by Spendlove this was in a bedroom looking out onto the road that ran across the polder.

The Dutchman's uncle was away but had left a key under a flowerpot by the kitchen door and his nephew was permitted to visit from time to time, thanks to an indulgent Nazi superior in the Todt.

At 02.00 the light flashed briefly in the bedroom window. Eric thought five minutes had never lasted so long but it happened again as planned.

He swivelled his head, glancing up and down the road, the other two waiting anxiously for his verdict, their warm breath misty in the freezing night air.

'Come on,' Eric whispered.

He rolled across the road, which hurt his elbows and knees but it was quick and silent. He was careful to protect the Thompson submachine gun with his forearms. The other two came across and they all ran the last few yards to the farmhouse, a light going on in the kitchen as they approached.

Piling into one another, chests heaving, Eric knocked smartly on the door with his knuckles. It swung back to reveal a tall, thin, fair-haired man – aged about 30 and wearing fawn corduroy trousers, muddy black ankle boots and a grey quilted jacket that had seen better days.

He looked anxious and the appearance of his visitors was somewhat daunting and scary as they tumbled in through the narrow door. Their fierce, camouflaged faces were heavily streaked with ash, under berets pulled hard down over over their right ears –

commando green with dull brass Globe & Laurel badges for Ted and Pilbeam and Eric's the lighter green Intelligence Corps beret and a brownish plastic 'Union Rose' – all three visitors clad in combat smocks over battle dress and festooned with the bulky accoutrements of war – submachine guns, grenades, daggers and ammunition pouches *et al.*

Blinded by the light, Ted uttered a loud curse as they were forced to shield their eyes, the Dutchman immediately turning it off. It would take at least 20 minutes to get their night vision back.

'Good evening,' the Dutchman said stiffly, the faint moonlight coming through the window picking out his wan, apologetic smile.

The two marines stationed themselves on watch – Ted kept a lookout through a window while Pilbeam stood by the kitchen door, which was ajar, listening intently.

Eric took the Dutchman by the arm and over to the kitchen table. 'Are you ready?' he asked.

'I am.'

'You have the materials?'

'I do.'

Eric nodded and enquired: 'Where?'

The Dutchman leaned down and picked a satchel up off the floor. 'These documents in here.' Eric smiled and was about to tell the Dutchman not to worry when Pilbeam hissed: 'Something's coming.'

He fully opened the kitchen door and stepped out, hugging the wall and sneaking a look up and down the road.

A faint squealing could be heard and Pilbeam saw two slits of light wobbling down the road, coming towards the farmhouse from the east. Pilbeam scooted back into the kitchen, closing the door softly behind him. 'Tracks,' he whispered, his forehead creased in a worried frown.

'Fucking Germans,' Ted hissed.

'Germans?' the Dutchman asked anxiously.

'Tank or half-track – maybe both,' Pilbeam ventured.

'Alright,' Eric suggested, trying to think of what to do, 'let's just stay calm.' Lights played on the kitchen window and the closer whatever it was got the more the squealing tracks put everyone on edge. Crouching low, Eric pushed the Dutchman down gently. 'Hopefully it will go past,' Eric whispered.

The squealing was now accompanied by the growl of an engine and grinding rumble; the vehicle crunched to a halt by the farmhouse. The engine was switched off, with the sudden quiet filled by loud voices and the sound of boots hitting the ground.

'In here,' the Dutchman urged in a whisper, grabbing his satchel and pushing open a door leading into a sitting room off the kitchen. Like crabs they scuttled in, closing its door just as the kitchen's was smashed open and somebody came in laughing oafishly.

Fortunately, the curtains in the sitting room were closed, so nobody could look in and see the three heavily armed men and a civilian crouching as close as they could to the floor. Hearts beating hard as adrenalin surged through their veins, Eric and the two commando NCOs stood up very slowly, mindful not to bump any furniture or knock over ornaments.

The muzzles of three Thompson submachine guns were pointed straight at the door to the kitchen. They hardly dared breath, hearing a drawer opened, cutlery rattled around and then it was slammed shut. What sounded like a cupboard door was opened and closed, too. The Germans were still laughing, chit-chatting without a care in the world.

The light in the kitchen clicked on, leaking under the gap at the bottom of the door.

'Fuck,' Ted gasped.

'Let's not have a Benny Goodman,' Eric whispered. Leaning down and gently pulling the crouching Dutchman closer, Eric said very quietly in his ear: 'You speak German…what are they saying?'

'They are looking for food,' the Dutchman whispered, 'and are delighted to find pickles, cheeses and potatoes in the larder.'

There was clinking of glass jars.

Pickles being taken away?

Then a thump and what may have been rolling.

The cheeses?

Eric noticed Pilbeam slinging his gun behind him, and pulling something from a scabbard on his waist belt. It glinted in the light from under the door - a Fairbairn-Sykes dagger.

The laughter exploded and the chatter increased in volume as a cupboard just the other side of the door was opened and then slammed shut. There was a metallic click as the catch of the sitting room door was depressed.

Pilbeam placed his feet evenly apart, pushed his left arm out in front, palm flat, fingers fanned. He pulled his stabbing arm back – like an archer stretching to hold a bowstring and arrow ready to fire.

The door began to open and loud German chatter flooded the room. A hand came in, fingertips feeling for the light switch.

Eric pulled the butt of the Thompson into the crook of his arm and caressed the trigger. Ted lifted his weapon to his shoulder, sighting it on the searching hand, which was just inches from the muzzle.

If Ted fired, the bullets would shred it.

Pilbeam shifted his weight onto his back leg, ready to spring forward. The Dutchman was absolutely terrified, clutching his satchel to his chest. Then the engine of the half-track or tank roared into life and somebody came into the kitchen barking orders. The hand withdrew without switching on the light. The door was shut, the latch clicking down. The light in the kitchen went off.

Eric and the marines still did not relax.

The back door slammed shut but they waited, with guns raised and knife poised. The squealing and rumbling got fainter and fainter and was soon gone, the Dutchman letting out a strangulated moan.

'That was bloody close,' Pilbeam chuckled darkly, sliding his fighting knife back into its scabbard.

'Too right,' Ted remarked, taking his beret off and wiping the sweat from his forehead with the back of a hand, his Thompson swinging down on its sling. Eric sat on the arm of a small sofa and let out a deep sigh of relief.

'I suggest we wait 15 minutes to ensure the coast is clear and then make our exit.'

'What if another one comes along?' the frightened Dutchman asked, flopping into an armchair.

Eric moved over to the sitting room window, parted the curtains and opened it. He was making sure it was big enough for them to climb out if needs be. 'The minute we hear anything we make a fast exit,' he explained, closing the window again but not drawing the curtains, so they could spot any looming trouble.

Eric scrutinised the luminous dial on his watch, then clipped the leather cover back over it. '2.15 a.m. – we should still make it back to the houseboat.' He sat down on the sofa while the other two kept watch - one by the sitting room window, the other at the open exterior kitchen door.

The Dutchman seemed to have calmed down.

Laying his satchel on the floor, he got up. Barring his way by stretching his legs out, Eric asked tensely: 'Where are you going?'

'Please, you must be hungry and perhaps we could all do with a drink?' Eric relaxed, withdrew his legs. A few moments later the Dutchman returned with four china cups and a small bottle of brandy on a tray, which he put on the coffee table in front of the sofa.

He disappeared again and returned with a loaf, two large wedges of cheese and a breadknife, all of which he placed on the table next to the tray.

'There is a secret store at the back of the pantry,' the Dutchman explained proudly. He poured some brandy into the china cups for Ted and Pilbeam who grinned broadly on receiving them. The Dutchman broke up the loaf and gave each of his visitors a hunk of bread and chunk of cheese.

'Edam,' he announced, proudly, 'My uncle's best, nice taste.'

He sat back down in the armchair and leaned forward, doing the same service for himself and Eric.

'I have to thank you for coming,' he said, with genuine, deep felt emotion while Eric sipped his brandy, wincing at the shock to his palate.

'We're not out of danger yet,' he informed the Dutchman, who nodded, drank some brandy and broke off a bit of bread, wrapped it around a piece of Edam. Eric was still a little dubious about the man's motivation and decided to test him.

'I hope you don't mind me asking, but why are you jumping ship and coming over to us now?'

The Dutchman was nonplussed.

'Jumping ship?'

'Giving up working with the Germans.'

'I did not work *with* them,' he said irritatedly. 'It was made clear that either I worked *for* them,' he paused to gulp down some brandy, 'or they would take my family away.'

Eric felt ashamed for asking.

'I'm sorry.'

The Dutchman poured himself and Eric some more brandy, remarking heavily: 'And the war is not over.'

'No,' Eric agreed, 'not by a long chalk.'

'A month ago, when I saw they had come up with this criminal plan, I could not bear the idea of the Germans getting an upper hand when my country was getting so close to liberation. I gathered my courage and sent word for my wife and child to live with relatives, to hide from the Germans. So, now I bring you documents of their plan to carry on making weapons, even terrifying new devices to attain victory. As I have seen before, the Germans never like to waste an industrial asset if they can squeeze something more out of it. Natural wastage is to be expected of course, but for them the end justifies the effort.'

Eric suggested: 'You mean the end justifies the means?'

'Sorry, yes the means – always with them the end justifies the means.'

The Dutchman lapsed into a gloomy silence.

Curious about exactly what the Dutchman had in his satchel – *these 'terrifying new devices'!?* – Eric wanted to enquire further, but checked this inclination. He knew from past experience that Spendlove and his expert debriefers did not like their pitch queered by nosy field troops.

Eric reached out to get some more bread and cheese, as he was now feeling rather hungry. The Dutchman leaned forward, tapping the back of Eric's hand with something.

'These are my family,' he revealed, offering a small photograph.

Putting the bread and cheese down, Eric held it up to moonlight coming through the window. He picked out only the indistinct shapes of what looked to be a young woman on a bicycle with a small boy placed on its handlebars. 'You are a lucky man,' was all Eric could think of saying before handing it back, flipping open the cover on his wristwatch to check the time again.

It was time to go.

As they now knew the lie of the land, the journey back was completed more quickly, even though they must still move with stealth. Scrambling along the foot of the raised road, splashing through soggy polder, they reached the turn just before it ran into trees.

They crouched down, wheezing from the effort in cold air.

The river seemed very quiet.

In the distance a few flares floated down under parachutes.

Tracer bullets snaked languidly into the sky; far away.

It was 3.15am.

They got up and took the risk of running down the road. Once into the trees they took a right turn onto a path down to the grassy bank above the river. Sliding down it they trudged along the beach, found the bushes and quickly uncovered the Folboats.

Pilbeam and the Dutchman were in the lead craft, setting off at a fair lick because time was running out. Fortunately, the current was with them. Eric and Ted got into their Folboat, the satchel containing the precious documents going in Eric's footwell.

The Dutchman had been reluctant to give it up, as if the satchel was his talisman but Eric assured him it was in safe hands – another expression that seemed to arouse puzzlement. 'And you will be safe with Pilbeam,' Eric added, as they helped the Dutchman put on an inflatable life belt under his quilted jacket. He nodded, still uneasy but a little less scared.

Further proof of Eric's incompetence in the art of paddling was provided, for, even with the current carrying them, he and Ted fell behind quite a way. Suddenly, up ahead, a searchlight from the German side flicked on, its fat, evil beam catching the lead Folboat cold. Eric and Ted stopped paddling and let their craft drift, for there was no point in hastening their entry into the same predicament.

Fire erupted from the German side - machine guns, rifles and then, with a insistent hammering that provoked instant, gut-wrenching fear - a quadruple 20mm anti-aircraft weapon firing low and level.

This was the weapon that had wrought such devastation in the ranks of British paratroopers trying to reach the Arnhem road bridge over the Rhine the previous September.

Cannon shells came in a fiery stream from the northern bank. Creating a forest of splashes, they tore the lead Folboat apart. One moment Eric and Ted could see the tiny silhouette of the canoe and the two men in it – Pilbeam's paddle whirling desperately – and the next it was eradicated by a cyclone of cannon shells and spray.

Heavy fire was coming from the British side now – much more intense than the Germans could muster. Artillery shells tore through the night sky to explode on enemy positions. Among the leaping flames and soil fountains Eric thought he saw a tree being tossed high into the air, turning end on end. Then it all stopped - like the light in a room suddenly being switched off.

Eric and Ted let the current take them down river, expecting to be blown apart at any moment. They slid through a pall of smoke drifting on the water, glancing around trying to spot signs of life. There were small fragments of wreckage but no sign of anybody - until there was a bump.

The Folboat's nose had collided with a body, floating face down.

Ted manoeuvred the boat so Eric could reach down and grab the corpse's quilted jacket. Stowing his paddle, Ted helped, and they turned it over. An explosion on the German side lit the scene with an orange flash, revealing the Dutchman's sightless blue eyes wide open in surprise. They tried to pull him out of the water – not easy in an inherently unstable Folboat - only to realise the body had been cut in half below the ludicrously intact life belt they'd made him put on. They gently let him go.

Ted got his paddle and steered them over towards the southern bank while the Dutchman's remains were carried off by the current into the smoke and down river. A flare illuminated the scene, some way off, while German green and white tracer bullets silently arced overhead, interlacing with red British rounds going the other way.

Stunned into angry impotence, Eric clenched his fists and punched the water on either side of the boat.

He didn't bother to paddle, his hands just trailing uselessly in the freezing water. Three owl hoots from Ted and he snapped out of it, for they had somehow found the houseboat on the British side.

One of the Cornish troops hooted back.

The boat bumped the beach.

'Time to get out Eric,' Ted said, his voice betraying no emotion at all.

Ted had seen plenty of people killed, not least in Normandy and while he was angry and bereft at the loss of his mate, for now he kept it under control. They pulled the Folboat up onto the shore, soldiers from the houseboat coming down onto the mud to help them drag it up to the riverbank. After it was laid down on the grass, Eric pulled the satchel out of the footwell. 'Fucking Germans, I hate 'em,' he spat.

Ted said nothing, needing all his strength to control his black-hearted rage. Eric, meanwhile, was wallowing in his own failure to look after the Dutchman. He felt great shame at surviving while the others were killed. In the aftermath, plunged into a deep, dark hole of self-loathing and depression, Eric wrote to Katherine explaining that he didn't think it was fair to keep her waiting for him as the war dragged on. She should just forget him. Better a short, sharp pain now rather than have her suffer a broken heart when he met his inevitable death.

20

A MONTH later Spendlove told Eric to fetch a jeep from the unit motor pool as they were going on a jaunt to the Allied Forces headquarters near Paris. Naturally, Eric got the driving chores.

Turning the wheel to swing in through the imposing gates of the palace at Versailles, an American military policeman checked their papers and directed them to a parking area.

Spendlove – alert and bright eyed while Eric felt quite worn out - explained that, despite the terrible impasse that followed the Market Garden failure, the war was reaching its endgame.

At some stage he expected the unit would operate in Germany on what he referred to as 'tasks of a special nature and sensitivity'.

Both of them uncurling their stiff legs and climbing out of the vehicle, Eric accompanied Spendlove through the grounds and into the Palace itself.

As they entered the famed Hall of Mirrors, Spendlove wittered on about 'bringing Hitler and his henchmen to book' and how much he would 'relish the task.' He explained that there were plans to potentially use Versailles again for the finale of this war – the natural sequel to both the Germans declaring their new Emperor in this very place on 18 January 1871 and the signing of a peace treaty of 1919 that formally ended the previous Great War. This time it would be the stage for a grand surrender by the Nazis.

Eric was impressed – it certainly was a spectacular setting.

Spendlove fell silent, looking vexed, and then announced he had to 'go and see a man about a dog' and disappeared, not even seeming to hear Eric's plea of: 'Shall I just wait here, then Sir?'

In showing off the Hall of Mirrors to his subordinate, Spendlove had forgotten an appointment in the nearby Trianon Palace Hotel, where elements of Allied high command were still ensconced, so hopped into the jeep and sped off.

Feeling at a decided loose end, Eric wandered around, pondering the war and all it had done to his family, his city and country. Eric felt angry. Looking at his reflection one of the mirrors on the wall facing the windows, through which a weak winter's light streamed, he saw a soldier – *no longer a jolly copper from the Plymouth City beat but a battle-hardened warrior* – and someone who had seen his share of death, some of which he felt responsible for. There were the Maoris, who had given their lives to carry him along the railway track at Cassino and the Dutchman whom he had failed to deliver safely. Eric let self-loathing and guilt wash over him.

Deciding he had to escape, Eric marched over to the nearest pair of French windows and wrenched them open. Out in the grounds Eric found a stone bench next to a flowerbed and sat down. Leaning back, wrapping his coat tightly around himself and with hands buried deep in its pockets, he closed his eyes. 'I hope Spendlove doesn't take much longer or I'll get piles,' was his last thought before sleep overwhelmed him.

* * *

Spendlove roused Eric with the nudge of his boot. Awakening with a start, shuddering at the cold that had crept into his bones, grimacing at his sore neck, Eric got to his feet. 'Come on Wise, we've got to go!' Spendlove bellowed, striding away towards where the jeep was parked.

When he got to the vehicle, Eric found Spendlove behind the wheel, so poured himself into the passenger seat. Spendlove reached behind Eric's side and hoisted a bulging briefcase up and over between them. Unclipping its lock while it was wedged between his tummy and the steering wheel, Spendlove pulled out a buff folder, passing it to Eric. After shoving the briefcase into the back Spendlove started the jeep engine and pulled away.

Eric opened the folder to find it contained air reconnaissance photographs of what looked like hundreds – *no, make that thousands* - of people being herded along roads - a great mass of humanity flowing through various types of landscape: flat, open country; hilly uplands; wooded tracts.

It was a latter-day migration out of Egypt – only this time away from a voracious Soviet tide sweeping in from the East rather than Moses shepherding his people across the Red Sea.

'That's the fruit of your mission across the Rhine!' shouted Spendlove as he botched the gear change, throwing an American sentry at the gates a salute as they kangarooed out onto the main road.

'A job well done despite the cost,' he added.

Ignoring this attempt at mitigation - feeling annoyed at having to juggle the folder in his hands to keep its content flying in all directions - Eric enquired: 'What *exactly* am I looking at?'

'That's the Nazis marching their slaves West away from the Red hordes.' Joggled by the motion of the jeep, Eric leafed through the images again, scarcely able to believe what he saw and something puzzled him.

'Why aren't they scattering when the aircraft flies over?'

'You'd think they would,' replied Spendlove, 'but that plane is too high to bother them – the camera lenses in those reconnaissance Spitfires are incredibly powerful. Gives you an idea of the sheer scale of their nasty little endeavour, all those poor souls snaking across the collapsing Reich. This is what the Dutchman passed us secret documents about - the Nazi plan to march their slave workers West, so they can be under the yoke in underground weapons factories.'

Lost in black thoughts of the inhuman efficiency of the Nazis, Eric didn't notice that instead of taking the road back to Holland, Spendlove was venturing deep into the narrow streets of Versailles.

The content of the photos made Eric feel sick to his core, something enhanced by the stop-start nature of Spendlove's driving as the jeep dodged around. Closing the folder, Eric's hatred of the Germans increased as, into his mind, flashed an image of the Dutchman smiling as he poured brandy into a china cup. There was now a widow and a fatherless boy somewhere in occupied Holland - all thanks to the Dutchman's decision to try and help the Allies end the war. His family remained – like millions of others - still held in bondage by Hitler and his gang. For his own sanity, Eric banished thoughts of their predicament from his head.

The jeep careered around a corner and lurched to a halt, Eric nearly losing control of the folder entirely. Tongue between his teeth for concentration, Spendlove eased the vehicle over the kerb and parked against the wall of a tall, grey stone corniced 18th Century building. The front wing of the jeep nudged a lead drainpipe, Spendlove turning the engine off.

'Can I ask, Sir, what we are going to do about this?'

Spendlove reached across, closed the folder for him, then, with a grunt of exertion, hoisted the briefcase out of the back again and shoved it inside.

'There's not a lot we can do Eric, and the Russians are nearer.'

'So, they can save these people?'

Spendlove cracked a humourless smile: 'I am sure Stalin's boys will do their best, while our Bomber Command chaps will no doubt digest the Dutchman's wonderful intelligence documents – especially the locations the slave labourers are being marched to. They will start pounding the underground weapons factories, using some of our delightful new Tallboy earthquake bombs.'

Eric was aghast.

'Hopefully before the slave workers get there?' Spendlove shrugged apologetically: 'It is not within my remit, but, yes, hopefully.'

Eric was not reassured and felt his mood blacken further.

With no further comment, but with a groan of effort, the major pulled himself out of his seat and went around the front of the vehicle, carrying the briefcase in his right hand. On looking out of the jeep to the left, Eric found Spendlove heading for a restaurant across the street called *Le Saint André*.

Eric climbed out and went across to join his boss on the pavement outside the establishment, which to Eric's eyes appeared closed, its grimy window shutters firmly shut. Spendlove knocked on the frame of the front door, which offered a 'Fermé' sign trapped between its large, single glass pane and some venetian blinds.

'Bloody super little place,' Spendlove purred. 'Excellent wine list, brilliant menu even in difficult times; bit of plonk and some hot food will cheer us both up.' The venetian blinds twitched, a thumb and forefinger prised two of them apart and a pair of dark eyes scrutinised whoever it was dared to knock. 'Better than your pea and ham soup!' Spendlove roared merrily over his shoulder at Eric. 'That *was* thunder-fucking awful stuff.'

Bolts clunked back and the door swung open to reveal a short, wiry man with a narrow, leathery face distinguished by an enormous hooked nose under which was a greying toothbrush moustache. He wore a dark double-breasted suit with a white shirt and red bow tie.

'Ah Michel!' Spendlove cried with delight, the two men embracing.

'Monsieur Saint Jean!' Michel exclaimed, beaming with delight, 'I have not seen you since the Boche arrived in 1940.'

'I made it out of town just in time!'

Michel's shoulders heaved with merriment.

'Come in Monsieur Saint Jean.'

Michel ushered them in, taking their caps and coats – with Spendlove retaining the briefcase - and handing them over to a waiter who led the two British Army officers deeper in.

Above the low hubbub of conversation, a jazz guitar and violin were languorously intertwined in *Out of Nowhere*, while under the dim lighting, Eric picked out other waiters bustling from booth to booth. As kitchen doors swung open and then shut at the far end, the smell of warm herbs and poached salmon wafted out, along with the loud, unintelligible voice of a chef bellowing orders.

Eric and Spendlove were shown into a booth.

Looking around, Eric noticed that nearly all the diners were Allied military officers, both male and female, with just a few civilians sprinkled here and there. Most astonishing of all, in another booth, was what looked like a Luftwaffe general flanked by a British and an American air force officer.

Eric was stunned by this amazing vision of such conviviality between officers of his own side and a leader of the very same organisation that had blitzed Plymouth. He wanted to ask Spendlove if his eyes were truly deceiving him, but the major's attention was firmly fixed on Michel as the latter explained there were, sadly, still limitations to the menu, but that today's *highly recommended* special was the Salmon *en croute* with provencal tomatoes and new potatoes.

'It is quite magnificent,' suggested Michel.

'Then we'll have that times two and a bottle of chenin blanc.'

'Excellent choice.'

Once Michel had gone, Eric whispered, his pulse racing and mouth dry: 'What's a Luftwaffe officer doing over there?'

Distracted by the two musicians playing on a small stage, Spendlove did not register Eric's enquiry.

'You know,' he mused, 'I think that is actually Django Reinhardt and Stéphane Grappeli playing for us...how splendid.'

'But, Sir, the German …'

'What?'

'At another table - over there,' Eric growled. 'A fucking German.'

Eric resisted the urge to point accusingly and so nodded in the direction of the booth in question. Feeling his blood boil, he sorely wanted to stand up, pull out his pistol and plug the German between the eyes with a 9mm bullet.

It was just as well their sidearms were locked in a chained down ammunition container in the back of the jeep - Spendlove's innovation for avoiding *the deeply uncivilised practice of toting them* in social settings when out and about behind the front line, *as the sight of them might scare off contacts with useful intel.* Eric had suggested the container might be *just the sort of intriguing thing somebody would feel compelled to steal* but that notion was breezily dismissed.

Now Spendlove's eyes were scanning the restaurant, alighting on the three air force officers - one in a Luftwaffe uniform - who were smoking cigars and enjoying brandies, and, so it seemed, sharing a good joke. Spendlove shook his head and remarked: 'I have no idea why exactly, but sometimes we parole prisoners and take them for a slap-up meal if they have been good boys and gifted us some secrets.'

Spendlove paused for a rueful smile and remarked:

'I bet the German recommended this place for their cosy lunch.'

'Nonetheless, Sir,' Eric suggested, 'if you had a pistol in that briefcase of yours under the table and I could get my hands on it, I think I'd like to shoot our German friend.'

The bottle of chenin blanc arrived in its ice bucket just in time to cool things down. The sommelier retrieved it and showed the label to Spendlove, who nodded his assent.

After pulling the cork and filling their glasses the sommelier withdrew, while Spendlove gave Eric a chilly smile and suggested:

'Have a drink and calm down Lieutenant.'

Sighing, Eric did as ordered, enjoying the cool, crisp wine, feeling it damping his fury. Observing Eric's jaw unclenching, Spendlove observed: 'In this job sometimes drinking on an empty stomach is the best medicine.'

Taking a sip of wine, Spendlove then confided in a whisper: 'I do have a handy little Beretta pistol in my capacious briefcase Eric and, much though I share your desire for instant vengeance on Herman Goering's pal over there, it would be impolite before we have even eaten.'

Resigning himself to the situation, Eric observed sourly: 'Shame we couldn't have brought the Dutchman here rather than see some bloody Nazi getting the Rolls Royce treatment.'

Spendlove nodded, letting out a heavy sigh that shivered the surface of his chenin blanc. 'Yes, it would have been preferable to seeing that swine over there,' Spendlove conceded, 'but don't forget Eric, the Dutchman served his overlords loyally for some years before risking his neck, so he was not clean either. As you are finding out, there's all sorts of shades of grey in our nasty little corner of warfare.'

PART II

1

The Huntsman's Lodge, May 1946

HAVING SPOKEN for an hour or more, Eric fell into silence, staring down at the empty shot glass as he turned it over in his hand.

His head was swimming from the process of telling his story and more alcohol on an empty stomach; his mouth was dry and throat sore. On the other side of the table Martin yawned loudly.

'Have I bored you?' Eric enquired sharply.

Laying the Walther pistol down, Martin stretched out his arms and brought his hands together, lacing his fingers and cracking their joints.

Heart beating wildly, Eric considered making a grab for the gun but the German saw where the Englander's eyes were resting. 'No, you have not bored me,' Martin remarked, picking up the gun and again pointing it at his captive. 'It has all been most fascinating, and now I would like you to get to your feet.'

Was this it? As he stared into the German's mocking eyes Eric burned with a mix of impotent fury and fear.

Smiling, Martin proposed: 'I think we could both do with some fresh air and a cigarette, yes?'

Eric saw a chance to get away, but was the German really that stupid? Surely he knew there was a risk his captive would make a break for it?

Martin holstered his Walther and picked up the sniper rifle.

'Do not try to make a run for it,' the German advised, 'as you will force me to put a bullet in your head – and I am a very good shot.'

'Ever the typical, arrogant German,' Eric thought.

As they came around to the front of the lodge, Martin instructed: 'Go slowly, captain.' The jeep was just a few yards away – *could Eric jump in and get away?* He brushed his right trouser pocket with his fingertips to make sure the ignition keys were still in there.

Spotting this, the German informed him: 'You would never make it.' Stopping and looking over his shoulder, Eric found Martin holding the sniper rifle at waist level, aimed squarely at his back.

'Please, go over to that tree Captain Wise.'

'Which bloody tree?' Eric asked sullenly.

Martin waggled the rifle to his right.

'The tall fir by the ornamental wheelbarrow.'

Eric tried desperately to summon the courage to make a break, but the idea of being shot in the back as he ran away did not appeal.

Once he was at the tree, Eric turned around. Pointing the gun straight at Eric's stomach, a matter of no more than six feet away, Martin enquired with a cool smile: 'Cigarette?'

'I don't need a last cigarette before my execution,' Eric observed with a weary sigh. Affecting a look of shock and surprise, Martin asked: 'You think I am going to kill you?'

Tired of the games, Eric closed his eyes and leaned back against the rough, warm bark of the tree - listening to the faint breeze through its branches - but there was no gunshot. Instead Eric heard Martin confess: 'Actually, I have been toying with you Captain Wise. Please turn around and look down, at the foot of the tree.'

Puzzled, Eric did as ordered, spotting a white pillowcase with grease stains on it. A few ants were crawling over it.

'Pick it up,' Martin ordered. 'It contains our lunch – and I don't know about you but I am starving.'

Back in the kitchen the German sat at the table again, pistol on Eric as the Englander put the chickens on a large chopping board.

'It is a cool day,' Martin observed pleasantly, 'and they were freshly roasted this morning, so still edible I am sure.'

Eric checked the roasted chicken over for insects, finding none, or at least not any that he could see.

Martin asked Eric to place it at the centre of the table. 'We can eat with our fingers,' the German proposed - keen not to put potentially lethal cutlery in the other man's hands - adding that there was some bread in the larder, which Eric should bring to the table.

'Let us sit down and eat,' Martin proposed.

Eric did so, eagerly tearing into a chicken leg, mind racing about what to do next. Also eating, and wiping greasy fingertips on his hessian scarf, Martin suggested politely:

'So, please, continue your account.'

Eric seethed at being held hostage and forced to tell his story, but it struck him the longer he talked, the more the German would tire of holding that gun on him. He pressed on, for it might give him time to save his life.

2

British Sector, Berlin, February 1946

THE BITTER COLD was barely relieved by the pathetic fire of Eric Wise's office in a building called the London Block near the Olympic Stadium where the Nazis had a decade earlier tried to showcase Aryan physical supremacy. Now the site hosted elements of the British military administration of the former German capital.

A telephone on the grey-painted steel desk rang shrilly. Grimacing at its tone, Eric picked the hand set up off its cradle to find Spendlove on the other end, requesting his presence forthwith for a chat about a pressing matter.

Eric paused at the door, tightening his tie knot against the collar of his shirt, then knocked, Spendlove's booming voice inviting him to enter.

The boss had a far bigger fire, which crackled and sparked merrily, filling his entire office with a jolly sort of toastiness, reflecting the mood of its occupant. 'Sit down,' Spendlove instructed, waving a hand towards the chair on the other side of the desk. As he talked Spendlove toasted crumpets on the end of a long fork over the fire.

Once he was certain each one was done, he deposited it on a large plate on his desk, itself next to a butter dish on which rested a silver knife. 'Be mother would you, old boy,' Spendlove ordered, pointing the fork at a tea set next to the crumpet plate.

Eric shifted his chair nearer to the desk, pulled the beige woollen cozy off the chunky, glazed brown china teapot and gently prised its lid off. Spendlove preferred the small bags containing tea leaves and Eric had to agree it was better than licking tiny brown bits off your tongue and gums.

'Two things to discuss Eric,' Spendlove revealed, turning a crumpet at just the right distance from the flames to make it golden brown, but not burned. Eric used a teaspoon to squeeze the teabags against the inside of the pot while Spendlove gingerly took another crumpet off the fork and placed it on the pile. 'One - we've got to assert our rights in the Soviet sector of Berlin as you know, so I want you to step up the "tours of inspection", to let those fellows know we have rights to access.'

Eric put the lid back on the teapot, lifted it and gently swirled its contents. 'I'll do one this afternoon, Sir.'

'Excellent. Be a good fellow and butter the crumpets.'

'And the second thing, Sir?'

Spendlove appeared not to hear as he inspected the browning of another crumpet. 'Am I'm being demobbed?' Eric ventured, more in hope than realistic expectation.

Taking the crumpet off the fork to do the other side, Spendlove smiled at his subordinate's cheek.

'No such luck,' he chortled, spearing the crumpet again. 'I'm afraid we'll need you for some time yet.' Smearing butter on a crumpet, Eric could not hide his disappointment: 'Oh, I was sure my time is up.'

Hurling the crumpet onto the pile, and laying his toasting fork to one side, Spendlove grinned broadly, barely able to control his mirth at Eric's downcast face. 'Actually Lieutenant Wise, you're being promoted to captain...'

Eric stopped buttering, shocked at his sudden elevation.

'Isn't that a bit irregular?'

'Oh yes, but your talents have been recognized, as have mine. I am to be a lieutenant colonel - for my sins. And while I stay here you'll soon be going to Austria to head up a new war crimes investigation unit.'

Eric selected a crumpet to butter, while Spendlove reached for the teapot, also marshalling two cups towards it.

'You forgot to be mother,' Spendlove noted reproachfully.

Spendlove poured the tea, shoving a steaming cup towards Eric. 'You'll be hunting down nasty Nazis – and other little jobs.'

While Eric picked up his cuppa, Spendlove seized a crumpet and took a big bite out of it, talking as he chewed.

'They'll let you know exactly what you're up to when you get down there…You'll still be reporting to me…and remain part of my little band of merry men – but at a distance. We up here …will continue to be Spendlove Group One, while you…will be S.G.2. I intend giving Ted Bodman to you…for company.'

'When does my pay go up, Sir?'

'Next pay day, you lucky beggar.'

'When do I leave?'

'Soon as you've tidied up your odds and ends here.'

* * *

The journey from Berlin to southeast Austria some weeks later went fairly smoothly, aside from one awkward moment at a Soviet checkpoint.

Ted Bodman was behind the wheel, as they passed through part of the Russian sector before entering the British one in the south. It was the sort of occurrence Eric had been accustomed to handling with tact and diplomacy (or threats if they did not suffice) during forays into the Soviet sector of Berlin. Smiling at the scowling Red Army sentry, Eric handed over their papers, which explained his and Ted's authorization in English, Russian and French. The sentry handed them straight back after only a cursory glance.

'Niet!'

'Niet!?' Eric asked incredulously. 'You didn't even read them!'

Detecting anger in the British officer's voice, the Russian raised his PPS-43 submachine gun, and poked it in Eric's face. Ted slowly lowered his hand from the steering wheel and surreptitiously undid the flap of his pistol holster.

'Niet,' the pasty-faced Russian snapped.

Eric grinned and nodded to show his understanding of where the power lay, glancing meaningfully at Ted, to ensure his sidekick didn't pull a gun on their Soviet friend.

The Russian soldier's solemn, bovine features remained blank but his eyes were hostile. Ted reversed the jeep back down the road, wary of careering off the edge into the gorge.

Parking up, he looked to Eric for further instruction.

'Well, what do we do now?'

Eric applied a match to a cigarette for a thoughtful puff as he pondered tactics. Ted reached into the back of the jeep to fetch a grenade from an ammunition tin behind the driver's seat. Eric shook his head and told him:

'I don't think we should be blowing up Russian sentries.'

'It won't hurt to be prepared,' Ted observed nestling the grenade in his lap, perhaps not the ideal place for it to be, but close to hand while he was driving. Eric, meanwhile, weighed up the situation. The sentry appeared to be alone and Russians were notoriously jumpy and intransigent when they didn't have someone else to tell them what to do. Initiative was positively discouraged at all levels. This character probably had a vodka hangover and just felt like relieving the boredom of his lonely vigil with a bit of obstructionism. Eric wondered if the Russian could read at all, and - if not -the documents handed to him earlier by Eric had been a frightening prospect – not the sort of responsibility he wanted.

The sentry had returned to his hut, pulled a little three-legged stool out from inside and sat on it, PPS-43 across his lap, scowling at the jeep and its occupants.

Eric decided they should give it another go.

When the jeep stopped at the barrier, the Russian stood up and held the gun ready to fire but at least did not yet poke it in Eric's face. He regarded them with deep creases furrowing his forehead, mutely trying to convey his dilemma. Eric decided to help him out. Even though he may not understand much, if any, English he would hopefully get the tone of voice.

'Soldier,' Eric said loudly, in a commanding tone, 'we are important people and you must let us through!'

The Russian's frown deepened, and he shifted uneasily from foot to foot, finger still curled lightly around the trigger of his weapon.

Out of the corner of his eye, Eric saw Ted slowly lifting the flap of his pistol holster. The Russian saw it too and now his PPS-43 was raised, pointing at Eric's face. 'We must go now, comrade,' Eric suggested quietly, staring straight into the other man's eyes, adding a Russian phrase he had found most useful in East Berlin: 'Eto poryadok.'

This is order.

The Russian suddenly comprehended that this Western officer was doing him the honour of taking charge, lifting the weight of thinking off his peasant shoulders. He gave a big grin, the gun dropping, leaning into the jeep and gathering Eric into a bear hug.

'Khoroshiy angliyskiy tovarishch!'

'Good English comrade.'

Nose twitching at the smell of stale cigarettes and cabbage impregnating the man's filthy uniform, Eric responded:

'Da, tovarishch Krasnoy Armii.'

'Yes, Red Army comrade.'

Letting go, the Russian stepped back, a broad grin on his face, saluting smartly before marching over to the barrier and raising it. Eric threw him a smile and a return salute, while Ted wasted no time in accelerating through and away down the road.

Using the wing mirror to check the Russian was not lifting his machine gun to shoot them in the back, Eric let out a sigh of relief. A bend in the road took them out of sight, racing away down the narrow road, snaking between the fragrant pine covered slopes and onward to the south.

3

Originally surrendered to the Russians - with not much damage from the fighting itself - large parts of Austria's second city of Graz had been levelled by earlier Allied bombing.

Its railway junction was a key point for distributing fuel to the Nazi war machine, so rolling stock, marshalling yards and train workshops had been pummelled. When bombs missed those targets – and they often did – thousands of homes were destroyed and two thousand civilian lives claimed. Yet, somehow the beautiful old university city's most historic parts – including the Schlossberg fortress at its centre - were untouched.

Graz was handed over to the British in July 1945 when each of the Allied powers pulled their troops back to respective demarcation lines, settling into allocated sectors of occupation.

Britain was awarded administration of Steiermark and Kärnten, with its main military base in Wetzeldorf, on the outskirts of Graz, and which during the war served as a Waffen SS barracks.

It had been home to both those troops and secret policemen who, before they withdrew in April 1945, conducted the slaughter of more than 200 Jewish slave workers and captured Yugoslav resistance fighters held there. For the sake of thorough house-keeping, they added a few captured British, French and Russian servicemen to the murder tally.

The barracks now hosted several hundred British troops, mainly from the 1st Battalion of the East Yorkshire Regiment, a unit whose story in the Second World War stretched all the way from Dunkirk to combat in the Reich itself. A number of non-infantry units called it home, too, including the Royal Military Police and the intelligence-gatherers of the so-called Field Security Sections.

When they arrived Eric and Ted found the soldiers guarding the gates of the base – these days known as Hawkesworth Barracks - were even less friendly than the Russian at the sector checkpoint, though at least they did not point guns at anyone. Despite a sentry's vague directions Eric and Ted successfully located the car park for the RMP Headquarters building.

Climbing out of the jeep, Eric pulled his kitbag from the back, telling Ted to go and find the Sergeants' Mess. Eric bounded up the steps and inside. Depositing the kit bag in an outer office, he was taken in by a fresh-faced subaltern to see Lieutenant Colonel Angus McFaul, Commanding Officer RMP Graz, who had his nose buried in some paperwork.

The colonel, a rather austere Scot, looked up and put the documents to one side, sliding them under a white marble paper weight with a silver wash metal Nazi eagle and swastika mounted on it. Taking his glasses off and placing them perfectly parallel with the edge of his blotter, before speaking the colonel cleared his throat with a loud phlegmy cough.

'Welcome to Graz, Captain Wise - please sit down.'

'Thank you, Sir.'

Eric sat on a straight-backed chair in front of the desk.

'Good journey?' the colonel enquired.

Taking his cap off and placing it on his knees, Eric admitted:

'Aside from having a gun poked in my face by a Russian sentry at a sector checkpoint, very pleasant.'

McFaul raised his eyebrows in surprise.

'Really? They're a rum lot these Russians. Makes you wonder if we were fighting the right people.'

Eric laughed, though he soon realized that was a mistake. Despite what he had taken to be a drily humorous tone, a glare told him McFaul was deadly serious.

'Well, Captain Wise,' the colonel suggested, 'I suppose I ought to give you a feel for the terrain.'

McFaul got to his feet, walking over to the office window and gazing out across an empty parade ground. 'We do have an enormous problem with bandits,' he remarked dourly. 'Murderous swine, running wild in the countryside robbing blind wherever they go, plundering villages and towns of whatever booty they can find. There is also a massive black market going on. We currently have a big ongoing operation to try and bring one of the kingpins to justice.'

Frowning deeply, the colonel span around, and with two steps was back at his desk. Opening a drawer, he extracted a file, which he put on the blotter and opened without sitting down.

Pulling his glasses on, McFaul scanned up and down, finger tracing his progress on the sheet of paper. He explained, almost absent-mindedly: 'Calls himself *die Falke* - if you are a German speaker - or *il Falco* – if you're an Italian. *The Hawk* to us, *the Falcon*...whatever you wish.'

The colonel gave Eric a steely, determined look. 'If we can bring him in, a lot of trouble might be cleaned up. Some help with *The Hawk* would be appreciated.'

The colonel sat down but swivelled his chair to gaze thoughtfully out the window again as he spoke.

'That won't be your main business, though. You may be Spendlove's man, but you take higher-level instructions from me. I am most keen for your new unit to hunt down war criminals and place them in front of a firing squad...' He turned his chair back around to look at Eric, a muscle in his cheek twitching as he added portentously: 'Or in a hangman's noose.'

The colonel opened another drawer, ferreting around in it until, with a grunt, he pulled out a dog-eared file, shoving it across the desk.

'And that's your starting point.'

Eric opened it and started to leaf through while McFaul elaborated. 'As the Russians approached in early 1945, the Germans decided they better try and remove evidence of what they'd been up to in the camps,' the colonel explained. 'They also aimed to retain vital slave labour to carry on war production – that much you have no doubt been briefed on by Spendlove, hopefully including the use of Liebenau labour camp near here?'

McFaul grimaced at Eric's blank look.

'That was not in any briefing, Sir.'

'Well it doesn't matter, as we've already dealt with it and the guilty parties are going to be executed soon, at Karlau prison – eight swine who in the spring of last year marched a load of Hungarians Jews from Liebenau to Mauthausen death camp in the north. More than thirty died on the way, shot and buried along the route, although we suspect many more were killed in the camp itself. The primary point of interest for you Captain Wise, in this new investigation, is that they decided to burn another such camp in Hungary - and force march those poor souls to an underground weapons factory, via Graz. We think the intent was to ship them by train from here to Saint Georgen an der Gusen - just next door to Mauthaussen - but nobody arrived as far as we can tell.'

Eric felt his pulse quicken as he realised this could very well be one of the marches he'd seen in the aerial reconnaissance photos at Versailles. Eric pulled a small map from the folder and opened it. Someone had drawn a red line from one X at Lake Balaton to another at Graz. A red circle had been drawn around St. Georgen an der Gusen.

As his finger traced the route, Eric remarked:

'It's a long way to walk from Balaton to Graz.'

'About 160 miles,' the colonel informed him. 'While the Nazis killed quite a few along the way when doing these so-called death marches, hundreds usually did survive in some god-forsaken camp or factory to tell the tale. This is a very strange case because we have a sole suspected survivor. Until the Russians hand over their files on this to us, all you have in that folder is the map and some case studies on other death marches for general swotting up on the Hun's barbarity.'

Eric was about to ask about the 'sole suspected survivor' but before he could open his mouth, McFaul pressed on.

'I want you to take a preliminary investigation group - pathologist and his team, one or two Field Security Section men, if you need them, along with some military policemen, plus yourself and your own S.G. chap of course - and retrace the footsteps of the march. Collect enough evidence to confirm a general line of thought on guilty parties, so we can bring someone to book for whatever happened. The main thing is to confirm the locations of burial sites, with a light touch – an exploratory exhumation prior to a full-blown investigation and graves registration unit to go in later.'

McFaul fell silent, seemingly lost in thought, the fingertips of his right hand tracing the outline of the Nazi eagle and swastika engraved into the paperweight, before lifting angry eyes and snarling: 'If I had my way, I'd hang, draw and quarter all the Nazi bastards who did this, without trial.'

Eric nodded in sympathy, observing: 'Yes, Sir, but aside from the general route have we got much to go on? You mentioned *a sole suspected survivor*?'

'There is a young woman at Bad Gastein who may, or may not be, from the march. She's too traumatised to get much sense out of her. You could pay her a visit – you might fare better. Bad Gastein is in the American sector.' McFaul cracked a thin smile as he added: 'Hopefully nobody will stick a gun in your face, though you never know with the Yanks.'

'Are the Russians alright about us entering Hungary, Sir?' Eric enquired.

'Full co-operation, allegedly, ' replied McFaul, 'though the paperwork has yet to be tidied up – but don't go in there unless you absolutely have to.'

'Can I take this file away for further reading?'

'Have it as long as you like. You should know that your pathologist is a naval Surgeon Commander called Jock Geddes and he's got a gang of women with him to do all the writing up and typing.'

This last bit was expressed with a distinct air of distaste and disapproval, McFaul adding: 'Four naval nurses and a Nursing Sister, an officer, by the name of Smith-Glosson who…'

McFaul paused on seeing a shocked look on Eric's face.

'Something wrong Captain?'

Wearing a wry smile, Eric shook his head.

'No, Sir.'

'Don't like the idea of working with a squad of females?'

'No, Sir, I am fine with that.'

Eric was just worried about one in particular, a ghost from his not so distant past. Katherine Smith-Glosson. 'Go across to Barrack Block C at some stage,' the colonel suggested, 'introduce yourself to the Surgeon Commander and his team. Other than that, I think the Field Security lot will probably make room for you in their offices.'

Eric stood up, put his cap on and saluted McFaul, who waved him away with a grimace, sat down and lifted the Nazi eagle paperweight to one side to resume his reading.

* * *

The sound of a familiar voice distracted Katherine Smith-Glosson away from her chat with a couple of khaki-clad nurses. After a few seconds of shock at seeing a former lover on the threshold of the office, she returned to her discussions, gaining time to restore her composure.

Colouring a little, Eric attempted to cover up his embarrassment by casually leaning against the doorframe, trying to ignore her slim figure under battle dress and the timbre of her voice, which still thrilled him. While waiting he surveyed the office. It was a spartan affair, occupied only by a small, highly polished dark wood desk and a single chair. A few shelves on the wall had box files on them while the desk was host to an olive green phone and a small portable typewriter, with a neat stack of blank paper and some carbon sheets beside it.

Katherine dismissed her nurses crisply.

'I think that's all for now.'

The nurses exited past Eric, keeping their eyes down, not daring to exchange any curious glances for fear of provoking the ire of their commander. Katherine gazed expectantly at him with a familiar challenge in her eyes. 'Well, what a pleasant surprise this is,' she observed with icy neutrality.

Eric nodded and smiled, still embarrassed but striving for a light touch. 'Sorry to shock you like that Katherine, but it seems we are to work together. I am the investigator who will go with you into Hungary.'

'No need to apologise,' she responded, keeping professionally polite, but then couldn't resist adding reproachfully: 'Even though you were rather brutal in finishing with me.'

Eric felt his heart sink, ashamed at the reminder of how he'd treated her. Flustered, and at a loss for words, he stepped over the threshold of the office, attempting an apologetic smile. Katherine retreated behind the desk, reaching up to the boxfiles. She started rearranging their order for no discernible reason, other than to distract herself from him and keep space between them. 'When I wrote that letter from Holland,' he explained guiltily, 'I thought I might be killed any day.'

She paused, looking down at the floor, right hand resting lightly on the shelf, the other dropped down by her side.

They lapsed into a pregnant silence but she did at least turn around, eyes watery but smiling, trying and failing to cover up the residual hurt. 'That's not much of an excuse, but, as you say, it was for the best.' Strangely crestfallen, Eric observed rather lamely: 'Well, anyway, I just wanted to apologise so we have no bad blood between us.'

Katherine nodded, giving nothing of her inner turmoil away. He backed out of the office, grateful to escape.

As Eric strode down the corridor he was optimistic that at least they could be civil to each other. Then, Eric realised he'd forgotten to go and see the naval surgeon, but that could wait – he just needed to get out of there as quickly as possible.

4

Getting together the people, vehicles and equipment would take several weeks. In the meantime, Eric and Ted worked with the Field Security Section and MPs to crack down on black marketeers, joining a raid to bust one of *The Hawk*'s hideouts.

A hoodlum disgruntled over a deal with the criminal maestro had given the game away by turning informant. He told British military authorities there was a contraband alcohol and cigarette store in a watering hole that had been established near the ruins of the Graz Hauptbahnhof, the main railway station.

It was very popular with Allied soldiers but below its rough-hewn floorboards was a cellar containing thousands of cigarette cartons and bottles of whisky.

Some of the raiding party went in through a cellar door while, much to the outrage of the establishment's proprietor, other raiders made their entrance by tearing up floorboards and going straight down.

Eric was one of the latter, descending through the hole on a knotted rope, in the process getting covered in ceiling plaster dust and cobwebs. Wooden crates toppled and splintered as the raiding party went about its business, breaking whisky bottles in a flood of golden liquid, packets of cigarettes kicked hither and thither by their ammunition boots.

There was a bout of savage fisticuffs with bandits amid intoxicating fumes and flickering torchlight, Eric twirling as out the corner of his eye he saw a figure lunging from the shadows.

An elbow in the face saw his assailant sprawling against a crate, knife falling from the man's hand. Seeing it in the dirt, Eric felt burning fury. Grabbing the stunned crook by the jacket collar, Eric hauled him to his feet. He pushed his assailant against some crates, one crashing to the floor with dozens more bottles shattering.

Sliding down into a heap, the man was about to receive some more rough justice, this time from Eric's boot in his face, when Ted Bodman intervened. Shoving past his boss, he hauled the black marketeer to his feet, pushing him into the waiting arms of two Field Security men who dragged him away. Picking up an intact bottle of *Johnnie Walker Red Label*, Ted unscrewed the cap and thrust it at Eric, who was staring glassy-eyed at his boots, alarmed at how close he'd come to doing the crook serious harm.

'Drink this,' Ted suggested.

Bringing his eyes into focus on the bottle of Scotch, Eric shook his head, remarking angrily: 'That bastard would have killed me for that.'

Eric closed his eyes and rubbed his forehead.

'After all we've come through…'

Ted shrugged. 'But he didn't – you got the better of him but we wouldn't have got much information out of him with a broken jaw.'

Ted took a slug of the whisky, put the cap back on. After patting Eric on the upper arm, he pushed past - pistol in one hand, bottle in the other - intending to explore the cellar further.

'Don't drink any more evidence Sergeant,' Eric called after him.

Half a dozen dubious characters were rounded up and taken away while Eric also had a poke around, finding the remains of a meal on a trestle table in a dining area beyond which was a bunk space. There was a small stove below a large, open rectangular window, its sackcloth curtains hanging in a disorderly fashion from an askew rail.

There was a large pot on the stove, Eric lifting the ladle and tasted the lukewarm contents; a hunter's stew but a bit too much paprika for his liking.

Eric put the ladle back into the pot and parted the curtains, finding a pair of boots belonging to a MP on guard outside. A chill breeze blew in and Eric shuddered. *Had the criminal mastermind himself been visiting that night?*

If so, this would have been the Hawk's escape route, but he must have waited until chaos ruled in the cellar.

That was very cool headed.

Turning around Eric noticed a cigar resting on the edge of an ashtray, still with wisps of smoke curling up from it but by now half consumed by ash. Eric poked it with a finger, the ash disintegrating, the solid part falling off and rolling across the table.

The haul of cigarettes and whisky was considerable, though the barkeeper claimed he had no idea it was all down there, which nobody believed. Maybe he was under threat of death from *The Hawk* whom, it was said, thought nothing of killing those who crossed him.

* * *

After the close call in the cellar, it was a relief to get back to barracks for a shower and afterwards Eric planned to do some background reading. Back from the showers, he found a bottle of *Johnnie Walker Black* sitting on the desk in his room. Frowning in disapproval, Eric vowed to again have a word with Ted about his habit of liberating certain contraband he came across. Declining to give in and have a dram, from a long drawer under the lip of the desk Eric pulled out the death march folder. The documents it contained offered background that might assist the investigation in assessing the Nazi modus operandi from Balaton to Graz. Eric switched on a lamp, for dusk was drawing on and the light through the window was fading rapidly. Not knowing quite where to start, he leafed through the tightly typed sheets of paper and the photographs.

Some of the latter were, like the Versailles aerial reconnaissance shots, of desperate humanity herded along roads. Others were of waxy corpses piled high in pits at liberated concentration camps. These were interspersed with images of SS guards standing along-side the pits, proud grins plastered across their faces. Eric shook his head and cursed under his breath. In the absence of any detailed reports relating to Austria, he studied a typescript entitled 'Death March – Berlin to Baltic'.

At the top was a tally:

'Estimated 33,000 inmates started.

18,000 finished.'

Did 15,000 really die along the way?

He would need fortifying if he was to read on.

Taking his toothbrush out of the glass on the sink, Eric swilled it out with tap water and then helped himself to a large measure of *Johnnie Walker*. Sitting back down, he read on, dreading what he would discover but also strangely eager to find out.

The starting point of one march was Sachenhausen-Oranien-burg concentration camp, to the north-west of Berlin. It was a time of great panic as the Soviets were already across the River Oder and knocking on the front door of the German capital. Departing on 20 April 1945, the prisoners - those lucky enough not to be liquidated in the camp's gas chambers - were marched around 60 miles to Schwerin, 31 miles from the Baltic coast. Around a fortnight later the town was taken by the Americans but soon declared part of the British zone of occupation under international agreement, though was ultimately handed over to the Soviets.

According to accounts gathered from survivors by Allied inter-rogators, during the march SS guards made the wretched captives sleep in the fields on cold nights. Many expired before morning but those who were alive, but unable to rise when ordered, were summarily executed.

Any that fell by the way while marching were also killed. Walking for 18 hours a day, receiving hardly any food - already worn down and close to expiration due to years of abuse - many succumbed. Eric seized his glass and knocked the whisky back, glad of its burning, numbing effect. Head spinning, he decided he couldn't face reading read any more documents and needed some fresh air.

* * *

Not far from the Hawkesworth Barracks officers' mess was a brook with a small water wheel. There were some benches next to it and Eric sat down on one of them, the refreshing breeze and the brook's babbling washing away his turmoil. Then, he realised there was someone sitting, quite still, on the next bench along, enjoying a cigar in the moonlight. Its end glowed red as he drew on it.

'Oh, I'm sorry,' Eric blurted apologetically, 'I didn't mean to intrude.'

The man exhaled smoke and observed cheerfully, in what sounded like a Yorkshire accent: 'No need to apologise, lad.'

Silence fell as they enjoyed the mild spring evening, Eric becoming heavy-lidded, lulled to sleep by the babbling brook. Suddenly snapping awake, for a few moments he wasn't sure where he was. Momentarily bewildered, Eric sensed the other man staring at him.

'Are you alright, son?' he asked.

'Must have nodded off,' Eric confessed.

'A tiring day?'

'Yes. What about yourself?'

After expelling smoke, which gave the illusion of masking the moon, the other man admitted: 'Fairly busy.'

From what Eric could make out, his companion was wearing a suit not a uniform. His curiosity was pricked.

'Would it be rude of me to enquire what you do, Sir?'

'It would lad,' the other man chuckled, 'but if you're a military policeman I suppose curiosity comes with the job.'

When the cigar smoker said no more, Eric got to his feet.

'So, I'll say goodnight then.'

The man pulled the cigar from his mouth, offering his hand, which Eric shook. 'Keep up the good work, son.'

Deciding to go inside, Eric headed for the officers' mess and, as he came through the swing doors, encountered McFaul, wild-eyed and red faced, the product of too much firewater.

'Ah, Wise!' the colonel exclaimed, making straight for him.

'Have you been outside?'

Eric thought that self-evident but merely conceded:

'Yes, I have, Sir.'

The colonel was swaying a little, eyes finding it difficult to focus and he asked in a voice laden with drunken suspicion:

'Did you see any civilians out there?'

'There was a gentleman in a suit by the brook, enjoying a cigar.'

'Sounds like him - the blighter needs to be on a leash.'

The colonel strode off, pushing the swing doors so hard they crashed back on their hinges. As he passed by the entrance to the officers' mess, Eric spotted McFaul's faithful subaltern - pale-faced and looked like he might vomit at any moment. 'Why is the colonel in such a flap?' Eric asked.

The subaltern initially seemed not to recognise him but then exclaimed: 'Sorry, Sir! It's bloody Pierrepoint…'

Seeing that Eric was bemused, the subaltern attempted to explain, despite his booze-befuddled state: 'Y'know, Sir…Pierrepoint, the executioner - here to hang some Nazis and other hoodlums, doing more tomorrow at the prison.'

The Subaltern's left hand flew to his mouth, trying to keep lips tight shut as his cheeks bulged. He lurched off in search of some toilets in which to be sick. Eric looked down at his right hand in amazement, clasping and unclasping it. Pierrepoint was Britain's chief executioner, had dispatched countless murderers and traitors – and a just few minutes earlier Eric had shaken hands with him. In a bit of a daze, he wandered back to his room and sat on the bed. Eric shuddered and then went to the sink where he washed his hands thoroughly, with plenty of soap and hot water. Nothing against the man - somebody had to do it - but it spooked him.

After drying his hands on a balding towel in his room, Eric sat down at the desk again. Opening the case file, he fanned the photos out, revealing their horrors under the lamp. Eric pulled out the map showing the death march route from Balaton into Austria that McFaul had given him. He reached for the whisky bottle, thinking with grim determination, as he unscrewed the cap, that he would do his utmost to solve the mystery of what happened.

5

THE FOLLOWING AFTERNOON, as Eric was preparing to set off on a research trip to Bad Gastein, he was called over to see McFaul, who was in a filthy temper about 'bloody Pierrepoint.' Doing the wall of death around his office, the fuchsia-faced colonel stormed, lips curling into a semi-canine snarl: 'He's a fuckin' menace!' Apparently, so McFaul informed him, the executioner had blotted his copybook during a stop-over in Vienna on his way to Graz.

'Can I ask what happened, Sir?' Eric enquired, turning around in his chair to keep track of McFaul's circuit.

'It was incredibly thick…that's what it was, and so we've got to keep him out of trouble here too - God knows what he'll do.'

Halting by the drinks cabinet, McFaul poured himself a neat whisky, not offering one to Eric and gulped it straight down.

Fixing Eric with a fierce look, the colonel ordered:

'You will pick him up from the jail in town and bring him straight back here, so there's no more of his shenanigans.'

McFaul said he'd get his adjutant to phone the prison with instructions for Pierrepoint 'to meet a motorised escort' outside the front gate.

Deciding to drive himself, Eric took the jeep and headed for the

Karlau Prison, a brutish edifice on the edge of the city centre. Parking up by the front gate, a few minutes later a slim, middle-aged man in dark blue suit – its unbuttoned jacket revealing a scarlet waistcoat and a silver watch chain – and all topped off with a light grey trilby, stepped out, blinking due to the sunshine.

He looked around for his ride back to the barracks - more like an anxious paroled prisoner than His Majesty's Executioner.

Eric pressed the horn to attract his attention. Pierrepoint grinned and waved, trotting over and climbing into the front passenger seat.

'Thanks lad,' he said.

'My pleasure, Sir.'

Eric started the jeep up and pulled away.

Pierrepoint suddenly laughed and remarked: 'Actually, even though they've given me the honorary rank of colonel you've no need to say, "Sir" to me.' As they came to a halt at a junction near the railway station, Pierrepoint observed: 'Do you know, I've had a rather stressful afternoon and I could do with a settler.'

'A drink?'

Pierrepoint nodded.

'I know somewhere near at hand,' Eric said, turning down a road that led to the place near the Graz Hauptbahnhof ruins.

* * *

Leaving Pierrepoint to light his cheroot, Eric went over to the bar of the otherwise deserted establishment. He ordered two whiskies from the barman, who wiped his hands on his grubby waistcoat before reaching for a bottle of *Johnnie Walker Black.*

Eric smiled, thinking it might be one of the bottles his team missed when they busted the place. Its spongy, creaking floorboards underfoot, reminded him of his dramatic entrance through the floor into the cellar below.

Pierrepoint moved his gilt cigar case and box of matches out the way as Eric placed the drinks on the round pine table.

Settling on a low, unsteady stool, placing his cap on the table alongside Pierrepoint's trilby, Eric noticed that close to the edge on his side someone had scratched 'Anschluss macht frei!'

Joining makes you free!

Eric wondered if its perpetrator was expressing a sincere sentiment or extracting the mickey…

'Thanks for the drink,' Pierrepoint said, lifting the glass and taking an appreciative sip.

'Do you recall our meeting by the brook last night Mr Pierrepoint?' Eric enquired. 'It was dark, so maybe not?'

'I do.'

'I'm Captain Eric Wise by the way.'

'My reputation often precedes me,' responded Pierrepoint with a rueful smile as they shook hands across the table.

Eric waited for him to say something further, but Pierrepoint appeared perfectly happy puffing on his cigar. Eric dreaded the answer but felt he had to ask: 'How did it go today, if you don't mind me asking?'

Pierrepoint gave him a funny sort of sideways look, took the cigar out and balanced it on the edge of the ashtray before replying: 'You mean the business with the Nazi war criminals in the prison?'

Eric nodded, taking a sip of whisky.

'Well, son, it was all about educating the Austrians.'

Pierrepoint sighed and added: 'It wasn't easy.'

'How do you mean?'

'Conveying the techniques through an interpreter about how the gallows equipment needs to work properly…'

Pierrepoint seemed tired suddenly, stifled a yawn, smiling apologetically before resuming his account.

'…but, anyway they seemed to pick it up and watched me very intently. Y'see Captain Wise, it's all about speed and humanity – put the cap over the head, slip the noose on and then straight away pull the leaver – and the drop breaks their necks, which is best really.'

To demonstrate he picked up the cigar and held it gently between his thumbs and forefingers. 'The higher the vertebrae are severed the better,' he explained, pushing up with the thumbs as if to snap the cheroot in two, some ash falling onto the table, 'giving a swift, clean end.'

Though feeling nauseous, Eric offered no exterior response.

Pierrepoint placed the cigar back on the ashtray, took a sip of whisky and continued. 'But, these bloody Austrians were giving them a short drop, then two of the buggers would go down below the trap door, where the poor soul was kicking his legs at the end of the rope, and they'd pull him hard down to make sure he choked.'

The executioner shook his head and sighed, looking quite upset, knocking back the rest of his whisky. 'Glad I showed them the proper way to do it.'

After digging a handkerchief out of a trouser pocket and blowing his nose, Pierrepoint got his cigar going again, inspecting Eric through the smoke. Though his face was impassive, Eric, who had seen the execution process in his mind as Pierrepoint explained it, was appalled.

He'd been involved in a few murder cases in Plymouth but never actually witnessed an execution. For all he knew, Pierrepoint had done the deed back then too.

'Did you meet the condemned?' Eric asked.

'I did,' Pierrepoint confirmed, 'and they were a miserable lot, in dirty clothes and not fed, so I told the Austrians they must clean them up, give 'em a meal. Only right to do that.'

Eric nodded, picked up the empty glasses to go and get refills at the bar. Still contemplating Pierrepoint's code of honour for the condemned, he had to concede it seemed decent enough treatment for war criminals who had not awarded their victims the same privileges.

Returning to the table, as Eric gave Pierrepoint his whisky, the executioner asked him: 'So, tell me lad, did McFaul ask you to be my baby-sitter?' Eric laughed.

'He did. Something about you going absent without leave in Vienna, which I find hard to believe…'

Pierrepoint chuckled, grinding his spent cigar into the ashtray, flicking open the gilt case to select another cheroot. As he did this he began to tell Eric the story behind McFaul's orders.

'It's daft really. I was in Vienna for a night and bored with my own company in the Hotel Sacher - a lovely place, but a room is a room, four walls and all that - so went out for a walk. I wanted to see what the Austrians looked like in their sackcloth and ashes - whether they might by now be cheery or still downtrodden and glum.' Eric observed: 'That probably wasn't a good idea – Vienna's the wild west, but with nice architecture.'

Pierrepoint smiled and nodded, lighting his cigar and blowing on its end to ensure an even glow. With it properly underway he took a puff and exhaled smoke.

'You're not wrong Eric lad, as I found out when these two drunken Russians accosted me and tried to steal my silver watch chain.'

To illustrate, he ran his fingers along it, still sitting there on his waistcoat. 'Anyway, one of them lunges for it, and I lashed out, got him square on the chin and sent him on his britches in the dust.'

Pierrepoint was laughing at the memory, and Eric smiled in amazement at the picture of a Russian soldier laid out by a besuited middle-aged Englishman.

'What happened next?'

'I legged it, of course, managing to hide behind this pile of bricks, getting grime all over me suit, while I could hear them looking for us. After the sound of their big clumsy boots faded I crept back to the hotel and back up to my room.'

Eric shook his head and whistled. 'You were bloody lucky.'

'Aye, but after I got to Graz, McFaul said the Russians had complained about some Allied civilian giving one of their soldiers a sore chin outside the Hotel Sacher. I'd also been spotted by a military policeman posted in the lobby passing by looking a bit flustered and with a very dirty suit.' He laughed again and remarked: 'They put two and two together and made me out to be Pierrepoint, loose cannon'

'Rumbled,' Eric observed drily.

'Aye.'

Giving Pierrepoint a mock reproachful look, Eric remarked: 'Well it's my job to make sure you get back to barracks today without getting into any fistfights.' Pierrepoint chuckled and shook his head, then ventured hopefully:

'Anyway, one more for the road?'

'Not for me,' replied Eric, 'mine's a tomato juice, if they've got it - but, if you want whisky, by all means do.'

Pierrepoint got up and went to the bar, still puffing away on the cigar. Eric studied the Englishman abroad in his dark blue suit, finding it hard to connect this person with his occupation, despite the grisly details just related. This was the same man who the previous December had famously executed the infamous guard at several concentration camps, Irma Grese. At Auschwitz, the blue-eyed Grese - according to one horrifying military report Eric read she was nicknamed 'the Blond Angel of Hell' - revelled in the job of selecting gas chamber victims. She loved inflicting a bit of torture on the side - whipping inmates and committing numerous other acts of sadism in pursuit of sexual gratification - or using a pistol to carry out summary executions for fun. Just the thought of her made Eric nauseous.

Pierrepoint returned with a whisky and, miracle of miracles, a tomato juice. 'I asked him to put a splash of Worcestershire sauce in, to pep it up,' Pierrepoint revealed proudly.

'Thanks,' said Eric, adding, 'I am amazed they have it.'

'Stranger things happen at sea.'

'So, I've heard.'

Pierrepoint settled down and blew on the cigar's end again, frowning as he did so. After a few moment's silence he looked up and, on finding a thoughtful look on Eric's face, gave a smile of recognition.

'Go on then lad…'

'I was just thinking about Grese.'

'Thought you might be.'

'What did you think of her – how could a woman do such things?'

'People are capable of anything lad,' the executioner ventured, balancing his cigar on the ashtray again, then continued. 'You could walk down an average British street, past your friends and neighbours – men or women – and, given the right circumstances, some of them would get involved. It could be pressure to join the biggest gang or gaining the power of life or death over other human beings. That appeals to such people – they have an evil streak. Others are delusional, capable in the right time or place of condoning, rationalising any monstrosity. Their idea of natural justice, no matter how unnatural.'

Pierrepoint paused, brow furrowed and lost in thought – Eric wondered if, in a moment of self-awareness, the hangman was pondering what he'd just said and worried how it might apply to him? Pierrepoint sighed and continued: 'Or maybe it's just they want a good wage and social prestige. She just happened to be extra special in the realm of cruelty. Irma Grese liked being a sadist.'

'The papers called her the "beautiful beast" - was she?'

'No lad - to me just plain and ordinary but with something dead in her eyes and an edge to her, a cold arrogance. I think a doctor would call her a psychopath, a diagnosis you might expect for a person such as that.'

Eric felt sick again, but also furious

'She deserved to die,' he remarked bitterly.

Pierrepoint ground out his cigar for emphasis.

'And to burn in Hell,' he conceded, 'to where I gave her a ticket.'

'Did she say anything beforehand?'

Pierrepoint nodded.

'One word.'

'Which was?'

'Just "Schnell" and no sign of nerves at all.'

'And were you quick? If you don't mind me asking.'

'I didn't break my cigar rule.'

Seeing Eric was mystified, Pierrepoint smiled almost sadly, lit up another cigar. Holding it daintily between thumb and finger he went on: 'Once I've had a few puffs in the place next to the hangman's cell, I lay it down on the edge of something.'

He balanced the cigar on the edge of the round table, holding

Eric's gaze, 'and then I do my business,' he revealed. 'And I am back within a matter of seconds to find it still going strong.'

Pierrepoint picked up the cheroot, blew on its end, which glowed afresh and resumed puffing on it, raising his eyebrows at Eric as if daring him to call it balderdash.

Eric believed him but said nothing, instead rubbing the words scratched into the table. They were surely a play on the slogan in the wrought iron arch above the gates of the Auschwitz death camp. He'd seen it in a photograph.

'Arbeit macht frei.'

Work sets you free.

The utter sods.

Pierrepoint continued studying Eric through the cigar smoke, sensing the young officer now wanted to say something, but content to wait rather than prompt him.

'You know Mr Pierrepoint, my job now is to hunt down war criminals and when I get them, I hope they receive a slow end longer than the life of a cigar.'

Pierrepoint took the cigar out, laid it down in the ashtray and took a sip of whisky. Shaking his head, he explained: 'That I could not do lad – because that would make me as bad as them. With me it's quick. We are both cogs in the machinery of justice, you and I, but we do it out of a sense of both justice and mercy, based on the law, for the greater good of humanity – not in pursuit of a corrupt ideology that views human beings as mere cannon fodder or grist in a monstrous mill. Or to satisfy some deeply perverted craving. Above all, there must be genuine due process appropriate to the crime – and sometimes it does not warrant a death sentence.' Pierrepoint paused to let his wisdom sink in and then asked: 'Hope you don't mind me saying that?'

Eric shook his head and decided he needed another whisky. At the bar, he asked the barman to fetch him the phone. He called Ted and told him to get a lift down to the railway station bar as he'd be needed to drive himself and Pierrepoint back in the jeep.

'Drinks all 'round then?' Ted enquired optimistically.

'Tomato juice for you to make sure you stay sober and get us home safely.' There was a heavy sigh on the other end of the line. 'You've got to drive me tomorrow too,' which provoked an even deeper sigh from Ted.

Eric put the receiver down and picked up the glasses, careful not to spill even a drop as he made his way back across the bar. Placing a whisky next to the cigar case, he told Pierrepoint. 'I have someone coming down to drive us back who will remain sober as the proverbial judge.' Picking the glass up, Pierrepoint smiled and said: 'Cheers lad!'

They clinked glasses, downing their contents in one, with Pierrepoint suggesting: 'How about another?'

6

A RECTANGULAR WOODEN sign on the desk revealed in gold lettering: *Surgeon Lieutenant Commander Samuel Darrow, United States Navy*. Disconcerted by this discovery, Eric sat fidgeting on the broad windowsill of an office on the second floor of a former casino turned Displaced Persons Hospital at Bad Gastein, a spa resort in mountains to the south of Salzburg.

In between nervously fiddling with his tie or cuffs, Eric stared through the red carnations in a flower box on the open window's small balcony at a torrent of water crashing by below.

A cooling wet mist hung in the air – *which helped his hangover* - yet the office seemed rather stuffy. Eric partially unbuttoned his battle dress blouse, tugged his beret out of the epaulette and left it on the windowsill. Maybe it was the unsettling discovery that someone from his past was in such an unexpected place that made him feel so hot.

Bloody Darrow.

The Yank naval shrink from Stonehouse Hospital.

First Katherine Smith-Glosson and now Doc Darrow. On Darrow's desk Eric spotted a well thumbed book, which he picked up.

It opened naturally at one particular piece of verse, which Eric found his less than perfect German could, nonetheless, handle. He scanned the lines, finding two of them softly underlined in pencil.

'He does not look below to the rocky shoals,

He only looks up at the heights.'

Eric leafed back through the book, finding someone had written the same couplet on the inside front cover. Closing it, turning the slim volume in his hands, the gilt lettering on the spine gleamed and revealed:

Heinrich Heine Gesammelte Verse

'Heinrich Heine Collected Verses.'

A door in the corridor creaked open and then banged shut, followed by footsteps getting closer. Eric put the book back, buttoned up his battle dress blouse and arranged himself nonchalantly on the windowsill.

Darrow strode into the room, white coat tails flapping, hair immaculately slicked back and face as nut brown as ever. On seeing who was waiting he looked shocked, but then his features broke into a wide, delighted grin. 'Good God Almighty!' he boomed, hand outstretched.

The doctor had just been sent back to Europe after a short time looking after the mental health of American occupying forces in Japan, and so he was delighted to see a familiar face.

'When they said a Limey officer was waiting I would never have guessed it would be you!'

Eric couldn't help but grin back and they shook hands enthusiastically. The naval psychiatrist gently shoved Eric into what looked like the same battered old chair from his office in the naval hospital at Plymouth. He went over to a coffee pot bubbling away on a hot plate.

'Cup of java?' he asked, a twinkle in his eye, for he recalled Eric disdained such 'Yank muck' in preference to tea. Surprisingly, Eric assented: 'Yes, thanks.'

'Hey, the man's a coffee drinker now!'

Once he had armed them each with a mug of coffee, Darrow threw himself into the chair behind his desk.

'What gives Eric?'

Eric told him about the death march and how it was his job to assemble eyewitness accounts and then retrace the route. 'There is supposedly someone here who we have been told may be able to give us some information – a young woman found wandering in the woods.'

Darrow momentarily drummed his fingers on the desk, looking deadly serious and admitted he knew the case.

'She's got a bad dose of trauma – can't even give us a name, physically, emotionally and mentally exhausted, *possibly* after wandering the woods and mountains for weeks, or so we can only assume. She was found on the Himmel Wand, a pathway by a mountain hotel, not far from here. But, you know, in an entire continent of traumatised people, her current state isn't that unusual.'

Darrow explained that all his team could manage was a sticking plaster approach, treating just the worst cases.

Often it was more interesting from a study point of view than to provide any real cure.

He took Eric down the corridor to a room where the patients were counselled – big, open, airy and neutrally decorated, with a few easy chairs and an oval coffee table.

'Sit yourself down and I'll get one of the nurses to bring her along for a gabble. I doubt you'll get more than a word or two, though she can speak English. Afterwards, if you have time, we'll pop into the local town for a film show.' Eric protested: 'I'm not here to enjoy myself!'

'Don't worry, you won't,' Darrow observed ominously. 'It's not Bogart and Bacall – but you'll find it educational.'

After Darrow left, Eric moved the furniture around, putting the table between two chairs so he could face her, talk and take notes.

A few moments later a male American army nurse brought in a malnourished, haunted-looking young woman who sat curled up in the chair opposite Eric's, a huge leather flying jacket enveloping her. Staring at the floor, her hands nervously gripped and released her bare feet.

'Can you tell me anything of the march?' Eric enquired softly, hoping that she would understand. It was worth a try, but her eyes remained fixed on the floor, long dark blonde hair falling across her face. 'A description of any guards would be helpful. Can you remember anything?'

She frowned, bit her lip, clutched herself, Eric waiting patiently for a reply. Then she looked directly at him, her penetrating blue eyes making him blink and momentarily look down at the blank page of his notebook. Raising his eyes again, Eric gently suggested: 'Why don't we start with your name?'

She ignored the question, instead looking up at the white ceiling on which sparkled silver flashing light, created by the reflection of the rushing water below the window.

It had been shut to keep the noise out, but even so, she spoke in such a whisper Eric found it difficult to hear what she said. 'I was nearly left for dead by the road,' she revealed in Austrian-accented English. 'After the black crows came.' Taking notes, Eric was surprised to hear the girl utter some familiar words. 'He does not look below…only looks up at the heights.'

Before he could ask if the book in Darrow's office was hers, she yawned loudly, stretched her arms, and tumbled out of the seat, stumbling a little against the table. Eric got up to steady her but she shrank from him. The nurse, who had been loitering in the doorway, came in and helped her out of the room.

Eric sat back down, rested his head on the back of the chair, watching the silver flashes dancing on the ceiling. His mind was suddenly filled with the sound and vision of hellfire in the Octagon at Plymouth all those years ago; he could even hear collapsing buildings, and smell the dust. And then there was the dead girl in the alleyway, who couldn't have been much younger than the one he had just tried to interview. In his mind Eric saw her again, seemingly asleep under the white chiffon shroud he draped over her.

* * *

Returning to Darrow's office, Eric asked the doctor where he'd found thc book of poetry.

The American picked it up, flicked through and shrugged. 'I think it was here when we took over,' he decided, putting it down on the desk. Exchanging his white coat for a khaki US Navy deck jacket, Darrow explained: 'This used to be a rehabilitation hospital for wounded warriors of the Reich. It was a casino before the war.'

Putting his garrison cap on, Darrow indicated his visitor should exit the office ahead of him, asking: 'Why the fascination with the book?'

'Something the girl said,' Eric remarked, pulling his beret on.

As they walked down the corridor he added:

'Might help if I had the book.'

Darrow laughed, still puzzled by the Englishman's request:

'Sure buddy, I'll get it for you before you leave.'

* * *

On the way down into town, along the Kaiser Franz-Josef Strasse, Darrow offered more thoughts on the case of the traumatised young woman. 'Obviously her experiences have left her a little unbalanced, as they would anyone. Getting even a few words out of her is an achievement.'

They stopped on the narrow pavement to let a group of laughing, chattering Jewish Kibbutz teenagers pass by – stocky lads in jackets over open-necked shirts, all of them sporting flat caps, with the girls in pristine white shirts and dark skirts, their long thick hair shining healthily in the sun. Eric studied them curiously while Darrow gave a nod and a smile to the youngsters. He remarked to Eric as they resumed walking down the street: 'Carefree kids, huh? Amazing considering what they have endured. Bad Gastein is home to numerous misplaced persons camps and Zionist collectives formed to sort of give young people an aim, which, I've heard is to prepare for a new Jewish homeland.'

'So,' enquired Eric, not wanting to be diverted from the topic of greatest interest, 'I shouldn't take what the girl says seriously?'

Resuming their walk, Darrow conceded: 'There's some truth in it – somewhere - if you can work out the riddle.'

The noise of the waterfall got louder and louder as the road bottomed out, leading onto a short, but wide, bridge - the Wasserfallbrücke – that linked one side of town to the other.

It was impossible to speak now, so Darrow shrugged his shoulders and grinned and they went over to the balustrade and stared down into the roaring waters. Eric found it quite hypnotic, his head beginning to spin and he was almost tempted to jump in, but shook that crazy notion off. Anyone doing so would instantly be dashed to pieces on the rocks. He was reminded of the poem. *'He does not look below to the rocky shoals…'*

Again, the mist was pleasant and cooling, with Eric suddenly feeling at peace amid the tumult, closing his eyes, letting his mind become swept away until Darrow tugged his sleeve.

'Stop daydreaming or we'll be late!'

They followed the Bismarckstrasse, with Darrow remarking, and pointing to the street name sign fixed on the side of house, 'you sure meet a lot of imperial German and Austrian head honchos on this route.' He next led them along a path wending its way up-slope on the other side of the town, which, so Eric noticed, was called Kaiser Wilhelm Promenade. The noise from the waterfall declined to a muted roar. Eric was beginning to sweat and itch in his woollen battle dress and enquired testily: 'Where are we going for this bloody film show anyway?' Darrow pointed ahead: 'Just up here.'

* * *

Townsfolk were packed into every corner of the hall to witness half an hour of gut-wrenching footage - projected onto a white bed sheet - revealing the terrible things Allied troops discovered at various liberated concentration camps: skeletal half-naked men and women stumbling around in a malnutrition trance, their huge eyes lifeless; hideously entwined pipe-cleaner limbs heaped in massive piles - the corpses of those who expired in the final hours under the Nazi overlords; SS guards forced to carry tangled remains to mass graves; an occasional rifle butt in the back for any who showed reluctance to clear up the charnel house.

Worst of all, to Eric's eyes, was that the prisoners had been stripped of all dignity and humanity…rendered less than human.

The camera panned across the naked corpses of women laid out in a row next to a burial pit, their shrunken breasts flopping down over cavernous rib cages. Next to them was a row of men, their genitalia similarly exposed for all to gawp at.

'Lord God Almighty,' Eric whispered. Darrow glanced at Eric and nodded, but said nothing.

A paroxysm of unease and revulsion went through the audience. American MPs stationed by the hall entrance and at the back by the projector, made ready to draw their batons at the first sign of trouble.

Eric had heard about the atrocities in the camps and, of course, just read a report on the death march from Berlin to the Baltic. Now he had seen the results of Nazi bestiality flickering into life on a bedsheet in all their horror and was sickened to his core. An intense loathing of the Nazis surged through him again.

When the film show was finished, the majority of the townsfolk filed out in silence - shocked and sombre. Many were ashen-faced but a few appeared unperturbed. Some even laughed and chatted.

Watching Eric's face intently, Darrow turned him to one side and said in a low voice: 'There's plenty of Austrian folk who are appalled by this, and truly hated Hitler as much as us. Others loved the Nazis but some simply don't believe it, or can't allow themselves to. They think these are communist propaganda films.'

As the last members of the audience left, Eric's burning eyes caught one or two defiant stares in his direction.

'Lügen!' an elderly woman hissed.

Lies!

A middle-aged man was chewing an apple as he passed Eric and Darrow, gobbing some of it out, making Eric clench his fists. Darrow, who had a surprisingly strong grip, grabbed Eric's forearm and squeezed hard to stop him from retaliating. Darrow pulled a handkerchief from a trouser pocket, kneeling down to wipe mushed apple and saliva from his shoes.

* * *

After retrieving the book of poetry from Darrow's office and bidding farewell to the doctor, Eric sought out the girl, finding her sitting on the bed in her room.

With the incongruous leather aviator jacket wrapped tight around her, she was staring down through the glistening, white-painted bars of the open window, at water rushing over the rocks below.

She looked at him for a second, cast a momentary glance at the male nurse standing watch in the open door of the room, then returned to her vigil as if nobody was there.

'I thought I'd get you this,' Eric told her, holding out the volume of poetry. She looked around, sweeping hair away from her face. She laid the book on her lap and it fell open at the same pages as before. Her lips moved silently and Eric saw her finger was caressing the title of a poem. *'Die Lorelei'*.

Looking up, her teary eyes shone and he couldn't help but be moved by the simple joy that had suddenly bubbled up within her. Dropping the book onto the bed, she took his right hand and held it against her cheek. Eric knelt down beside the bed, fighting an upwelling of emotion himself.

He was so glad this girl had not ended up like the poor wretches on the screen. 'Can you tell me what happened?' Eric asked softly.

The happiness fled from her eyes and she looked away, out the window, dropping his hand. Eric stood up and, as he departed, saw she was reading the book of verse again, lips moving silently.

7

THERE WAS something unknowable about the Russians and Eric supposed it was because they came from a vast, alien country that was a world within a world; a law unto itself, too.

Right now - in the aftermath of a terrible war that had brought so much misery and destruction - the Soviet Union was a great, glowering bear squatting on the front doorstep of Central Europe. For eyes the Russian Bear had glowing coals of loathing for the West, peering out over a black, gaping maw filled with masses of sharp teeth. Having consumed the Baltic States, Poland, Czechoslovakia, Hungary, Bulgaria and Romania, the Russian Bear was ready to gobble up more countries, given half a chance.

That imagery asserted itself in Eric's mind as he sat in a cracked old leather bucket seat to the left of McFaul's desk, looking on as the colonel held forth about 'Allied Powers Sector Protocols'.

Eric tried to recall something from a speech Winston Churchill had just made in America. It was very striking...about an Iron Curtain from the Baltic to the Adriatic.

The target of McFaul's monologue was a rather tough-looking Russian Army officer sitting stiffly in the straight-backed office chair, his black chrome leather riding boots shining wetly in harsh morning light streaming through the window.

Eric's gaze moved up to the peaked cap sat on the officer's lap, glimmering red star badge enclosing gold hammer and sickle lustrous on the hat band. The Russian's olive green cotton twill tunic was immaculate, not a hint of lint.

The brown leather belt, supporting a black pistol holster, was pulled tight. The man's square jaw was clean-shaven, his wide, thin-lipped mouth a non-committal slit. His broad, flat nose must have been flattened in some long-ago boxing bout. The cold blue eyes either side were inscrutable and Eric realised they were looking straight at him, returning the scrutiny.

The Russian sphinx returned his attention to McFaul. Passing a well-manicured hand over his tightly cropped pepper and salt hair, in only faintly accented English, the Russian stated: 'Colonel, there will be no need for us to arrange your protocols for entering into the Soviet Union's zone of control.'

McFaul's face turned crimson and Eric noticed a vein in his left temple starting to throb. McFaul loathed communists and found it very difficult to conceal it, especially if he'd had a skin full of Scotch the night before, which, so Eric judged from his superior's sweaty, red face, was decidedly the case here.

'I'm sorry Major Dostoyevsky,' McFaul said in a slightly strangulated voice, 'but if we are to investigate properly then it may require a visit to your neck of the woods.'

Dostoyevsky smiled beneficently and waved a hand.

'I am here to help,' he claimed, with brazen irony, 'and make that tiresome adventure unnecessary.'

The Russian leaned forward stiffly - trussed up as he was by his immaculate uniform - pressing the cap onto his lap with his left hand, while reaching down with the right to pick up a leather map case.

Looking straight at Eric, Dostoyevsky requested:

'Please, captain, give this to your chief.'

Eric rose from the bucket seat, taking the map case off the Russian and placing it on the colonel's blotter. McFaul's bloodshot eyes swivelled up to give Eric a disapproving look for so eagerly doing the Russian's bidding. 'Open it,' he ordered through clenched teeth.

Eric unbuckled it, lifting the flap to discover a pouch containing a folder. Pulling that out, he laid it gently on the desk and then withdrew, returning the map case to its owner.

'Thankyou,' Dostoyevsky said pleasantly.

McFaul had, meanwhile, opened the folder and started leafing through neatly typed documents – all of them in English – accompanied by maps and photographs.

Eric settled back into the bucket seat, watching the colonel's frown deepening as he read on. Major Dostoyevsky coughed again, but failed to clear his throat. 'Would you like a glass of water, Sir?' Eric enquired politely.

The Russian smiled and nodded, still coughing.

Eric went over to a drinks cabinet on the far side of the room, turning over a glass and pouring in some water from a jug that McFaul kept there for diluting whisky.

He handed it to Dostoyevsky, who smiled and took a big gulp, handing the empty glass to Eric who took it back to the drinks cabinet and then sat down.

'What you have, colonel, are the case files of our own investigation into the death march from Lake Balaton into Austria,' explained the Russian, 'as it is our sincere desire to assist our British friends in bringing war criminals to justice.'

McFaul closed the folder, giving Dostoyevsky a mistrustful look.

'That's most kind,' he remarked, adding sarcastically: 'and naturally we would expect no more or less from our deeply respected Russian allies.'

A sly smile played along the Russian's lips again and he nodded, his eyes crinkled into narrow slits.

There was a knock at the door.

'Enter!' McFaul bellowed irritably.

The clerk from the outer office stuck his head into the office, looking at Eric. 'There's someone here for Captain Wise.'

McFaul growled back: 'Well, it's bloody inconvenient, corporal – go and tell whoever…'

Before McFaul could finish his sentence, the corporal was pushed out the way and Spendlove rolled in, exclaiming: 'Awfully sorry, but I must grab Captain Wise for a chat!'

Standing up, Eric was unable to avoid grinning broadly at the lack of tact shown by his boss while Spendlove wore a surprised look, apparently totally flummoxed at finding a Russian present.

As Dostoyevsky got to his feet and turned around, the smile on Spendlove's face vanished for a split second, his eyes widening fractionally. Then the façade dropped again, and he wore a sickly, insincere smile. 'A Russian friend,' Spendlove remarked fruitily, 'how wonderful.' Dostoyevsky tweaked the corners of his mouth up and then, turning his back on the intruder, sat down again. McFaul, meanwhile, glared at Spendlove who, undeterred, suggested: 'Can I borrow my man for a moment?' The colonel grunted his assent.

Following hot on Spendlove's heels, once they were in the corridor Eric was grabbed by an arm and spun around into a huddle, Spendlove hissing conspiratorially: 'Have you got a thunder-fucking office where we can talk unheard?' The breathless urgency in Spendlove's voice was quite alarming.

'My room?'

'That'll do.'

Spendlove hauled him off down the corridor.

* * *

'So, he's calling himself Dostoyevsky, is he?' Spendlove enquired excitedly, knocking back a shot of *Johnnie Walker* as he sat on Eric's bed.

Declining to pour himself a whisky, Eric screwed the top back on the bottle and pushed it away across the desk. Turning in the chair to face his boss, he enquired with a trace of irritation: 'Can you put me in the bloody picture, Sir?' Spendlove placed the empty glass on the bedside table, unbuckled and took off his belt, unbuttoned his battle dress blouse and leaned down to loosen the laces of his boots. Eric sincerely hoped *they* were not coming off.

With a sigh of relief, Spendlove straightened up and asked: 'When did he turn up?'

'Out of the blue, an hour ago.'

'I never forget a face, so it was a bit of a heart starter when I walked in and found that fizzog staring back at me.'

Spendlove loosened his tie, clearly intent on spinning a long yarn. Sometimes Eric enjoyed them and often he did not. He was prepared to sit this one out if it meant discovering more about the Russian visitor. As the junior officer it was his duty to listen, anyway.

'Last saw him back in the summer of 1942,' explained Spendlove, 'when I was still in military intelligence, seconded to the staff of General Brooke for Winston's visit to Stalin in Moscow, though I don't think our friend recalls me. I was somewhat slimmer in those days…'

Spendlove gave a self-conscious smile and patted his tummy but Eric didn't think anyone could put on *that much* weight in just four years. Eric smiled at the conceit, having first met Spendlove in the summer of 1941, when he was already quite portly.

'Or maybe he hid his recognition very well – he's a poker-faced cove. Gave a bit of a Cheshire Cat smile didn't he? Anyway, my job in Moscow was as a bag carrier.'

Eric felt certain that was not *all* Spendlove was up to.

'And of course, we had to attend various dreary functions where there were endless vodka toasts relieved only by little eats – pickled green beans, whole garlics, small gherkins and other such fripperies.'

Food did seem to hold an undue fascination for Spendlove, thought Eric - *and he wondered why he'd put on a few pounds?*

'Anyway, this chap Dostoyevsky is a bloody scoundrel …' Spendlove held his glass out for a refill, so Eric grabbed the bottle and did the honours. 'What I mean,' Spendlove elucidated, 'is that our friend Dostoyevsky is in all likelihood a murderous bastard.'

'What makes you say that, Sir?'

'I was loitering at one of these toasting sessions in the Kremlin, as was my job, and there he was at Stalin's right hand, whispering in

Uncle Joe's ear as he chatted with Brooke and Winston. The point is the bastard was wearing the uniform of an officer in the NKVD – the Narodnyy Komissariat Vnutrennikh Del to give it in the full Russki lingo.'

Eric, of course, knew of the NKVD - the secret police tasked with internal repression (including purges). It was hard to keep track of all the various reorganisations of Soviet espionage and state control bureaucracy. It was *a continual process of musical chairs* with the NKVD now known as the MVD. Whatever they were called - and Eric had met some of them in Berlin - they were brutes, and, in his view, killers all.

'I know *them* alright.'

Spendlove grinned and nodded.

'The dirty buggers who put a bullet in the back of your head if Stalin don't like the look of you, but our friend didn't have a secret policeman's uniform on today, did he? I'll wager he's up to no good.'

Spendlove chuckled and slapped his knee with the open palm of his left hand, juddering the glass in his right and spilling some whisky on Eric's bed blanket. 'Of course!' he exclaimed, having suddenly realised something.

'The cheeky sod.'

Eric was bemused and also displeased at having Scotch sprinkled on his bedclothes.

'Back then he was calling himself Captain Mishkin y'see.'

Eric sighed. He was beginning to get a headache.

Spendlove gave him a withering look: 'Don't you see Eric, he's extracting the urine. Mishkin is the hero of a Dostoyesvky book – *The Idiot* – so Mishkin – Dostoyevsky.... And we're the idiots!'

Eric merely conceded a puzzled frown, so Spendlove pressed on.

'Well, we made some discrete enquirics about Stalin's little helpers to see if it would enable us to get the edge with juicy gossip on 'em. Other than his name and NKVD uniform that was about all we could find out about our friendly interpreter with the killer's eyes.'

Spendlove put his glass down on the bedside table, rubbing his hands together as he pondered the present-day situation. 'This could mean trouble,' he decided, taking his spectacles off and pinching the bridge of his nose.

Spendlove suddenly seemed rather tired but, putting his specs back on, leaned forward and resumed his tale. 'The drunken banquet of the century took place in the Kremlin – I mean *big* eats, not little ones – and all sorts of booze, from aviation fuel vodka to sublime Crimean champagne and disgusting Georgian red wine that tasted like jam. I well recall this huge pig on a spit, mountains of tomatoes and cucumbers and a gigantic Caspian sturgeon on ice – do you know those fish can live for more than a hundred years? Imagine, swimming around since the middle of the last century, quite happy and then ending up on Stalin's buffet table in the Kremlin…'

Eric hoped Spendlove would soon get to the point.

Sensing Eric's impatience Spendlove swiftly pressed on:

'The Russians were rolling out the whole shooting match and to hell with the rationing. This was of course to bamboozle us - get us pissed and farting – and then outwit us. Most vivid in my mind is what occurred with this American diplomat who was rather chummy with Stalin – or thought he was, because nobody is really pals with that beast. Anyway, the Yank expressed interest in the latest Russian tommy gun – something about its allegedly astonishing rate of fire - and so Stalin ordered that one of them should be brought in by Marshal Voroshilov, who gives it to this Yank. The silly so and so starts waving it about and aims it at another American diplomat – I forget who…and someone puts an apple on that chap's head. Stalin looks on, his avuncular push-broom moustache twitching and black shark's eyes narrowing with cruel amusement. All the while this Dostoyevsky-Mishkin feller is whispering and sniggering in his ear. Uncle Joe was certainly enjoying these idiot capitalists playing William Tell. Winston, meanwhile, stood by smoking a cigar and scowling like an angry bulldog.'

Spendlove laughed and slapped his knee again.

Goodness, he was enjoying himself.

'Anyway, this Yank squeezes the trigger…'

Eric let out a gasp, Spendlove smiling with satisfaction at the effect on his subordinate.

'But, fortunately it only clicked! Stalin, our friend and everyone else roars with laughter. Uncle Joe remarks, with perfect timing – translated and delivered very coolly by Dostoyevsky-Mishkin – "you should be very careful aiming a gun at someone in the Kremlin." And the Yank shoots back: "Why should I care – it's not my apple!" – which caused more uproar. So, anyway Dostoyevsky-Mishkin steps forward and knocks the apple off the Yank's head, catches it in his hand and takes a big bite out of it. Stalin finds this hilarious, slaps his man on the back, which causes him to spit it out, landing in a bowl of borscht. Well, of course this was all very hilarious to the Russians and appalling to the rest of us – I mean who would want that soup now?'

Eric was again astonished by Spendlove's ability to spin amazing yarns – but he did wonder what the point was. Guessing this was in his mind, Spendlove sat back, waving his hands.

'That's by the by I suppose, other than to fill you in on our Russian friend's history and connections – but the point is that he is not who he says he is, and likely now assigned to nefarious external security duties. Must have an ulterior motive in offering their help. Russians don't even take a leak without authority, so he must be here on the highest orders. Bearing in mind his place at Stalin's side - that he survived four years in the Kremlin court without being executed - he must be well trusted and not without powerful friends, possibly even Uncle Joe himself as patron. And that, Eric, makes me feel the Soviets are taking an unparalleled interest in this Nazi leftover you are about to poke your snout into and for which I came down to add my two penny-worth.'

Spendlove fell silent, lost in thought as he turned over the angles.

Eric suggested: 'Hadn't we better warn Colonel McFaul about the Russian?' Spendlove seemed not to hear.

'Sir - the colonel?'

'Sorry - yes, you're right, let's pop along and advise McFaul.'

Spendlove tightened up his bootlaces again and, as he grunted and groaned through the process, began to reveal the real reason he'd come down to see Eric. 'Before we return to McFaul and the Russian there is a detail I need to apprise you of, which is that towards the end of the war Saint Georgen an der Gusen hosted a facility for producing the fuselages of those Me 262 fighter aircraft that had us all worried so much.'

'The so-called Nazi wonder jet?'

Spendlove finished with the laces and, as he buttoned up his battle dress blouse, went on: 'Yes, a really tricky foe for the mass bombing raids on the Reich. It is likely the fate of the people being marched across Austria you are looking into - had they survived - was a troglodyte existence in some underground slave labour camp in vast caverns.'

Hauling himself onto his feet, Spendlove twisted to grab his belt off the back of the chair. Eric asked: 'What's that got to do with the price of butter, Sir?' Clipping his belt together at the front, Spendlove gave Eric a puzzled look. 'I'm sorry?'

'Whether they were making wonder weapons or bayonets underground, what difference does it make to the investigation?'

Spendlove responded with the tone of voice an exasperated school master might use with an insolent pupil. 'Because it shows how dreadfully important it was for their war effort that they got some slaves from point A to B. How many times have you criticised me for not keeping you in the picture on essential detail Captain Wise?' Thinking Spendlove a pompous twit, Eric restricted himself to just observing bitterly: 'I wish we'd had wonder jets to defend Plymouth against the Luftwaffe instead of bloody antique biplanes.'

* * *

By the time they got down to McFaul's office the Russian had gone and the Scotsman was in an even worse mood. 'There's something fishy about that bastard,' McFaul sneered. 'Well, quite,' observed Spendlove, with a smug smile before briefing McFaul in a concise and anecdote-free fashion about his suspicions.

He left out any reference to the Russian being in the Kremlin or his high-up connections, merely suggesting Dostoyevsky was definitely not what he appeared to be and probably worked for Soviet military intelligence, adding untruthfully: 'This was precisely the warning I came down to convey to you Colonel McFaul.'

The red-faced military policeman tightened his jaw and scowled.

McFaul briefed them that originally more of the suspected death march route had passed entirely through Russian occupied territory.

When they pulled back to the current demarcation lines between zones of occupation most of the suspected burial sites then fell under the jurisdiction of the British. Apparently, according to Major Dostoyevsky, notification of a completed Soviet investigation had been delivered to the Allies some time ago, but must have gone astray in Vienna. McFaul suspected that was a lie.

'I believe as soon as they realised we were about to start an investigation they thought they ought to own up to their own,' the colonel observed sourly. 'Major Dostoyevsky says it's all in there,' he snorted, 'and wonders why we feel the need to go over the same ground again – literally.'

'It's bullshit of course,' Spendlove observed happily.

McFaul glared at him, leaning back in his chair, which creakily protested. 'Of course, if you say so Spendlove,' McFaul remarked sarcastically, like a dismissive head prefect. 'You would know.'

Eric wondered what *exactly* the Russians could be trying to hide. Distrust was an ever-increasing facet of dealings with the Soviets, not that it had been absent during the war. Even then the British and Russians spied on each other and sought to use 'brotherly co-operation' to secure as much intelligence on each other's deepest secrets as they could.

With the death march, though, it could be they were being mysterious for the sake of it, which was their habit. 'After all,' thought Eric, 'those who possess knowledge have power – and those who give it away too easily are fools.'

8

A LEADEN ATMOSPHERE under stormy summer skies, with not even a hint of a breeze, covered the clearing and the metallic *clack-clack-ting-thunk* rhythm of a typewriter being worked was unnaturally loud.

The focus of activity was a pair of trestle tables in its centre.

At one, examining a cadaver, was Surgeon Commander Jock Geddes, the naval pathologist, calling out the cause of death for the nurse at the other table to hammer his words onto paper.

Sighing at the sheer effort of changing sheets - wrestling a slippery piece of carbon paper between them - she called out miserably: 'Hold on, Sir!' While he waited Geddes straightened up and rubbed his sore back. The nurse resumed her typing, determined to carry on, yet ashen faced from the stench and sheer horror of it all.

Whenever the team had paused to investigate a burial site the smell and the sights had been dreadful - this was the fifth such grave.

Beyond Geddes, four khaki-clad figures wearing rubber aprons and gauntlets - military policemen McFaul had assigned to Eric's investigation group - sweated profusely under the hot sun. With deep distaste etched on their faces, they partially excavated a mass grave – just a narrow strip to exhume a few of those suspected of lying there - gently wielding entrenching tools to uncover them, then bayonets and spoons for more precise release of the dead from the earth. As each of the remains was exposed a naval nurse stepped forward with a camera and took photographs. A ground sheet was then used to carry one at a time over to the examination table.

The numbers were beyond the capabilities of Eric's team to do more than gather sample evidence. After exhuming half a dozen of the remains - Geddes conducting a cursory survey to identify means of death - they were carefully reinterred.

The pathologist continued to recite his findings in a deliberate monotone, gingerly lifting a mud-caked, rotten limb or skull, or, with the aid of a nurse, rolling a cadaver over to inspect its back.

'I would say, based on the pelvis,' Geddes decided, 'that here we have a female. Penetrating, fatal injury to the back of the head; a bullet. Execution style.'

The pathologist nodded at two military policemen loitering to one side, who stepped forward and picked up the ground sheet with the presumed woman's remains on and took it away. They returned with a small cadaver. Lumps of earth fell off as it was gently placed on the table

'Child,' the pathologist assessed, as he leaned over the table.

'Cause of death…' Geddes fell silent, momentarily overcome. 'Very close-range pistol shot. Back of head. Execution style'

When there was no sound of the typewriter in response, Geddes turned around. At the other trestle table the nurse was slumped over the keys, shoulders heaving as she wept silently, doing her best not to make a scene but unable to carry on.

Katherine had been on a cigarette break and, returning to the clearing instantly understood the scenario. She walked over and put an arm around the nurse's shoulders, gently easing her up out of the canvas chair. 'I'll carry on - just go and have a break,' she said softly.

Another nurse came over and led her away.

She was taken to a truck parked a little down the road – away from the dreadful smells and sights. It was where they went every now and then for a breather, to have a nerve settling smoke and restorative mug of tea.

Eric contemplated these events from the passenger seat of his jeep, deciding there had to be a way of alleviating the distress, at least for the naval surgeon and whoever was doing the typing.

An idea popped into his head and, climbing out, he went around to the back of the jeep, reached in and loosened the neck of his kitbag. Digging around, he found a fresh pair of long green military socks. Pulling a commando dagger out of the scabbard on his belt, he used it to rip holes either end of each sock. Grabbing a bottle of Scotch from a box in the back of the vehicle, he drenched the socks in alcohol.

Eric walked over to the pathologist, holding out one of the socks for him and revealing: 'Here, I've made this.'

Geddes looked up, annoyed to be disturbed as he investigated a cadaver. The pathologist looked at what was being offered to him with deep suspicion.

'Put it on,' Eric insisted.

'It's wringing wet,' Geddes observed, holding the sock gingerly between thumb and forefinger.

'Whisky, to filter the stink.'

Geddes grinned.

'In that case I'm only too pleased...'

Eric walked over to Katherine at the typewriter and offered the other sock, careful not to let it drip on the paper. She did not object but had difficulty putting it on, so Eric helped. She initially recoiled, appalled by the alcohol fumes but it was better than the stench of decay.

Eric stepped back to admire her, nodding approval.

'You look lovely,' he remarked, 'and I hear it's the latest fashion.'

He couldn't really tell if it cheered her up, but it looked like Katherine's eyes smiled. She nodded and began typing as Geddes called out details.

Soon everyone was wearing a sock mask soaked in whisky and becoming a little woozy.

Returning to his vigil, Eric looked across the clearing at a GAZ - a Soviet copy of the jeep - and in which lurked Dostoyevsky and his bull-necked driver, Sergeant Ivanov.

They stared morosely through the windscreen, passing a bottle of vodka back and forth, gulping alcohol down between furiously puffing foul, unfiltered Belomorkanal cigarettes.

Dostoyevsky and the driver had joined the investigation group at the Austro-Hungarian border ten days earlier. Providing maps and supposedly precise locations of death march burial sites, they expressed hurt at the British for not taking the original reports – autopsies and whatnot – at face value. Dostoyevsky told Eric it was all *so unnecessarily tiresome and distressing* going through the business of digging up those who had already been buried twice – originally by the Germans and then again by the Russians after their own investigations. With a shrug of the shoulders he sulkily remarked there was no need for - how did he put it? - 'bourgeois corroborating evidence.'

Did they not trust their Russian allies?

'Simple answer,' Eric thought, 'absolutely not.'

He wondered if the Russians, so brazen and skilled at telling bare-faced lies to opponents – a practice called *vranyo* – actually told the truth to one another in private.

Outwardly Eric merely gave a mirthless smile and observed:

'Just following orders Major.'

To soothe his bruised pride Dostoyevsky was allowed to lead the way down the main route west and, with only a couple of days break, it had been a gruelling schedule.

* * *

Eric turned to place the whisky bottle in the back again, the vehicle jiggling as Ted dropped heavily into the driver's side. This made Eric drop the bottle, which rolled under the passenger seat.

'Bloody hell!' he exclaimed furiously.

Before Eric could tear his head off, Ted told him: 'Sir, there's something you should see over in those trees,' also suggesting: 'Bring your weapon.'

Sensing it must be serious, Eric forgot about the whisky bottle and grabbed his Thompson submachine gun, climbing out of the jeep, following Ted across the clearing, all the while feeling Russian eyes burning holes in his back.

It took about a minute to reach the spot, Ted explaining how earlier he'd wanted to get away from the stink and have a cigarette and a piss, but not necessarily in that order.

And that was when he found it.

Ted halted by a shallow, recently filled-in pit in a fairly large space between the trees. It was full of sand, along with white powdery ashes but when Eric's eyes adjusted better to the poor light, he also saw bone fragments scattered here and there, having been dug up, so he guessed, by animals.

Eric made out a lower jaw, a thighbone and a skull with its black, empty eye sockets *and were those finger bones?* Kneeling down to closer inspect the surface of the pit he discovered damp, burned fragments of wood and even smaller bits.

It had rained hard a couple of days ago, and perhaps this also helped expose the bones? Then, in his peripheral vision, Eric noticed Ted was holding something up.

It was a large green petrol can with Cyrillic lettering on it.

Red Army issue.

He took it off Ted, put his nose to its cap – the lingering petroleum fumes made his nostrils twitch.

A snapping twig made Eric spin around to find Dostoyevsky and Ivanov standing there on the other side of the pit, their own guns slung over their shoulders – *but looking terribly displeased.*

Eric decided there was no point in prevaricating, so asked bluntly:

'Tell me, Major Dostoyevsky - why would the Red Army burn these remains?'

'They were diseased,' explained Dostoyevsky, rather too calmly, 'so we had to dispose of remains after we dug them up - to prevent a plague if some kind of an animal ate them and then was consumed by a human. Is it not in the original documents that we gave you?'

'I didn't see it.'

The Russian shrugged and suggested:

'I am sure it is in there, if you look hard enough.'

He could tell this was not enough to reassure the Englishman.

'And if by some chance it isn't I will ask our headquarters in Budapest to submit a fuller report.'

Yes, Eric felt certain there was more to this, if *he* looked *hard enough*. That Dostoyevsky and sidekick - who generally affected an air of watchful boredom throughout the whole process - had hotfooted it into the woods spoke loudly of something suspicious going on.

Eric smiled and pretended acceptance of what Dostovevsky proposed.

'Alright then major, let's see what Budapest yields.'

The four of them walked back through the trees in an awkward silence, the cheery song of birds in the trees in stark contrast to the grimness of discovering the ashes and bones pit.

Returning to sit in the jeep to wait out the rest of the afternoon, Eric resolved to not let the matter of the pit rest. He would carry on with the charade of co-operation until they reached the final burial site, sending the Russians home, with deep thanks for all their help. The British would then double back to check the ashes pit out further.

Ted twisted uncomfortably under the steering wheel of the jeep, trying to get enough space to unbuckle one of a large ammunition pouches on his chest webbing. He pulled a brass cannon shell casing - about five inches long and an inch in diameter - out of it.

Ensuring his body blocked the view of the Russians from their vehicle on the other side of the clearing, Ted handed it to Eric.

'Souvenir hunting?' Eric enquired.

'Look at the base, Sir.'

Eric turned the casing over – there was Russian writing stamped into it. 'I found that during my little walk earlier,' Ted explained, 'lying on the forest floor – along with quite a few others.'

Eric frowned, knowing that it meant something important and sensing it was somehow connected to the pit in the woods.

But he couldn't quite work it out…yet.

Eric sensed it was the real reason Dostoyevsky and Ivanov were along for the ride.

9

THEY WERE ten more miles down the road to the west, with the wagons circled in another clearing and tents pitched in neat lines, but this time there was nothing to excavate. Their labours were, according to Russian information, at an end and the time had come to say goodbye to Soviet friends.

Gathering around a big fire on a glorious summer's evening, a cobalt blue sky turning to violet and purple as the sun sank, they roasted a couple of wild boar Ivanov had hunted and killed that morning using his Mosin-Nagant sniper rifle.

While everybody else had a restorative kip, caught up on paperwork or did their laundry in a nearby river, the Russians had been working on preparing the feast since noon - digging a pit, chopping wood and burning it therein to make extremely hot embers, before assembling their spit and slowly roasting the animals.

There were pots of boiled spuds and cabbage to accompany the meat, all served up on aluminium plates while the Russians seemed to have cheered up considerably, producing several bottles of vodka to join the Scotch provided by the British.

The sheer relief of the ordeal being over seemed to unite the war allies again, making a convivial group sat on logs around the roaring fire. Sergeant Ivanov, despite very limited English, tried his best to chat up the nurses – he was full of laughs and incomprehensible stories – but was getting nowhere. His meaty hands were batted away whenever they strayed where they shouldn't. They were canny enough girls and, if he got too cheeky, some of the British soldiers were secretly quite eager to give Ivanov a bashing, though that would be regrettable, for it would spoil the party mood.

As for Dostoyevsky, he was charm personified – relaxed and genial, installed between Eric and Katherine. His green army shirt was unbloused over his best blue cavalry britches, riding boots firmly planted in the ground, almost like a Tsar holding court.

With great enthusiasm Dostoyevsky ripped into the wild boar and noisily sucked in slivers of cabbage, all washed down by vodka. Lifting his bottle, its contents sloshing noisily he bellowed: 'Let us toast the successful reaching of our mission's objective and, once again, the end of German fascism!'

From his British comrades Dostoyevsky received bemused smiles. They wondered if the man before them could be the same surly Soviet officer they were used to. Eric lifted his enamel cup of whisky and returned the toast with all the false jocularity he could muster: 'To our valiant allies!'

The rest followed suit, Dostoyevsky giving Eric a sly sideways glance that showed he wasn't as drunk as he was making out.

'So, it's back to Moscow now for you, Major?' Eric enquired.

Dostoyevsky pursed his lips, laid his plate of food on the ground, wiping his hands on the tail of his shirt. This made Katherine wince in distaste, though Dostoyevsky couldn't see that, for he was giving his full attention to Eric, calculating what lie to tell next.

Picking the vodka bottle up, he shrugged, remarking mildly:

'I make my reports and go wherever I am told.'

Eric drained his glass and put it down by the log, holding his hands out for the fire's warmth. It was getting really chilly now.

'And you Captain Wise, one day back to civilian street?'

Still staring into the flames, in his head Eric saw Plymouth burning. 'Possibly,' remarked Eric, 'if there's anything to go back to.'

He glanced past Dostoyevsky at Katherine but she looked away, embarrassed by the directness of his stare.

Picking up on this, the Russian turned to look at her, enquiring with a playful smile: 'And you, Lady Katherine?'

She looked shocked at being asked, for Dostoyevsky had barely said more than a word to her during the whole investigation.

'First of all, Major Dostoyevsky, I am not a Lady anything,' she replied icily but then thawed and smiled, 'thanks for asking, but I have no idea what I will do after all this…'

With his left-hand Dostoyevsky reached out to try and grab a spark flying up from the fire. Failing, he sighed.

'The future is so uncertain, so hard to grasp.'

Eric wanted to laugh at such pitiful melodrama but kept staring down at his dirty boots, listening intently to what else might transpire in Katherine's exchange with Dostoyevsky. 'You Russians have the souls of poets,' she observed, with Eric appreciating the ironic tone 'Bad ones,' Dostoyevsky chuckled.

Before the war Eric had spent many an hour giving evidence to His Honour Judge Smith-Glosson at Plymouth Crown Court – he still found it hard to imagine Katherine was the daughter of that rather severe deliverer of justice.

True, the old boy had been reasonably friendly when they met during that Cornwall leave two years ago, but, all in all, she was kind and empathetic, whereas old Smith-Glosson sent more people to the gallows than anybody else on the Devon circuit. Some of them deserved to hang alright, but others? Probably he'd like to hang Eric for the brusque fashion in which he had finished with his daughter.

Dostoyevsky's voice interrupted Eric's thoughts. 'And Captain Wise, you were just a simple policeman before the war, no?'

Eric found Katherine looking right at him and a smug smile on Dostoyevsky's face. He experienced a surge of anger at this smart-arse Russian, remarking acidly: 'Though not a *secret* policeman like yourself, *just* a humble copper.'

Dostoyevsky shrugged.

'You are mistaken - I am just an army interpreter and liaison officer, but before the war, I was in, how you say, import-export, which is how I picked up my excellent English.'

A likely story, thought Eric who laughed at the boldness of the bullshit. Dostoyevsky beamed – for he was surely pleased with his barefaced lie. To defuse the situation, Katherine enquired: 'Do you have a wife and children back home, waiting for you major?'

Dostoyevsky looked suddenly very sad and properly so, which was a surprise. 'No,' he remarked mournfully, staring into the embers of the fire, 'my family was killed by the fascists.'

Katherine leaned forward to touch his arm.

'I'm so sorry.'

Dostoyevsky wiped away a tear with a thumb.

Eric still didn't buy it.

He wanted to smash the Russian's face in for playing on Katherine's sympathy like that.

'So many were lost,' Eric remarked quietly.

Dostoyevsky nodded, thinking Eric was commenting on Russia's losses, adding: 'Yes, it was a terrible struggle.'

Katherine gave him another sympathetic look, but Eric felt only contempt. Then the Russian changed tack.

'And you Captain Wise, did you kill many to achieve vengeance?'

Eric found Dostoyevsky wearing a curiously open look, but was there also a hint of mockery?

'Directly or indirectly?' Eric asked guardedly.

The Russian roared with laughter, wiggling his almost empty vodka bottle ostentatiously, taking a swig, then hurling it into the fire, where its dregs made the flames flare up.

Wiping tears of laughter from his eyes, Dostoyevsky persisted.

'How many did you kill – how many fascists?'

'I suppose quite a few indirectly with artillery bombardments...'

'Big guns, yes?'

'Yes, big guns...'

This seemed to make Dostoyevsky very happy. He again roared with laughter: 'That must have killed more than a few! And directly, eye to eye, with their stinking breath in your face captain – how many of *them* did you kill?'

The chatter and laughter around the fire stopped. Now everyone was staring at Eric, waiting for his reply. Dostoyevsky leaned forward, arms crossed and elbows on knees, staring intently at Eric.

Katherine shifted uncomfortably, started playing with a hairpin, not sure she wanted to hear what came next but also not wanting to miss it.

Eric felt angry at being put on the spot. He would ordinarily have told anyone who asked such a thing to fuck off, but he couldn't let this Russian get away with thinking all the killing had been on his side, could he? The problem was that Eric couldn't confess to something he had not done.

Not breaking the Russian's gaze, he told him: 'Truth to tell, when I had the chance – face to face with a German in Italy - I could have blown his brains out, but I didn't.'

Katherine was relieved but the Russian looked crestfallen, which made Eric smile. 'Disappointed, major?' Straightening up, stretching and yawning, Dostoyevsky confessed: 'A little – it left more scum for us to eliminate.'

'Don't you worry,' Ted Bodman assured the Russian from across the other side of the fire, 'I killed a few of the buggers eye-to-eye and don't mind ending the life of any foreigner who threatens my country.'

A chill descended that wasn't caused by the night air and dying fire. 'And how many did *you* kill?' Eric asked Dostoyevsky calmly.

The Russian responded with a sly smile and a non-committal shrug, so Eric pressed on: 'Germans or Russians – face-to-face, or back of the head?' In an ice cool tone Dostoyesvky replied:

'As a mere staff officer, my opportunities for wiping out the human stain of traitors and fascists were sadly limited.' Getting to his feet, not unsteady in the slightest, Dostoyevsky bowed.

'Goodnight ladies and gentlemen – we have a long drive back to Budapest tomorrow.'

Dostoyevsky rapped out an order in Russian to Ivanov, who jumped to his feet and fell over a log, causing a few titters. Picking himself up, red-faced Ivanov scurried after his boss into the dark. To break the tension, Surgeon Commander Geddes remarked jovially: 'I think I'll have one more wee snifter and be off to ma scratcher.'

Geddes, in the lingo of his native land, was heading off to bed.

The doctor walked around to sit in the gap created by Dostoyevsky's departure, holding his empty mug out. Eric replenished it, also offering a refill to Katherine.

She shook her head and, with a tired smile, got up.

'I think it's time to turn in.'

'Goodnight then,' Eric said, hiding his disappointment behind a smile. The nurses followed suit, leaving Eric, Geddes and Ted along with half a dozen MPs and Field Security men to carry on drinking. 'It's just us boys then,' Eric observed with a heavy sigh.

10

Early the following morning, slumped in the passenger seat of the jeep with a sore head, Eric's mood was not improved by the good cheer of Ted behind the wheel, seemingly impervious to hangovers. Ignoring him, Eric scrutinised a dot on the map sitting on his lap.

It was a village a mile or so off the main road and he wondered 'had anyone there seen the death march?'

It could not have just stopped such a long way from Graz, and the survivors vanish into thin air. The Russians had not declared burial sites further to the west, nor did anything in their paperwork suggest where the survivors went. *Did Dostoyevsky and his masters really think the British would leave it at that?*

Parking the rest of the team at the side of the road, and with two Field Security soldiers in the back of the jeep - and with Ted at the wheel - Eric headed for the village. Its pretty, multi-coloured pastel-painted houses were like something straight out of the Brothers Grimm, with ginger bread and pink, lime green or white icing sugar exteriors.

Taking Ted and one of the Field Security men with him, leaving the other to guard the jeep, Eric headed for the post office.

Finding nobody behind the counter, he dinged the bell.

A middle-aged man emerged and, judging by his forest green loden wool jacket with brass Posthorn badges on each lapel, he was the village postmaster. Blinking fearfully, remaining safely behind his counter, the postmaster smiled nervously. Assuming a deceptively cheerful air, Eric told him, using his very basic German:

'Guten morgen.'

The postmaster nodded, giving an uneasy smile.

'Sprechen sie Englisch?'

The man nodded again.

'I am Captain Wise of the British Army,' Eric continued, 'and I would like to ask you about events in early 1945, particularly a column of prisoners that came this way.'

The postmaster blanched. 'The only columns we have seen are Russian and British.' Certain from the man's reaction that his hunch was correct, Eric told the postmaster: 'I think not.' The postmaster went even paler and admitted rather fearfully: 'Yes, Sir.'

* * *

Evening was coming on when, finally, after they had been driving up and down the road for some time, the postmaster finally recognised a spot that looked likely.

Leaving everyone else in the jeep, Eric took his Thompson submachine gun and gently urged the postmaster through a line of trees into the clearing the man had explained lay beyond.

It looked like it might have once been a picnic spot, what with its tables and barbecue grills and stunning view of the mountains. The postmaster stopped by one of the tables, leaning on it - head down, breath coming in gasps - and then calmed himself enough to provide an explanation. 'Some of the guards had come into the village for bread and water, but later, on the main road, we heard shooting.'

'Go on,' Eric suggested quietly.

'But, you see, when we got there – I came with Schulz the innkeeper, in his carriage - we found only the bodies of Germans.'

Eric frowned, stepped closer to the man, who gave him a fearful sideways look.

'Are you sure?

'Yes, Sir, only German soldiers, all dead – so a few others and myself buried them. We saw no prisoners…at any time.'

'Where did you bury them?'

The postmaster raised his right arm and pointed, wavering as he swept it in an arc. 'Ich kann mich nicht erinnern,' he said in abject misery.

I cannot recall.

Eric wanted to slap the man, but instead, without comment, took the postmaster back through the trees to the road. He told the two Field Security men to get out of the jeep and loiter by the road as markers while he, Ted and the postmaster went back to the village. Eric and Ted took him to an inn to find his friend Schulz and discover what he had to say. Eric sat them both down at a corner table for an interview while Ted took notes.

Eric let the postmaster translate his questions and the innkeeper's responses, so he had time to study the man's facial responses.

'So, you found the Germans in the clearing?' Eric asked.

Schulz nodded, a slight quivering of the man's upper lip.

'What about march survivors? Your friend says he saw none – but did you?'

'Nein,' Schulz claimed.

'He saw none,' the postmaster explained, a little too helpfully.

'Are you absolutely sure there is nobody who would know more about this march?' Picking up on Eric's angry tone, the innkeeper looked very uncomfortable, raised a hand to rub a sweaty forehead. In a bid to shift attention away from himself – *from his village* - the postmaster ventured: 'Well, there is the huntsman.'

The innkeeper frowned, licked his dry lips, wondering what his friend was saying. 'Sei vorsichtig was du sagst,' the innkeeper urged his friend.

Be careful what you say.

The postmaster went on regardless.

'He appeared not long after the march went through.'

Losing his courage - worried the huntsman might visit his wrath on the village folk for being given away - the postmaster added: 'But there's no point in bothering him. He had nothing to do with any of it - of that I'm sure.' Eric pulled him up sharply.

'I'll decide that. Where does he live?'

'I'm not sure. We see him in town when he brings in game he's shot to barter for bread and beer.'

'Think,' Eric suggested, 'and show me where.'

He opened his map case and laid it on the table. Schulz could sense the fear and tension in his postmaster friend and said something that Eric's basic German skills could not catch.

'Sei vorsichtig, der jäger rächt sich nicht an den schafen die einen wolf schicken ihn zu sehen.'

'What did he say?'

'Nothing of importance, believe me,' the postmaster replied, 'but I will tell you the huntsman lives in an old lodge at the end of narrow track off the main road, about a mile west from where we found the dead Germans.'

The postmaster grabbed the map case, took the chinagraph pencil out of the holder, and marked the clear plastic waterproof membrane protecting the map - a big, black X indicated a spot in the woods beyond the village.

Bidding the innkeeper and postmaster an icy farewell, Eric led Ted back to the jeep. As he started the engine, Ted turned and asked: 'Did you catch any of whatever that pub landlord said?'

'Something about sheep being careful not to send the hunter a wolf because he might seek revenge.'

Turning the wheel to pull out into the road, Ted laughed:

'So, they were shitting themselves!?'

Eric sighed, not sure he liked being called a wolf.

'Delicately put, as ever, Ted.'

* * *

That night in the clearing ghosts crowded around Eric: his father looking dapper in his best naval uniform; brother Bert and his cheeky grin; the girl and her sailor boy lover from the alleyway; the Maori troops cut down carrying him to safety at Cassino after he'd been wounded; the poor dead Dutchman. Sitting on the edge of his camp bed, Eric cracked open a whisky bottle and toasted them all.

Leaving his tent, with oil lamp in one hand and bottle in the other, Eric made his way over to the now partially excavated mass grave, climbing down a ladder. About 30ft-long and eight feet deep, it had taken them an entire day to disinter most of its dozen occupants.

Austrians liked to keep things tidy and, so it transpired after later questioning some other locals, villagers had dragged the corpses of various assorted others – the postmaster called them Hungarians - they found in nearby ditches to join the German guards in this grave. Could not have been a pleasant job. Nor was it wonderful digging them up again.

Due to the comparatively modest number of remains, the smell was not as strong as previous sites and, anyway, they'd all got used to it by now. The lamplight revealed a claw-like hand with a gleaming Nazi party signet ring on it poking out from an unexcavated layer of earth.

Eric heard someone approaching, swinging around to find Geddes climbing down. They stood in silence for a few moments looking at the claw sticking out of the earth, Eric offering the bottle to Geddes and putting the lamp down on the floor of the pit.

'How could they do it?' he asked Geddes.

'Kill all those people on the march?'

Geddes guzzled some whisky before responding.

'They lost sight of their humanity.'

The doctor lowered himself to the floor of the grave, sitting cross-legged, while Eric slid down and rested his back against the damp earth of its sides. 'You were a uniformed copper on civvy street weren't you?' Geddes asked. Eric nodded. 'Well, anybody who has dealt with the dregs of society knows the capacity for this barbarity is in all of us,' suggested the doctor, 'even the most mundane little mouse. You can do anything if you justify its logic to yourself.'

Vision swimming, Eric shook his head, observing:

'This march wasn't a case of domestic murder.'

The Scotsman unleashed a smoker's raspy laugh, adding.

'Wasn't it, though?'

Eric had no idea what the man meant, particularly with his mind befuddled by booze. The pathologist tried to help him understand.

'Hitler killed German humanity in the home before he inflicted his evil on the world. All those "Good Germans" who never fired a shot in anger, but supported the Nazis have a guilty secret in their hearts.' Eric took another swig and shook his head. 'I don't have a clue what you're talking about.'

Eric stared at a pair of moths frantically beating their wings as they bounced off the searing hot glass of the oil lamp.

With a heavy groan, Geddes got to his feet.

'Come on, it's no good torturing yourself down here.'

With a 'one...two...three' Geddes shoved Eric up the ladder and out of the pit, then climbed out. Behind them in the burial pit, the moths continued their dance of death around the lamp.

Overcome by the booze, by mental and physical exhaustion, Eric found he could not get to his feet while Geddes was unable pull him up.

Nonetheless, Geddes panted and groaned, tugging at Eric's arms, cursing and trying to get the bigger man at least on his knees.

'But the big question is,' Eric slurred, stars spinning dizzily overhead, 'who killed those Germans we found in the pit? Not that they didn't deserve it ...' More pairs of hands arrived to assist Eric to his feet and he found Ted and Katherine raising him up.

Back in his tent the last thing he remembered before blackness descended was her leaning over him, loosening his tie, while somebody else took his boots off. Tears leaking from his eyes, he told her: 'Sorry...I'm such a fool.'

She smiled and kissed him on the forehead, a gesture that did not go unnoticed by Ted, who diplomatically chose to say nothing.

11

Never one to feel sorry for himself for too long, Eric decided the best form of defence when attacked by alcohol poisoning was to get up early and head for a quiet spot in the trees where he could throw up.

Next would be a walk to clear his head and get away from those whom he was too ashamed to see. Ted tagged along, though, as it was never wise to go too far solo, what with roving bands of cutthroats skulking in the woods. Eric was in no fit state to defend himself, yet protested that he didn't need an escort. Ted maintained that nobody in Eric's condition would be able to shoot straight, so he should shut up and put up.

The sounds of digging in the clearing and a radio tuned in to the BBC Overseas Service faded behind them and, not long after, Eric sensed something bulky and dark looming overhead. Looking up, he was amazed to discover aircraft wreckage roosting in the trees, like some big bird of prey.

There was a hollow, metallic clank. Looking down and around, Eric found Ted kicking at something that had become detached from the aircraft. Eric walked over, finding part of a green-painted wing. Some it had flaked off, revealing bare metal.

To one side of the wing part, something glinted on the floor of the forest. Eric knelt down and brushed away the mulch, discovering a silver thread Nazi eagle badge on faded grey fabric – he wiped away some more, finding the sleeve of a coat. Eric tugged, but it wouldn't give – so he pulled harder and the decayed fabric came away in his hand, sending him flying onto his backside, head pulsing with pain.

Ted had been gazing up at the aircraft wreckage but span around on hearing Eric curse, and couldn't help but laugh at what he found. Not finding it funny in the slightest, Eric got to his feet, still holding the sleeve, which had come away at the shoulder seam due to rotted stitching. 'That must be the pilot,' Ted remarked as Eric's tugging had revealed human remains under the coat remnants.

Ted went over and poked it with his boot, then stooped down and gingerly extracted the skull, still with dried shreds of flesh on it and clad in a flying helmet. Laughing, Ted observed: 'Alas poor Ivan, I knew him well.'

Ted presented it to Eric, who shook his head and retorted angrily: 'Don't muck about – put it back.'

Looking shame-faced Ted returned the skull to where he'd found it.

Staring up at the aircraft wreckage again, sleeve still dangling from his hand, Eric wondered why a coat with a Waffen SS eagle badge had been draped over a dead Russian pilot. Ironic, thought Eric, that the pilot probably survived the crash in the trees, then fell and broke his neck, but who came along and covered him with the coat?

Another image leapt into his head: The fragile young woman at the hospital in Bad Gastein curled up in the chair – *wearing a flying jacket with cracked, undernourished leather.*

Pulse quickening, a sudden burst of adrenalin chasing the dregs of the hangover away, Eric looked up at the wreckage again, circling below it, squinting against the bright light. A phrase the young woman uttered came back to him. *After the black crows came.*

The dripping, rusting, smashed up aircraft, all jagged with bits of cables and metal rods hanging down - body and wings wrapped around the trees was very crow-like. Not realising he had said anything out loud, Eric noticed Ted giving him a very puzzled look.

'The black crows?'

Eric tried to explain: 'Do you remember when you drove me to Bad Gastein? And I questioned someone who might have survived the march who said she'd been left for dead "after the black crows came"?' Eric looked up again, and so did Ted, remarking with a smile: 'Yes, it does look like a bloody big crow up there.'

As if the summit of a mountain had emerged from mist into bright sunlight, Eric felt something solid asserting itself in plain view at last.

She had been here, he felt sure of it, but how it all related to the pit of ashes back down the road he was not yet certain. The lower slopes of the mystery remained hidden in the shadows.

'What shall we do about the pilot, Sir?'

'Nothing,' Eric suggested, rolling up the coat sleeve and slipping it inside his trouser map pocket.

'And telling the Russians?' Ted asked as they returned to the clearing.

'I think we should keep this to ourselves,' Eric suggested, 'old Dostoyevsky has gone back to their sector and that's where he belongs. I hope I never see his ugly mug again.'

In the privacy of his tent Eric placed the coat sleeve with the Waffen SS eagle on the floor and the Russian shell casing beside it. On the walk back he'd ordered Ted to take one of the naval nurses with a camera to photograph the wreckage in the trees and the remains of the Russian pilot. He sat on the camp bed, staring at the two artefacts, trying to piece together a theory. The death march had for some reason come to a halt near this clearing, not the earlier one – the one the Russians said was the final destination without bothering to explain where everybody went.

Had Russian aircraft attacked the column, killing the guards, so the prisoners melted away? But how could a strafing Russian aircraft just kill the guards? A ground attack aircraft was a blunt instrument, not a precision tool of slaughter. Where were the bodies of dead prisoners who had also been cut down by the aircraft? There were none, at least not at this site. At other burial sites there had been prisoner bodies but no Germans. And none of the corpses exhumed anywhere had suffered from being torn apart by heavy machine gun or cannon fire. Then there was the pit of the burned remains at the other place, which the Russians had not admitted to in their files. They were diseased, said Dostoyevsky. Or were they? And why would the Russians burn bodies that were not? Prisoners killed by ground attack aircraft? Germans? Who exactly was in the pit of ashes and bones?

His head was spinning, so he stepped out of the tent, glad of the cooling breeze on his face.

'Are you alright?'

It was Katherine giving him a concerned look. She had seen him return and so came over to check on his welfare.

'You're very pale,' she suggested.

'Coming around the bend now.'

'Good.'

She smiled and he felt his heart lift a little.

They began walking across the clearing towards where the trestle tables were set up. Geddes was bent over the cadaver with the claw from the pit, a naval nurse poised at a typewriter on the other table. Looking up from his labours, Geddes observed: 'Lazarus rises.'

Ignoring the comment, Eric asked: 'How did they die? The people we've found here? Remind me.'

Laying down his scalpel and wiping his hands on the apron, Geddes replied: 'Bullets puncturing vital organs and blood vessels – your normal combat death. Shreds of clothing point to them being soldiers of some kind. Of the others - no wounds, no uniform, so likely to be prisoners…maybe they just died of exhaustion.'

'Not executions, back of the head style?'

'No.'

Eric asked: 'And not ripped to shreds by cannon fire or heavy machine guns?' Geddes shook his head. 'Why do you ask that?'

'Just curious.'

Eric turned around and walked to his tent and a few moments later Katherine followed him. Opening the flaps she was amazed to find him buckling on his webbing belt and holster.

'Where on earth are you going?'

Closing the brass clasp of the belt, he revealed:

'To find some answers from someone I sense knows what happens in these woods.'

'I don't understand. Who? Where?'

Eric pulled out the Browning pistol, made sure it was fully loaded then shoved it back into the holster.

She stepped aside to let him out, walking with him to the jeep, deep concern etched on her face. 'Are you fit to do this?'

He climbed into the vehicle, the peculiar look in his eye not making her feel any better. 'On your own, Eric?'

The vehicle's engine turned over.

'Let me come with you.'

Realising she was genuinely worried, Eric reached out for her hand, giving it a squeeze. 'No fear, can't take you on this ride – but thanks for looking after me last night.'

And with that he drove out of the clearing, Katherine watching as the jeep turned right to head west. Looking around, she could find no sign of Ted Bodman.

Where was he?

Somebody had to do something to stop Eric killing himself.

* * *

Hurtling along the road in the jeep, a fatalistic mood took hold of Eric. He felt that he was rushing at high speed to whatever destiny might offer. He would find the huntsman and get some answers, even if it killed him – he owed it to the poor souls murdered by the Nazis. If the huntsman was a war criminal Eric would bring him in dead or alive and he'd show bloody Dostoyevsky that, when it came down to it – delivering face-to-face justice – he could handle it; with satisfaction.

PART III

1

There was a heavy stillness in the hunting lodge as Eric - with almost heart stopping anticipation - awaited the German's response to the conclusion of his tale. Up until this point, under the gun, Eric felt the idiot – giving things away for nothing in return. Yet, as he reached the last part of his story, he'd observed the Waffen SS officer's arrogance deflating.

The facial features had softened; the eyes lost their hardness, dropping occasionally to stare at the table.

As though contemplating past sins?

The gun wavered and Eric pondered another attempt to turn tables, making a grab for the pistol and wrestling it off the German.

However, the gradual transformation in the other man's demeanour showed that Eric's alternate strategy was both keeping him alive and getting under the skin of his prime suspect.

Then Martin lowered the gun, keeping it still in his hand, but resting on the table. Eric ventured hesitantly, playing a hunch: 'The girl in the Bad Gastein hospital…'

Martin smiled wistfully – or was it sarcastically?

'Ah, yes the one you gallantly gave the book of Heinrich Heine poetry to *Die Lorelei.*'

'Did you know her?'

Martin's face tightened up and the gun was raised again, Eric once more finding himself staring right down the barrel.

Nonetheless, he had to press his advantage, to confirm that the huntsman villagers feared, but needed so much, was connected to the death march. 'How were you associated with the killings?'

The German's finger tightened fractionally on the trigger, his eyes burning. Martin exploded, slamming his left hand on the table, making the dirty plates and chicken bones jump, but, curiously, putting the pistol down on the table and getting up.

'You think you know *Die Lorelei* – you think *you know!*?' he shouted, banging the table with both fists clenched, making Eric recoil.

The pistol was tantalisingly close to his fingertips now, but before Eric could take it, Martin had the K98k rifle at his shoulder, lunging forward to press the muzzle against Eric's forehead, making the British officer rigid with fear. In a low, menacing voice, Martin suggested: 'Just a fraction more pressure on the trigger and it is you who are history.'

Eric did not react but Martin sighed heavily, lowering the rifle, leaving a small red circle on the other man's forehead.

'You must know Englishman that I am very picky about who I shoot.'

Martin placed the rifle on the table next to the Walther while Eric slumped in the chair, lowering his hands to his lap so the German could not see them shake. Martin pulled the beer flagon over and refilled the glasses.

'So, do you admit to knowing her?' Eric asked.

Martin shook his head and took a sip.

'I cannot say that I knew her.'

Suddenly the German erupted into laughter, verging on hysterical, throwing his head back, shoulders heaving.

'Nor did she know me!'

Eric knew this was a decisive moment, so he reached out and touched the man's forearm. Martin pulled it away, glaring at Eric.

'I killed those guards on the march,' he revealed in a flat voice, adding, 'they deserved to die.'

Eric's head throbbed with pain, and he looked away, finding it hard to focus. The bloody hangover was back with a vengeance and he felt sick.

'Lorelei was my lover,' Martin confessed, voice cracking with emotion.

'What?' Eric whispered disbelievingly. 'Her name is actually Lorelei? But you said you didn't know her…'

Now Martin leaned forward and grasped *his* forearm.

'I must confess until your story I had no idea she was alive – and inside my heart and soul has been in turmoil as your tale has been laid before me.'

Eric looked at the German, incredulous, feeling sickened by Martin's sudden transformation into an excited, lovelorn schoolboy.

'But now you have told me, I am happy, do you see?'

Eric shook his head.

'You were in the Waffen SS? How could *she* be *your* lover?'

Martin sighed heavily.

'It is a long story.'

Eric suggested, his voice dripping with sarcasm: 'I am not going anywhere – I don't want a bullet in the back or in my forehead.'

Martin shoved the Walther across the table.

'There – and if you think at any stage I deserve to die during what I am about to tell you then please shoot me, because I have just realised that all along my purpose has been to wait for you.'

For Eric shooting the German was a *very* tempting prospect.

Finally, he was face-to-face with one of those who had brought such misery to the world – to his family. He was being gifted an opportunity to even the score, with the enemy's stinking breath in his face, as Dostoyevsky might have put it. *There would be one less German to worry about – a death march murderer given a suitable justice. And this SS officer screwing one of the poor abused prisoners was just further evidence of the corrupt bestiality of the Nazis.*

Eric picked up the pistol and closed his palm around the grip, finger gently caressing the trigger. 'Go on then,' he suggested, pointing it right at Martin, 'tell me your story.' The German fixed him with a cool look, nodded and stated calmly: 'Alright, I will.'

2

THEY STORMED on throughout the summer and autumn of 1941, legions of death laying waste to anything or anyone that stood in their way, but Comrade General Winter checked them before Moscow.

Halted on the outer edge of the city, at the village of Katyushki – confronted by rows of tank traps made from girders on the road to the Russian capital - Martin and his men froze in thin summer tunics as they waited for Arctic warfare clothing to reach them up the supply chain.

Lying in the bottom of a foxhole shivering under a tarpaulin, back to back with his senior sergeant, Bruno Schwarzerde, to share body heat, Martin often dreamed of the warm, soft Italian girl he had made love to during a languid Croatian late spring.

Was it really just seven months ago?

It felt like a century, a different life entirely.

Now, Martin's company was awaiting assault engineers who would help them create holes in walls – both exterior and interior - of tenements on the edge of the city itself, a mere six miles away.

When the order to attack came they would go through the buildings rather than be exposed to fire in the streets. But the engineers' trucks had broken down due to a lack of anti-freeze - Moscow may as well have been on the Moon. The whole idea of some final big push on the enemy capital was the stuff of fantasy.

Later, while standing on the turret of a Panzer III - gritting teeth to control shuddering as a sharp blast of Siberian air cut through his thin tunic and sheepskin over vest - Martin used binoculars to scan the bleak, snow-covered landscape. Sweeping them back and forth over the roofs of the shabbily constructed village buildings, they appeared devoid of life.

No Russian troops had been seen for days, but that didn't mean they were not out there somewhere. Lifting the focus of the glasses higher, a break in the low, slate-grey clouds allowed through a rare shaft of sunlight.

Was that a gold leaf dome in the Kremlin that he could see glittering on the horizon? Perhaps it was a mirage? He adjusted the focus of the binoculars but a curtain of snow was drawn across the dark, brooding landscape.

* * *

The 2nd SS Panzer Division *Das Reich* withdrew from Moscow to enable its supplies to catch up and shortly afterwards the Red Army's hordes swept in from the East and hurled the Germans even further back, inflicting massive casualties. In the aftermath of the Moscow battle, still exhausted by the huge effort, the 2nd SS was withdrawn to rest and refit in France.

The following summer's thrust south for Stalingrad, the industrial city on the banks of the Volga, became the defining folly of Hitler's war in Russia. Hundreds of thousands of men's lives were thrown away because the Führer would not let them retreat when the Reds girded up their loins and threatened to trap them in the city. The metal sea of Nazism broke on the ragged, granite shores of Stalinism.

Having recuperated and been reinforced, the *Das Reich* returned to the Eastern Front. It was awarded a role in retaking the key city of Kharkov in the Ukraine, recently snatched back by the Soviets.

The brutal tenacity of the *Das Reich* – equipped with the mighty new Tiger tank - would be applied as part of an SS Panzer Corps. At the very tip of the spear thrust between the Red Army's ribs was Martin Walder, by then a newly promoted and decorated hauptsturmführer, and his 200 men.

Kharkov, Ukraine, night of 15 March 1943

A lightning flash tore open the heavens, freeze-framing Martin against a wall, listening intently, bricks either side of his helmet glistening wetly from recent rain. To his left, he saw that Bruno had taken off his helmet and was massaging his scalp. Looking to his right, Martin found Schütze Wilhelm König with his eyes closed, muttering a prayer.

The sound of thunder got louder and louder, reverberating through the brick wall that loomed over Martin and his men, by then whittled down by combat casualties to a mere twenty-five.

It trembled, dislodging dust and moss, making some of them cough. Martin tugged Bruno's sleeve.

'Let's move,' he mouthed as more lightning ripped the sky, the order passed up and down the line, soldiers cautiously edging their way along.

Fingers of his left hand stretched out, caressing the brickwork as he moved forward, Martin's other hand tightly gripped a MP40 submachine gun. There was a very loud, stuttering burst of heavy machine gun fire in an adjacent street, the echo lingering as it rebounded off nearby buildings while lightning crackled again, but this time further away.

The thunder returned, but even more strongly, slates falling off the roof of the tenement they were moving past to shatter on the ground. Some nearly hit Martin's men, causing some loud cursing.

'Shut up you pigs!' Bruno bellowed.

A few yards ahead, the tall garden wall between Martin's men and the next tenement building collapsed as a Tiger tank burst into the street. Crouching down to protect themselves from a shower of shattered masonry, the SS soldiers were at least glad to see it wasn't

Russian. Grinding bricks and mortar into dust beneath its squealing treads and swinging out into the street, the Tiger's turret swivelled. Its 88mm gun halted just above Martin's head, twitching up and down. Lightning illuminated the scene, revealing the identity of the soldiers to the Tiger's crew who had been peering anxiously through their periscopes at the figures huddled in the street – they let out a collective sigh of relief on finding friends rather than foes.

Climbing up onto the panzer as a hatch opened, Martin spoke to its commander, telling him to head east down the street. Martin climbed down and waved his men forward, scrambling into cover behind the steel beast as it moved off, engine roaring and exhausts belching smoke.

The Tiger came to the end of the block, pivoting to the left, but lurched as an enemy shell hit it with a loud *clang*. Ricocheting off into the night, the glowing projectile inscribed a tumbling arc down the street, embedding itself in the road surface with a flurry of sparks.

The Tiger's 88mm roared and spat flame, its hull-mounted machine gun chattering – its foe was a Red Army T34 tank, lying in wait at the junction. The Russian was hit and shuddered but not destroyed; its supporting infantry scuttling away in all directions, like cockroaches scattering when a kitchen light was suddenly switched on. An angry swarm of bullets from the Tiger's coaxial machine gun buzzed around them.

'Into the building!' Martin shouted, his men climbing through shattered windows and kicking down doors. On the other side, Russian soldiers made their own violent entry.

The Germans groped their way through the darkened interior, illuminated every now and then by the flash of the tank guns and lightning.

Each room was investigated, an SS man either side of a door, a third entering ready to kill. In a kitchen they found a mother and her children cowering under a large wooden table; in a sitting room an elderly man made a statue by fear, sunk into an armchair below a large, framed poster of Comrade Stalin. The elderly man clutched a photograph of Lenin to his chest, like a protective breastplate.

Ignoring them as he trod lightly through, Bruno slung his MP40 behind his back, pulling out a specially sharpened entrenching tool from a case strapped between his shoulder blades. Back in the kitchen, König picked up a carving knife from a breadboard while Martin held a bayonet in one hand and Walther pistol in the other. Any fighting that transpired would be hand-to-hand with no room for wielding rifles or submachine guns.

As they came in from the opposite side of the building, the Russians also prepared themselves for a savage fight to the death. An officer rolled up his sleeves, took his watch off and placed it in a trouser pocket; one of his NCOs seized a heavy metal iron from a shelf and hefted it in his hand, smiling with grim satisfaction at the potential lethality of its weight.

In the street outside, the mortally wounded T34 charged the Tiger, attempting to lock horns. The Tiger backed off, and then rammed the T34, shoving it back, both tanks' furiously whirring tracks gouging the road surface.

Inside the building, the grim ballet of death unfolded in all its visceral barbarity, Russians and Germans pirouetting around one another with savage, homicidal intent. There was the occasional flash of a gun being fired, but it was otherwise a clash of elbows, fists, knives, boots and tearing teeth. Bruno hacked viciously at a Russian soldier's head, blood jetting from a severed jugular vein. In the kitchen the Russian NCO battered König with the iron, which made a sickening squelch as it sank into the young German's face. The carving knife fell to the floor, its shining white blade hypnotising the mother and her children cowering under the table.

In another room, Martin thrust his bayonet into the Russian officer's throat, the man's warm blood gushing over his hand. Placing his pistol against the Russian's temple, Martin squeezed the trigger.

* * *

In the aftermath of the wrestle to the death a heavy silence was punctuated only by the far-off sound of fighting in another street. Inside the building, amid pools of blood, shattered furniture and broken glass, were ludicrously intact items – wilting flowers in a vase; an untouched cabinet of books, polished glass still pristine.

Offsetting these was a horribly mutilated German corpse lying half in a fireplace and a Russian soldier's lifeless body sprawled on a ripped-apart sofa, a poker stuck in his chest.

The elderly man had remained in his chair, alive but frozen in place, still clutching Lenin. Meanwhile, Stalin's portrait lay broken on the floor, a rapidly spreading pool of blood masking the dictator's genial smile. Swallowing sobs of fear, the mother ushered her children from under the kitchen table and through the wreckage.

Martin was slumped in the corridor by the kitchen door, gasping, his helmet having been ripped from his head, face covered in gore and hair matted by sweat. Groaning, he pulled himself to his feet and came face-to-face with the mother.

She stared wide-eyed with terror at the slaughterhouse apparition swaying before her, still clutching its bloody dagger and pistol. Martin moved aside. Gathering her children, murmuring fearful prayers, she slipped by, the youngsters clinging to her skirts for protection. Clucking to cool their fear, the mother ushered her brood through a door and into the comparative safety of the night.

Bruno emerged from the interior, leaning against a doorframe to survey the T34 and Tiger, still locked together but apparently devoid of life. The rear end of the Russian tank was now ablaze, its four crew rousing themselves from their stupor and climbing out, amid much shouting and wild gesticulation.

Bruno ran down the steps of the tenement building and into the street. Pulling around his MP40, he hosed down the Russians with hot lead. As the Reds twitched on the ground, he slung the MP40 again, pulled a pistol from a holster and moved from man to man, squeezing off a single shot into each one's head.

Inside the building, Martin slowly mounted some stairs, passing corpses of his men and Russians locked in death's embrace.

Here and there a German soldier sat in shocked silence, smoking a cigarette and staring into space. Martin patted each survivor on the shoulder as he passed by.

'Anyone else?' he asked a corporal on the second floor landing.

Too exhausted to speak, the soldier gestured along the corridor to an open door. Just inside the room Martin found his man – dead, with a neat bullet hole in his forehead. Sprawled against the far wall, under a window, was a mortally wounded Russian, gently whimpering.

Martin was surprised to find it was a woman, a sniper's rifle lying beside her but with a pistol resting in her limp right hand.

Life was rapidly seeping out of her, a massive, slippery slick of blood covering the bare floorboards, shimmering as a series of explosions - the burning T34's ammunition cooking off - illuminated the room so brightly it was like day. Martin knelt down and, acting on a strange impulse, took one of the wounded Russian's hands in his. He noticed her eyes were fixed on a religious icon hung on the wall to one side the window. In the flickering light from the blazing tank, the Madonna and Child – with gold leaf halos - seemed to come alive; Martin was momentarily transfixed by its simple beauty – the pink-skinned cherubic Christ with golden curls looking up with shining eyes, safe in the enfolding arms of Mary, whose face wore a beatific smile.

Getting up, he removed the icon from wall and brought it over, kneeling and offering it to her lips. The sniper kissed it, releasing a deep sigh as she finally let go, her dark brown eyes going dull. Martin placed the icon face up on her chest, folding the sniper's hands over it, his face betraying no emotion at all.

Western Ukraine, 15 February 1944

Bruno looked so peaceful, almost angelic.

Once upon a time his eyes had burned with fascist flame, especially when Jews were driven from their homes and businesses during the terror of the Kristallnacht pogrom in 1938. He was there with the rest of them, hurling bricks and obscenities.

Following the glorious conquest of France in 1940, Bruno seduced the fair maidens of Paris who gave unto the victors their spoils – whether willingly or unwillingly in their hearts or minds, he didn't really care.

His eyes had been pitiless with contempt at the plight of Russian peasants burned out of their pathetic hovels in the summer of 1941.

During the titanic struggle at Kursk in 1943 - just weeks after the Kharkov fighting - he, alongside Martin, was magnificent, rallying men as wave after wave of Red tanks surged across the great plains to brush aside the panzers, including the *Das Reich*'s own damned Tigers that so often broke down due to mechanical imperfections.

Bruno had executed his masters' bidding with utter ruthlessness but by early 1944 the glory days of conquest were long gone and now so was he. Now his eyes were devoid of any spark. He was fast asleep - that was for sure. The sleep of eternity and, in some ways, Martin Walder envied him.

He twiddled the knob on his binoculars to get a sharper view of his company sergeant's head. It was poking up through the snow in no man's land in front of German trenches outside Ternopil - a ruined city on the meandering River Seret, currently under ice.

Ternopil had switched hands over the centuries between Germans, Poles, Austrians and Russians, and no doubt would be yielded back to the Soviets. The SS panzer division's lines were no more than a frail ribbon stretched to breaking point by the Red Army juggernaut.

Sooner or later it would snap.

Bruno had led out a fighting patrol a week ago, which ran into trouble and during the mayhem of a skirmish he was wounded in the leg. He told the others to go back as he'd take care of himself.

The tough-as-nails NCO crawled as far as a tree stump, no more than 100 yards from the German lines. While gathering his strength for a final effort he froze to death.

They didn't go and get Bruno because they couldn't have buried him anyway. The ground was too hard to dig and even dynamite could not have excavated a grave. So, they left him there – as if the snow was a comforting blanket pulled up tight beneath his chin.

* * *

In no man's land a white-clad figure crawled up behind the shattered tree trunk against which Bruno lay. It was a Russian sniper who carefully placed his rifle barrel on the frozen corpse's shoulder, using it as a rest to steady his aim. Over his head the Russian sniper wore a white gossamer camouflage net, which served to soften the outline of his helmet and cover his face while the weapon was wrapped in ragged strips of grubby bandages.

Meanwhile, Martin dropped his binoculars and pulled his grey woollen scarf up until only a thin slit across his eyes was exposed. He raised the binos again, humming *Lili Marlene* as he scanned the terrain, unaware of the Russian zeroing in on him.

'Who will stand by the lamppost,
With you, Lili Marlene?'

He smiled, and thought of that Italian girl in Croatia, feeling a warming glow, but such daydreams were, of course, a potentially lethal distraction. And, anyway, thinking of her always made him sad as it was not an affair that had ended well.

The Russian sniper's cross-hairs were now square on Martin's head but he cursed the German's binoculars, which were blocking a clean shot of the target's face. It was already tricky enough and the glare off the snow didn't make things any easier.

Martin banished thoughts of sex. Snorting with disgust at himself, he reflected that he was more likely to find a blanket of snow than get between the sheets with a woman. He twiddled the focus knob as there was something odd about Bruno's head…something that wasn't there a minute ago.

The Russian sniper cursed, fearing the German was onto him. Calming himself, he took a deep breath and slowly exhaled, allowing the barrel of the rifle to rise fractionally until perfectly aimed. His finger caressed the trigger.

It wasn't easy to get a sharp focus with binoculars while wearing gloves, so Martin bobbed down to pull them off with his teeth.

The Russian hissed, stifling an urge to withdraw. Would he manage to get a shot off before the bastard finally realised he was staring death in the face? It had to be a perfect shot, too, as so little of the target was available.

A bullet right between the eyes.

The sniper exhaled to calm himself again…

Martin raised the binoculars again, realising what he was looking at.

It was death, come to collect on a debt. A high velocity round smashed the binos to pieces. Lens fragments and metal casing were driven into Martin's face sending him sprawling unconscious to the bottom of the trench.

As a member of Hitler's special elite, Martin was assured the best of medical care. Handpicked doctors pieced the Waffen SS officer's head back together again with their vinegar and brown paper. He'd live, but whether or not Martin would regain his eyesight was another matter.

After treatment at a casualty evacuation post, and then a field hospital in Chernovsty, they decided to ship him back to the Reich.

It was just as well, for Comrade Stalin's barbarian hordes were closing in fast and the wounded were being slaughtered in their beds. Such were the rules of war on the Eastern Front.

3

Bad Gastein, Austria, 20 July 1944

MAJOR ERWIN SCHMIDT sat in the window of the room he shared with Martin Walder in the convalescent hospital, caressing new scar tissue over a wound caused by jagged glass that had torn into the hamstring of his right leg.

It was very tender to the touch and Erwin could feel its ridges through the thin fabric of his cotton pyjama trousers. He badly wanted to scratch it, but resisted.

Posted to the 5th Gebirgsjäger Divison in late 1943, he soon saw action - and received the wound - at Cassino in Italy. It happened during a grapple with an Englander who could have blown his brains out but, strangely, chose instead to put this hole in his leg.

The Mountain Division officer - silver haired, despite being only in his late 20s - tapped the tip of a cigarette on the window ledge. The ash was snatched by the breeze and instantly disintegrated into nothing. Below, the Gasteiner Ache river thundered through the centre of the town and, as ever, the raw power of the water amazed Erwin. He leaned forward in the window, saved from plunging to his death by a tiny, narrow wrought iron balcony strong enough only to take a few potted plants. Flicking the moist petals of some geraniums, Erwin stubbed his cigarette out in the black, peaty soil of a pot. He'd dreamed of geraniums when fighting in the white wastes of the Caucasus mountains in southern Russia.

Erwin had been one of the soldiers of the 1st Gebirgsjäger Division who, in the summer 1942, placed the Nazi flag on Mount Elbrus, the highest peak in Europe. According to a well-placed staff officer Erwin knew, Hitler was enraged to hear of it, demanding to know why lives had been sacrificed to that end and not in seizing the oil fields of Baku. Erwin thought that when it came to war strategy, it was the only thing upon which he and the Führer agreed.

And now Erwin was keen to get back into the mountains. He glanced back into the room, where Martin reposed on his bed reading a book. 'I fancy exploring the local scenery,' Erwin announced. 'Werner, that mountain guide fellow, has offered to take us. Fancy it? I need to get my mountain legs back.'

Absorbed in his book, Martin gave only a grunt.

'Did you know,' Erwin pressed on, 'that Werner's grandfather used to take our Kaiser, Austria's Franz Josef and Bismarck hunting here? That's something. Imagine the three of them settling the fate of Europe while slaughtering mountain antelope and drinking schnapps.'

Again getting no reaction, Erwin shook his head and enquired: 'An absorbing book?' Still not looking up, Martin mumbled, 'just some poetry.'

The incongruity of a Waffen SS officer reading poems amused Erwin, who observed sarcastically: 'Of course.'

Realising he was perhaps being rude, Martin finally looked up.

'What were you saying about the scenery?'

'I was suggesting we get some fresh mountain air.'

* * *

Distant thunder but a cloudless sky overhead with no sign of storm clouds away to the far horizon. It was a real puzzle and it couldn't be an avalanche as there was no snow except on the summits. Nor could it be artillery fire, for the war was still far away. It would have to be a mighty big waterfall to make such a sound, to reach them up on the high pasture above the Kötschach Valley. The three climbers had paused on the track to pass a water bottle around and, wiping the top before giving it to Martin, Erwin mused: 'What the hell can it be?'

'I have never heard anything like it,' Werner remarked.

'Onwards and upwards?' Erwin enquired.

Looking at the pair of wounded heroes in his care, Werner was doubtful. 'Are you up to it?'

Erwin stuck up for his friend.

'It's his eyes that are healing, not his limbs.'

Taking the water bottle from Martin, the mountain guide elaborated.

'I meant you, with your leg. It's been fairly easy so far. From here it's hard. These are proper peaks, not your Bavarian pimples.'

'I've tackled harder mountains than this under fire,' Erwin scoffed.

Werner slipped the water bottle strap over his head.

'I'm sorry major, you're my responsibility and I'm not sure you're strong enough.' Erwin glowered at Werner, looking for support from Martin, but he appeared distracted. Suddenly, Martin pointed to the horizon and shouted excitedly: 'Look!'

It was a fast moving, Swift-like shape tumbling in the sky. The noise they had taken for thunder emanated from its cigar-shaped engines, one under each swept back wing. With a bunsen-burner roar, the aircraft swooped down into the valley, its dark camouflaged upper surfaces lost for a moment against the black forests and bright grassy slopes.

It seemed as if the mountains had swallowed it up and nature's peace reigned. Then, with engines howling, the aircraft leapt high, its pilot throwing it up over the spot on the trail where the three men stood.

Showing its pale blue underside, it pulled around, black German crosses plainly visible on its wings.

They watched open-mouthed – *no propellers!* - as the

extraordinary machine circled, dived, levelled its wings and flew past just below them. The pilot, clearly visible in his cockpit, gave them a wave as it shot by, wings waggling in salute. 'My God!' shouted Werner, waving back vigorously, 'how can we lose with wonder weapons like that!?'

As swiftly as it had arrived, the aircraft – actually the Luftwaffe's new, revolutionary Me 262 'Schwalbe' jet fighter - disappeared, its roar bouncing off the mountainsides then fading away. 'Yes, the Führer has given us some wonderful weapons,' Erwin remarked drily, looking at Martin, who seemed to be studying the dirt of the path intently. Werner continued to scan the mountains for more signs of the noisy Swallow.

'What would von Clausewitz have said I wonder, eh Martin?' Erwin asked. Martin looked up, fixed Erwin with a puzzled stare.

Erwin tried again.

'What do you think about our wonder weapon to smite the enemy?' With not a flicker of a smile Martin quoted a well-worn phrase by von Clausewitz drummed into every German army officer: 'Never forget that no military leader has ever become great without audacity.' Erwin grinned uncertainly, not sure if Martin was joking or being serious.

* * *

Werner had arranged for a pony and trap, with driver, to wait at the bottom of the trail, and for that they were very grateful as their convalescence clearly still had a way to go. Erwin's leg was getting very painful, while Martin found he had no physical stamina, or at least not compared with his old self.

Even a long walk back down via an easy route had tired the wounded warriors out, but not Werner. The wiry, tough 50-year-old had spent his entire life in the mountains, including combat against the Italians above Trento during the last war.

Turning into the gates of the Casino Convalescent Hospital, they found a large black Mercedes 260D blocking the way. The car's florid-faced driver was dozing in his seat, head resting against the window; Werner dismounted and rapped on it with his knuckles. The driver was startled, setting off the car horn by accident. Werner jerked his thumb and mouthed: 'Get out the way.'

The driver nodded, started the engine, moving the Mercedes across to the other side of the small car park. Werner climbed back up onto the trap, whose driver tugged the reins, pulling it around to the front steps of the hospital, his passengers dismounting.

'Thanks for the adventure,' Erwin said, reaching up to shake the mountain guide's hand.

'Any time lads.'

As the two officers entered the hospital lobby, they didn't notice a slim, blonde-haired man in a well-tailored black double-breasted suit sitting in a winged chair by a table loaded with magazines.

On seeing the two men in mountaineering gear, the female receptionist called out: 'This is them Herr Hecht!'

Pulling himself out of the chair, Hecht strode forward, hand out towards Erwin. 'Hauptstürmfuhrer Walder?' he enquired, broad grin on his well-polished face.

Erwin shook his head.

'Afraid not.'

Turning to Martin, Hecht said:

'Please accept my apologies.'

He reached inside his jacket and pulled out an identity disk, which he flashed at them, revealing himself to be Kriminalinspektor Alois Hecht of State Security. Martin frowned, feeling his gut tighten.

An emissary from the Gestapo…

This did not promise good things.

Seeing the perturbed expression on Martin's face, Hecht laughed self-consciously. 'Oh forgive me...it's nothing to worry about. I've merely been sent to take you to Berlin, Haupstürmfuhrer.'

'Because...?'

Hecht beamed, even reaching forward to give Martin a reassuring touch on the arm, but sensing a certain frostiness, withdrew his hand.

These two military officers were not the least bit awestruck by his title or the organisation he worked for.

Pulling himself up, tugging his suit jacket down at the front - keenly aware onlookers were watching the exchange with great interest - Hecht beamed, and announced rather too loudly: 'The Führer himself is to award you the Knight's Cross with Oak Leaves and Swords for your outstanding bravery in the fight against Bolshevism.'

Turning to look at Martin with renewed curiosity, Erwin observed: 'You kept that quiet.'

Martin continued to frown and Hecht shifted uneasily from foot to foot, grin fixed on his face.

'What for?' Martin asked coldly. 'I was shot in the head.'

'I'll see you later,' Erwin suggested, heading for the stairs.

Steering Martin over towards the entrance, Hecht explained eagerly: 'In such challenging times the Reich needs every hero it can get.'

Pointing at the black Mercedes parked outside, he added: 'Your car awaits. So, could you please go up and pack a bag, so we can get this show on the road.'

Martin closed his eyes, listening to the river crashing through the town, which somehow calmed him. Yet, he knew that any dreams he had of a few more weeks healing body, mind and soul - and maybe even the chance of some romance with a particular girl - had disappeared with the arrival of this bastard in a bespoke suit. Martin sighed, opened his eyes, and fixed Hecht with a glare.

Swallowing nervously, Hecht grinned and offered: 'Cheer up. It's a medal from Adolf, not a firing squad.'

Without a word the SS officer exited to get his things.

There was something about Martin that unsettled Hecht even though they'd only just met. There again, he'd *never* been totally at ease in the company of soldiers, no matter how well he hid it.

But, if he was to succeed in delivering a satisfactory outcome of his investigation into Martin's parents - and their harbouring of an enemy of the State - he had to somehow manipulate him into doing his bidding.

4

As a child Hecht had been forced to endure several long rail journeys with his mother and an aunt who never stopped talking, so he was quite happy to travel in silence and study the landscape from the front passenger seat, or even just snooze.

On the first leg of the return journey to Berlin - deliberately not the most straight forward, fastest route like via Munich, as Hecht fancied stopping at Prague overnight to observe and work on Martin - they wound their way down past Salzburg, including using the short stretch of West Autobahn, whose further construction had been frozen for a couple of years.

Hecht couldn't help but remark aloud that it was the Führer himself – *an Austrian of course* – who had turned the first sod when they started the West Autobahn's construction in 1938. Martin did not react while the heavyset, beetle-browed driver seemed to not even notice the remark.

Kriminalassistent Gunther Kruger, was a real Trojan, never complaining despite his many hours behind the wheel. A simple man, he was the son of a tram conductor and a washerwoman. Born in Leipzig, as a youngster he'd served as a trooper in the 18th Uhlans, who started the First World War as cavalry, but ended up as infantry in the trenches. After the Armistice Kruger joined the Freikorps and terrorized the Ukraine, before his talent for dishing out rough justice took him into the Prussian constabulary in the mid-1920s. By 1931 he'd transferred into the political squad, based in Berlin, a useful human cudgel for use against undesirables like the Bolsheviks. In 1933 Kruger was sent to Department 1A as a driver come strongarm man (on round-ups of communist agitators) and general dogsbody to investigators. In his early days in the Prussian force he had knuckle-dusted his share of Nazis too, but that all changed under Hitler's rule.

By 1934 Department 1A had been transformed into the Gestapo and, after a turf war in the upper echelons of management, it had become a wing of the SS.

Kruger first met Hecht in the spring of 1939, and they became a good team. The investigator - *clearly a son of the upper class* - had been some kind of dissolute young lawyer prior to the war and provided the smooth for Kruger's rough.

He'd first set eyes on Kruger as the latter waited outside the Gestapo headquarters in Berlin – at Prinz-Albrecht-Strasse, home of the Reich Security Main Office.

A substantial three-storey former 'Museum of the Decorative Arts', it contained cells in its basements where interrogators, torturers and executioners performed their service to the Reich. They were virtuosos in the art of keeping a suspect on the fine line between life and death until all that could usefully be gleaned from them was obtained...and then despatched the miscreants to Hades.

As he loitered, Kruger found himself instinctively disliking what looked like *a right ponce on the other side of the road.*

It was actually none other than Hecht, whose light mac was flapping in the breeze, revealing a fashionable pin-striped suit, but the Kriminalinspektor's cherry brown brogues came to a halt just as he was about to step off the kerb.

A hand passed over the carefully slicked back hair – checking for even one strand out of place - and Hecht adopted a pleasant smile for an old lady he decided to help across the street. As he took her by the elbow she likely felt a little anxious where she might end up, but fortunately her fears were unfounded. Having said goodbye to the old dear, Hecht turned and came up the steps, spotting Kruger, guessing this must be his new assistant. With the smile from his good deed wiped instantly from his face, Hecht observed rather sternly: 'Ah, you must be my new factotum?'

Kruger had *no fucking clue* what that was.

He soon discovered the man who, on first look he'd dismissed as *a bit of a fairy*, was a hard-as-nails, ruthless operator who needed a blunt instrument to back up the scalpel of his investigator's cunning intellect.

Not that Hecht couldn't apply lethal force. Once, when clearing out an illegal campsite of gypsies, they found themselves engaged in a brawl. Then, as three angry Romanies came hell for leather at them through the trees - wielding knives and clubs with nails embedded in them - Hecht wasted no time in pulling out his Mauser HSc and shooting them all dead. It was not easy to hit a man at that range with a pistol, especially with the target flitting between trees.

Kruger decided Hecht was a most uncommon Nazi, one who read English language novels and poetry and had a taste for jazz, a music form considered offensive by the regime due to many of its exponents being black or Jewish. Kruger let the dubious cultural leanings slide, admiring the sheer drive of Hecht, who possessed a fanatical determination never to let a case beat him.

Kruger felt he and Hecht shared the same world view: Hitler had pulled Germany from the sewage pit of history, so any bastard who tried to push it back down there deserved to get all that was coming to him. Sometimes Kruger did wonder about what went on in Hecht's head. There was the occasional crack about the Führer and his henchmen that bordered on sedition, but Kruger took them as jokes to ease the stresses and strains of the average day. Nothing serious. Banter.

Hecht didn't really mean that Goebbels was a braying jackass or that Heydrich was really no more than an ambitious pervert. Hecht never exposed himself like that in front of anyone else anyway, so it didn't matter.

When it came to personal details, Hecht knew all about Kruger's record. Kruger knew only that his boss came from Munich and, yes, had been some kind of lawyer before joining the Gestapo. Whether Hecht was married or not, Kruger had no idea. The invites extended for Hecht to come over for dinner with Kruger's family never seemed to result in anything. There'd been no opportunity to strip away some of the Kriminalinspektor's highly polished veneer and see what lay beneath.

* * *

Glancing in the rear-view mirror, Hecht noticed Martin had closed his eyes, but he thought this was perhaps a ploy to avoid being engaged in conversation, which was fine. Martin had, meanwhile, drifted off into his own recent past, to an event not long after he'd arrived at the convalescent hospital.

* * *

It was the afternoon of the Heroes Dance, a special social occasion hosted by the Hotel Schöner Berg on its Grand Terrace with its superb view down the Kötschach Valley. Erwin and Martin sat at one of several tables which had been laid for a celebratory lunch, the debris of which now lay scattered across its surface.

An oompah band dressed in feathered hats and traditional Austrian tracht pumped out tunes enthusiastically, but too loud for Martin's liking. Erwin, with a cigarette clamped between his teeth, banged a hand in time on the table, making cutlery and plates clink and dance. For their outing, both men were wearing plain grey double-breasted suits with open-collared white shirt, the invalid uniform for officers recovering at the Casino Hospital. While by this time the bandages covering his eyes had gone, Martin still wore sunglasses to protect them.

Erwin leaned forward, suggesting: 'We can leave, if all this is too much.'

Martin shook his head, for he was enjoying the sun.

'I'm fine.'

'Are you sure?'

'Go and dance with a pretty nurse, that one you've had your eye on.'

That would stop Erwin hammering on the table.

'Please, do.'

Erwin beamed at this excellent idea.

'Nurse Gottlieb is very appealing.'

Erwin made a beeline for his target while Martin took his sunglasses off as they were irritating him. His face appeared undamaged, aside from a few slight scars above and below the eyes, but his vision was still blurred. He reached for a glass of water, in the process brushing the sunglasses off the table without noticing. Martin surveyed the surroundings, which were an indistinct mass of shapes in browns, reds, yellows, greens and blues.

He blinked hard, his vision sharpening then going out of focus again.

'You've dropped your sunglasses.'

Turning to see who owned the voice, Martin's eyes focussed sharply.

He was instantly captivated, heart thumping, every detail of her beautiful face shocking in its clarity. The waitress placed his sunglasses back on the table but he didn't put them on.

She was the picture of radiant beauty: long blonde hair tumbling in to her shoulders; flawless pale skin; full, sensuous lips; crystal clear blue eyes. All this registered in seconds, an overwhelming flood of sheer emotion surging through him. Martin had never felt anything like it. He knew she was clear, cool water in which he could wash off the grime of war.

Far from finding this unsettling, there was something about his frank gaze that she liked. He was handsome enough, in a lean way, but it was those penetrating blue eyes. Something stirred inside her and Lorelei tried to hide her inner turmoil with a bland question: 'Would you like a drink, Sir?'

'No, thanks.'

She blushed and moved on, feeling his eyes following her as she navigated between the tables. Lorelei looked back, then quickly away again. He was still staring at her.

* * *

Desperate to escape the nerve-jangling music and shocked by the intensity of emotions the girl's beauty provoked, Martin got unsteadily to his feet. He carefully made his way between the tables and down steps leading to a stream that bisected the hotel village. He paused on the low, stone-clad bridge spanning the stream, still shocked at the clarity of his restored sight.

Below, trout flicked slowly to and fro, Martin wincing from light dancing on the water. Crossing the bridge, he paused at a sign beside the path leading down into the woods. It showed a crudely painted troll pointing west.

Within a speech bubble, the creature declared: 'Flusspfad!'

River path!

Once into the woods Martin's eyes flickered anxiously from side to side, initially fearful of shafts of light, but he was determined not to retreat.

He cautiously edged forwards until the toe caps of his shoes were inside a bright circle, but holding the rest of himself back in the shadows. He reached in, as if plunging a limb into a pool of water, swirling his arm around. Closing his eyes, he stepped into it, throwing his head back to bathe in the warmth.

* * *

Martin had no idea how long he'd been in the woods, stopping every now and then to stare in wonder at some fragment of loveliness.

One such - a vivid, purple orchid - flashed him back to his childhood, when, as a five-year-old, exploring woods near his home he had come across a clearing carpeted with orchids of every colour.

Martin knelt beside this orchid, afraid to reach out and touch the flower, for fear of it vanishing. He found courage, fingers caressing the petals of the delicate flower. It was quite the most stunning and beautiful thing he had seen in his life, except for the waitress at the Schöner Berg. Suddenly he was afflicted with terrible sadness. Tears leaked from Martin's eyes; bitter, hot tears of regret, a longing for that which he knew could never be his. Closing his eyes, he tried to recall the pure, unsullied wonder he felt as a young boy during his wanderings in the woods. For a few, brief seconds he was again back there, amid the orchids of his childhood.

* * *

Time and distance again passed in a blur. The trees receded up the slopes and in a meadow he came across a small, deserted lodge with animal traps hanging from its eaves. This unsettled him, disturbing his bucolic dream with the hint of a bad memory that lurked in the shadows but did not yet force its way into the light.

Moving on, Martin found the trees pressing down on the path again. Stepping off, he went down towards the stream. He stood dead still watching the water wash gently over rocks. A gap in the canopy allowed another shaft of light to hit his face, Martin turning his head away, but then staring up again, was unafraid. His eyes went from cloudy to clear blue, the scars around them washed out.

* * *

Martin's head had been filled not with thoughts of war, for he seemed to have entered a new born state - filled with everything and nothing all at once. A child's cry pulled him back to reality and, staying on the dark edge of the treeline, he slowly edged along parallel to the path, discovering another lodge, this one occupied. By it a young mother was gathering in washing from a line strung between two trees, singing to herself - happy as a lark in the alpine sunshine. The child cried out again, not a brief protest, but a prolonged, insistent wailing for attention; for someone to soothe away pain.

The mother stopped, momentarily disappearing from view.

She reappeared with a baby in her arms, stroking its hair and kissing one of its hands. This scenario stirred something deep and terrifying lodged within the darkest recesses of Martin's memory, dragging him back to a world of turmoil from his pantheist daze. The smell of burning flesh filled his nostrils, the screams of the dying were in his head, along with the crackle of all-consuming flames - he was dipped into a cold sweat of shame.

The woman took the child inside the lodge and now Werner the mountaineering huntsman who sometimes worked for the Schöner Berg appeared at the door, eyes scanning the woods.

Spotting someone loitering on the edge of the trees, Werner's brow darkened and he shouted something – what exactly Martin could not make out.

Reaching back inside the lodge, Werner grabbed a rifle, which he held across his chest. Werner shouted again and this time Martin heard him: 'Are you lost!?' Nodding, Martin stepped out from the shadows into the light. Noticing the wounded warrior suit, and realising this was a poorly boy from the Casino Hospital, Werner shouted back: 'I'll get you home!'

5

When he awoke, dry-mouthed and with a throbbing head, Martin found Hecht asleep in the front passenger seat, mouth agape. Kruger was hunched over the wheel, folds of flesh on the back of his close-cropped head creased, chewing his lip to stop himself from dropping off.

Noticing via the rear-view mirror that Martin had stirred, the Gestapo driver grimaced in an attempt at a friendly smile, provoking a nod of acknowledgement from his passenger.

Martin turned his head to stare blankly out the window at a passing landscape of vibrant green fields and forest but soon nodded off again. Arriving very late in Prague, which, since 1939, had been capital of the Reich Protectorate of Bohemia, Kruger drove them up a winding street to the top of a hill upon which clustered Hdraçany, the Castle District, pulling to a halt at a roadblock manned by leather-coated SS Field Police troops. One of them leaned in at the open front passenger window, MP40 slung across his chest and silver gorget at his throat flashing in the torchlight.

'What's going on?' Hecht asked equably, handing over his identity disk. After scrutinising the ID with a comrade over by the barrier the SS policeman returned it. Helmet rim knocking against the window frame, he shone his torch into the back of the car, revealing someone in a scruffy suit and open necked shirt. Martin shielded his eyes against its glare with a cupped hand.

Hecht shoved the torch back out the window, opening the door forcefully and stepping out. Kruger stretched, yawned widely while Martin observed what unfolded via the side window. Hecht engaged in a very animated conversation, jabbing an angry finger at the SS policeman who looked embarrassed and nodded. Then the SS policeman said something that visibly stiffened Hecht who, looking shocked, immediately stopped berating him and turned on his heels. Climbing back into the car and leaning over the back of the seat, he revealed breathlessly: 'Some bunch of fuckers tried to kill the Führer.'

Kruger gasped, unable to believe it.

Martin sat forward, gripping Hecht's shoulder hard and asked: 'Can that be true?'

'There's a lockdown all over the Reich,' explained Hecht with a grimace. Releasing his grip, Martin sat back.

Kruger gunned the engine as he swung the Mercedes out past the roadblock while Hecht massaged his arm. 'Where to boss?' Kruger enquired solemnly.

'Let's try and get some rooms at the Savoy,' Hecht suggested.

* * *

The Kriminalinspektor was at his most charming during a short chat with the manager of the hotel, but would anybody ever dare refuse the Gestapo? Some Wehrmacht staff officers were turfed out of their suites and sent across the city to a barracks. With many of their comrades being taken in for questioning over the attempt to kill the Führer, they departed eagerly rather than share the hotel with the secret police.

Kruger was sent to fetch the luggage, which wasn't much - just Martin's carpetbag, which he had borrowed from the hospital, Hecht's weekend bag and his own small case.

An obsequious waiter escorted Hecht and Martin across the

vast, empty, dimly lit restaurant, placing them at a table under an ornate skylight. He brought them a bottle of red wine and two glasses, whispering something in Hecht's ear. Martin stared up at the stars and, for a moment, was back on the vast Russian steppe, below a vaulted night sky.

The waiter poured the wine, left the bottle in the centre of the table and backed away. Hecht picked up one of the glasses, gently clinking it on the rim of the other to attract Martin's attention.

'Haupsturmführer?'

Martin gave him a quizzical look.

'It's a pinot noir,' Hecht told him, with a freeloading grin, 'compliments of the management.'

Reaching for the remaining glass, Martin asked:

'Will the medal presentation still go ahead?'

Hecht shrugged, poured and sipped some wine.

'We should proceed to Berlin.'

Hecht pulled a slim, silver tin from his jacket's inside pocket, opening it to reveal cigarillos.

'A smoke?'

'No thanks,' Martin responded, trying the wine, which even his unsophisticated, soldier's palate appreciated.

'Shocking news though, isn't it?' Hecht suggested, blowing smoke out the left-hand corner of his mouth, then sipping wine with the right.

'Who did it?'

Hecht sighed heavily.

'Some Wehrmacht swine.'

'How did they think they could get away with it?'

'They almost did,' Hecht revealed, grabbing a Bohemian crystal ashtray and moving it closer. 'Apparently the Führer was injured by a bomb, or so the SS Field Police told me at the roadblock.'

'Fuck,' Martin observed.

Hecht nodded.

'Fuck indeed.'

The waiter returned, carrying three menus, with Kruger lumbering along in his wake. He presented one of the menus to

Hecht, then scurried around to Martin's side, opening a menu, placing it in his hands. The third one he left on the table. Kruger sat down and opened it to scan the offerings voraciously, for he was a man who enjoyed his food and was famished after the long drive.

'What the hell are *you* doing?' Hecht asked.

Startled by Hecht's angry tone, Kruger looked over the top of the menu, eyes wide. 'If you go to the kitchen I'm sure they'll give you some garlic soup,' Hecht suggested, the rudest he had ever been to a subordinate, prompted by the underlying anxiety of chaperoning Martin.

'Come on, Hecht,' Martin pleaded, shocked by the Kriminalinspektor's lack of care and respect.

Hecht sighed, realising the long drive had made overly irritated.

'Alright Kruger, but eat with your mouth closed this time.'

'Yes, Sir!'

Looking dismayed, Hecht turned the menu around so the other two could see and jabbed it with a finger.

'Dumplings with everything. I bet they're dry, too.'

* * *

As a Central European city, Prague could be unbearably hot during the summer, but in the park on Petrin Hill, it breathed.

Just along from where Martin reposed on a bench, the passenger carriages of a funicular railway crawled centipede-like towards the top and, mind blank, he was content to watch their progress up and down for a few minutes. Turning his eyes away from the funicular, he found the red-tiled roofs of the houses in the Mala Strana district - sprawling along the west bank of the Vltava River, which bisected the city - glowing as the burning orb of the sun broke free from a passing cloud.

Martin got up, crossed a bridge over the funicular, which rumbled away beneath his feet, and walked along a path through some trees to the Petrin Lookout Tower.

An inferior copy of Eiffel's, it was built in 1891, after some locals were impressed by the Paris edifice and decided to create their own as part of a Prague version of the World's Fair. It became a proud boast that, with the assistance of the Petrin Hill, the top of their tower was the same height as the French one.

Martin found the entrance hall open but there was nobody behind the ticket desk, so he began his ascent up the steps to an observation platform. Finding it more tiring than the mountain climb, the higher Martin got the more he needed the handrail's assistance.

At the top, after grimacing and wheezing, Martin laughed at being an idiot to even bother. The view through the windows was worse than it had been from the bench - distorted, with the colour of the Prague panorama obscured by grime. Martin heard a footfall on the steps and somebody coughing and cursing, then Hecht emerged, looking very sweaty and hot in his suit.

Martin smiled, enjoying the other man's discomfort.

'Are you unfit?'

Hecht nodded, holding his heaving ribs.

Joining Martin at the window, he tugged down his tie, crying out in anguish: 'All this way to find out the Czech swines don't clean their windows!'

Martin reached up and with a finger wrote in the dirt:

Long live the Führer

The man had been so much part of his life since he was a teenager. To suddenly not have him there, to even think of no more Hitler would have been strange. He would never escape the Führer, as his very soul was stained by the deeds he had committed in that man's name, but what of this oily Gestapo functionary? How loyal was he in the wake of the assassination attempt – what might he write in the grime?

'So?' Martin enquired.

Hecht looked at the writing on the window and was bemused.

'What?'

'Full stop…or question mark?'

Hecht frowned, recognizing the nature of the test – following the assassination attempt every German's loyalty to the Führer would be doubly scrutinised. And by posing this question Martin revealed he may not be as straight-forward to manipulate - a means to an end - as Hecht had hoped. He pursed his lips and then add an exclamation to the end.

Long Live the Führer!

Martin was impressed.

This Gestapo man was a born survivor.

* * *

On their way through the park, Hecht noticed a dingy building with the façade of a Bohemian fairy tale castle, and a fancy sign above an entrance arch declaring it to be a 'Mirror Maze.'

'I haven't been in one of those since I was a kid,' Hecht remarked.

Giving his companion an imploring look he asked:

'Can we? A bit of fun before we head off?'

Martin was in no hurry to be trapped for hours in the stuffy Mercedes, so raised no objection.

'If you want to.'

The Gestapo investigator gave an elderly man huddled in a kiosk some Protectorate Crowns, for which he appeared pathetically grateful, pulling aside a cordon barring the entrance with a profusion of bowing and scraping.

They passed into a vaulted hall, both blinking at the sudden brightness, for its walls were covered in mirrors framed by wooden pillars, which reflected multiple versions of the two men, going away into a dizzying infinity.

Making their exit they found themselves in a smaller room, in which yellowish light bathed everything, courtesy of three small, fake crystal chandeliers suspended tenuously from a low, Prussian green-painted ceiling. Turning to one of the mirrors, Hecht broke into a fit of giggles, as he was confronted with a squashed version of himself - face all stretched out sideways and with a tractor tyre for a waist.

The neighbouring mirror made Martin into a stick insect, the effect not appearing to amuse him in any discernible fashion.

Hecht thought maybe it insulted the Waffen SS officer's dignity, or perhaps Martin was laughing on the inside? Either way it pleased him after Martin's trick with the writing in the dirt of the tower window. Moving on to another mirror, Hecht exclaimed with a laugh:

'Look at me, a human squeezebox!'

Martin did not look, as he was scrutinising a chandelier hanging directly overhead. Coming over, Hecht filled the contemplative silence by asking sarcastically: 'Do you think they were inspired by Versailles?'

Martin circled slowly underneath the chandelier, examining the way that even a fake refracted the light in green, cobalt blue and white.

'You know, The Hall of Mirrors,' Hecht persisted, his voice echoing hoarsely, 'where we took the French surrender in 1870?'

Martin stopped circling and shot the Gestapo man a mocking look.

'A schoolboy error Herr Hecht for the French had already surrendered at Sedan. The Hall of Mirrors was used by Bismarck to declare a unified Germany.'

How pale the other man suddenly looked.

Couldn't stand to be wrong, eh?

'We all make mistakes,' Martin told him, moving away to inspect himself in a mirror down the far end.

To get over his embarrassment, Hecht looked up at the chandelier, a kaleidoscope of colours dancing on his face while loud, almost hysterical, laughter exploded from Martin.

The Gestapo man was amazed at the dour soldier's sudden surrender to hilarity and went over to see what was so amusing.

It was the final mirror before the exit and Hecht was disappointed to discover that it was just a normal reflection, yet Martin continued to laugh as he looked at himself: a tall, spare young man, unshaven and in badly tailored suit that hung off him.

Feeling rising irritation with his soldier companion, Hecht remarked sharply: 'We really must do something about your attire.'

The Gestapo man turned and strode away, headed for the exit, leaving Martin staring dazedly into the mirror. He did not see himself, though but rather the waitress as he'd first laid eyes on her at the Heroes' Dance; shining blonde hair framing her lovely face.

Lorelei.

Martin had obtained her name via Nurse Gottlieb, who had a friend who worked in the kitchens of the hotel village. He intended to ask Lorelei out, once he could pluck up the courage.

Even her name appealed to his ideas of valour and romanticism.

From his teenage years, Martin had been fond of the traditional German tale in which a beautiful, mysterious maiden named Lorelei makes a knight fall in love with her. The knight then wanders the woods under her spell, while she uses her siren call to lure him to his death in a boat on the rocks of the turbulent Rhine.

A battle hardened warrior who had sated his lust from time to time, but was still, in many ways, an adolescent in matters of love – Martin had been drawn to day-dreaming of winning Lorelei's heart. Still looking at his reflection in the Prague maze of mirrors, a tidal wave of irrational emotion suddenly surged through Martin and he was swept to another place.

Choking it back and closing his eyes, images from battle-ravaged Kharkov flashed through his mind: a tank exploding in the street outside the tenement as its ammunition cooked off; the shimmering icon of the Madonna and Child on the wall; a dark pool of blood spreading across the floorboards; life fading from the female Russian sniper's eyes.

* * *

'Haupsturmführer Walder, are you alright?'

On realising Martin had not followed him out of the exit, Hecht returned to find him leaning against the mirror, eyes closed and pale-faced. The Gestapo man's interruption echoed harshly.

'I'm fine!' Martin snapped.

As they walked back along the path across the top of Petrin Hill, a breeze carried the sound of the Vltava sweeping over a weir up to them - it blanked out Martin's thoughts, filling his mind with a rushing roar he was grateful for.

Later, in the car and with Prague falling swiftly behind, the residue of Martin's meditation distilled into a cruel realisation. He had always assumed that death would come on some battlefield, in honour of the Fatherland.

He had accepted that fate a long time ago.

Now he wasn't so certain. That he deserved to die for his sins Martin was sure - for what soldier who'd fought in the East remained unstained?

6

HEADING NORTH, skirting Dresden, they stopped once at a roadside inn for Hecht to use the telephone. He was keen to try and find out more on the attempt to kill the Führer and fill a coffee flask that he extracted from a duffel bag.

On reaching the outskirts of the German capital an hour or so before dawn, they continued to make good speed, for there were few cars or trucks, or anything else, on the pre-dawn roads.

'I thought you might like a diversion to the AVUS,' revealed Hecht, 'as I think it's best to stay away from Gestapo Headquarters in the Prinz-Albert Strasse for an hour or two more as they'll be very busy right now with suspected plotters.'

The truth was that, when studying Martin's old Hitler Youth files, Hecht spotted that as a youngster he liked watching motorcycle and Grand Prix motor racing.

The Automobil-Verkehrs-und Übungsstraße, or AVUS, was a racing circuit finished in the early 1920s and incorporated into the Berliner Ring, an autobahn that served as an orbital major traffic artery. Its two sides formed an arrow straight, tree-lined highway feeding traffic to the edge of the city centre itself, where older roads filtered off.

At the northern end of the AVUS, Kruger brought the Mercedes off the road, coming to a halt beside a concrete spectator tower that had four tiers of balconies running around its exterior.

Uncurtained windows punctured the white tube at the core of this structure, some of which were already reflecting the cold light of dawn.

Beyond the steeply banked curve of race track that peeled away from the road lay Berlin's suburbs, awaiting an ascending sun burning off the night. Martin noticed as they entered the tower that the concrete was sweating, making the green mould in the shady crevices of its roughened surface glisten. The two men leaned against the balcony of the lower tier, the sun's rays slowly creeping around the AVUS. Hecht produced two white-enamelled metal mugs from the duffel bag, which he had brought with him from the car, handing them to Martin, who was shivering in his thin suit.

'This will warm us up,' suggested Hecht, whose coat kept him only a little better insulated against the dawn chill.

He pulled the brushed metal flask from the bag, unscrewing the stopper. Hecht added, with a note of triumph: 'None of this Acorn shit, real coffee, so the innkeeper told me. I should imagine he was keen to please State Security, though too stupid to realise I could have arrested him for profiteering.'

Teeth chattering, Martin tried to keep his shaking hands steady as Hecht poured steaming black liquid into the mugs.

The Gestapo man put the flask down and lit a cigarillo – Martin was offered one but again declined. He was surprised at an official of the Nazi state smoking so brazenly in front of someone whom he did not know. Members of the police or security forces were banned from smoking in public, and it was frowned upon by the regime, whose scientists claimed it caused cancer.

As the sun finally reached the tower Hecht smiled, took one of the mugs from Martin and luxuriated in the coffee's warmth and his defiant cigar. Martin sipped his coffee hesitantly, for it was very hot, the heat transmitting through the handle and burning his hand, so he held it gingerly between thumb and forefinger. Below, Kruger walked up and down beside the car, which was still in the shadows, stamping his feet. Every now and then he glanced imploringly at their balcony, but Hecht did not invite him up.

'I see the Gestapo is consorting with an enemy of the people,' Martin observed archly. Hecht looked puzzled, narrowing his eyes as he blew smoke away out the corner of his mouth and enquired: 'I'm sorry?'

Laughing at the expression on Hecht's face, Martin suggested: 'Didn't Hitler condemn tobacco as "an enemy of the people"?'

'And yet,' Hecht remarked, with a shrug, more sure of himself this time, 'it's not illegal and wherever you go from the Dover Straits to darkest, deepest Russia, our boys are sustained by cigarette rations - are they not hauptsturmführer?'

Martin nodded, observing: 'You're right. God bless nicotine.'

'Did you ever come to see any racing here?' Hecht asked to change the subject. 'Yes, as a boy,' Martin admitted.

Taking a sip of coffee, Hecht revealed: 'I came to see the Olympics cycling here in 1936.'

'I was there, too,' Martin responded, looking rather wistful.

Hecht exhaled more cigar smoke, carefully blowing it away from them. Martin was not forthcoming on any further details.

It suddenly occurred to Martin that the Gestapo man had looked deeply into his background, even into his teenage hobbies.

Of course he had, for that was what snoopers did.

What else had Hecht dug up?

Out of curiosity he decided to play along.

'Most of all, Herr Hecht, I remember the smell of the hot fuel and the roar of car engines when there were races here. Quite intoxicating. The sheer power put into the air was an assault on all the senses.'

Hecht smiled and nodded, impressed by Martin's lyrical turn.

Martin decided on a direct question.

'Might I ask, while we're being so chummy, why anyone would send a Gestapo man on a messenger boy errand to fetch me to Berlin for a medal presentation?'

This put Hecht slightly off balance, so he took his time responding, blowing out cigar smoke and taking a long, slow sip of coffee.

He then tipped what was left in the cup over the side of the balcony, putting it back in the duffel bag, which was at his feet. Straightening up he found Martin giving him a hard, penetrating stare.

'So?'

Hecht grinned self-consciously, but resisted the impulse to shrug again, which would be too deliberately nonchalant.

'I'll be blunt haupsturmführer; this is all part of a big morale-boosting publicity stunt.'

Martin had suspected as much but it still stung a little to hear his cynicism confirmed.

'It's like this: the Führer is briefed on your heroics at Kharkov, along with all the wonderful deeds of many others. Reichsführer Himmler is reluctant to single you out, but the order comes down to us anyway, to me - as I am apparently at a loose end – to go and fetch you to Berlin for some good news creation.'

Martin sighed, drained his own mug and then tipped it over the edge of the balcony, shaking the dregs out.

As he took the empty mug off Martin and slid it into the duffel bag Hecht explained: 'It's a big deal, greater now I suppose, in the wake of the attempt to kill the Führer. It will become even more important as a demonstration he is still in charge, and that the troops of the Waffen SS in particular remain loyal. Your visit is serendipitous.'

Martin felt like chucking his guts up and wished this Gestapo prick would shut his bloody mouth.

Then Hecht said something that further darkened Martin's mood: 'I wonder if you'd like your parents there?'

Martin ignored the question, choosing to seem as if he was enjoying the view across Berlin but Hecht wouldn't let it go.

'Would that please you?

'That won't be necessary.'

'It's up to you,' suggested Hecht, 'I just thought…'

'I'll play along with this stupid medal ceremony,' Martin snapped, 'but don't get my family involved.'

'Are they not proud National Socialists?'

Martin gripped the concrete balustrade hard, his knuckles turning white. 'Loyal and proud,' he responded frostily.

'My dear haupsturmführer, it's all about what you want and if you'd like your mum and dad to be there.'

Hecht shrugged, adding: 'Or not.'

He placed a reassuring hand on the other man's tensed forearm, a deliberate provocation. Martin shoved Hecht's hand away and walked around the balcony. He halted, looking south across the city towards Dahlem, where his parents lived, his head spinning.

While his father was a Protestant pastor, and by instinct against much of what the Nazis stood for, he had never been one to raise his head above the parapet. Martin had been estranged from his parents for some years – it had been a choice of Party or family and he had picked the former. That Hecht was so keen to have them attend the medal ceremony aggravated him intensely.

* * *

With the Mercedes getting closer to the city centre, there were more and more roadblocks manned by nervy-looking troops with itchy trigger fingers.

Hecht usually climbed out to have a discussion with the commander, showing his ID and explaining that he was bringing a hero of the Reich to meet the Führer. In each case, after a fusillade of shouted orders from the officer or NCO commanding, the barrier was removed to let the car pass through.

As the car proceeded it was clear to Martin's eyes the bunting clad, arrogant days of triumph in the German capital had been replaced with ruination.

He was shocked at the battered and scruffy state of central Berlin, with rubble where familiar buildings used to be and many of those left standing were scorched and partially demolished; according to Hecht residential areas further out had been devastated.

Martin saw combined squads of elderly men and boys of the Hitler Youth bending to the neighbourly task of wielding brushes or lugging debris in a bomb-blasted street. They were creating mounds of detritus beside lorries while others shovelled it onto their tippers. The bright morning sun through a cloud of dust made spectres of them.

One of the checkpoints was run by Waffen SS troops and from the back of the car Martin couldn't help inspecting their uniforms with a professional eye – their neatly pressed tunics, highly polished boots, helmet chin straps at the precisely correct angle under the chin passed muster.

With a sinking feeling, Martin realized that he recognized the untersturmführer in charge - a kid named Lehmann. He shrank down in the seat, wanting to avoid being seen but that bloody fool Hecht, deploying his usual patter, only encouraged the keen young officer to come over. Lehmann took off his cap and poked his head in through the open front passenger window of the car. With a grin of recognition, he declared: 'It really is you Haupsturmführer Walder!'

An arm shot into the car.

'It will be an honour, to shake the hand of a hero.'

Martin leaned over the seat, taking the other man's hand, remarking with false jocularity: 'Lehmann, from the Leibstandarte, who we got out of the shit near Minsk.' The youngster's grin got even broader and he glowed at being remembered by a hero, but, taking in Martin's generally gaunt appearance, there was a flicker of dismay.

This was not how Waffen SS heroes were supposed to look.

Withdrawing from the car Lehmann ran back to the barrier, shouting at his men to move it aside. As the Mercedes swept by, Lehmann threw his right arm into the air, screaming: 'Heil Hitler!'

Martin's eyes met Lehmann's for a moment, finding a fanatical light that his own could no longer reflect. In that moment, Martin crossed the Rubicon, knowing he would never again feel like the eager young stormtrooper.

* * *

Not long after, Kruger swung the wheel violently, the Mercedes sweeping around in front of the grand columns of the Brandenburg Gate, the car easing to a halt outside the Hotel Adlon.

'These are your lodgings,' Hecht revealed with a pleased smile.

Martin was genuinely impressed, remarking:

'Quite a change from a foxhole or a hospital.'

'I should bloody well hope so,' Hecht snorted. 'If it's fine enough for Charlie Chaplin, it's good enough for a hero of the Reich.'

Jumping out, Hecht opened the door for Martin while Kruger fetched the carpetbag from the boot.

They escorted him into the lobby, the receptionist initially bemused by why two Gestapo men - *surely State Security, as they reeked of it* - were bringing a raggedy-looking prisoner into *his* hotel.

Hecht clarified things, explaining that a booking had been made and the Adlon must ensure this brave Waffen SS officer was settled into one of the best suites. State Security would pick up the bill. Coughing nervously, the receptionist assured the Kriminalinspektor this would most certainly happen.

Clicking his fingers, the receptionist summoned a bellboy not a day under 70-years-old whose arthritic hand grasped the handle of the carpetbag, hoisting it away from Kruger.

Martin felt he had slipped into a bizarre alternate world, so far removed from the blood, mud and bullets of his recent life that it was the stuff of farce.

But he may as well play along with Hecht's design if it got him a suite in what was, even now - after four years of war - still one of Berlin's finest hotels.

'Go upstairs, have a bath and a sleep,' Hecht proposed. 'We'll be back this evening to take you out, to a rather good tailor I know.' Looking Martin up and down, he added: 'Because you can't turn up to get your medal in *that* outfit.'

* * *

Nobody answered the door and there were no lights on. Hecht rang the doorbell of the tailor's shop again, while Martin waited patiently beside him, watching searchlights trailing lazily across the night sky.

'They should be here,' Hecht remarked, deeply embarrassed.

He turned to look at Kruger, sat behind the wheel of the nearby Mercedes picking his nose. 'Did you *really* telephone them and make the appointment?'

Flicking the results of his nasal excavation out the window, Kruger nodded. 'Yes Sir, I did.' Disgusted by the nose picking, Hecht asked harshly: 'Are you sure?'

As if in reply, lights went on in the shop.

Rubbing his hands together and showing a triumphant smile, Hecht revealed to Martin: 'Since we started resettling the Jews there have not been many tailors of the right calibre, but this firm remains superb. Italians, but we won't hold that against them. They make suits better than they fight.'

Once inside, the Gestapo man sat in a chair sipping a cup of coffee, looking on approvingly as Martin was measured for his new Waffen SS officer's tunic, along with trousers, cap and helmet. Again, Martin gave in to the flow. *He was still a soldier under orders, so who was he to argue?*

The tailor – persuaded by money and the implied threat of serious trouble if he didn't comply – agreed that he and his team would work through the night to have the uniform ready for the morning.

Returning Martin to the Adlon, Hecht accompanied him up to the suite, whistling at the opulent, classical décor and furnishings.

'This is some *fancy* barracks,' Hecht remarked in open admiration.

He stopped at a large window in the main salon, which looked down onto the Pariser Platz. Peeking between its heavy blackout curtains, Hecht saw the brooding silhouette of the Brandenburg Gate opposite.

Turning away, he found Martin standing on the other side of the room staring at a huge print of an engraving by Carl Wilhelm Kolbe, totally absorbed in the scene.

It depicted a gnarled, dead oak tree, its disfigured branches clawing the sky. Gargoyle-like faces were contorted horribly in its knots and burls.

A pair of storks crowned the monstrosity, settled on a huge, unruly nest, a fresh, green branch sprouting just beside them. In a glade beyond the tree two young boys lay on the grass staring into the distance – *youth looking to the future and not the past.*

Hecht was distracted by a bottle of champagne chilling in an ice bucket on a coffee table in the centre of the salon. Martin turned away from the engraving and yawned, easing himself down onto a chaise longue by the table. Hecht extracted the champagne bottle, trailing a finger down the outside, making a clean dark line through the condensation.

Turning around to suggest a toast in honour of tomorrow, Hecht found Martin asleep. He touched Martin's knee with the base of the bottle, prompting the soldier's eyes to flicker open.

'I'll be here tomorrow morning, early.'

Martin nodded, closing his eyes again.

'Perhaps you would like some female company tonight?'

This received a shake of the head.

'Alright then. You're lucky as it looks like there's not going to be an air raid this evening. You ought to haul yourself off to bed.'

There was no response. Hecht couldn't believe Martin was going to sleep where he lay, nor fail to drink the champagne or even take a companion to bed with him. With a resigned sigh, Hecht fetched a blanket from atop the wardrobe in the master bedroom and draped it over the slumbering warrior.

7

22 July 1944 – Late Morning

MARTIN'S FINGERS flew up the front of the field grey, silk-lined dress uniform tunic, thumb and forefinger of his right hand pushing the buttons through their holes.

Reaching the dark green collar, he decided to leave that one undone.

This left a nonconformist gap between double lightning flash 'runes' - made from silver wire, on a black wool collar badge - to the right, and, on the left, rank insignia of three silver pips and bars on black.

He lifted his left arm to study the black silver-edged cuff title with the words *Das Reich*, and above it the silver bullion wire eagle with swastika. On each shoulder were the silver braid epaulettes with two silver pips and the insignia of the division, the *Wolfsangel* - the 2nd SS heraldic symbol, in Germanic lore a means of deterring wolves.

Martin's gaze drifted down to the bottom left hand corner of the long mirror. In his mind's eye he imagined Lorelei sitting in front of the mirror at the dressing table of his bedroom in the Hotel Adlon, brushing her long blonde hair, which shone in bright light coming through the window.

In this daydream he leaned against a doorframe, admiring the graceful curve of her neck as she lifted her hair. She was watching him in the mirror and he didn't look away, but returned her smile openly and confidently.

A cough brought Martin back to the tailor's fitting room and, in that mirror, he found Hecht at his shoulder, a black leather belt in his hands and quizzical look splashed across his face. Martin turned and took the belt, clipping it around his waist.

His daydream had been pathetic really, for he didn't know her at all, had never even spoken to Lorelei properly, but she represented something pure and unsullied in a world of chaos and decay. He needed someone or something new in which to invest his faith.

Martin closed the buckle as the Italian tailor reached up and placed the cap on his head. The silver death's head on the black band above the peak grinned wickedly, Martin reaching up with both hands to adjust the angle of the cap until it suited. There he was at last in the mirror: a warrior of the Reich, though wearing straight uniform trousers and shoes rather than the jodhpurs and boots favoured by some. On the belt a ceremonial dagger in a scabbard was suspended from the left-hand side. Martin leaned closer to the mirror, fingertips of his left hand gently caressing the small, barely visible, white scars around his eyes.

A touch on his arm and he turned, to find the tailor holding out a new steel helmet, with SS flashes in a shield on its right-hand side. Martin handed the tailor the cap, took the helmet, pressing it down on his head, fastening the chin strap. Its weight was now so strange, whereas in Russia he had not even noticed it. Martin made the animation drain from his face as he gazed into the mirror, finding a teutonic knight staring back. He smiled, not sure he was convincing even himself but Hecht beamed and delightedly declared: 'Every inch a killer!'

Martin made no response, adjusting his collar, closing the button off. The tailor stepped forward to fasten a ceremonial Knight's Cross at his throat, just to see how the real thing would lie.

Hecht sat down in a winged chair on the other side of the room, picking up a delicate Dresden china coffee cup from an occasional table and daintily sipping from it. The tailor stood back, a satisfied smile on his face.

'You look very smart.'

Martin nodded his thanks, reaching up to take off the helmet.

There was the chink of cup on saucer, then Hecht leapt out of the chair. 'A fine job, Enzo!' he exclaimed. The tailor bowed, a relieved grin on his face, glad to have pleased the Gestapo. 'Thankyou Herr Hecht.'

The Kriminalinspektor clapped the tailor on the back.

'Send us the bill as soon as possible!'

Martin unfastened and handed back the pretend Knight's Cross.

The tailor withdrew, collecting his measuring tape and tailoring box as he went. With just the two of them left in the fitting room, Hecht pulled himself up, giving a comical click of his heels, which provoked a dour look from Martin. Despite this Hecht stated cheerily: 'And now, the Führer awaits.' Martin placed the cap on his head, then unfastened the top button of his tunic. It didn't look proper, so he reluctantly did it up again.

Tucking the helmet under his right arm, he turned to Hecht, looking down to make sure there was no lint on his jacket front, brushing his decorations – *for bravery under fire, for blood, sweat and no tears* - with the fingertips of his left hand: the buttonhole ribbons for the Iron Cross and Eastern Front Medal; the Iron Cross 1st Class itself in the centre of his left breast pocket; a Close Combat Clasp above the same; the wound badge.

'Are you ready now?' Hecht asked, disturbing the fingertip inspection. Martin swallowed his irritation, remarking neutrally: 'Yes, I am.'

Emerging from the shop into sunlight, Martin recoiled, turning his head away from the sun. Then, tilting his head up, but careful to ensure the peak still shaded his eyes, he stared into the cerulean sky, his head empty of thoughts.

* * *

Above Martin's helmet encased head, hanging from poles that pierced the walls, were blood red flags emblazoned with strident black swastikas in white circles. They drooped flaccidly in the heat, which was stifling even in the vast grandeur of the neoclassical Marble Gallery of the Reich Chancellery.

Martin was arrayed at attention in line with a dozen other stiff-backed elite SS troops. All had their heads tilted slightly up to the left, gazing towards the end of the hall.

A trickle of sweat ran down his neck, until the, by now, throat-throttling collar of his tightly buttoned tunic soaked it up.

There, below a gigantic granite German eagle, was a podium upon which Adolf Hitler stood behind a lectern draped with another flag, this one showing the silver runes of the SS against black.

Face impassive, Martin surreptitiously scrutinized the Führer.

Hitler's eyes offered no spark of interest as he focused somewhere ill-defined over the heads of the arrayed medal-winners. His face was marked with little cuts from the bomb that had nearly killed him a few days earlier.

It was not the first time Martin had seen him in the flesh, as Hitler had inspected the *Das Reich* division before the invasion of the Soviet Union.

Martin had to suppress a smile at the memory of the division's officers forced to eat a sparse vegetarian lunch to suit the Führer's taste, in a large, airless tent in a forest clearing in western Poland. *And them all confirmed carnivores.* However, he was The Leader – a genius who had saved Germany from her Versailles humiliation and they were willing to forgive him foibles such as vegetarianism.

The Hitler the *Das Reich* officers dined with in early summer 1941 promised to lead them to victory and their deeds would be immortalised in a 1,000-year Reich. He had fired them up with a table-thumping monologue about how the Bolsheviks stabbed Germany in the back at the end of their fathers' war. Eyes blazing with fire - veins bulging in his neck, flecks of spittle flying - he told them it was 'time to pierce the dark heart of the enemy with the long lance of German martial might.'

The Waffen SS - the pure ideological warriors of National Socialism - were the tip of that lance, said Hitler, and their sharpness, already honed to perfection by war in Poland, the Balkans and the West, 'would be buried deep in the black heart of the Bolshevik dragon.'

Furthermore, he urged them to recall that 'in snuffing out the abomination that was Poland' Germany deployed 'righteous brutality that was absolute and cleansing.'

Burning with fervour, Hitler swept his eyes across the faces of the *Das Reich* officers, fixing them with a look that, he hoped, showed total personal confidence in them. He urged them 'not to recoil from crushing Russian scum with the same sacred brutality.' In that moment they would all have plunged into the depths of Hell. In time they did.

* * *

It seemed as if a century had passed since all that talk about slaying Bolshevik dragons. This Hitler before them on the podium was pallid and sagging, his eyes glazed, the toothbrush moustache under the nostrils flecked with grey; a different Führer altogether. 'With such men as you, final victory for National Socialism is assured,' he told them, which Martin felt was delivered with less than total conviction.

Tightly gripping both sides of the lectern, Hitler somehow dredged up some of his old energy and barked: 'The scum who thought they could prevent our triumph will soon dance on the end of meat-hooks!'

This provoked thunderous applause from the audience and a desperately eager fusillade of 'Heil Hitler!'

A beam of light falling through one of the windows caught dust particles as they danced, 'on a current of the Führer's hot air,' thought Martin, somewhat treasonously.

Hitler stepped down so that Joseph Goebbels, the weaselly Propaganda and Public Enlightenment Minister, could mount the podium to deliver a lecture to the gathered bigwigs about the heroism of the young men and foul natures of the cowering bed-wetting Allies. There was a lot of bored coughing and people struggling to keep drooping eyelids open while a trio of propaganda photographers for *Signal* – the Reich's foremost military news magazine - dashed about, firing off shots, their flash bulbs crackling and popping.

A trumpet call - a full-blown fanfare no less - woke everyone up, followed by a drum roll from a Waffen SS band clustered by tall windows that opened out onto the Courtyard of Honour.

It seemed to galvanise the Führer, who shuffled along the line of stormtroopers while trailing in his wake were flunkies with cushions on which nestled small black leather-bound cases containing medals.

Martin stiffened his posture in anticipation, throat parched, pulse racing and sneaked a sideways glance down the line. No less than Heinrich Himmler - little piggy eyes blinking furiously behind wire-rimmed glasses - was accompanying the Führer, introducing medal recipients by rank, name and unit. Martin thought it impressive the SS boss even knew who they were.

More flashbulbs exploded as the photographers captured each moment of presentation while those cursed drums were still banging away.

'Haupsturmführer Walder, *Das Reich* Division.'

The Führer seized his right hand, Martin looking down, directly into Hitler's cold grey-blue eyes. They seemed far away, showing no emotion, no sign of even recognizing Martin as a fellow human being.

'The Reich thanks you,' Hitler rasped.

A firm handshake; the medal case slipped into his left hand by Himmler; one of the flunkies gently turned Martin towards a photographer.

The flash as the picture was taken for a few seconds propelled Martin back to the room in the Kharkov tenement building, as he pressed the Madonna icon onto the chest of the dying Soviet sniper, closing her hands over it…

The Führer let go of his hand and, even as Martin fell back into line, his right arm reflexively shot up in a Nazi salute, his voice roaring:

'Heil Hitler!'

Boredom set in, Martin's eyes drifting to the Nazi flags hanging lifelessly overhead on the other side of the hall. With a trumpet fanfare the Führer exited. 'Parade at ease!' a guttural voice bellowed, echoing off the marble lined walls and columns.

Martin relaxed his stance, waiting to be dismissed.

He brought his eyes down, scanned the rows of seats to his right, which were still packed with VIPs chatting to each other. Nobody paid the slightest bit of attention to the medal recipients, except for Hecht. He was studying Martin keenly from a few rows back.

Looking away, shifting the medal case from left to right hand behind his back, Martin glanced up and down the line, finding the other medal winners much the same as himself.

Impassive.

Unsmiling.

It had been a strange affair, subdued and without any true feeling of celebration; just for the cameras, exactly as Hecht had suggested.

Martin felt completely detached from his surroundings, as if he was standing outside looking in on it all. He hadn't experienced this since he attended his grandfather's funeral as a lanky teenager – fulfilling duties as one of the pallbearers - another event from which he was absent in mind if not body. His grandfather was in the coffin but it felt light as a feather on his shoulder, which of course it was. *He wasn't actually in there, though, was he?* Grandad's mortal remains were, yes, but his soul had flown…his mind, his personality and all he had done - the substance, the weight of his life and being - had vanished into the ether.

Maybe it took a rebellious, convention-questioning teenager to see the absurdity of funerals? Standing up for hymns at the front of the church, looking at the coffin on its stand, surrounded by wreaths, the lid open to reveal the cold, dead bewhiskered face, Martin felt like laughing out loud. He wanted to turn to them all and roar with laughter: 'Can't you see!? Why are you so sad? He's not here anymore! Stop your weeping!'

And today, here in the heart of the 1,000-year Reich, he should have shouted, laughed in the face of mass stupidity: 'Can't you see, *he's* not with us anymore!? The Führer is here, in the bloodied flesh, but not in the spirit, not with the fire in his eyes. He's gone!'

Martin sighed, the disappointment mingled with relief.

This God who had saved Germany in the aftermath of the disaster and shame of the Kaiser's war; the man who had offered Martin hope amid the turmoil of his teenage years, was just a frail human after all.

It was all too ridiculous.

He could see that now.

Life.

War.

The search for glory.

A gust of wind came in from somewhere along the gallery, stirring the flags. Someone must have opened a few windows. Martin was suddenly reconnected to where he was.

The parade commander roared: 'Dismissed!'

Martin took his helmet off, the fresh air feeling very cool on his sweat matted hair. He closed his eyes, turned his head towards where it was coming from. Martin inhaled deeply, in his head a vision of Lorelei smiling at him.

'Happy?' someone enquired, disturbing his reverie.

Opening his eyes, Martin found Hecht giving him an enquiring look. The Gestapo man observed excitedly: 'Meeting the Führer is *truly* inspirational.' Martin said nothing.

'May I?' the Kriminalinspektor asked, gesturing at the medal case in Martin's right hand, which the Waffen SS officer handed to him. Flipping the lid up, Hecht's eyes gleamed. 'Very pretty.'

Martin suggested: 'If you like, you can have it.'

Hecht's mouth dropped open in shock, as if he believed it.

'You're kidding?'

Martin laughed and took it back off him.

'I didn't see you killing any Ivans.'

Martin thought Hecht now looked overly serious and, snapping the lid shut, slid the case into a tunic pocket. Other soldiers were proudly slipping their beribboned medals over their bare heads and around their necks but Martin just didn't feel in the mood.

'Aren't you going to put it on?' asked Hecht.

Martin cradled his helmet in the crook of his left arm, his right hand gently taking the Gestapo man by the elbow, guiding him through the crowd. 'What I really want, is for you to take me for a drink on the Gestapo, somewhere far from the crowd.'

Hecht was surprised by the usually sombre soldier's sudden enthusiasm for enjoying himself. For his part, Martin was relieved to get it all over and done with, released for a return to Bad Gastein and to finally ask Lorelei to walk out with him. *But, first there was the matter of that drink…*

8

As the Mercedes slowed to a halt in the Potsdamer Platz, Martin could see that Allied bombs had ripped the covering off Haus Vaterland's magnificent dome - exposing the steel skeleton beneath, smashing in many windows along its frontage.

For those in the know, according to Hecht, hospitality was available within its despoiled layer cake interior – the Gestapo man knew people in low places and so there was still a drink to be had in the Rhine Terrace bar.

Leaving Kruger in the car, Hecht led Martin, who had swapped his helmet for the cap, across the road to give a special knock on the wonky brass-clad double front doors, the sound summoning a bewhiskered, elderly concierge.

Making their way up a broad marble staircase, they dodged water dripping from where the roof had disappeared and then, on the third floor, entered a short, dark, fetid corridor.

To fill the silence, Hecht remarked over his shoulder that he felt the Führer had looked remarkably well during medal presentation, especially following his near brush with death. 'So lucky just to get away with scorched trousers and burst eardrums,' Hecht observed with Martin unsure if he was being genuine or sarcastic.

The concierge held open a door and stepped to one side, so Hecht and Martin could squeeze by and into the capacious Rhine Terrace. Overall, it was remarkably unharmed by the war's ravages, though the blistered ceiling sagged. Martin surprised the Gestapo man by handing him his peaked cap and making a beeline for the spectacular careworn kitsch of the bar's Rhine panorama at the far end, dodging through dusty tables and overturned chairs. Meanwhile, from somewhere in the Vaterland's bowels appeared a bartender in a Prussian blue waistcoat and crisp white shirt with black bow tie, producing a bottle of Obstwasser and two glasses, which Hecht ordered him to set up on a table before wandering over to join Martin at the wooden rail running around the edge of the elaborate panorama

'Did you ever come here as a boy?' Hecht enquired.

Martin nodded.

'Yes, it was quite a show,' he said, an image of an absurd oompah band of fat men in lederhosen and dancing girls in dirndl flashing through his head. Hecht laughed. 'The rosy-cheeked Rhine Maidens stick in my mind,' observed the Gestapo man. 'And the pimps taking time off from their turf.'

'But a child did not notice such people,' Martin pointed out, slightly irritated. 'True,' Hecht conceded.

Martin felt sad on surveying the current state of things - the sound and the fury absent - thunder and storms; trains dashing by on overhead rails; a ship dancing on Rhine – behind-the-scenes clockwork machinery stilled and silenced. The tin waves and thunder-clappers neither bobbed nor clapped. Martin pointed at the panorama's painted realisation of the famous Lorelei Rock.

'You know the story?'

'I read the Mark Twain version,' the Gestapo man replied, adding in a disdainful tone: "the faint air cools…the peaceful flowing Rhine with the sunsets flooding wine" - Lorelei combing her golden hair on the rock and a doomed knight trying to save her. Not really to my taste. Soppy.'

Martin glared at him and said dismissively: 'Clearly you are no romantic,' adding, 'anyway it's better in the German original.'

Hecht wanted to laugh in Martin's face – so serious! - but thought better of it. The admiration of a Waffen SS officer for Heinrich Heine, a Jewish poet, was rather fascinating, an interesting insight into the true nature of the Nazi knight in front of him. A brutal sentimentalist.

Martin and Hecht made their way over to the table where the fruit brandy waited and, after a couple of drinks, the suddenly talkative Waffen SS officer recounted a walking holiday from Rudesheim to Bonn with his boyhood pal Fritz Fleischer, when they were both seventeen.

With a dreamy smile, Martin recalled a farmer giving the footsore teenagers a ride in his empty tractor trailer and a meeting with a group of women cyclists by the road, pausing in their ride to share around an Asbach brandy bottle concealed in a brown paper bag. They offered the boys a swig, laughing at the youngsters' shocked looks as the booze burned down their throats. With a suggestive tone in his voice, Hecht asked: 'A case of also sharing something more?' Martin smiled and shook his head.

'We were just hopeless. Hadn't got a clue when it came to women.'

Martin also told how he and Fritz tramped under an intense sun, up the dusty paths, through vineyards; until they reached the very top, sitting down to rest awhile, taking in the winding, slow-moving, sparkling Rhine, finding themselves on the same eye level as a turreted castle across the river. 'It was truly spectacular,' Martin recalled, momentarily lost in that long ago summer's day.

He gestured towards the far end, 'the very thing you see in the panorama.' Hecht smiled indulgently while thinking that could hardly be the case.

Martin related how he and Fritz descended the slopes to make a pilgrimage along the banks of the Rhine to stand in the shadow of the Lorelei, gazing up awestruck by the massive, looming outcrop.

'We were poised between the Lorelei and the river itself.'

Martin laughed and shook his head.

'It was a very hot day and do you know what I remember most

about our hike to the Lorelei?' Hecht shook his head, picking up his schnapps for a sip to let Martin continue.

'The sweet sickly stench of dead rats rotting by the roadside. Now, that's a smell I have come to know well, Herr Kriminalinspektor. The stink of rotting flesh.'

There was no response from the Gestapo man, other than a faint smile and refilling glasses, with Martin thinking he really ought to have had more of a breakfast than just coffee, for the Obstwasser was going straight to his head.

Martin also blamed his giddy feeling on the head-spinning odyssey from Augean front line to Olympian pantomime in the Reich Chancellery. It would knock anyone off their axis.

But, it was time to leave and Hecht picked up his own hat and Martin's cap, leaving some Reichmarks on the table, ushering his charge back down through the Haus Vaterland and across to the Mercedes.

Kruger waited behind the wheel with the window down, puffing on a foul-smelling cigarette.

'Put that fucking thing out!' Hecht snarled. Kruger spat the cigarette onto the pavement, looking shame-faced at being caught.

Not that smoking always seemed to bother Hecht, what with his cigarillos.

Swaying slightly, Martin suddenly felt amity for the Gestapo investigator, grabbing him by the shoulders and asking:

'Do we have to stop now and break up the party?'

Hecht shrugged him off and opened the rear passenger door.

'Regretfully I have paperwork to do.'

'Oh, come on – eat, drink and be merry...'

Hecht pushed Martin gently into the back of the car and climbed into the front passenger seat.

As he eased the Mercedes out into the traffic - squeezing between a truckload of blank-faced troops and a fire engine - Kruger was careful not to let a ladder mounted on the back of the latter smash through the windscreen.

Hecht said to Martin over his shoulder, with a suggestive smirk: 'Tonight we can certainly exceed your expectations.'

Martin liked the sound of that. Letting his head loll back against the seat and closing his eyes, he mumbled drowsily: 'We who are about to die salute you.' Not catching it, Hecht glanced into the back of the car, finding Martin in an inebriated slumber.

'How did he get so pissed in less than half an hour, Sir?' Kruger enquired incredulously. 'It appears our hero has no head for alcohol,' Hecht remarked with satisfaction.

* * *

They dropped Martin off at the Adlon for a good sleep and picked him up again several hours later. Clean shirt, freshly shaved, refreshed and bright eyed, Martin was again immaculate in his Waffen SS uniform, now with the Knight's Cross at his throat and cap at a rakish angle.

Their destination was a short drive away: Club Eros, which for the young combat officer would prove a stunning revelation. Who'd have thought the Zoo flak tower – a gigantic castle keep 13-storeys high, so called because it was next door to the city zoo - had such a place buried beneath it?

Under the constant bombing from the Tommies, who visited the city almost every night, Berliners looked for solace, and a steadier nerve, in their minor comforts and major vices.

As Hecht and Martin were dropped off in the shadow of the Zoo Tower, Hecht told Kruger to go and get some dinner. He should then come back and wait for them in the car or, if the bombing got too hot, seek refuge in a shelter. Kruger assented resentfully and pulled away, leaving Hecht grinning self-consciously at Martin.

They waited in line to enter, alongside bauble-bedecked Nazi Party officials, senior military officers and their ladies in evening dress finery – although the term *ladies* could only be applied loosely to some of them judging by the coarse laugher and voracious crotch-grabbing crudity.

Martin craned his head back to study the battlements high overhead. Searchlights located at various sites across the city traversed the night sky. Every now and then – at the apex of the concrete monstrosity – against their beam was visible the silhouette of an upraised 12.8 cm Flak 40 anti-aircraft gun, barrel training around as it waited for targets.

Some tiny white faces under helmets heads peered down – crews of the smaller calibre AA guns around the rim of the tower's firing platforms who were curious about the fortunate elite going safely underground.

Part of Martin would prefer to be up there, preparing to hurl hot metal at the British 'terror flyers', as Goebbels called them. Martin returned his gaze to Earth and, not for the first time, wondered why Hecht was going to all this trouble. Any further attempt to unravel Hecht's web of cordiality was swept away as the doors of the nightclub opened with an ostentatious *clang*, provoking a ripple of applause from the waiting revellers.

They started to shuffle in, Martin removing his cap and slipping it snugly under his left arm. There had already been a few impressed glances in the direction of the Knight's Cross with Oak Leaves and Swords at his throat, with a return smile for the women and a steely look for the men. Hecht had enjoyed it, too, grateful Martin was acquiring a pride in trinkets – a good sign that he was not immune to flattery, which could be useful later.

High above, on its top platform, the flak tower's sirens started to wail. The guns pirouetted on their mountings, their crews responding to orders from a battery commander whose headset was being fed instructions by radar stations detecting incoming bombers, with the guns laid on target using the human eye.

The queue moved along a little more swiftly.

The flak guns fired with an ear-splitting crack, prompting some to jump in their skins and sending nervous laughter pulsating through the queue. People pushed those in front, telling them to get a move on, but they didn't dare touch the Waffen SS officer and Gestapo man.

Martin shouted in Hecht's ear:

'I commended mirth, because a man hath no better thing under the sun, than to eat, and to drink, and to be merry!'

It took a second or two for the words to sink in.

'A quote from Ecclesiastes,' Hecht realised, which was appropriate for a pastor's son he supposed.

The hellish bombing raid symphony began in earnest: sirens, the bark and thump of the guns, screaming bombs and incendiaries tumbling from the bellies of the bombers somewhere far overhead. The triangulation of the flak tower weapons was calculated to throw a protective dome over the centre of the German capital, or that was the idea. Thousands of rounds a minute were spat into the sky, out to a distance of a dozen miles, the enemy respecting the ferocity of fire thrown up by Berlin's flak towers and doing their best to stay away from their parabolas of death.

Earlier, as they headed across town in the car, Hecht had reeled off the virtues of the Zoo Tower – *a brutalist, over-size version of a medieval redoubt he'd suggested, his eyes afire with enthusiasm at the sheer wonder of the Reich's architectural prowess – taking from the old but with a modern twist.*

'Albert Speer is a genius!' he declared.

Hecht had boasted there was little point in bombing the flak towers themselves, for their reinforced concrete walls were *very* thick, so tough precious artefacts of city museums had been deposited within for safe keeping. Apparently, so Hecht claimed, there was even a fully-fledged hospital in each, while the Reich's propaganda service broadcast defiance from an invulnerable studio in the Zoo Tower. That last point had provoked a grim smile from Martin. He had often wondered where the outlandish pep talks were emanating from when listening in from some godforsaken Russian hovel.

What inventive volley of curses would Bruno have unleashed had he known the bastards were being very brave behind metres of concrete?

More astonishing, though, was Hecht's stage whisper revelation that deep within were secret storage rooms, with their own dedicated heating and ventilation systems, their function to preserve stolen art treasures of the Reich. Now Martin and Hecht were descending into the bowels of the Zoo Tower, leaving behind the orgy of destruction above ground for a riotous party. In the elevator everyone was pressed up against each other, the air rapidly becoming unpleasant due to hot bodies and breath – some not so pleasant. Martin turned his head away from a corpulent Nazi official in a shit brown uniform whose halitosis was of epic proportions. He found himself looking into the hungry eyes of a platinum blonde. The doors opened, the blonde swept away amid the rush, Hecht laughing and clapping Martin on the back as they entered the portals of Club Eros.

9

THEY WERE TRANSPORTED into a parallel universe, where all the things an allegedly ascetic Nazi leadership publicly railed against seemed in the ascendant. Martin simply could not believe his eyes – it was scene straight out of the debauched Weimar era.

Laid out before him was a sea of tables, each one covered with a scarlet tablecloth, the yellow glow of a lamp at its centre. Groups of men or couples were hunched around them, engaged in intimate discourse and, in some cases, Martin thought, even actual intercourse, with the women astride the men's laps. Meanwhile, penguin-suited waiters hurried to and fro with amazing speed and dexterity, holding aloft trays carrying plates of food or bearing silver buckets crammed with ice.

A jazz band began pumping out the Charleston, the dance floor soon heaving with couples – one or two females together, but mainly men paired with women – all hurling their limbs about. 'What the Hell is this?' Martin gasped, his mouth hanging open.

Hecht laughed, yelling in his ear: 'Götterdämmerung, eh!?'

The House Manager, his bouffant white hair quivering and waxed moustache twitching, lunged out of the crowd, coming up the steps to the waiting area with his hand out-stretched. 'Herr Hecht! How nice to see you! The usual table?'

Hecht grinned and nodded.

The House Manager led them across to the right-hand side, between tables populated by SS officers and their women. The House Manager pulled their seats out, melodramatically dusting them off with a white handkerchief pulled from the breast pocket of his jacket.

The Charleston halted abruptly, the dance floor clearing, and an orchestra replaced the jazz musicians, striking up the Blue Danube. Out came twirling and leaping dancing girls dressed in red basques, black stockings and white ballet pumps.

It was among the most ridiculous things Martin had ever seen, but somehow fitting for the gauche, tasteless Club Eros - for bacchanalia on the edge of a volcano. A waiter brought over a silver bucket with a bottle of sparkling wine rammed into a small mountain of ice, plonking it on the table along with a pair of flutes.

Sitting down, Martin looked up at glittering chandeliers – such massive affairs, so different in scale and quality from those puny efforts in the Prague mirror maze – but the two places shared a certain distortion and exaggeration. This Zoo Tower club was so decadent, so profligate with brazen electricity while the rest of Berlin was plunged into blackout.

Hecht seized the bottle of fizz, artfully undid the restraining wire on the cork, twisted and extracted it with a submissive pop. He poured the pétillant golden liquid into the glasses, shoving one of them across the table. 'It's not as fine as the stuff in your hotel, but it's good enough,' he explained. 'So-called Crimean champagne and, so I am told, a vintage the last Tsar was particularly fond of.' Martin hoped Hecht would stop trying so hard.

The orchestra changed gears and broke into a crazed version of Glenn Miller's *Chattanooga Choo-Choo*. 'I thought this sort of thing was only the preserve of corrupt Americans?' Martin asked, nodding towards the dancers.

'Never mind that - tonight, enjoy the fruits of glory!' Hecht exclaimed, with loud, mock sincerity. 'You deserve them.'

Leaning back in his chair, Hecht caught hold of a passing waiter.

'Yes, Sir?'

'Menus please.'

'Yes, Sir.'

But Hecht retained his grip.

'And more champagne.'

The man was finally let go.

Hecht and Martin settled back to watch the dancing girls who had finished their frenzied American routine and now, bosoms heaving and glistening, were gracefully describing *Swan Lake*, cheeks flushed from exertion. Martin found it all rather too ridiculous.

The waiter deposited another bottle of the Crimean bubbly in an ice bucket on the table and took the old one away, leaving menus by Hecht's elbow. The Gestapo man poured Martin another glass, which was gone with a flick of the wrist. 'Steady on,' urged Hecht, 'savour it - we've got all night.'

Hecht handed him a menu and, as he did so, noticed two elegantly dressed beauties - one honey blonde, the other raven haired - on the threshold of the nightclub, checking their wraps in at the cloakroom.

'Excuse me,' Hecht told Martin, 'I've just spotted someone.'

Martin reached across for the bottle of Russian sparkling wine, poured himself another glass and gulped it down. Meanwhile, Hecht intercepted the women, redirecting them to the table. Seeing them approach, Martin rose from his seat. 'Ladies, I would like you to meet a hero of the Reich, Hauptsturmführer Martin Walder, who was only today presented with the Knight's Cross with Oak Leaves and Swords by the Führer himself. Martin, this is Hannah and Elise, both of whom work in administration at my office.'

With a rush of bubbles in his bloodstream, Martin grinned broadly and bowed. Delighted by Martin's sudden loosening up, Hecht declared: 'Bravo!' Hannah - the raven haired one - sat by Hecht, while Elise - the honey blonde - slid in beside Martin, the Gestapo man leaning over the back of his seat and snaring another passing waiter to ask for more sparkling wine.

* * *

The wreckage of a sumptuous meal lay on the table while the dancers had gone, to be replaced by couples gliding by – including Hannah and Hecht, cheek-to-cheek, floating on a smoochy *Begin the Beguine*. Elise and Martin were leaning in towards each other, heads touching, both very drunk, also intoxicated by the sexual heat they were each giving off.

'What does it feel like?' she asked.

Martin glanced away to pour them both another drink.

Placing a glass by her hand, he looked directly into her eyes and enquired: 'What?'

'Tell me what it feels like to kill,' she pleaded. Putting his glass down, Martin shot her a foxy smile and Elise laughed.

'You're not going to tell me?'

Caressing her cheek Martin gently shook his head.

'It's not the sort of thing an officer and a gentleman shares with a pretty young woman, especially in a decadent nightclub.'

She was undeterred and insisted: 'But, I *must* know.'

* * *

The roar of explosions and gunfire was deafening, bombs marching towards the Adlon making the furniture and ornaments rattle. There was a hammering on the door, a muffled voice shouting hysterically from the other side: 'To the shelters! To the shelters!'

The blackout curtain was open, the room starkly lit by the flashes of explosions while the glass panes in the windows trembled.

Yet amid all this Martin's face was impassive - a diligently labouring machine as he fucked Elise. In the deathly silence after the air raid Martin and Elise lay entwined on the bed, a slight breeze occasionally lifting the nets in the windows, which had lost most of their glass. With her head nestled on his chest, Martin finally yielded to Elise's morbid curiosity, telling her about the first man he had killed, when he was serving as a junior officer in the *Germania* regiment of the Waffen SS.

'In modern war, you rarely see the enemy, at least not alive, not as you kill him,' Martin explained in a matter of fact fashion.

'The first man I saw as I actually killed him was a Pole, on a farm outside Lemberg. The regiment had paused and my platoon rested there as we thought it was entirely abandoned. I went to urinate behind the barn and, as I relieved myself, peering through the slats, noticed a pair of boots poking out from a pile of straw.'

Martin gave a hollow, mirthless laugh at this memory of the Pole's pathetic give-away. Fingers brushing back and forth across his taut stomach, Elise urged: 'Go on.'

So he resumed his tale.

'Very slowly and carefully I crept around the side, in through a door, and over beside the platform on which was heaped the straw under which this Pole was hiding. I poked the straw with my pistol and this rather short and scrawny officer emerged very slowly, his hands up.

'He chose that moment to try and kill me with a pitchfork, which he grabbed from where it leaned against a wall - actually threw it at me. Didn't strike me the way he intended, instead hitting me flat on the chest, knocking the pistol out of my hand. He then tried to get away through the door, but screwed it up, couldn't get it open… I was winded and furious, as you can imagine – after all somebody had just tried to kill me. It seemed so personal…not like when you fire rifles at the enemy on the other side of a field or in a town. Raging mad, I got to my feet, picked up the pitchfork and ran at him. He turned around and tried to fend me off as I rammed it in under his rib cage, pinning him to the door…I didn't know my own strength. I was so furious that the bastard had actually tried to kill me.'

With a heavy sigh he told her: 'So, now you know what killing is about.' She said nothing - *was Elise shocked into silence?*

Martin had never regretted taking the other man's life – if someone tries to kill you then you'd be a fool not to respond in kind. Telling the story did not make him feel good especially – he had told it many times before to comrades-in-arms around various camp fires – but he now wondered what his parents would think of him.

This girl's opinion didn't matter – he actually felt nothing but contempt for civilians who had never seen combat showing undue fascination with the killing or being killed – but that night, the close proximity of his mother and father across the city made him feel ashamed.

10

23 July 1944 – Afternoon

MARTIN AND HECHT talked as they walked along Unter den Linden, many of its trees no more than shattered stumps, most of the benches broken and scattered, a few bomb craters here and there still smoking.

Hecht had a dreadful hangover, looked very pale, while Martin seemed fresh as a daisy, and *once again* unbearably immaculate in his uniform. Hecht groused good-naturedly: 'How is it that you, a mere novice drinker, get away scot free and me, a veteran, receive this?'

Hecht spotted a still intact bench.

'Please, can we sit down?'

Martin couldn't understand why the Gestapo man had taken such trouble to call on him if he felt so ill.

'Martin, I need to ask you a favour.'

'Oh?'

'I want you to go and visit your parents.'

A muscle twitched in Martin's cheek, his world knocked a little off-kilter again by this sudden and unexpected request - *or rather order* - from State Security.

'I know you didn't want them at the ceremony,' Hecht pressed on, not wanting to give Martin time to think, 'but I think they should know the Führer himself regards their boy as one of Germany's shining sons.'

Martin shrugged, seemingly indifferent but actually all churned up inside. 'Why the hesitancy?' asked Hecht. 'Is it because they don't approve of you being in the Waffen SS?'

His heart was beating hard and, sensing dangerous ground, Martin said, as casually as he could manage: 'A clash of personalities, that's all - the usual father-son stuff.'

Hecht touched his sleeve so that Martin looked at him, discovering hardness in the other man's stare that he had not seen before. 'Well, right now your father is being very foolish,' said the Gestapo man, in a tone as cold and sharp as ice, making Martin inwardly shiver in fear for what his parents had been doing.

'What on earth do you mean?'

Hecht was concise: 'He and your mother are sheltering an enemy of the State.' Martin felt the ground open up beneath him.

'I find that very hard to believe,' he protested.

'A Jew,' Hecht sneered, 'a young boy.'

Martin shook his head, angry and astonished.

'Go and talk some sense into them,' suggested Hecht. 'Get them to give up this stupidity.'

Stunned, Martin nodded, so Hecht decided to ram his advantage home.

'The last thing we want to do is take drastic action against a man of God, the father of a hero decorated by the Führer or, indeed, against your mother. There has to be a way of solving this without any untoward effects.'

Martin's face flushed red with anger and he leapt to his feet, pulling his cap off. 'I can't believe it,' he gasped, pacing up and down beside the bench then sitting down again, hands clasping and unclasping the cap.

Hecht sighed, rising with a groan. Dizzy, he steadied himself with his right hand on the back of the bench, his left beckoning Kruger and the Mercedes, which slid to halt at the kerb.

'Let's go,' Hecht suggested. 'I'll drop you around at your father's place.' Summoning up as much ersatz empathy as he could manage, he added: 'Give him the sermon according to patriotism for me, would you?'

Martin hauled himself to his feet, dropping his cap as he did so.

It rolled away but he stooped nimbly to pick it before it came to a rest. Hitting it with his hand to shake off the dust, snatching a few seconds to compose himself, Martin walked over to the car. Hecht stood next to the nearside rear passenger door, which was open and ready to swallow him up.

* * *

It seemed a lifetime since Martin last stood in the leafy suburban street in Dahlem that was host to the church of St. George and the pastor's house where he grew up. The church itself was a half-size version of the Marienkirche in Kaiser Wilhelm Strasse in the centre of Berlin.

A tightly woven red tiled, high-peaked roof above a mix of original sandstone and latter-day clay bricks, this house of God was topped with a English-style square medieval tower.

Originally an Anglican house of worship and part of the Church of England in Europe, Martin's father had been the first, and, so far only, pastor since its reopening in 1926 as a German Protestant outpost. Its congregation before the outbreak of war in 1939 had been cosmopolitan, including British, Swedish and American diplomats along with other expatriates. They had gradually disappeared until only the Americans joined the German worshippers. They ceased coming after Pearl Harbor in December 1941.

Pastor Jonathan Walder suspected his current congregation often contained the occasional informer eager to assist the Gestapo.

The church and its pastor had only really provoked the keen interest of the secret police since a Jewish boy went missing from a 'resettlement' train during a stop on the outskirts of Berlin to replenish its water tanks.

A vigilant local had spotted 'a strange looking boy' playing in the graveyard one afternoon. It was 'most odd', so said the same neighbourhood informant during a call to the Gestapo, who were always grateful to freelance snoopers. This intelligence was passed along to Hecht, as he was assigned to the case. The graveyard sighting chimed with other aspects of the affair that pointed towards the involvement, in some capacity, of the pastor Walder. Hecht's preferred method was to gather up all the conspirators via a gradual process of trawling for information, then tightening the net when appropriate. Hecht's superiors had lately begun to lose patience in his slow methods and so the investigator had hit on the idea of using Martin to flush things out.

* * *

The sky had become overcast and, as Martin watched from across the street, lights flickered on inside the church, their glow filtering wanly through the windows. He glanced back down the road, to where the Mercedes was parked under the trees, occupants watching but hidden within its dark interior. According to Hecht time was running out for his parents, unless he could persuade them to give up the boy.

Head throbbing from the hangover now beginning to assert itself, Martin crossed the road, taking the main path through the graveyard.

He couldn't help but smile at recollecting a childhood fight with Grossman, his nemesis – a large lad who thought he could bully the pastor's son until challenged to a fight on top of a tomb.

Chanting, laughing choirboys gathered around its base as they grappled until – with a triumphant groan - the smaller Martin hoisted his chunky foe off his feet, sending him tumbling into a holly bush with loud screams – the harder he struggled to free himself the more Grossman was pricked. Leaping up and down in triumph, Martin's exultation was short-lived. With Grossman whining and blubbering, the other boys suddenly scattered, surplices billowing. Martin looked down and there - staring up at him with furious, bulging eyes - was his father.

* * *

Fourteen years later a determined push on one of the large oak doors provided admittance to the church; that peculiar and familiar smell of polished leather and musty mothballs invading Martin's nostrils.

It instantly pulled him back to those far off days as a chorister under his father's stern eyes, robustly belting out hymns. The extra money for singing at weddings had appealed more than devotion to God.

Today, gathered for their Sunday afternoon service in the wake of the attempt to kill the Führer, the small congregation was nervously listening to Herr Pastor Walder – his flinty blue eyes sparking, craggy, lean features animated and even his close-cropped silver hair quivered as he made what some might see as a politically unsound sermon.

'These are difficult times,' he told them solemnly - head down, hands gripping the rim of the pulpit, his voice echoing beseechingly around the cavernous interior. 'Times of doubt when perhaps we are finally asking questions which we should have addressed long ago.'

Looking up and scanning the upturned faces of his flock, he continued: 'This includes myself. If we examine home truths perhaps we might be able to decide where our morality lies in the wider context. We cannot be good Christians in our hearts, in our homes and then owe allegiance to that which is ungodly.'

It made the parishioners squirm uncomfortably in their pews, exchanging worried glances. Confirming their worst fears, there, in front of the gently swinging inner doors was a young man in Waffen SS uniform. One or two gave apologetic smiles, but the SS officer remained stone-faced, eyes hidden under the peak of his cap. The pastor's voice trailed away, astonished as he was into silence by the unexpected arrival of his son.

His flock fled the wolf in their midst, shuffling anxiously out of their pews, heading for the door, squeezing past the soldier as if touching him – even brushing against him – would make them burst into flames.

Jonathan Walder gathered up his sermon notes and dismounted from the pulpit. As his father came down the aisle, Martin took his cap off and sat down in one of the pews, Jonathan sliding into the one in front, pushing the notes and a glasses case along. Draping an arm along the back of the pew, he scrutinised his son's face, noticing the scars around his eyes.

'You've been wounded?'

Martin nodded.

'When?'

'A few months ago.'

'And you didn't think to write and tell your mother?'

'Would she care?' Martin enquired resentfully, getting no answer.

Martin picked up a hymnbook, the gilt words on the spine catching the light. Leafing through its pages, studying them with pretend interest, he asked his father: 'Is she still drinking?'

'No, she stopped the day you left,' was the lying reply.

Martin closed the hymnbook, put it back, stared at his shoes.

The bottle had become his mother's solace for the loss of her first-born son, Manfred, who was taken from them by the influenza pandemic in 1919 - the *Blitzkatarrh* - while still a baby. Her subsequent reliance on alcohol was something Jonathan Walder enshrined by pretending it was nothing out of the ordinary, that there was *no reliance* on booze in *his* house.

He would rather ignore her tipsy nights than fight her, though Martin, as he reached his teenage years, recognised it for what it was and bitterly resented her choice of the bottle over him.

Studying his son's downturned face, Jonathan told Martin: 'Your mother is still consumed by dread that one day she will read your name in the casualty lists or receive a telegram.'

Martin looked up, shook his head, but kept his silence. Even his deep and abiding resentment about his mother's preference for a dead child (and the bottle) over him had to be laid to one side when confronted with the threat from Hecht. Rising, he told his father in a commanding tone: 'I need to talk with you both about something important.'

Jonathan felt the hairs on the back of his neck rise – this sounded very ominous, but he still did not connect his son's return to the fugitive boy.

With Jonathan leading the way, they went out of the church and around the back of the pastor's house to enter via the kitchen.

Elsa was at the sink, doing the dishes.

On hearing the door open, she turned to smile at her husband, brushing an unruly lock of grey hair out of her eyes.

'We have a surprise visitor,' announced Jonathan.

On seeing Martin, she dropped a china bowl in the sink and, without stopping to wipe her hands, rushed forward to enfold him in an embrace, leaving soap suds handprints on the back of his beautifully tailored tunic.

Looking at the two of them together, a lump of emotion rose in Jonathan's throat but suddenly he felt fearful. Where was the alleged fugitive boy? Might their secret blunder in at any second?

There had been no advance warning of strangers in the house to send him off to his hiding place in the loft. With Elsa still holding Martin tight in tearful embrace, Jonathan slipped out of the kitchen and crept upstairs to make sure David was hidden.

* * *

Later, with the boy safely secreted, all three Walders sat around the main kitchen table, drinking tea and eating cake. Elsa gently turned Martin's head so she could inspect the scars around his eye and he didn't resist her touch.

'It doesn't hurt?'

'Not now,' he admitted, pulling his head away from her hand.

'You should have written to us.'

'What was the point in worrying you?'

'Five years is a long time for us not to see you,' Elsa remarked with a sniff, grabbing his hand. 'Surely you had leave?'

Martin looked away, inspecting the spotlessly clean tiled floor.

'I didn't think I was welcome in this house.'

Jonathan sighed, brow furrowed.

'As our son, you are *always* welcome Martin.'

Jonathan suddenly felt sympathy for his boy – like father like son, suffering in war, just as he had in the trenches 20 or so years earlier, his world also narrowed to a patch of blood-soaked mud.

Getting up from the table, Jonathan decided to give mother and son a moment or two alone. 'I have to look at some urgent parish matters in my study,' he claimed. After Jonathan had closed the door, Elsa squeezed Martin's hand again. 'I heard him in the church,' Martin told her.

'He shouldn't say those things. He can get you both in deep trouble. You shouldn't have to suffer for his opinions.'

She bridled a little at this.

'Are they wrong Martin?'

'The Führer has hauled Germany up by her boot-straps, restored her power and pride to where it should be. He's taken a stand against the evil of communism to save us. They're no friends of God you know, the bloody Reds. Tell him he has to keep his opinions under control. Germans need to keep faith in their Nation or the Bolsheviks will be in our homes.'

Even as he said these words, Martin realized that he no longer believed them, or that Hitler had achieved salvation for Germany – quite the contrary. It wasn't a matter of Germany stopping the Reds anymore, but of holding off the Soviet steamroller as long as possible, to delay annihilation. But, doing Hecht's bidding might be the only way of giving his parents some way out of this mess. The noose was around their necks and they didn't even know it. So, he said these things, hoping they might give the boy up and receive the clemency Hecht had implied would be forthcoming.

Feeling resentment at being plunged into this situation in his heart, with hot tears of angry frustration welling up, Martin suggested harshly: 'But, some enemies of the State are already in our homes, aren't they?'

Elsa stiffened, withdrew her hand from his.

'Why are you hiding a Jewish boy in your home?'

She turned pale, but said nothing. This, then, was the reason he had come home and she felt burning betrayal, shaking as she got to her feet without saying anything and left the kitchen.

Martin gave a deep sigh, feeling dreadful but also sure he had done the right thing to bring them to their senses.

In the study Jonathan was at his desk, apparently engrossed in paperwork, but he had been listening to the murmur of voices and then felt his gut tighten as he heard the kitchen door open. Looking up he saw his wife was white as a ghost, closing the study door softly behind her.

'He knows about David,' she hissed.

Jonathan was dumbfounded.

'How?'

His face darkened with anger. He got up and gently took Elsa to the chair by his desk, sat her down and told her to stay calm. In the hallway outside the kitchen door Jonathan paused to compose himself. On entering he found Martin standing by the window.

'Is this why you came?' he asked his son, voice infused with fury.

Turning around, Martin's eyes blazed.

'You don't deny it then?'

Jonathan laughed contemptuously:

'Since when have children been enemies of the State?'

'You'd be surprised what children are capable of, father.'

Red-faced, Jonathan spat back: 'I know what children are capable of!' Martin shook his head in disgust at his father's naivety.

Jonathan lifted up one of the chairs and slammed it down.

'My eyes are wide open boy!' he roared.

'They see with absolute clarity what you are!'

Martin held his temper in check, fixing his eyes on a photographic portrait on the shelf of a kitchen cabinet – it was his mother as young woman, holding a babe-in-arms – not Martin, but Baby Manfred, before the Spanish influenza took him, gurgling and beaming up at his mother, who smiled down at him, blissfully.

It had always been impossible to compete with a dead baby brother who had become a saint, felt Martin. That angelic child never got to live long enough to anger and disappoint his parents.

No longer able to contain his fury, Martin yelled: 'You don't know what's coming from the East!'

'Evil begets evil!' Jonathan barked.

Martin smiled bitterly.

'For once maybe you and I agree.'

He sat down at the table, placing his head in his hands.

Jonathan, who had consigned his son to the past, wished he was still there and had not materialised in the present. His wife pined for the son she once knew, but Jonathan understood what war could do to a man's soul and that chances of survival in the infantry were slim. Jonathan had never expected to see his son again, not this side of Heaven or Hell.

To have Martin invade their lives on such a mission was unbearable and he observed, with barely suppressed rage: 'That you, my own son, could come into our house – and into God's house – on a mission to find a child for the Nazis to murder sickens me.'

Martin offered no rebuttal, held his palms up to his eyes to suppress more tears of anger and sorrow.

Cautiously re-entering the kitchen, Elsa expected to find they had murdered each other.

She pulled up a chair by Martin, not touching him, but staying still with her hands in her lap, looking anxiously from father to son, studying their faces for clues as to what had just happened. Her heart was torn between wiping away her boy's tears and holding fast to supporting her husband.

Martin looked up, avoiding her eyes. He was ashamed – of himself, and scared for them. They wouldn't give the boy up.

He reflected bitterly that the lad was probably more of a son to them. In truth, admitting to their misdeeds would only earn them execution – Hecht's clemency offer was a dirty lie. Nazi justice was savage, especially with those who assisted enemies of the State.

Martin got up, the chair scraping back noisily, which jarred his parents' nerves. With conflicting emotions, for a few silent moments he regarded them with sorrowful eyes; anger at what they had done surging in his blood; knowing that they had no tomorrow unless he could convince Hecht there was no boy in the pastor's house.

Though not one to seek God's help, he might even pray for a miracle. Martin grabbed his cap, turned on his heels and pulled the kitchen door open forcefully.

It crashed shut behind him and Elsa began to weep. Jonathan folded his arms around her, wondering how long it would be before jackboot heels and rifle butts bashed the door in.

11

Martin had the few seconds while he crossed the road to Hecht's car to get himself under control again and decide what to do.

Anger had been such a feature of his internal life for so long. There was the long held and deep-seated fury at his parents, particularly his mother for her pining after poor lost Baby Manfred - *seeming to love the dead child more than her living son*; and anger at the lack of respect shown to his country by the world.

It had combined to propel him into the Hitler Youth and then the Waffen SS – a gesture of defiance against his parents – *he'd show them!* – which was also of pride and patriotism in the New Germany the Führer forged. And now there was more anger - at the failure of war to bring him glory, disappointed its fires had not cleansed his soul, but rather burned him.

His stupid parents made him furious again for their lack of reality – their hopeless gesture of saving the Jewish boy…and he could not shock them out of their folly. Now he had to purge himself of impulsive rage, for Martin realised, no matter what, he could not, in the end, betray his mother and father. There was deep sorrow in his heart, the like of which he had not known since the day he left home to join the Waffen SS. As Martin approached the Mercedes, the Gestapo investigator climbed out, opening a rear passenger door and following Martin in to sit beside him, examining the soldier's inscrutable face for signs of what had transpired.

'Will they give the boy up?'

'They deny it.'

'What?'

'They said it's all lies - they would never give refuge to an enemy of the State.' Martin held Hecht's disbelieving eyes steadily, giving nothing away. 'They were outraged that I could suggest such a thing when their first loyalty is Germany.' Hecht responded sceptically: 'That may be so, but...'

The Gestapo investigator had gambled on the stormtrooper being persuasive and the result was, well, disappointing. Or was Martin telling the truth? Hecht shrugged and remarked resignedly: 'Oh well…but I don't suppose there's any point you going back in and talking to them again?'

Martin knew any chance his parents retained, when it came to evading the full force of the Gestapo's further investigation, resided in his vouching for them.

Meeting Hecht's hopeful stare with a deceptive façade he told the Gestapo man: 'For what it's worth I believe them, but our relations are so shattered it would be futile.' Hecht nodded and then with a regretful sigh observed: 'It is what it is.'

* * *

Hecht felt Martin had reached the end of his usefulness and so, after calling at the Adlon for him to pack his carpetbag and check out, they headed for the Friedrichstrasse station, Hecht walking him to the platform.

'Thankyou for all your help,' the Gestapo man said, extending a hand, which Martin declined to take.

'Did you arrange for me to get my medal from the Führer just so you could send me to see my parents? The medal was horse shit wasn't it?'

Hecht looked genuinely shocked, giving a beautiful impression of being so. 'Of course not; how can you think that?'

The Gestapo man couldn't resist gilding the lily.

'We don't misuse Germany's heroes; just a happy coincidence Martin. Serendipity.'

Martin didn't believe a word but merely told him wearily:

'Goodbye Hecht.'

A railway porter grabbed Martin's bag and opened a carriage door, climbing up to put it on a shelf above the seats.

'Goodbye hauptsturmführer,' said Hecht, 'it's a First Class compartment – so, enjoy.'

Hecht turned and walked away, Martin's contemptuous eyes boring into his back, as he climbed up into the carriage. Martin settled into a seat and, as the train entered the tunnel that ran under the Spree and Landwehrkanal, he reached up to pull the window down.

Standing up and bracing himself against the doorframe, from a tunic pocket he pulled out the case into which he had placed his Knight's Cross.

He lifted the lid, pulled on the ribbon, dangling the medal, watching it twist and shine in the carriage lighting before extending his arm out of the window and opening his hand. The medal fell, ribbon trailing, swallowed up by the darkness.

* * *

Clad again in his baggy wounded warrior suit and open-necked shirt - uniform and accoutrements shut away in a wardrobe - Martin sat on the windowsill of the room in the Casino Hospital at Bad Gastein.

Even after his roommate entered - clad in mountaineering gear - Martin did not drop the book he was reading, though sighed at having to squint in order to bring the text into focus.

Only when Erwin dumped his climbing ropes on the floor did Martin look at him, not terribly pleased to be disturbed.

'How did it go with the optician?' Erwin asked as he sat on a bedside chair to untie his boots and take off socks, rubbing his sore feet. Martin had been unable to go up the mountain with Erwin and Werner due to the ophthalmic appointment.

'The tests were inconclusive.'

Martin gestured with the book towards the table under a large mirror. 'There's some mail there for you.'

Erwin got to his feet with a groan, hobbled over to pick up the envelope and opened it. After reading whatever was in the letter, he carefully folded it up and put it back inside. Curious, Martin dropped the book into his lap and enquired:

'What is it?'

'Ordered back to my regiment in the 1st Gebirgsjäger Division.'

Martin spotted a silver lining for his friend.

'You can take Nurse Gottlieb out for a big farewell dinner and maybe get your leg over before you go?'

Shocked by Martin's earthiness, Erwin laughed and reached forward to tap him on the head with the envelope before depositing it on his bedside table. 'Anyway, never mind me,' Erwin said, 'what about that waitress with the blonde hair at the *Schöner Berg*?'

Martin gave no response, picking the book up and carrying on reading. He had taken a walk up there shortly after returning from Berlin only to discover she was no longer working at the hotel. Lorelei had vanished, so it was presumed she had returned to Vienna. This was not long after her cousin had turned up out of the blue. Martin's notions of romance had therefore gone out with a whimper but he wasn't going to admit that.

Erwin grabbed the jug of water on his table and poured some into a glass. He drank it down in one, poured himself another, then sat on the edge of his bed looking expectantly at Martin: 'Hey, I didn't get time yet to ask you for a look, so where's the medal?'

Not raising his eyes from the book, Martin responded in a flat voice: 'Packed away.'

'Get it out.'

'It's a piece of metal Erwin, that's all.'

'Come on, let's see it.'

'I left the medal with my parents.'

Erwin was not convinced. He couldn't make Martin out these days. There was the change in his reading matter for a start. Instead of von Clausewitz, he was into Heinrich Heine, the Jewish-born poet - *a banned writer no less* – and where Martin had managed to find such a book Erwin had no idea. He had warned him not to read it outside the room they shared or leave it lying around.

Martin replied that Heine was a perfect German patriot no matter what the Führer thought. Erwin thought that *very* dangerous talk. He now disapprovingly tapped the top of the book with a finger, which earned him a glare

'What can Heine teach you that old von Clausewitz can't I wonder?' Erwin enquired. Getting up and throwing a towel over his shoulder, Erwin grabbed a wash bag as Martin read aloud from the book.

'He does not see the rocky reefs,
He only looks up to the heights.'

Turning at the door, Erwin observed drily:

'A cheerful couplet.'

Martin laughed, a full, genuine expression of humour so unlike the Waffen SS automaton of even a few weeks ago. With Erwin gone, Martin returned to his book, holding it up for better light. Below the window, raging waters crashed and roared over the rocks.

PART IV

1

The Huntsman's Lodge

Martin paused in the telling of his tale to make a request.

'My mouth is dry - may I get myself something?' Eric nodded, so the German got up and went over to the sink where he drew off some mountain spring water via a tap.

'I'll have a glass, too,' Eric suggested, as he too also felt rather fatigued and dehydrated.

Martin began the hunt for a pair of glasses, opening and shutting cupboard doors with a loudness that aggravated the British officer.

Eric had long since laid the Walther pistol on his lap, surreptitiously ensuring the safety was on so he didn't accidentally shoot himself in the groin. The German had been so engrossed in his story that possibly he had not even noticed, though Eric wasn't entirely sure it wasn't all just some long-winded plan to lull him into a false sense of security. Martin's story just seemed bullshit by a Nazi trying to show that he was *a good German* after all.

Would family ties and the life of a Jewish lad in hiding have really conquered a fanatic's loyalty to the Nazi state?

Martin placed a glass of water in front of Eric, then sat down and sipped his own, declaring: 'That is good!'

Martin opened a drawer on his side of the table and, with a heart-thumping jolt, Eric realised this could be it – the German's move to finish him off and get away. Eric dropped his glass on the table and scrabbled for the gun in his lap. Water spilling across the table, the glass rolled off the table's edge and shattered on the hard floor, Eric raising the Walther.

'Don't move!' he screamed.

Eyes fixed on Eric's finger curling around the trigger, Martin put his hands in the air and said quietly: 'I am not going for a gun.'

Eric got up, keeping the Walther on Martin, coming around to the other side of the table. 'Get back!' he shouted.

The German pushed the chair back with his legs, Eric pulling the drawer fully open, finding it contained a packet of cigarettes after all and some matches – but also, of course, his Browning pistol. Eric pulled the Browning out and put it back in his holster.

'I promise you that I was only interested in the cigarettes,' Martin protested.

'Get me more water,' Eric ordered, going back to sit on his side of the table, keeping the Walther pointed at Martin.

'After you've done that sit down and no tricks and let's hear the rest of your tale? Why don't we do that?'

And so, Martin resumed his story.

Having sat through all the rest – *rose-tinted rubbish or not* – Eric wanted to hear the remainder of the SS officer's tale, in case it helped solve the mystery of what happened to all the poor souls on the death march.

Even Germans, responsible as they were for so much suffering, should be allowed to give their testimony. Yet, if Martin tried to lull him into a sense of ease and escape, a bullet would be Eric's response.

2

Hungary, September 1944

To the north of Lake Balaton was a railway halt in the middle of nowhere to which a ramshackle train brought Martin Walder whose dignity and olfactory sense was affronted by travelling in such close company with peasants and poultry.

Just weeks earlier he had been honoured for his bravery by no less than Adolph Hitler, but now he was being transported in a style fit only for pigs who, indeed, also made up some of the cargo.

As even Martin had to concede, he had treated his Knight's Cross with such disdain that perhaps he could expect nothing better.

Shuddering, with the straining steam engine letting out an agonized gasp, the train coughed to a standstill. Relieved to quit the rancid, cigarette smoke filled carriage Martin threw the door back and, grabbing his bulging suitcase from the rack above his seat, lost no time in dismounting. Belching clouds of steam, the train hauled itself away, pigs squealing at the terrifying vibrations transmitted through the frames of its trucks and carriages.

It disappeared around a bend in the track leaving behind a sultry silence, broken only by the whisper of wind through the trees and hum of insects. After the cacophony of the train, Martin found it was a welcome relief. Unbuttoning the top of his lightweight field jacket, he took off his cap – a mountain division one presented to him by Erwin. Martin wiped the sweat from his brow using a white cotton handkerchief then scanned his surroundings.

Aside from a sign announcing the halt, there was no other indication this was somewhere that people alighted – no platform, no picket fence around it, or shelter; just the track cutting through the woods.

A pathway led away from the railway track through the trees and Martin hoped it would take him to a road where he would find some form of transport waiting, or that something would soon turn up. Martin put the cap back on, picked up his suitcase, the stones of the ballast crunching under his feet as he crossed the line, a thin film of white dust coating his brown climbing boots.

He needn't have worried, for parked up by the road was a Horch staff car, its driver snoring behind the wheel, an Organisation Todt field cap tipped over his eyes. Martin dropped his case on the back seat, making the soldier wake up with a start. Walking around to the passenger side, Martin opened the door and climbed in, enquiring: 'You're from the camp I presume?'

'Yes, Sir!' the Todt man cried out, retrieving his cap from the foot well, jamming it on his head and turning the key in the ignition.

* * *

Through the windows of the Commandant's office, beyond a screen of trees, Martin could see guard towers. Scanning to the left, he took in neat rows of huts where the inmates live.

It all looked rather like a seedy holiday resort, which, so the Horch driver had informed him, it had been before the war. But this was no longer a site of relaxation and recuperation for city workers, but a place of hard labour for Jews and other undesirables who had, so the Nazis felt, been loafing when the Hungarians were in charge. Germany had now occupied Hungary, and so sent in the Todt to run this place.

Martin suspected his assignment in the labour camp was Hecht's little joke, arranged as a place fit for an uncooperative hero. No longer considered the ideal Aryan soldier – due to his less-than-perfect eyesight – Martin was to provide useful service putting some spine into Todt guards – the so-called Schutzkommando personnel - making sure their weapons training and discipline was up to scratch; or even just adequate.

On the other side of a large oak desk, the Commandant's sweaty bald head was bent over a folder, reading Martin's service record. 'Very impressive,' he remarked, not sounding that impressed.

'Thankyou,' replied Martin crisply.

Looking up, the Commandant, or Oberleiter in the Todt paramilitary hierarchy, gave Martin the same queasy smile with which he had greeted him earlier; shaking his hand was like grabbing a slippery fish. 'We have very few combat veterans here and no holders of the Knight's Cross,' the Commandant observed, mildly perturbed. 'The report does not specify, so may I ask why exactly you are assigned to us?'

Martin smiled apologetically.

'It was my eyes, Sir.'

The Commandant closed the folder.

'A shame…do you need spectacles now?'

'No, Sir.'

That was a lie. The report said Martin needed glasses for close work. The Commandant gave a satisfied little smile at finding a weakness in this elite warrior.

'Have you offended someone?'

Martin's gut tightened and suddenly he had a vision of Hecht's shit-eating grin in his head but he met the Commandant's enquiring gaze steadily and wore his best poker face.

'Not that I am aware of, Sir.'

The Commandant opened the report again and ran his finger down the top sheet as he spoke.

'You received the Knight's Cross with Oak Leaves and Swords

from the Führer himself, yet you don't wear it?' He looked bemused: 'Is this out of modesty?'

Martin nodded, face straight, though actually rather amused by the way this idiot's mind worked. 'Yes, Sir. Modesty.'

The Commandant was not convinced.

'It wasn't taken away for some misdemeanour not listed here?'

Martin swallowed his irritation and lied again.

'My parents have the medal.'

The Commandant gave an insincere smile.

'Your mother must be *so* proud.'

'Yes, Sir, she is.'

The Commandant closed the report, opened a desk drawer and put it away, observing: 'I suppose if you'd been a naughty boy it would say so in your record. And you'd be in a penal battalion in Russia, not here.' The Commandant leaned back in his chair, pulled open the drawer on the other side and extracted a bottle of peach schnapps and a couple of shot glasses. He poured the drinks and pushed one of them across to Martin, giving a tight smile. 'Welcome aboard Hauptsturmführer Walder,' he said, with no trace of warmth. 'Any questions?'

'What exactly does the camp do, Sir?'

The Commandant downed his schnapps with a flick of the wrist, then smiled coyly.

'We clean up society.'

'How?'

Martin knocked his schnapps back, the Commandant refilling their glasses. 'We are meant to provide criminals and undesirables; prisoners of war, foreign internees…for working parties, to be employed on useful projects – road construction and defensive barriers - and then, when they are no longer useful we send them away to the resettlement camps.' He added with barely concealed anger at the higher ups: 'Lately we have ended up with young women and the elderly, as if they can do such work…it is a disgrace.'

The Commandant threw back his second schnapps.

Martin's remained untouched.

'You are not much of a drinker?'

'Not much, Sir.'

The Commandant poured himself yet another.

'Everybody here drinks,' he revealed. 'Not to excess while on duty of course, but it certainly helps to oil our machinery. We work very long hours and sometimes, I will admit, it can be quite taxing. We work hard and play hard. So, drink up, for tomorrow we die, as the saying goes.'

Martin frowned at the fool's faux bravery.

What did he know of war?

The Commandant took satisfaction from irritating this hero of the Reich, for the backbone of Greater Germany was in his view provided by the hard work of the Todt. The Commandant lifted his glass and exclaimed enthusiastically: 'Prost!'

* * *

They found him a spot in one of the holiday camp administration huts that had been closed since just before the war but recently reopened to host the ever-growing Organisation Todt bureaucracy.

Martin's office had belonged to the former entertainment manager and was bedecked with posters of beaming, muscle-bound athletes leaping over pommel horses and doing acrobatics between rings.

There was even one showing a family enjoying a picnic on the green slopes by Lake Balaton, clustered on a tartan rug and helping themselves to bounty from hampers – all rosy-red cheeks and grins.

'The smug bastards,' thought Martin sourly.

His desk and chair was made from bamboo, in keeping with the exotic, so-called holiday theme of the pre-war camp. A long-faded framed photograph on the wall above a rusty filing cabinet depicted a beach of what must have once been blinding white sands fringed by tall green palm trees – except everything was now a uniform dirty blue.

None of this improved Martin's mood and he felt a slow, creeping despair. An inventory of the camp armoury, for instance, had revealed a shockingly poor level of weapons maintenance, though Martin had managed to salvage an MP40 submachine gun for himself, some ammunition and also a few grenades.

For the day when the Russians swept into Hungary could not be far away. He still half entertained the notion that he might be able to organize a fighting unit out of the guards - a 120-strong company of men, including some who had fought in his father's war. A bunch of derelicts. He was again thinking what a slimy bastard the Commandant was when the man himself entered the office, to check on his latest recruit. He loomed over the desk, displaying that queasy smile of his.

'You should learn to relax Martin,' he observed. 'This kind of work has its rewards but really, everyone needs to relax some time. Have you visited our bawdy house yet?'

This description was delivered with a lascivious smirk.

'No, thanks,' was Martin's stony response.

This was not good enough for the Commandant.

'Some of these women are the most shockingly compliant,' he remarked with a lascivious grin. 'You must spend some leisure time there. It will take the edge off you.'

Perhaps he should, as the nights alone in his room were becoming Martin's very own Hungarian purgatory.

He had turned in on himself, drinking to gain release, to blot it out, but it wasn't until he gave in to the entreaties of the Commandant to partake of some carnal relaxation at 'social club' that the screw really turned.

Entering its stinking, tawdry confines Martin's stomach was turned by the sickening combination of cheap cologne mixing with alcohol fumes, and absurd décor - red and black flock wallpaper, naked nymph-shaped wall lamps and, naturally, Austrian drapes.

Martin let the Commandant buy him a drink at the bar to explain how it worked. As he spoke, with a meaty paw the Commandant indicated the stage at the far end, explaining that before the war this was a clubhouse where magicians and conjurers entertained the kiddies while their parents got pissed.

Nowadays, each evening the girls would first entertain the officers with a rendition of classic songs, such as *Eidelweiss*. According to the Commandant they had lovely voices.

After the songs they would descend from the stage and mingle with the officers, who would choose whomever they fancied for sex, or 'relaxation' as the Commandant termed it. Martin died a little more inside.

A nervous coughing and scraping of chairs indicated a group of musicians dressed in ill-fitting black tie had entered and were arranging themselves below the stage.

They began playing *The Blue Danuben* and the curtains parted, the Commandant and other Todt officers applauding.

Martin was, though, entranced by the stage's massive backdrop depicting towering, sharp-edged, snow-topped Alps above dense green forests. It was incredibly well realized and he could pick out a massive waterfall and also a small train puffing its way towards the heights.

The girls trooped out – all skin and bones, their drawn faces daubed with make-up that didn't hide their poor state of nourishment, nor could the thin, ill-made dresses hanging loosely from their bodies.

They began singing *Lili Marlene*, the tune cutting straight to Martin's core in a fashion that quite surprised him. The purity of their voices - the contrast with the squalor of their predicament - made him want to weep.

Martin scanned the singers, feeling his stomach drop through the floor. For there, in the second row - her still beautiful face lifted as she stared with glazed eyes over the heads of the ghastly audience - was Lorelei.

Martin turned away, slugging back a pear schnapps, his glass immediately refilled by the barman. He knocked that back, too, put his glass on the bar and fought to get his emotions under control.

The visit to Berlin had prised open a chink in his armour, but finding Lorelei right in front of him was a dagger thrust penetrating his heart and soul behind what remained of the protective carapace. Martin grabbed his refilled glass and retreated to a table in a dark corner. A wave of sadness hit him, a yearning for the paradise of the mountains - but the dream of the perfect, golden girl had evaporated and he struggled in his head to make sense of it.

How on earth had she turned up here?

When the girls came down from the stage, they sat in a long line on stools at the bar. Allowed a schnapps as a reward for their fine singing they were poised primly, to await selection. In the majority of cases their faces were devoid of animation, though one or two pretended eagerness.

The Commandant, typically boorish, sought out Martin and suggested that, as the newest officer, he should make his selection first.

Feeling sick with disgust and fear as he walked down the line, Martin was thankful Lorelei had not, so far, recognized him. Trying to appear as casual as possible, he stopped and gently took her hand.

As she slid off the stool the other officers jeered and catcalled. Martin showed her to a table in the shadows at the back. He said nothing, patiently waiting for her to react.

Lorelei's eyes slowly lost their glazed aspect, acquiring lachrymose recognition, provoked by his presence and being a reminder of a time when she was free in the mountains. He dug into a trouser pocket and offered her a handkerchief, which she hesitantly took - for she feared he was an apparition.

Suddenly feeling anxious, Martin looked around, finding the Commandant at a neighbouring table wearing a disapproving frown; there was something very odd about his new officer, and his suspicions had increased when he saw the man offer the Jewess a handkerchief to dry her tears.

He suspected this Waffen SS hero found the camp's business all too distasteful. That just wouldn't do and, if the Commandant could catch Martin out, he would see him end up in a penal battalion after all.

Martin went over to the bar, paid for a whole bottle of schnapps, and, taking Lorelei's hand, led her from the brothel. A few Todt officers wolf-whistled and made crude suggestions. Martin wanted to rip their throats out but repressed his fury.

* * *

Stunned and fearful of what might happen next, Lorelei stood by the window while Martin took his tunic off and hung it up in the wardrobe.

'Please, remove that ridiculous wig,' he told her.

Shaking like a leaf, she did so, revealing her shaved head.

He took the wig and put it in the bottom of the wardrobe.

'Take those clothes off,' he ordered.

With trembling fingers, she started to slip the dress off.

'Wait. Move over by the bed.'

Lorelei meekly did as she was told, head spinning at finding the handsome wounded officer she had flirted with in the mountains here in a labour camp - and in an SS uniform. *Might he now fling her on the bed and rape her?* Instead he reached inside the wardrobe for a dressing gown and handed it to her. 'If you want to wash, please use my sink.' In order to afford her privacy, Martin went over to look out the window.

3

THAT FIRST NIGHT she had eventually settled and he let her sleep in his bed while he nodded off in an armchair.

When he woke early the following morning she was staring at him; a deer in the woods watching a sleeping wolf. Hauling himself out of the chair he went over to the sink and brushed his teeth, avoiding her stare by not looking in the mirror.

It was the rule that bed companions had to be returned each morning and in Lorelei's case that would be to her job in the main kitchens of the camp – a privilege for the lucky few chosen to serve in the brothel. They would last longer than those doing hard labour.

Over the following days a pattern exerted itself and there were complaints about him monopolizing this one woman, but nobody really wanted to argue with a combat-hardened Waffen SS officer.

The Commandant glared suspiciously but did nothing, though if he had known of the previous connection between Martin and the girl he might well have taken some action.

It was a perplexing situation. Since breaking with his parents' morality and ways - giving himself to the Nazi party – Martin had been taught to hate anyone who was not of pure Aryan blood. Lorelei had appeared to be the epitome of a healthy Germanic maid…with her long blonde hair, fair skin and blue eyes. The girl he'd met in Bad Gastein represented his supposed ideal. It stunned him to find her shorn and traumatised…and he was bewildered.

The Todt jackals may have believed he was screwing her, but, in reality each night Lorelei would just sleep in his bed, Martin watching over her for a while, slowly getting hammered on schnapps, until he dropped into an uneasy slumber.

Sometimes into his dreams a vision of her riding a bicycle down a mountain road – beautiful, free, so alive and full of life – would intrude, or it might be the female Russian sniper dying in a pool of blood. On other occasions it might be an ochre disk sun behind the smoke of a burning Belarus village.

When he watched her sleep, Martin's thoughts were equally troubled as he pondered the situation with his parents – the anguish and sorrow but above all the fury and frustration of their suicidal harbouring of the boy - and despair at the possibility they had already met a cruel fate.

There was also misery at even his idealistic dream of Lorelei turning to ashes. He sat forward in the chair, trying to force the tears back into his eyes with the palms of his hands.

* * *

Lorelei woke, watched him but when he looked up she closed her eyes, pretending to be asleep. Drifting off, when she surfaced again, Martin was standing at the window, staring up at the stars, slugging back spirit direct from the bottle. On hearing her stir he turned around and, as Lorelei stretched, gestured towards some food on a small table by the bed.

'Eat.'

She took the plate of bread, cheese and sausage and tucked in while Martin returned to staring at the stars.

'Would you like some schnapps?' he asked.

'Yes, please.'

He went over to the sink, took a glass from the shelf above it and poured some, placing it on the table.

After a few minutes silence while she ate, Lorelei enquired:

'Why are you doing all this?'

Martin sat down in the armchair, watching her eating while he again drank from the bottle. 'I thought you were a soldier,' she ventured after a minute or two.

'I was.'

'How did you end up here?'

'My eyes.'

'Your eyes?'

'They were not perfect after my wound, so I could not be returned to combat with my unit. They sent me here.' He sighed and then added sarcastically: 'They think of it as an honourable way to serve the Reich...but, if I may ask, how did you end up here?

'My mother is Jewish.'

'And they put you in here for that?'

'She and my father divorced in 1933. To all intents and purposes we were thoroughly Aryan. My mother lived in America, out of sight and out of mind. Father was even a Nazi party official in Vienna and we believed in Hitler - we were loyal to the Greater Reich and anything else was irrelevant but then my brother, Peter deserted from the army after being badly wounded at Stalingrad. He absconded from a hospital in Berlin, but when he got back to Vienna he discovered that one of our neighbours had told the authorities that we were Jewish. My father had been arrested.'

The old Martin – before his head wound – would have felt enraged at hearing of an army deserter, especially one with such impure blood.

But now humanity crept into his soul – the scales had fallen from his eyes. Anyone who got home from the almighty catastrophe of Stalingrad deserved credit no matter who they were. Even a half Jew.

'I went into hiding.'

'Bad Gastein?'

'Yes.'

'Why?'

'We used to holiday there, although no one really remembered me. I was only a girl. A friend of the family told Peter where I'd gone, so he came to get me - pretending he was a cousin. We planned to go over the mountains through Austria and Italy into Switzerland, then to America but things didn't quite go according to plan.'

* * *

Werner Schaffhausen disdained telescopic sights, preferring the iron sight on the end of his hunting rifle barrel, aided by an unerring eye that had served him well since his father first took him hunting as child.

As a young man in the mountains above Lake Garda he'd stalked Italians who cared more for their comfort – lolling about in the open - than concealing themselves from his roving huntsman's eye. They were easy prey compared to this chamois, a mature male, whose pale rump bobbed infuriatingly out of range on the crags above. It had taken him all morning to finally bring the magnificent little mountain goat within killing distance. The chamois was the prey of kings – Emperor Franz Josef himself hunted them in these very mountains. The emperor must have been a fit old goat himself, for the chamois was a most demanding quarry, requiring the hunter to be swift and sure of foot across treacherous rocks.

Once or twice Werner believed the animal knew he was stalking it.

He'd taken a detour through some woods, hoping to get into a shooting position above. With utmost stealth, despite his stiff, aching middle-aged joints, Werner leopard crawled to the edge of the tree line, rifle braced across his arms.

The chamois stood proud on rock outcrop in the Gastein Valley, its senses straining to pick up danger, sniffing the air. Werner was well-placed above, the chamois against some fluffy white low clouds and he ever so slowly raised the butt to his shoulder, pulling it in tight, thumb gently pushing the safety off. This rifle was an old friend. Its bolt action was smooth and noiseless as the bullet was rammed home. Werner remained in the shadows at the edge of some trees, the gentle breeze ruffling his grey hair, reminding him to allow for windage.

He laid the sight on the goat, which was now head down, nibbling at some vegetation. Werner inhaled, the barrel dipping, then exhaled, bringing it back up to target and holding his breath. One shot should do it, aiming for the belly line, so penetrating the heart and lungs, killing the animal with minimal pain.

But, before he could squeeze the trigger, the chamois detected a presence that made it uneasy, scenting something on the wind, from down slope.

It bounded away across the rocks, Werner cursing under his breath.

Getting to his knees with a groan, he switched the rifle's safety back and his ears picked up the faint sound of voices.

* * *

'How much further!?' Peter called out, his attention suddenly attracted by a flash of brown and white bouncing across the slopes above.

Narrowing his eyes against the glare, he saw it was a chamois, which momentarily paused to look down at him, horns quivering and then it was gone, bounding away into the dancing heat haze.

Peter felt dizzy, he thought probably due to dehydration, so he sat down on the grassy slope, disturbing a bee gathering pollen from edelweiss. Batting the irritated insect away, Peter closed his eyes and enjoyed the sun's warmth on his pallid skin, which had seen too few summer days. Looking back down the narrow mountain path he found Lorelei also resting.

'How much further?' he asked again.

'Not far.'

He got to his feet.

'Well, stop sunning yourself and let's go.'

They reached their destination; a mountain lodge. In summers past, once the snows thawed, it would have seen a lot of through traffic. Since the war visitors had become few and far between – the last one, a few weeks earlier was Lorelei when she tested the route and decided it was an ideal location to secrete provisions.

The front door was stiff, but Peter's shoulder got it open, the hinges creaking and dust stirring underfoot as it suddenly gave way and he stumbled inside. Coughing, Peter staggered to one of the windows, fingers scrabbling for the catch on the shutters. With an alarmed cry, Lorelei rushed across to stop him. 'Hey!' he spluttered as she pulled his hands away.

A fierceness in her eyes showed she meant business.

'It's best not to draw attention to ourselves. The dust will settle.'

She dragged him into the kitchen area, and crouched on the floor, running her fingers over the floorboards.

There was something desperate, something urgent in her that Peter had never seen before. Peter realized his sister's double life had imposed a great strain on the seemingly carefree person he'd known in Vienna. His frown of bemusement turned to amused curiosity when she lifted up part of one of the floorboards, then another section beside the first. Peter crouched beside her as she reached in.

Like a magician extracting a rabbit from a hat, she pulled out a hessian sack and, from within it, a bar of real chocolate, of the like he had not seen for years – big, chunky and wrapped in gold foil. Edible bullion. These days it was surely worth as much as precious metal?

As if that miracle was not enough, she pulled out not one more but three.

He took them off her, piling them up, enjoying the glint and substance of the glittering pile.

'This is treasure indeed,' Peter remarked in awe, 'but how did you get them?'

'The head chef of the Hotel Schöner Berg has a secret hoard,' and revealing with with a cheeky grin: 'I sweet-talked him.'

Next she handed him a smoked sausage.

'And who did you sweet-talk for this!?'

'I stole it from the breakfast buffet.'

'And no one noticed?'

Lorelei grinned devilishly and next pulled out a bottle of Asbach brandy. 'Goodness,' said Peter admiringly, as he turned the bottle over in his hands before placing it beside the pile of other goodies.

'The brandy I bought from Herr Greim who owns the hotel. He got it on the black market for me. He knew you were coming and thought...'

'... that cousin Peter should have a welcome fit for a hero.'

Going over to a kitchen cupboard, Peter pulled down a couple of glasses, trying to blow the dust out of them, but this didn't do the trick. Turning on a tap over the sink, all he got was a clanking of empty pipes.

Peter put the glasses back in the cupboard.

'But, you, know, I think that right now I'd actually rather have some tea.' Lorelei delved into her hiding place and retrieved a packet of tea. 'Voila!'

Peter pulled his sister to her feet, giving her a hug.

'My little Lorelei...I am so proud of you.'

'You're crushing me.'

He released her and she exited the kitchen, coming back with her rucksack, pulling out a packet of matches. He shook his head and sighed: 'But there is no water.' Lorelei went over to the sink, opened a cupboard beneath it, reaching in to turn on a stop cock to release the flow from a fresh water tank up slope connected to a stream. She let it flow for a few moments, grinning and then producing a copper kettle from somewhere Peter was amazed again, shaking his head and smiling in wonderment; could this be the same Lorelei?

* * *

As far as Werner knew, nobody had used the lodge since he last led climbers up this way several months ago. And so he'd watched with extreme interest as two tiny figures entered it, some shutters momentarily opening then closing.

Werner saw a wisp of smoke curl up from the lodge's stovepipe – Lorelei in her excitement had overlooked that give-away. Werner felt he should investigate; it could be escaped Allied prisoners of war attempting to make Switzerland.

They had caught two a few weeks back, but that was on the border. As a veteran of the first world war, Werner had the skills to handle any fugitives – he remained very fit for his age, still had his aggression. He could kill them, or they could come quietly and he'd give them a schnapps before handing them over to the authorities.

If they chose to resist, he didn't mind shooting them.

Today he'd rather bag a chamois.

* * *

Having secreted their escape supplies back below the floorboards - Lorelei and Peter were sat either side of a big wooden table in the dining area, sipping their cups of tea while Peter revealed his worries about potential pitfalls in their plan for escape. 'A young man of service age who isn't in a uniform sticks out like a sore thumb,' he suggested but she insisted: 'We must wait at least a month until the weather is warm enough at night.'

'You should have come to me.'

'Switzerland's easier from here.'

'But, what will I do for a month?'

'You can scivvy in the kitchen.'

Peter scowled, letting out a deep sigh, conveying submission to something he didn't agree with at all. Turning the china cup around in his hands, Peter looked away from her, the light seeping through the shutters turning his usually cloudy blue eyes clear. He snapped his head around, a deep frown on his face as he stared at the stove glowing in the kitchen.

Lorelei enquired: 'What is it?'

'I was just wondering if you lighting the stove wasn't also a bit of a give-away? The smoke…'

She opened her mouth to respond, but before any words came out, the front door crashed open, revealing Werner, hunting rifle in hand, ready to shoot. Lorelei dropped her empty cup, which bounced on the bare floorboards but did not break, rolling against Werner's boot-clad foot.

Werner lowered his gun and roared with laughter.

'Lorelei, it's you!'

Inside Lorelei was fearful but returned his jolly delight by laughingly exclaiming: 'Werner! You scared the life out of us!'

On unsteady legs, she got up from the table, going over to the kitchen, a means to hide her shock.

'Tea, Werner?'

Lorelei grabbed the edge of the sink to still her fear.

Werner grinned and nodded, plonking himself on the bench across from Peter who betrayed no inner feeling at all on his face, though his heart was beating so hard it felt like it would burst out of his chest. Placing his hunting rifle on the table between them, Werner extended a hand and enquired: 'So this is your cousin Peter, huh?' Werner's huge paw nearly wrenched Peter's arm off as they shook.

Sounding as light-hearted as possible, as she washed out a china cup Lorelei informed her brother: 'Peter, this is Werner, one of the Hotel's huntsmen and mountain guides.'

The adrenalin still coursing through his veins gave Peter the urge to grab the rifle and crush the hunter's skull with its butt, but he somehow resisted.

Studying Peter through narrowed eyes, Werner remarked:

'My sister's boy was at Stalingrad too.'

'Really?'

'They say it was hell.'

Peter shrugged, offering a modest smile.

'Depends on your idea of hell. What happened to your sister's boy?'

'He never came back, maybe the damned Reds have him in Siberia.'

Werner spat on the floor and massaged the spittle into the floorboards under the toe of his right boot for extra emphasis. Softly, with hushed respect he stated: 'Thank God some of you got out.'

Peter observed, he hoped as nonchalantly as possible: 'I was lucky. One of the last evacuation planes.'

With her hands by now steady, Lorelei brought the tea over, placing the cup in front of Werner and going around to sit beside Peter.

Werner sipped from the cup, so dainty in his large hands, and smacked his lips in delight. 'My goodness that's damned refreshing!'

He roared with laughter again and winked at Lorelei.

Under the table Lorelei gave Peter's hand a reassuring squeeze.

Patting the rifle on the table between them, Werner asked. 'I bet you could have done with a good huntsman or two out there? Levelled the score?'

'Might have helped,' Peter conceded.

Silence fell, as Werner slurped the tea, scrutinising the two of them. There was something covert going on here and he wondered if they were lovers, not cousins after all, but it was really none of his business. Draining the cup, Werner got to his feet, picking up the rifle as if it was made of balsa wood, hefting it from left to right hand. He glanced around the lodge to make sure everything seemed correct. Nothing out of place at all, except for the two youngsters.

'I'll take my leave now,' he told them, a sly smile playing across his lips. 'Make sure you leave it all in good order.' Werner made for the door, turning on the threshold with a broad grin on his face. 'Behave yourselves, children.' The door banged shut after him, with Lorelei and Peter holding their breath until they were sure Werner was well gone, then letting out huge sighs of relief.

* * *

After recounting her story to Martin, Lorelei was on verge of tears, but managed to control herself, changing the topic of conversation.

'Anyway, what's your job here?'

'It is of no importance.'

Martin wouldn't be diverted – he needed to know the source of that upset. 'But Lorelei, about Peter? Where is he now?'

'We came back down to Bad Gastein and decided to make our escape a week or two later. He did some odd jobs around the hotel – chopping wood, cleaning dishes and so on - but could tell that people were suspicious, so one night he just disappeared. He left behind a note saying it was for the best. "You must hide out for the rest of the war," he wrote, supposedly to avoid "dragging me to a terrible fate." In truth he wasn't strong enough to make across the mountains. It was my silly dream, which he played along with, nothing more. He got caught in Vienna, or that's what they told me when they came to arrest me. I assume Peter was taken away and shot - that's what they do to deserters… isn't it?'

Her beseeching eyes cut into him but Martin said nothing, turning his head to look out the window, across the camp. *Peter likely gave her up under interrogation, and a beating.*

Lorelei sat forward on the bed, almost as if she was about to pounce on him; there was a mad gleam in her eye. Chin jutting out defiantly, she asked: 'Why haven't you tried to fuck me?' It was a shocking question, making Martin gasp.

'Please, Lorelei.'

She shifted back to the top of the bed, seizing the pillow and, holding it in front of herself, challenged him: 'But Martin, that is what your brother officers do to everyone else.'

He shook his head.

'They are not my *brother* officers.'

'Partners in crime then.'

Martin reached for the bottle of schnapps and took a swig.

She wasn't going to let it go.

'So, why not me?'

He shrugged.

'Maybe I'm trying to salve my conscience?'

She didn't buy it.

'Don't you want to screw me?'

Martin did not respond, so she persisted.

'I'm reasonably fresh meat - my body's still not bad.'

Martin took another swig.

Lorelei picked up her glass and held it out to be filled again while remaining defiant. 'I think I'd like you to.'

He offered no response, except to look away.

His head was spinning from her interrogation and he felt unable to deny that he didn't want her, so it was better to say nothing.

She seemed to be enjoying his discomfort.

'Doesn't the fact you won't make you suspect? Wouldn't it send you to the firing squad?'

Now that made him laugh. *After all that he'd come through, to be executed for his cold heart melting over some half-Jew girl in a Hungarian labour camp?*

'The Commandant is already a little suspicious about me,' he admitted.

'Then we'd better have some sex, to make sure his suspicions don't get any worse.'

He shook his head.

'It wouldn't be right.'

Now she laughed, hollow and derisive, but not at him, rather at her predicament. 'What's right or wrong in this place? If I screw you or any other officer, don't I improve my chances of staying alive? Maybe I should go with another officer. All my life I have been at the mercy of men – whether it's my father's desire to see me married off to some dullard, or his foolish compromises with the fascists – or the filthy pigs in the brothel of this hellhole…or you, right now.'

She laughed harshly and added: 'Only my brother has shown courage.'

Martin didn't say anything – he was a bastard alright and a child of The Beast, so he had to accept all that she said was true - but with her provocative talk, his smouldering desire for her grew - the fact that she too clearly needed some kind of release - *and, yes, the alcohol…*

Her eyes burned with fierce determination to break down his defences, to unleash all her burning yearning to obtain contact and a cathartic explosion - even with Martin, a Waffen SS icon of the Reich that had destroyed her family. 'Well then?' she asked. 'Should I go with another?

And again he gave no response.

Maybe in doing her own deal with the devil - taking the protection offered by

Martin as a means to escape the nightly meat auction - Lorelei could achieve some tiny measure of control over her life? The bargain could give her the most precious commodity of all - time...to survive...to achieve escape. And a measure of control – if you cannot gain command of the big things in life then sanity and preservation lie in controlling your destiny in the smaller things that are, nonetheless, of fundamental importance to your heart and soul. The personal decision-making, day-by-day was surely a means of changing fate, or fighting back for the otherwise powerless?

And she had taken back some measure of control by fleeing Vienna and hatching the ambitious plan for a getaway with Peter. This was Lorelei's logic.

She sat up on the bed, let the robe slip from her, the glow of light coming through the thin curtains casting pale relief on her naked body.

While preserving his unemotional outer face Martin was spellbound by her physical beauty and vulnerability. She came over and sat astride him, could feel his ardour.

'You're telling me you don't want it?' she demanded, breathlessly, then bemused: 'Don't want me?'

He lifted her up, gently pushed Lorelei back onto the bed, knelt beside it and, as she trembled, brushed the fingers of his right hand along her body. He kissed her on the mouth and she returned his passion. Martin stood up and took off his clothes, leaving them in a heap of the floor, while she got under the blanket. He climbed in beside her, suddenly shivery while she took his head between her hands and wrapped her legs around him, softly kissing the white scars around his eyes.

And so, it began.

The flames of desperate lust consumed them. Martin became determined to atone by saving this one girl from a grim fate – to salve the dark sins that lay buried deep inside him.

Of which she must never know.

4

MARTIN WONDERED if they should just disappear one night, though with the camp tightly guarded and the Commandant suspicious already, that would not be easy.

As Martin lay in bed with her in his arms, he dreamed of making it to Austria, finding a lodge in the high pastures of the Gastein Valley to hide out. There they would let the tsunami of the war's end crash through, safe on their mountaintop, in the bright sun above the dark forest. Just contemplating that possibility stirred up conflicting feelings of hope and despair, for he knew in his heart it was unlikely.

On this night - with the room warmed by the glow of the wood-burning stove in the corner - the curtains were open so they could stare at the stars. 'You'll think I'm crazy,' she told him, 'but I've never been happier than now.' Lorelei pulled him in tighter but his eyes were attracted to a tumbling, tiny glowing orb on the far horizon - above and beyond the swaying black mass of the trees surrounding the camp. Then there was another – and another.

Not shooting stars.

Tracer shells.

The war was getting ever nearer and the rumble of heavy

fighting had been audible for some time. Martin made no comment about the latest sign of the war closing in - no point in destroying her momentary happiness.

Earlier Lorelei had showered in the officers' accommodation block, Martin standing guard so she could relax. He had secured a bar of creamy French soap from an illicit hoard in the care of an Organisation Todt trooper whom he persuaded to give it up under pressure of his superior rank (and fear of the consequences if he didn't). The rascal had hoarded many luxury goods to buy the favours of girls in the local villages, so he wouldn't miss a bar of soap - nor the lipstick and a face powder compact Martin suggested he should also give up.

Lorelei's hair had grown back darker - not the same lustrous blonde - and, as she lay in his arms, Martin inhaled its apple scent, which was thanks to some shampoo he'd managed to also obtain.

Later, tearing himself away from her warmth, pulling on his field uniform - the cold in the folds making him shiver - Martin left her sleeping while he went out to forage for food. As he crossed the parade ground towards the social club, Martin was surprised to see the windows of the camp's main administration block blazing with light.

He could see the Commandant and a group of Todt officers crowded around a desk. Edging a little closer, keeping in darkness just beyond the boundary of illumination, Martin realised they were studying a large map but he couldn't see what it depicted.

Anxious not to be caught spying, he moved on. As he gently tried the handle of the social club's kitchen door, he glanced around to make sure he wasn't being observed, spotting the motor transport shed was a hive of activity. Lights had been rigged outside so more vehicles could be worked on, their bonnets up, with mechanics bent over engines - little trolleys carrying petrol pumps sat beside them. Martin's gut tightened. This could mean only one thing.

Organisation Todt was pulling out.

Thoughts racing, he decided he would grab as much as he could.

Whatever happened next, he and Lorelei would need provisions.

Stepping through the kitchen door, Martin hunted out a potato sack, emptying its musty old wrinkled contents onto the floor, kicking the detritus under a nearby fridge. He had to be careful not to take too much, or to leave a messy trail, taking only a loaf of bread, a Würstl and bar of chocolate. Those Todt arseholes would probably do an inventory before they left and, even when fleeing the Red hordes, they could be relied on to exact punishment for thieving. Walking over to the inner door, Martin peered cautiously through its circular window, checking nobody was in the bar area. Coast clear, he pushed through and made his way over to the counter, taking a brandy bottle from behind it.

Thanks to the lights outside the window, the gigantic panoramic alpine backdrop was alive in all its glory and Martin again studied its pristine peaks above dark green forests - fluffy clouds floating in a blue sky, lodges nestling in bucolic splendour - and with virgin white smoke trailed by the train crawling up the valley. It inspired him to think that, perhaps, there might, after all, be a chance of making it to Bad Gastein and hiding out in the mountains. And to make amends for someone else's death, an event that he'd buried in the past, until whatever this was with Lorelei raised that ghost from the grave.

Split, Croatia, morning of 28 May 1941

Always at the edge of the sea.

Never voyaging across it.

A perpetual stranger on the shore.

Clad only in a towel around his waist, Martin leaned on the rail of the balcony of his suite in the Hotel Splendide, an Austro-Hungarian relic nestled on the waterfront in imperial ostentation amid trees, surrounded by flowerbeds packed with exotic plants. Some palms imported from New Zealand loaned the hotel an air of tropical romance during the summer, but were hardy enough to survive the severe winters.

Beyond the deserted boulevard, its lamps flicking off one by one as the new day came on, a cloudless blue sky merged seamlessly with the Adriatic.

It reminded Martin of another view across a different sea.

As he played absent-mindedly with the pfennig that hung on its fragile silver chain around his neck, Martin's thoughts drifted back to that other morning.

A year ago exactly, at the time an Obersturmführer in command of 50 Panzergrenadiers, he had been enjoying the cool water of the English Channel gently washing over his sore feet, looking at the smoking hulk of a British corvette peeled open like a sardine can by a Luftwaffe bomb.

A dead sailor lay not far away, rocking gently in lapping waves, face up, the crispy black, burned head nodding. The sailor must have burned like a roman candle as he staggered ashore, only to die at the water's edge.

Why didn't the stupid ass just submerge himself?

Turning away from the sea, Martin's eyes fell upon a surrendered British Army officer speaking to Bruno, the two of them standing by a machine gun team sprawling at ease among the dune grass at the top of the beach.

The German sergeant couldn't speak the enemy's language, so brought the prisoner down to Martin, who had learned English as a child.

Coughing nervously before speaking, the Englander rather pompously told Martin: 'I know you are angry at the price you paid in your fallen comrades, but if you want to punish anyone, then it should be me.'

Martin sighed, recognizing from the grimy white dog collar around the man's neck that this must be the British unit's chaplain. They had put up some pretty stiff resistance to try and hold back the German tide, inflicting a lot of casualties.

'Are you offering to sacrifice yourself to save your men from our revenge?' Martin enquired, with a thin, mirthless smile.

The British chaplain glanced to one side, eyes resting momentarily on the bloated corpse of the sailor, so Martin pressed on:

'Do you think that we would execute brave men for fighting well?'

The chaplain swallowed nervously, his lips very dry, but not as parched as his mouth. 'There have been stories about…atrocities.'

Martin's rage exploded.

'Not by my men!'

Bruno punched the chaplain, felling him, then grabbing him by the scruff of the neck, hauling him back up and onto his feet and then away along the beach. Martin noticed the Englander's dog collar had come loose, peeling away to lie limply on wet sand flecked with sea foam. He stared at it, as the swash came in and the backwash carried the dog collar away, leaving behind air bubbles popping on the sand. Martin closed his eyes, raised his face to the sun, undoing his helmet's chinstrap, taking it off with his right hand while ruffling his sweat-matted hair with the left. There had been so many miles of brutal Blitzkrieg between the Ardennes and the English Channel. Suddenly, with the soothing hiss of the sea over his bare feet, and the cool summer breeze, here was peace.

A strange kind of contentment.

Martin walked into the water until the bottom of his rolled- up trouser legs kissed the foam. He squidged wet sand between his toes and it felt good. As a boy he never went to the beach because his mother hated the sand – it got every-where! - *and the sun, which soon burned her fair Nordic skin.*

Overhead a couple of weaving Luftwaffe fighters interrupted the lullaby of the sea, their machine guns chattering infernally as they swooped. Martin shaded his eyes to try and pick out their prey.

They had pounced on a small fishing boat, which even now was catching fire, thick black smoke curling heavenwards. Martin sighed again, this time from the opposite of contentment, and turned away, to find Bruno rooted to the wet sand watching the same drama. His eyes afire, he exclaimed with lip-smacking satisfaction: 'Boy are they giving those Tommies some hate!'

Martin put the helmet back on and pulled his water flask out from the holder on his belt but only got a few drops from it.

'Did they deliver water today?' he asked Bruno.

'Why don't you just fill it here?'

Martin laughed, but that changed to incredulity when he saw Bruno was serious. 'Are you mad?' The NCO frowned, not understanding at all.

'You Bavarian peasant, don't you know the salinity of sea water will drive you insane?'

'The what?'

'The salt. Dehydrates the brain, though maybe the sun has done that to you already?'

Martin clapped his platoon sergeant on the back and roared with laughter. 'Come on, let's radio those bastards at battalion headquarters and find out what they want us to do with the prisoners.'

As they began to walk back up to the top of the beach, Bruno suddenly stopped, staring back at the cadaver in the surf.

'What about that,' he asked, 'shouldn't we bury it?'

Martin felt no pity.

'Fuck him, he should have abandoned ship quicker, or baptized himself to put out the flames.'

Martin's words were harsh, but, deep in his soul, even he - hardened by the long, bloody march to the Channel - felt a pang of sorrow for the dead sailor's fate. He already regretted what he'd said, looking away to the horizon, careful not to let Bruno see the weakness in his eyes.

* * *

Martin's shoulders slumped, his forehead kissing the rail of the Hotel Splendide balcony. Suddenly he was very weary indeed. He still felt bad about the English sailor and what he had said that day, but it couldn't be helped. That was war. And Mars was his God. Death came in many different ways and what was left behind was just…well, nothing.

Decay.

Detritus.

The person was gone, so who gave a toss?

After waiting in vain to make a Channel crossing to subjugate the English, the men of the 2nd SS Panzer Division had been withdrawn in early 1941 to start preparing for operations in the East, which was when the Führer came to lunch and told them to stick their lance into the heart of the Bolshevik dragon.

But, in March, the Italians had bungled an invasion of Greece, setting the Balkans alight, with Martin and hundreds of SS Panzer Grenadiers sent south into Yugoslavia. They stormed Belgrade, a vicious battle in which there were many casualties. Withdrawn from the Serbian city, what remained of Martin's battalion was sent for some rest and recuperation on the shores of the Adriatic.

The vehicle column that snaked its way down through the mountains to the coast was attacked several times by the partisans. Martin's men were aboard vehicles in the middle, so had neither seen the attacks nor taken part in the retaliation. But, as they motored on the consequences were revealed. Revenge had been meted out with true German efficiency, leaving behind burning villages and ferocious black-clad Balkans widows vowing savage retribution.

This was not a war with much honour to offer – and certainly none to be shared among the thieves they had all become.

Raising his head and gazing once more out across the Adriatic, Martin couldn't resist a harsh, brutal laugh.

Stealing whole nations.

There again, why not?

The ancient port of Split and elsewhere on the Dalmatian coast had just been annexed by the Italians, but they couldn't be trusted to run anything properly, in the view of the Germans. That trouble was in store for the latest interlopers was made clear as the first Das Reich *armoured vehicles and lorries wended their way through narrow streets towards the main waterfront.*

Slogans were daubed on ancient Roman and Venetian walls, including one that declared: 'German and Italian pigs – you will burn in hellfire!'

Despite that promise from unfriendly locals, Martin had chosen to stay at the hotel. It was possibly a foolish decision – the rest of the German troops were in barracks. A Waffen SS officer would be an ideal target for assassination and several officials installed by the Italians had already been shot, knifed, blown up or run down by Croatian partisans. But the chances of romance in the barracks would have been zero, so Martin took the chance, though went appropriately armed.

As he scanned the Riva – the broad avenue running along the waterfront – just down from the hotel Martin spotted a small group of men crowded around a tiny car. They were all smoking cigarettes while offering advice to someone exerting himself to jack it up and change a tyre.

One of the men in particular attracted Martin's attention. He was wearing a pair of black baggy trousers and a brown leather jacket cracked from undernourishment and years of punishment, over a white open-necked shirt. His dark hair was slicked back and he sported a thick moustache – and he'd looked over his shoulder at the hotel more than once.

Catching sight of Martin watching him from the balcony, Baggy Trousers quickly looked away, showing intense interest in the tyre change. Shifting from one foot to the other, Baggy Trousers dropped his cigarette, ground it underfoot and, with a furtive last look up at Martin, strode away down the Riva.

Martin wondered how many watchers there were out there, hiding in innocent-looking little groups having a chat while they strolled, or perhaps sat alone at a café reading a newspaper while sipping coffee – possibly covert lookouts for a killing squad? If Baggy Trousers was one such, he'd made a poor job of it and should Martin see him anywhere near the hotel again he'd do something about it.

A knock at the door of the room drew Martin away from the balcony. Slipping through net curtains billowing in the light breeze and which threatened to become entangled with his towel – he swept them aside and sidestepped the chair by the dressing table. The German-speaking Italian girl he had picked up in the hotel bar the night before - a secretary in the main office of the Governatorate - stirred under the bed sheets, mumbling something he did not understand.

'Go back to sleep,' he murmured.

The knocking became more insistent, the girl protesting at the racket, turning onto her side to present her bare back to the door, pulling a pillow over her head.

Taking his Walther pistol from the holster that lay on the bedside table, Martin, with left hand around his waist to make sure the towel stayed in placed, went over and put his eye to the peephole. He was careful not to tread too heavily on the floorboards in case they creaked, giving would-be assassins a signal to put some hot lead through the door. It wasn't easy to tell in the feeble glow of the corridor lights if death had come calling and he was relieved to find it was Bruno.

'Hang on a minute!' Martin shouted, making the girl in the bed pull the pillow tighter against her ears.

Turning the lock with his left hand, Martin gently put the pistol down on the carpet and opened the door a crack.

Bruno was grinning lasciviously, assuming that his commander had got lucky, thumbs in the belt around his uniform jacket, cap cockily pushed back from his forehead. 'Time to stop playing Rudolf Valentino and get your arse back to barracks, Sir.' Martin felt a surge of excitement in his blood and Bruno smiled at the gleam in Martin's eye.

'I think it's Russia,' the NCO whispered melodramatically.

'How long have I got?'

'The boss wants you back by nine.'

Martin frowned – he had completely lost track of time and his watch was over on the bedside table.

'Which is?'

Bruno grinned at Martin's discomfort and looked at his own wristwatch.

'Just over two hours, Sir.'

'I will be back before then.'

Bruno clicked his heels and saluted, still wearing that awful grin. He turned away and went back down the corridor.

Martin changed his mind – if Bruno left he'd have to persuade some

Wehrmacht officer prig to lend him a staff car and driver to get out to the barracks.

'Scharführer - hold on!' he called out, using his rank, causing Bruno to halt and turn around.

'Yes, Sir?'

'Wait for me outside and I'll return with you.'

Bruno snapped off another salute and turned around again to head for the lift, his form soon swallowed up by the ill-lit corridor.

Martin closed the door, letting the towel drop to the floor, unhooking a cotton robe from the back and pulling it around himself. Going to sit on the edge of the bed, he brushed the fingertips of his left hand down the line of her spine. She shivered and shoved his hand away, grabbing the sheet and wrapping it around herself, the pillow falling off her head revealing tousled black hair. Slipping the bathrobe off, Martin slid under the sheet, spooning her insistently, lifting her hair up so he could kiss the nape of her neck, he murmured: 'I have to go now.'

Feeling his urgency, she giggled sleepily: 'So I see.'

Playfully slapping her bottom, and laughing, he shoved her.

'Go and shower.'

Later, as he passed a comb through his hair and then fastened the collar of his uniform jacket, he used the dressing table mirror to watch her dress. He enjoyed a last glimpse of her ripe, shapely body. My God, her lovely olive skin had been so warm and soft to the touch, and so welcoming.

She came over to him, placing her hands on his shoulders and they looked into each other's eyes – a fleeting second of honest intimacy. He smiled, turned around, reaching for some notes on the dressing table. Taking one of her hands, he pressed the money into it.

She looked hurt.

'You must,' he ordered softly.

She looked away. Still leaning against him, she banished any thoughts of their encounter being anything else but a few drinks, a good meal and sex. Martin had been an efficient lover, but always she sensed somehow distant and withdrawn. What else would one expect of a soldier? Far worse, probably.

Turning her chin back towards him, he explained: 'I am leaving here forever, so this money is no use to me, whereas you are stuck here playing secretary to that fat oaf governor.'

Now she felt emotion, a tear welled.

Another lover lost to war.

Martin disliked sentimentality, but hid his irritation, and wiped away her tear with a thumb and gently kissed her on the lips – a gesture of consolation rather than deep feeling.

'Do you know, I don't even know your name,' he whispered.

'Azzurra,' she replied sulkily, breaking away, sitting down on the bed to pull on her red shoes with their small black silk bows on the heel.

'It means blue,' she added with a shy smile.

'Like the Adriatic,' he suggested lamely.

'Your name?' she asked, retrieving her handbag from the dressing table.

'Jonathan,' he lied, 'as in a son of King Saul.'

'Truly? Or a lie?'

He smiled and shrugged.

She came over to him and kissed him on the cheek.

'And is Azzurra your real name?' he asked, suddenly stirred up, turning back to the dressing table to hide it.

'Perhaps,' she teased, with a wistful little smile.

'Don't let the slob screw you,' he instructed, watching her in the mirror as she crossed behind him but the girl's face had already become a mask, and she exited without a further word.

Crossing to the balcony, he leaned on the rail and watched her leave, escorted by one of the Italian soldiers who guarded the main entrance of the hotel to a military car waiting at the kerb. As she climbed in, the girl looked up.

She did not smile and he did not wave.

Martin raised his eyes to take in the view across the Adriatic to the melting horizon - for one final time - enjoying the warm sun on his face – a few seconds of solitude and peace before he returned to the war. Then, looking down the Riva he noticed the group of men and the little car had gone.

Martin closed the windows, carefully rearranged the net curtains, walked over to the bedside table, picked up the holster containing his pistol and clipped it on his belt. A last look in the mirror, to place his cap on his head and make sure it was straight; the silver eagle clasping the swastika glinted.

The death's head badge below it gleamed, mocking his night of softness with its grin. Martin frowned, took the cap off, stared intently at the skull badge, rubbing it with the same thumb he had wiped the tear from the girl's cheek. Shaking his head to dispel the last vestiges of vulnerability, he put the cap back on. Straightening it, he pulled the peak down slightly to shade his eyes. To be a soldier, not a lover was his destiny. He leaned down to pick up his MP40 from where it lay in the footwell of the dressing table – never lean a weapon against something, always put it flat. You don't want it falling over and going off accidentally.

The double entendre of that thought made him laugh.

Sitting on the edge of the bed he checked the gun over, removing the magazine to work the weapon's mechanism and make sure it was well oiled. Slotting the magazine back in, slinging the MP40 around his right shoulder, he got up and went over to the wardrobe. Martin opened it to pull out a bulging field green canvas bag. With a grunt, for it was rather heavy, he hoisted it onto his left shoulder and made his exit, sparing the room not even a wistful glance before letting the door slam behind him. It made a very loud bang that resounded throughout the hotel, making many a slumbering guest stir with a wildly beating heart.

* * *

Bruno was waiting on the Riva just across from the Hotel Splendide, in the battered, dusty kübelwagen that served as their usual mode of transport. A small, tough vehicle, manufactured by Volkswagen, it looked like an angular bathtub on wheels – not pretty, but it had never let them down.

Martin slung his bag in the back of the vehicle, placing the MP40 gently behind the passenger seat and climbed in. Bruno flicked his cigarette into the dusty gutter and swung the wheel to pull away, heading along the waterfront. It was a route that would take them past plush waterfront villas set back from the road.

'Hello, what's this?' Bruno asked as they came around a bend to find a makeshift roadblock of two horse-drawn carriages manned by nervous-looking Italian military policemen. Bruno eased the speed down, bringing the kübelwagen to a gentle halt, Martin climbed out and walked over to investigate. Without even the courtesy of a friendly smile he asked the Italians: 'What's the problem?'

Seeing the SS flashes on the German's collar, the Italians shifted nervously aside, enabling Martin to see more clearly down the road.

A squad of Italian military policemen was clustered behind a truck parked in the middle of the street, some of them dodging out every now and then to shoot at a villa to the right screened partially by palm trees. More Italians were lying prone on the verges, or sheltering behind trees, snapping off rifle shots every now and then.

A little way past the truck was another vehicle, an ambulance with its doors open. By its tailgate a body lay on a stretcher covered by a white sheet. Two ambulancemen were hiding under the vehicle's back wheels. Martin heard return fire, then a clang and a tinkle of shattered glass as bullets hit the truck. There was some excited shouting and Martin spotted what must be a senior officer crouching in a huddle with his NCOs behind the truck, for he was forcefully berating them. The officer was now gesticulating wildly, as if urging his men to grow some balls. Going back over to the Kübelwagen, Martin found Bruno very relaxed, eyes closed, enjoying the sun and the breeze blowing off the sea.

'Are you asleep?' Martin enquired incredulously, reaching behind the passenger seat for his weapon.

Bruno shook his head but did not open his eyes.

'No, Sir, just enjoying the last moments of my summer leave.'

Martin snorted, taking his cap off and throwing it onto the back seat. He leaned into the kübelwagen and pulled his helmet out of the green canvas bag, clamping it onto his head. Leaning down again he extracted some stickgrenades from the bag, which he stuffed into his waist belt.

Wondering at the commotion, Bruno opened his eyes and what he found perked him up a lot.

'Are we getting in there?' the NCO enquired eagerly.

Martin nodded.

'Looks like it,' adding with grim determination: 'It seems it will be our job to help these Chianti lovers sort out their little problem.'

With a broad grin Bruno climbed out and assembled his own tools of war. Some easy blood-letting would do him fine. *It had been too long without action for the veteran street brawler who had received his bloody baptism cracking communist and anarchist heads in the bierkellers of Munich. Bruno slipped the sling of his MP40 over his head, then put on his helmet.*

'This all sounds like a nice bit of exercise to me, Sir,' the NCO pronounced with almost lip-smacking relish.

Martin grunted, turned and began running down the road, followed closely by Bruno. The Italian military policemen swung the roadblock aside, puffing their chests out and saluting melodramatically as the Germans dashed through.

Neither of the Waffen SS men acknowledged them, their minds focused on the fight ahead.

Italian military police troops cowering behind the truck watched open-mouthed as the brazen Germans trotted in, their commander greeting the intervention with angry eyes, his top lip, with its pencil moustache, twitching with indignation. These Nazis could just go and fuck off.

Speaking German, the Italian officer enquired, with a tinge of sarcasm: 'Good afternoon gentlemen, and to what honour do we owe your arrival?'

Martin was impressed at the man's fluency but less than admiring of the tactical predicament. 'We thought we might give you a little help,' he suggested. The corners of the Italian officer's mouth turned down and he shrugged as nonchalantly as he could muster.

He winced as a bullet holed the bonnet of the truck while the Germans did not even seem to notice it.

'I think we can handle these scum momentarily,' the Italian officer suggested too lightly, convincing nobody, especially his own men.

Bruno snorted with open contempt, though Martin pressed on diplomatically. 'How may we help?'

The Italian looked around at his motley crew of middle aged, overweight military policemen, either lying face down on the road or hiding behind the truck's large rubber wheels. He shrugged again, this time to signify his helpless situation. After a resigned sigh he explained: 'Partisans, killed someone from our military secretariat,' he jabbed a finger towards the villa, 'they're in there.'

Martin peered under the truck and across the road – the villa possessed a Moorish aspect and above the trees he could see elaborate crenellations along the edge of its flat roof. There was a copper dome atop a turret on its right front corner. 'Some neighbours heard the screams and called us,' the Italian officer continued, 'so we came hoping to find her alive, but it was after the fact. It appears that act was merely a lure - their intention was to ambush us.'

'How many partisans?' Martin asked with a frown, something about the Italian's account provoking a feeling of unease.

'Two, three, four – or more.'

Looking past the officer, Martin saw a shoe lying in the road and his unease turned into nausea that he struggled to fight down.

It was red, with a small black silk bow on the heel.

A vision of Azzurra putting on her shoes in the hotel room flashed into

Martin's mind and he felt as if he had been punched in the gut. For a few moments Martin felt numb disbelief before rage began bubbling in his veins. 'Stay here,' he ordered Bruno, sprinting out from cover towards the stretcher lying behind the ambulance. As he ran Martin scooped up the shoe.

Some shots rang out from the direction of the villa, ricocheting off the surface of the road, missing him by a wide margin.

Kneeling by the stretcher, staring at the body's bare left foot, his mind plunged momentarily into stasis. Letting the shoe fall onto the stretcher, Martin reached over to gently lift the sheet, flinching at what he found. Her face was all bruised and battered, puffed up, purple, black and blue. The lipstick was smeared obscenely across her cheek. Her dark brown eyes stared lifelessly at him, no spark where just a few hours before they had been laughing with mischief and horniness.

Now…

She was decay.

Detritus.

He dropped the sheet, unaware of the bullets zinging past his head.

She meant nothing to him.

Didn't she?

Just a girl he picked up in a bar.

That was all?

The fruit of German supremacy over Europe plucked ripe from the low hanging branch, a mere Italian of easy virtue. This was what he was meant to feel and think, and his orthodoxy told him so, yet he could not but feel sorrow that his warm, beautiful Azzurra wasn't on this Earth anymore. Her cold, dead remains were an accusation.

To her killers she was nothing, an Italian invader consorting with an even more loathsome German officer, and while Martin could understand their hatred for him, Azzurra's murder seemed so spiteful. He frowned at the unexpected strength anger and shame welling up.

Doubling over, he vomited onto the road – he would later tell himself it was to purge weakness. Then, shaking off mental impotence and sentiment, he let the rage rise. He glared at the two ambulancemen cowering under their vehicle. Stepping over the stretcher he stuck his face in theirs, screaming: 'Get up you cowardly fucks and put her in the back of your vehicle!'

They didn't understand the words, but sensed his fury.

With fearful glances at the submachine gun in Martin's right hand, they rolled out and grabbed the stretcher, jabbering at each other fearfully as a couple of bullets cut through the trees overhead causing leaves to fall.

Sliding the stretcher in the back of the ambulance, they made to close the doors, but Martin stepped forward and growled: 'Wait.'

The shoe had fallen off the stretcher, so he placed it beside her bare foot, his fingers brushing an ankle, its skin stone cold.

* * *

The plan was very simple. The Germans would charge the front of the house, kick the door down, so to speak, and kill the partisans, the Italians following on.

Martin and Bruno made a crouching run to the villa using the cover of the trees to hide from the eyes of the partisans. Before departing they had told the Italians not to increase their rate of fire or the partisans would suspect something. The gunfire remained correspondingly desultory.

Edging up to the entrance, Martin and Bruno gathered all their energy and sprinted along the gravel driveway, the crunch of their boots barely heard above the loud burble of a large ornamental fountain that was the front garden centre-piece.

To their surprise, as they approached the front door, it swung open, its frame filled with two partisans planning an aggressive foray – or to flee – guns down and decidedly not at the ready. Their faces were a perfect picture of shocked surprise: mouths agape, eyes wide open in surprise as death crashed into them. Martin and Bruno – not pausing for even a heartbeat – shot them with staccato bursts from their MP40s, felling both partisans.

Jumping over the two corpses, sliding along the marble floor of the entrance hall, the Germans rolled in under a spiral staircase that curled up inside the domed tower. Chest heaving, his rib cage bruised from the force with which he hit the floor, Martin strained his senses, waiting for more partisans to appear. Above the hot metal and cordite smell of his smoking gun he detected the Italian girl's perfume impregnating the air. Below an antique table, beside a long mirror on the other side of the hall, a bottle of scent had been smashed into fragments along with a vase shattered, its flowers scattered and trampled on. Seeing such callous disregard made him even more furious, his eyes blazing fiercer. Panting as he crouched beside Martin, Bruno raised his eyebrows as if to say 'what next?'

They heard voices raised in anger and another partisan came into view – first his scuffed brown brogues and black baggy trousers with frayed turn-ups, then a broad back clad in a cracked brown leather jacket over a dirty white shirt. The sleeves of the jacket were rolled up to reveal tanned forearms sporting tattoos including a fouled anchor.

He carried a British-made Sten gun, which he angrily jabbed in the air on seeing the corpses of his comrades lying in an untidy heap in the doorway, his slicked back dark hair flopping forward.

Martin realized this was the watcher from earlier by the little car on the Riva. Thinking it was the Italians outside who had killed his comrades – the baggy-trousered partisan went over and slammed the door shut, berating the dead men, kicking their lifeless bodies.

They were fools, but he would make some of the occupiers pay for it.

A partisan shouted from the front room, no doubt asking what was going on. Martin restrained Bruno from pulling his bayonet out, shaking his head; he extracted a grenade from his belt and, with a grin of understanding, Bruno did the same. The baggy-trousered partisan went to join his shouting comrade taking pot shots at the Italians. Martin and Bruno dashed out and hurled two grenades in after him, taking cover again under the stairs

The boom of the grenades exploding was followed by screams of agony, which continued as Martin and Bruno stormed into the room.

The baggy-trousered partisan was sprawled on a sofa that had been ripped in several places, and was now soaked in blood from wounds in his legs and back. The other partisan lay over by some French windows, rolling from side to side clutching his stomach.

Kicking the partisans' guns away to a safe distance, Martin dealt with the one on the sofa, using a savagely jabbing elbow to break the man's nose – adding insult to injury and provoking an indignant roar of pain, blood gushing onto his moustache. Bruno stamped his mastery on the other by administering two hard kicks to the ribs that provoked screams.

Bruno pushed the French windows open, with what little glass was left in them falling out of the frames to shatter on the ground. He grabbed his partisan by the collar of a ripped and smouldering grey woollen jacket and dragged him out, screaming, into the villa's front garden - Martin followed suit, drawing on his residual fury to bundle the baggy-trousered partisan off the sofa and then shove him out into the garden.

* * *

Ashen-faced and clothes soaked in blood as they slumped against the fountain, both partisans were swallowing their pain down now – giving the Waffen SS soldiers malevolent looks as they shifted uncomfortably.

Martin wanted to execute them here and then, but that would be too easy and as an officer he felt he must show some restraint.

'Stand guard over these while I go and see what's delaying the damned Italians,' Martin told Bruno, 'they can decide on what justice these bastards need. We must get back to barracks.'

Martin returned a couple of minutes later with the Italian officer in tow, to find both partisans lying motionless at Bruno's feet.

Martin's eyes were caught by something in the water of the fountain; a blood cloud, which soon dissipated and was gone. Saying nothing, he stared at Bruno who was showing his best poker face. Martin noticed the leather scabbard of Bruno's dagger was gleaming with wetness. He must have cleaned the knife in the fountain water.

The Italian military police officer looked very uncomfortable, bending down to look at the partisans, frowning at the jagged red slits across their throats, but he did not confront Bruno; didn't say a word to either German.

For all his battle-hardening, Martin was shocked – feeling that the efficiency of due process had been subverted - but he also couldn't help thinking the partisans got what they deserved.

'Come on,' he told Bruno, who followed him like an obedient bull down the driveway. As they exited the two Italian ambulance men came in, grunting and sweating even while carrying an empty stretcher.

Putting their weapons and helmets in the back of the kübelwagen, Martin and Bruno climbed back in, this time with the NCO in the passenger seat. Bruno offered his water bottle and Martin did not object to the schnapps it contained.

The Italian officer came over to say a wary goodbye and delivered grudging, horrified thanks for their assistance.

'It was most efficient,' he observed uneasily.

Martin nodded, responding with an emotionless and insincere tribute to Axis amity. 'We were glad to help our Italian brothers.'

That made the Italian smile mirthlessly.

He saluted, turned on his heels and marched back over to shout at his useless men who were milling around their truck aimlessly.

Martin watched the last of the dead partisans being loaded into the ambulance, thinking it sickly ironic the men who had killed Azzura were being put in the same vehicle as her for the journey to the morgue. Bruno spat over the side of the kübelwagen into the gutter and cursed volubly. 'Fucking bastards – given time I would have gutted them like fucking fish.'

He glanced at Martin to see if there was any reaction, but could detect neither approval nor disapproval in the officer's blank face.

Martin felt he should have taken action to kill the baggy-trousered partisan in Split when he spotted him acting suspiciously on the Riva.

It filled him with deep regret whenever he thought about it even though they later gave him a medal for killing the partisans.

* * *

Nearly three years later, lying in his labour camp bed holding Lorelei in his arms, contemplating past sins, Martin wondered what else he could, in reality, have done back then?

He never should have taken the Italian girl as his lover for a start – he made her a casualty. As for Bruno…*hadn't Martin been complicit in that final act of savagery - prizing his loyalty to a comrade-in-arms above all? By not saying anything, by keeping faith with the Nazi orthodoxy, which instructed that all non-Aryans were just filth to be cleansed?*

It was difficult to shake off the mentality of all those years of blood and so-called honour, from a boyhood in the Hitler Youth to his actions in war.

He still loved Germany and would defend it from invaders to the death of course, but the rigidity of his belief was sagging.

During the medal presentation in Berlin, Hitler had been a pathetic husk of a man, and so, as the Führer declined, then so did the force of the ideology.

Martin's sorrowful eyes revealed growing doubts about the

worth of it all…unless he could find something to believe in and some means of taking action, someone to place his faith in again and fight for?

It would be Lorelei and this time it would be different.

But, the chances of the mountain hideout dream becoming reality declined precipitously after a knock on the door of his room, Martin opening it to find his nemesis in the corridor.

The Commandant explained stonily: 'You are to go to Simontornya and assist with the defence of the road bridge over the Sio Canal.'

Martin nodded dumbly, looking down at his bare feet, ensuring his bathrobe-clad body firmly blocked the view through the door of his room.

'And you are to hand over your whore first,' the Commandant sneered. Still looking down - thunderstruck at being so abruptly torn away from Lorelei - Martin pulled the bathrobe cord tighter, imagining it to be a ligature around the Commandant's neck.

There was no point in trying to buck orders, for if he was taken away for an instant field court martial and a firing squad it would not protect Lorelei. She would probably soon join him in the grave. He had no choice but to do what he had always done in such situations – fight his way out of things by reverting to type; a born killer.

Martin raised his gaze, staring directly into the Commandant's eyes, implying, without saying a word that he would like to rip the other man's throat out. Shifting uneasily and backing away, the Commandant placed himself snugly between two equally worried looking Todt guards. After swallowing nervously, he rasped: 'Your transport leaves as soon as you are ready.'

The Commandant turned around and withdrew with his escort, not daring to look back. Waiting a few seconds to regain his composure, Martin tried to figure out what to say when he went back into the room. *They should have made their escape immediately he returned with the food.*

He found Lorelei with her eyes tight shut, chin resting on her knees as she sat up in his bed. She had heard everything.

He let the robe slide off, slipped under the bedclothes, pulled her down. They lay like that for some time, she was quite still with her eyes closed, cheeks damp but no sobs. Martin's eyes were dry, his head strangely empty of thoughts. He wanted to physically savour the moment, the warm softness of her body, the smell of her, as he may never hold her like this again. Putting her head on his chest, Lorelei could hear his heart thumping calmly and evenly and marvelled at his control.

After a few minutes Martin sat her up in the bed. Offering what he hoped was a fair attempt at a reassuring smile, he told her: 'Once you are on the road it will be easier for us to disappear when I catch up.'

She nodded, but her eyes and heart were full of doubt.

'But what if…'

'Nobody has been able to kill me yet.'

Even so, her energy appeared to drain away, the life going out of her, so he helped Lorelei dress, finding amid his sparse wardrobe some thermals, a shirt, his old wounded soldier's suit. Like dressing a child, he put her into those clothes, then military ankle boots, pulled on over two pairs of socks. They weren't the best fit. He found a scarf and also put her into his best uniform overcoat, then tucked it in around her neck. The coat's pockets were soon stuffed with food and a flask of brandy.

Martin stood back and inspected her.

'There you go, ready for a winter stroll.'

She smiled, seeming to regain some strength.

It was very strange, him clad only in pyjama bottoms and her swaddled in bits of his cast-off uniforms. She glanced down at the silver thread eagle and swastika badge on the left sleeve of the coat. Lorelei rubbed it, inspecting its glimmer in the feeble light coming through the curtains.

She sat on the bed and watched as he transformed himself into a warrior. Over his own set of thermals he pulled on a thin field grey uniform trousers and service jacket - the latter with the SS lighting strikes and rank insignia on black collar - then a quilted jacket taken from a dead Russian during winter fighting in the Soviet Union. He pulled on his mountain boots very battered and scuffed – then bloused the trousers over their tops. Next, he pulled on a camouflage combat smock - patched many times, as it had seen much campaigning - with the same Waffen SS eagle on the left arm.

Then an equipment belt, with the ammo pouches on its front, water bottle clipped on its back and pistol in a holster on the left. Martin hung binoculars around his neck and, finally, put on the camouflage covered helmet, his face becoming hard and unsmiling, making her inwardly shiver. He stepped over to the wardrobe and pulled out his main weapon – the MP40 submachine gun. The Teutonic knight was now clad in his armour and fully armed. Martin caught sight of himself in a mirror on the wall and wondered who this person was, so long had he been out of full combat uniform. He also noted via the reflection that Lorelei wore a look of mute shock on her face – he hoped at the situation and not in fear of himself.

He turned away from the mirror, slinging his weapon behind him, taking off his helmet and laying it on the floor beside the bed. He knelt on one knee before her, taking Lorelei's hands between his and looking up into her eyes. 'Stay alive no matter what and I will find you,' he promised her in a soft whisper. Lorelei looked far from certain but put on a brave smile and nodded.

Then he frowned, remembering something. After taking off the smock and unfastening the quilted jacket, he dug into the left-hand pocket of his service jacket to retrieve his lucky pfennig, which he'd also worn throughout the fighting in Russia. Pulling it out, dangling on its silver chain he took her hand and opened it, palm upwards. 'Take this…my lucky pfennig,' he urged. 'It kept me safe.'

She shook her head.

'No, you should wear it, to make sure you stay safe also.'

Lorelei slipped it over his head and around his neck, so it lay against his jacket, glowing in the light.

* * *

Going out onto the parade ground they found chaos - screaming Todt guards rushing around all over the place, some with snarling dogs straining at leashes, shepherding a thousand fearful prisoners into a long column. The brothel building and main camp offices were ablaze, with columns of white, grey and black smoke twisting into the overcast sky. Outside the building were filing cabinets, their drawers pulled out all askew, with Todt officers hurling papers onto bonfires.

Martin saw some of the women from the brothel being helped up into an Opel Blitz truck on the other side of the parade ground. The Todt were ensuring their chosen sex toys were safely transported, presumably, to provide pleasure at a new camp. He instantly realized this offered an opportunity to give Lorelei a chance – for to place her in the column would surely see her perish, either at the hands of the guards or other prisoners – ripped to pieces for being a Nazi collaborator - or claimed by the rigours of the march.

'Come on,' he said, taking her by the arm, trudging through the mud to the back of the truck, where he found the Commandant's Aide assisting one of the women up over the tailgate. Turning around to find a grim-faced Waffen SS warrior standing there, the Aide reflexively recoiled.

'I want you to take care of Lorelei,' Martin told him.

The Aide nodded and smiled ingratiatingly. 'Of course - we are taking care of *all* our ladies.'

Martin helped Lorelei up into the truck and she sat down on the bench seat near the tailgate, her eyes searching his face, looking for reassurance.

He smiled, reached up and squeezed her hand – but even that was too much emotion, too much care between a loyal Nazi and a prisoner. The Aide frowned. Fucking a sub-human was fine, but to feel love for one of them. *That was most suspect.*

Any words of reassurance would be mere platitudes anyway and they both knew it. Lorelei pulled down her own blank mask – the better for surviving whatever lay ahead.

She must not think or feel but just try to survive. After a last lingering look, he turned away, almost overwhelmed by emotion.

Martin took the Aide by the shoulder, almost dragging him around the side of the truck. Towering over the Todt officer, Martin told him in a low, menacing voice: 'Once I have killed some more Russians I will catch up with you. Look after Lorelei or I will kill you, too.' The Aide gulped, grimacing at the vice-like grip of Martin's hand. Let go, he eagerly withdrew, climbing up into the back of the truck while shouting at two Todt men to close the tailgate.

The truck's engine roared into life and it bounced past, Martin raising his eyes to find Lorelei's. They held each other's eyes for a moment and then she was gone - swallowed up by the darkness of the vehicle's interior as the distance opened. The truck headed out through the gates, taking the road west. Three more trucks followed, one carrying the Commandant and his loot and the other two with Todt officers aboard.

The barking of the dogs got ever louder, the guttural shouting of the guards and low murmuring fear of the inmates gathered, as the column – a dark shuffling mass of misery - began to snake through the camp gates. Martin's nostrils twitched at something familiar: the smell of fear – urine and excrement, soiled clothes and sweat. Shuddering he closed his eyes and turned away.

Opening them again he saw a pair of trucks on the far side of the parade ground around which milled the two dozen unfortunate Todt men selected to fight under his command. As he walked towards the vehicles Martin reflected with a heavy heart that he and these wretched amateurs were surely the walking dead.

5

15 March 1945, the road bridge at Simontornya, Hungary

On the far side of the Sio Canal, beyond a square-towered, shell-pocked Renaissance castle and smouldering baroque Roman Catholic church whose tower had been decapitated by Soviet shells, plumes of smoke rose above the rooftops of the houses.

The hellish sound of battle was all around, the sharp crack of high velocity shells fired by duelling tanks and anti-tank weapons mingling with the thump and cough of mortars - all underscored by the incessant metallic pop and chatter of rifles and machine guns.

This symphony of war was completed by kettle drum-like explosions, windows shattering from shock, the contents of buildings thrown around and ripped apart…the blatter-smash of ornaments and crockery shattered and fittings ...walls collapsing with a roar into the street and dust billowing into the air.

As yet the Russian attack had not succeeded in getting across the iron arch bridge over the canal, which connected Lake Balaton to the Danube. The wreckage of destroyed tanks, half-tracks and other military vehicles intermingled with the torn remains of humans and horses on the bridge was evidence of an earlier attempt - followed by withdrawal of Soviet forces to lick wounds. Now they were renewing their bid to vault across the narrow, but crucial, water barrier.

An even fiercer fight was taking place not far away, around the railway station with much blood being spilled over who owned another bridge over the canal.

For a few hours there had been a steady stream of exhausted Waffen SS, including walking wounded, retreating via the road bridge, but suddenly it ended. The volume of fire fell away, indicating the part of town on the other side of the canal was no longer to be contested, a miniscule indicator the end was nigh for the 6th Panzer Army's massive offensive in Hungary.

It had aspired to prise Budapest free of the Soviet grip - Stalin's troops had taken the Hungarian capital that February after laying siege to it for more than a hundred days. A lunge was also made for Romanian oil fields (seized by the enemy in August the previous year), a move also hopefully stopping the Russian advance on oil wells near Vienna and in Hungary (not least around Lake Balaton).

For the Führer had declared securing oil supplies as the major priority, in order to fuel the divisions assembling to protect Berlin by hurling the Russians back across the Oder.

Oil and its associated products were also needed to send aloft swarms of Me 262 jet fighters to annihilate the American and British bombers by then mercilessly pounding German cities night and day. There was no point in having wonder weapons if there was no aviation fuel to get them off the ground, though it was all becoming rather moot.

While the majority of the divisions Hitler moved around on the map table in his Berlin bunker to defend the German capital were phantoms the real ones he threw into action in Hungary were his – and the 1,000-year Reich's - last best hope of surviving a few weeks more.

Spring Awakening - a romantically optimistic name for the death rattle of Hitler's legions - used whatever fit young (or middle aged) men the Reich could scrape together and press into service in the Waffen SS legions.

It also gobbled up output in tanks, assault guns and ammunition produced by slave-labourers, the latter driven ever harder by their beastly overlords in the underground weapons factories.

Thousands of men lay dead in the mud and the snow of Hungary, with hundreds of the new panzers already blackened shells or abandoned after running out of fuel or suffering machinery break downs.

The Red Army had recoiled initially, hard pushed to contain the enemy assault, but prevailed and was now rolling back the fleeting German territorial gains, corralling some Waffen SS units into pockets and then squeezing the life out of them.

Only a fanatical rear guard of Finns and Estonians from the 5th SS Panzer Division *Wiking* remained on the other side of the Sio Canal. They nurtured a hatred for the Russians going back decades, if not centuries, and would make the Red Army advance as painful and bloody as possible. After the last few holdouts were overwhelmed - and that would surely happen very soon, with the Reds taking no prisoners - it would be down to Martin and his motley crew, and scattering of snipers, to delay the Russians getting across the canal.

The Ottomans were the last occupiers of the small town that came from the East, in the mid-1600s, and they had stayed for more than a century. It seemed the new overlords would be the Soviets, kicking out the Germans once and for all. Hitler had sent in his troops to seize control of Hungary in 1944, after which began an eradication of the Jews, assisted by homegrown fascists.

The vengeance-hungry hordes of Moscow's armies would cut that process short…though the Grim Reaper's scythe continued to claim anyone caught up in the harvest of death, regardless of who they were. They included a Hungarian civilian, his wife and what may have been their teenage son, who ventured out onto the far end of the canal bridge to carve up a horse for its meat. Setting to work with cleavers, they were themselves soon torn in half – with blood and guts flying everywhere - by a sustained burst of MG42 fire.

It came courtesy of a trigger-happy straggler from the 9th SS Panzer Division *Hohenstaufen*, whom Martin had collared as the lad sprinted across the bridge on his own.

Shoving him into a slit trench by the road with a good field of fire down the centre of the bridge, Martin assumed that, compared to his Organisation Todt amateurs, this Waffen SS kid would have a cool head behind a MG42. 'Why the fuck did you do that!?' Martin screamed, hurling him off the machine gun and into the bottom of the trench.

'They were clearly not Ivans!'

The boy whimpered, curling his hands over his helmet, pulling it down over his eyes. Sighing heavily, Martin grabbed him by the webbing straps, hauling him into a sitting position. Like a guilty schoolboy the youngster still wouldn't look up at him.

Climbing down into the trench and leaning against its back edge, Martin tapped him on the helmet and suggested:

'It was a waste of bullets – didn't they train you to conserve fire?'

Looking up, the kid – and Martin suddenly realised this rosy-cheeked youngster was still in his teens – looked very sheepish. Wondering how such a skinny, unimpressive specimen could have been taken into the Waffen SS, Martin enquired: 'Where did the *Hohenstaufen* get you from, son.'

'Gotenhafen, Sir. I was a rating under training in the cruiser *Prinz Eugen*, but ordered ashore for special duties.' Incredulous, Martin enquired: 'You're a sailor!?' The kid nodded miserably.

'Alright, well do me a favour, when I go out onto the bridge in a moment, do not press the trigger – in fact do not put your hands anywhere near that machine gun until I get back.'

* * *

Festooned with magazine pouches and stick grenades, MP40 slung across his back, Martin carefully picked his way through the carnage, just managing to avoid putting his boot into the guts of a disembowelled horse.

His eyes searched left and right until he finally found what he was looking for - a junction box set into the structure of the bridge, on the right-hand side. It contained switches that needed to be pulled down to complete the demolition charge circuits. As Martin prepared to make a sprint for it, three T34 tanks, each carrying Red Army soldiers, roared onto the other end of the bridge, squealing to a halt when they discovered there was no easy way through the wreckage.

There were loud shouts above snorting tank engines - white smoke exuding from their exhausts - and the troops were ordered off. Martin thought better of his bid to blow the bridge up right there and then, making a crouching run back across, dodging between burned out vehicles and abandoned artillery guns.

One of the T34s opened fire with its machine gun, bullets hitting the bridge superstructure, sending sparks flying and making that familiar, almost comical, *peeeow* sound.

The scratch force of Todt troops of which he had been awarded command watched his antics incredulously and passively, with no covering fire to assist Martin's escape. Just behind their trenches was a sandbagged 88mm anti-tank gun, pointing straight down the centre of the bridge, its Luftwaffe crew in a fatigue-induced stupor.

'What are you fucking waiting for!?' Martin yelled.

The 88mm barked, its shell tearing through the air to strike one of the T34s, which exploded in flame and smoke - the turret torn off to tumble and twirl, splashing into the canal.

A Russian heavy artillery shell landed with breath-taking precision behind the 88mm, the explosion and shrapnel dismembering the gun crew. Although their ears rang, no shrapnel came the way of Martin or the kid behind the machine gun while a Waffen SS sniper on the girders of the bridge killed a Russian infantry officer trying to lead across rather unenthusiastic troops who scattered and hid among the burned out vehicles.

The sniper fell from his nest - nailed by a Russian bullet.

Still attached to the bridge via his harness, he swung back and forth - a blood-dripping ragdoll. The fire coming from the Russian side rose in weight and volume – the lead flying back from Martin's side not so impressive.

Girding up his loins again, Martin sprinted and dodged over to the balustrade on the right-hand side of the bridge, flipping open the junction box. Martin sensed the Russian infantry were getting ever closer but ignored them. He pulled the demolition charge switches down.

Nothing.

They had failed.

This was damned inconvenient.

A Russian shell landed nearby, the hot shrapnel tinkling on the bridge superstructure, making Martin flinch and press his helmet down on his head.

There was a lull in incoming fire - but no outgoing either.

Cautiously standing up, careful to use a bridge support as cover, Martin looked around. Of the Todt men and assorted waifs and strays he'd gathered, the only one who'd stayed at his post was the teenage Waffen SS stormtrooper, wide-eyed and frozen with fear in his slit trench behind the MG42.

As enemy bullets buzzed all around again Martin took his chances and dodged fast as he could between the wreckage, jumping into the trench beside the kid. 'Now you can fire that bloody machine gun!' Martin roared.

The kid squeezed the trigger, mowing down a gaggle of Russians who had been foolish enough to emerge from behind the wreckage of a truck.

Beaming with pride at his handiwork, the kid took his helmet off to wipe sweat out his eyes. He looked around to smile nervously at Martin, who was himself busy squeezing off a burst of MP40 fire.

A Soviet high velocity bullet drilled into the kid's right temple, exploding out the left, spreading skull fragment, brains and blood all over the inside of the trench, leaving him in a lifeless heap. Wiping blood and brains off his face, Martin shook with rage at whoever had sent such a hopeless specimen into combat.

He decided it was high time he made an exit, rolling out of the back of the trench and scrambling down the road embankment before sprinting for the protection of the nearby town.

* * *

Behind a long row of houses stretching away on the other side of the bridge, Martin came across a parked-up convoy of assorted German military vehicles - kübelwagens, half-track armoured personnel carriers, a King Tiger tank, even some open-topped staff cars.

Inside the latter were Waffen SS troops, sleeping the sleep of the dead - heads lolling, mouths open, snoring. Not even Pervitin - a methamphetamine enabling soldiers to go for days without sleep - could keep this lot fighting, at least not any longer. The more it was taken the more exhausted troops got in the end.

Astonished, Martin walked slowly down the length of the convoy.

He shook the shoulder of an officer behind the wheel of a kübelwagen – in fact, its sole occupant - but got no response. Martin took his Walther PPK pistol out of its holster, fired two shots into the air. No one in the convoy stirred, so he holstered the pistol, raised his MP40 and loosed off a few more rounds. Again, no reaction.

With a bemused smile on his face, Martin was walking away when a sleepy voice enquired: 'What's all the damned noise?'

Turning back, Martin saw it was the officer in the kübelwagen, whom, so he was amazed to realise, was Lehmann the young Untersturmführer of the *Liebstandarte* from the checkpoint in Berlin last summer. Now in a stinking, grimy field uniform, looking wrung out, Lehmann inspected the fierce-looking hauptsturmführer before him through bloodshot, uncomprehending eyes. 'The Russians are just down the street and coming this way,' Martin explained. 'Couldn't blow the bridge.'

Stretching and yawning, Lehmann merely observed:

'My men need their rest. They haven't had a break for days.'

'The fucking Russians are almost upon you,' Martin hissed in exasperation. Lehmann waved him away, closed his eyes and tried to resume his slumber.

Martin decided there was no point in this lot just using their vehicles for sleeping, so he opened the door of the kübelwagen and hauled Lehmann out. 'Hey!' Lehmann protested angrily at being dumped on the cold, wet muddy road. Martin chucked his MP40 and other kit in the back, jumped into the driver's seat and switched on the engine.

'You can sleep anywhere Lehman, I need this vehicle. Good luck!'

Martin swung the steering wheel, pulled away from the side of the road, gunned the engine and departed to the west.

Meanwhile, Lehmann settled down, the kerb providing a pillow. Comparative silence returned, but within seconds a shell hit a building a few hundred yards away with an ear-splitting crash. Still no one stirred in the convoy of slumbering troops.

* * *

Martin stopped the kübelwagen amid the debris of war in a village several miles along the road - burned out tanks, trucks, cars, and charred corpses were strewn everywhere. He helped himself to a petrol can - *a rare find!* - from a truck that was somehow unscathed.

The air was filled with the roar of a low flying aircraft and Martin pressed himself against the side of the vehicle for cover.

The black shadow of a Junkers troop transport flashed over, something plummeting from the open cargo door, hitting the top of a house, sending wooden shingles flying.

It was a torpedo-shaped supply container, which cracked open, raining down Iron Crosses on neck ribbons, which dangled from various pieces of wreckage like so many Christmas tree baubles. Martin took one of them from its hanging place, let it dangle from a finger, the medal twirling and winking mockingly in the sunlight. The insane absurdity of discarding his own Knight's Cross in Berlin, only to be bombarded with hundreds of medals amid the carnage of *Spring Awakening's* inevitable demise - crushed by the gigantic clunking fist of the huge and relentless Red Army - was irresistibly hilarious. Martin broke into a hysterical laugh, which he could not control, even after he climbed back into the kübelwagen and sped off.

6

As THE KÜBELWAGEN silently coasted through an abandoned customs post on the Austro-Hungarian border, Martin was more than ready for an ambush. He had placed grenades on the passenger seat alongside the MP40. Senses straining, he scanned black, empty windows and yawning doorways.

It appeared nobody was home.

Martin let out a sigh of relief, fingers brushing the ignition key, about to turn it and restart the engine when a voice suddenly called out: 'Hey!'

Martin slowly turned his head and was stunned to find a familiar face. It was Erwin, in a doorway, wearing a big grin - no longer dressed in the ill-fitting suit of a wounded warrior but in full combat uniform. Emerging on all sides from customs post buildings were Erwin's men, all armed to the teeth.

A few minutes later found the two officers leaning against the frame of a shattered window inside one of the buildings, drinking steaming ersatz coffee from purloined Red Army white enamel mugs.

Outside, some of Erwin's men were posted on guard, eyes

watching the road east, surveying the terrain to both sides and also the skies. Others were dotted around, inside and outside buildings, cleaning their weapons and checking equipment, swapping jokes as they worked. 'They're a good bunch,' Erwin observed with pride, draining his mug.

Martin nodded towards the rank insignia on Erwin's epaulettes, which had been revealed when he took off his camouflage smock.

'And they've promoted you to Oberstleutnant, which I personally find incredible.'

Erwin grinned and shrugged: 'Every other officer was dead, so they didn't have much choice.'

'And where's the rest of your battalion?'

'This is it my friend, all of us that survive. Twenty-five men. We're exhausted beyond belief but determined to get home.'

Martin enquired: 'And then what?'

Erwin shrugged, his eyes seeming a little troubled.

'Keep the Russians at bay long enough for the British and Americans to occupy as much of our territory as possible. And you? Still fighting for the glory of the Reich?'

Martin laughed but offered no comment.

'Come with us,' Erwin suggested.

Handing his empty mug over to Erwin, for a moment Martin appeared to be giving the idea serious consideration.

Erwin went over to a chair and picked up an open knapsack and put the mugs inside.

After doing up the buckle on the flap he pulled it on. It strained at the seams due to the sheer weight of equipment contained within. 'You belong with fighting troops Martin,' Erwin suggested.

'If you've got to make a last stand wouldn't you rather do it alongside us?'

Martin shook his head.

'I'm trying to catch up with someone.'

'Someone?'

Martin didn't elaborate – it would be too difficult to explain how he and the girl from Bad Gastein had become lovers in a labour camp. Erwin hoisted the bulging knapsack onto his back, reached forward with a grunt and picked up his Gebirgsjäger cap from another chair.

'Have it your way. We've got to get going.'

Erwin went over to the window and shouted:

'Hummel, we're moving out!'

An unteroffizier sitting on a groundsheet by the building opposite cleaning his StG44 assault rifle, looked up and yelled back: 'Yes, Sir!'

Swiftly reassembling the weapon, not even looking at what his hands were doing, Hummel roared at the troops: 'Alright you lot - we get moving in five minutes!'

Erwin again beamed with pride, but then looked sombre, filled with an urge to ask Martin a question that had been on his mind for some time, though he was wary of pushing the point too hard.

'Tell me something Martin…'

'Anything.'

'Were you ever afraid during all this business?'

Martin smiled, though his eyes were wary.

'How do you mean?'

'Does a Waffen SS warrior like you ever feel fear?'

Martin probed his memory for an instance he could relate, then nodded. 'It was early '43 and we were on the outskirts of Kharkov, pinned down under heavy artillery fire and losing quite a few men, but I couldn't do anything about it, except get very angry at my sheer helplessness. We just had to lie there, shaking with fury and fear, pressing ourselves as close as possible to the quaking earth as it soaked up our blood.' Martin's eyes had taken on a far-away look, lost in recollection of that moment. 'I must admit I was grateful for the protection of my lucky pfennig that day.' He returned to the present, asking Erwin: 'What about you?'

The other man grinned and replied: 'Oh sure, several times, not least under fire up some blasted peak with bits of shattered rock nicking my face and hands – shredding my nerves also – or hanging in space, dangling from a piece of string after a cliff fall, thousands of feet of thin air below my boots.' Erwin shuddered and reflected with a rueful smile: 'And yet, while many others have perished both you and I are still here.'

* * *

With Martin back behind the wheel of the kübelwagen, Erwin leaned in to say farewell, offering his hand: 'Good luck my friend.'

Martin gripped it firmly and they shook.

'You too, Erwin.'

The vehicle's engine roared into life and Martin pulled away, not looking back. Erwin watched him disappear down the road to the west, then slipped the sling of his MP40 over his head, the weapon nestling against his stomach. The mountain troops were already moving out, not taking the road, but heading in single file up a trail leading into the forest.

In the distance, shining in the brilliant morning sunshine, were the towering mountains of Austria and beyond them was Bavaria.

As the mountain troops melted into trees still wreathed in early morning mist, someone started singing 'Lili Marlene'. One-by-one the other soldiers took up the song. Erwin, with long strides made his way up the column to join his radioman in its centre.

Even after the mountain troops had all vanished into the woods, the sound of the song wafted down the slopes - not strident, but a lullaby.

'Give me a rose to show how much you care,

Tie to the stem a lock of golden hair…'

Then it faded, leaving just the sound of wind whistling through the shattered windows of the forlorn customs post buildings.

* * *

Daylight had faded into darkness when a drowsy Todt guard leaning against a tree by the side of the road was jolted awake by the sound of a vehicle approaching.

He raised his rifle, waiting for it to become visible – but there were no headlights, not even with slits, which was doubly suspicious.

Its engine was suddenly cut, the guard making out a low dark shape as it coasted to a halt just a few yards down the road.

'Who goes there?' the guard shouted into the darkness, voice high-pitched with fear. 'Friend or foe?'

'Friend - Hauptsturmführer Walder!' came the response.

The Todt guard escorted the Waffen SS officer across a large clearing that was covered in the supine forms of sleeping and, in some cases, dying prisoners. They found the Commandant wrapped in a blanket, sitting on a log by a crackling fire. He actually looked pleased to see Martin – grateful to have a real soldier among his men again. If the Russians made a foray along the road, he would need somebody to sacrifice leading a rearguard action while he got away. The Commandant offered Martin a hip flask.

'Schnapps?'

Martin declined with a shake of the head. Taking off his helmet, resting it by his feet, Martin sat down on the log too, holding out his hands towards the fire, rubbing them together. He stared into it, fearing the loathing in his eyes might be too apparent if he looked directly at the Commandant. Cunning was needed if he was to spirit Lorelei away.

Meanwhile, the Commandant regarded Martin with a sly sideways smile. The other officers gathered around the fire looked at Martin with great suspicion, not knowing if it was a good or bad thing the Waffen SS officer had joined them. 'We never thought we'd see you again,' the Commandant remarked with forced casualness. 'How was the battle? Our troops fought bravely against the Bolsheviks? Like lions?'

Looking into the fire Martin remarked sardonically:

'Oh yes, like lions.'

'Well it has been no stroll in the park for us,' the Commandant responded sullenly. Not wishing to hang around and hear a sob story, Martin picked up his helmet and left the Todt officers to huddle around their fire. As he disappeared into the darkness, the Commandant spat, his phlegm sizzling on a hot rock.

* * *

Martin was on a quest to find Lorelei among the prisoners, the blood rush thumping in his ears, anxious to be reunited with her. As he moved from group to group of pathetic, shivering people he peered closely at each one, deliberately not calling out her name to avoid arousing the attention of Todt guards. He came across one of the other women from the 'social club', curled up in a foetal position on the ground, and who stared up at him eyes wide with fear.

'Lorelei, is she near?' Martin asked in an urgent whisper.

She didn't answer.

'You shared her hut at the camp, didn't you?'

She remained silent, but a voice remarked defiantly from the darkness:

'There'll be no comfort for you tonight.'

Martin went over to its owner, an elderly man sitting on the ground.

'What do you mean?'

'She's free,' he observed with a harsh laugh.

Martin's heart leapt.

'She got away?'

'Escaped, killed, whatever – she's not here anymore. You won't be able to get her.' Martin slumped to the ground, completely stunned and overwhelmed, his helmet rolling from his hands, which lay useless in his lap, palms open. After a while he asked the old man to tell him how it happened

* * *

With the sun not far past the highest part of its arc across the sky, a new horror made its entrance – prowling Soviet fighter aircraft. Their low throb in the distance grew to a roar, punctuated by the clatter of heavy machine guns and hammering of cannons.

They swooped along the length of the column, the guards not slow to take cover in ditches either side of the road or hide in the trees. The shells ripped people caught in the open to shreds, a primeval howl of fear rippling through the stumbling press of prisoners, dozens of them falling only to be trampled underfoot.

The Commandant leapt down from his truck and flung himself into a ditch. The horses that had been pulling it since running out of petrol, tried to bolt, but could not escape with such a weight attached to them. They thrashed helplessly in their makeshift harnesses, nostrils flaring in distress, issuing blood-curdling whinnies, flanks glistening with the foam of sweaty terror. The other two trucks – also horse drawn by now - were hit with cannon fire, bursting into flames.

The animals pulling them were hit and dropped dead in their harnesses, while some human occupants tumbled onto the road as flaming torches. Hands over his ears as he pressed himself against the bottom of the ditch, the Commandant screamed: 'Don't let any of the prisoners get away!'

They tried to run for shelter but from the trees and ditches, the rifle and submachine gun fire of guards felling some on the road, which ran red with blood. In the chaos a number of prisoners still manage to escape, though dozens more were killed.

Todt guards found they were caught in a terrible dilemma: following orders to get as many slave workers as possible to the underground factories in the Reich – under threat of a firing squad if they failed - or simply melting away into the forests to save themselves from the Soviet scythe. Lorelei was among several of the social club girls who took their chances and simply vanished. By that time the guards were less interested in hunting down escapers than getting the march moving before the Russian aircraft returned.

* * *

As the old man finished this sorry tale, it occurred to Martin that the storyteller hadn't actually seen her being claimed.

'You saw no corpse?' Martin asked.

'She's free – dead or alive.'

Martin clung onto a shred of hope that Lorelei actually got away, and was still alive. But what the old man didn't tell him was that Lorelei took her revenge before she melted into the woods.

In the panic of the air attack some of the guards dropped their weapons, and from the roadside ditch - peering fearfully between his fingers - the old man had watched as Lorelei stopped by the mewling curled up ball of a Todt officer, picking up a discarded submachine gun.

Lorelei squeezed the trigger, unleashing a burst of fire into his body, then threw her head back to unleash a primal scream, letting the weapon fall from her grasp. The old man hauled himself out of the ditch, going over to Lorelei, to offer comfort and to explain that it was alright, that he too would have done such a terrible thing, to gain his own revenge…if he'd possessed the courage. Eyes still burning with anger, she brushed his hand off her shoulder, and without a word turned and crossed the road to be swallowed up by the darkness of the forest.

7

THE FOLLOWING morning the Commandant decided it would be a good idea to finish off those he felt were now unfit to go on.

In that way they would all hopefully make better progress.

Four Hungarian Arrow Cross party thugs, who had joined up with the march, unwillingly dug a large pit into which the corpses would be thrown. Responsible for many atrocities in Budapest and elsewhere, the Hungarian fascists may have grumbled and groaned but it was better than being left behind to face the Russians.

The Commandant called Martin over and, studying his face intently, told him: 'I want you to take care of the cleansing today and then bring the squad up to the column.'

Martin revealed not even a flicker of insubordination in his eyes, though all through the night he had wrestled with hot rage and cold fury. Returning to the kübelwagen, which he had moved around into the clearing, Martin sprawled along the back seat, throwing a blanket over himself. Tossing and turning, he'd barely suppressed an urge to leap out and slit the throat of every Todt bastard in their sleep; but no, he wanted to *see* them die – and they should know it was him, via something more kinetic and explosive than a knife in the night. Lorelei's departure had liberated him to do whatever he wished. They must not know of the storm that was coming and by morning ice ran in his veins.

With the slave workers who had survived the night and could still move herded out of the clearing and onto the road, a dozen of the living doomed remained.

Gathered into a group in the centre of the clearing were old men and women and a few sickly children. There was some quiet weeping among those marked for death, but otherwise they were too exhausted to rail against their imminent demise. Three Todt guards, armed with MP40s and pistols stood by them, looking very bored. One of the guards walked over to Martin, who was standing beside the kübelwagen, putting his own MP40 back together, having just cleaned it to ensure maximum killing efficiency.

'Sir, shouldn't we be getting on with it?' the guard asked.

Martin nodded, leaning into the vehicle to place the MP40 on the back seat. 'I'll be over in a minute,' he told the guard in a voice devoid of emotion. Pulling his pistol from its holster, Martin checked it also.

Plenty of bullets would be required for whatever happened next.

Retrieving the MP40 from the rear seat and cradling it in his arms, Martin turned and walked past the guards to prisoners.

A tremor of fear ran through them and they huddled even tighter together, the smell of sweat and piss causing him to gag.

They repulsed him, but not as much as the Todt guards, who looked at Martin expectantly, lifting their weapons to the firing position.

Their faces took on a confused look as Martin raised his MP40 and pointed it at them rather than the prisoners.

He pulled the trigger, spraying them with bullets and all three fell, two dead and one wounded and groaning in agony. Martin slung the MP40, then squeezed off a round from his pistol into the head of each guard.

Martin went over to the prisoners, who shrank from him in fear so he holstered his pistol and held up both hands, to show he meant no harm.

'You must disappear,' he told them. 'Maybe you won't make it, but maybe you will. At least now you have a chance rather than a bullet in the head.' He pointed West. 'Go that way.'

They didn't move, suspecting a trick, but as Martin climbed back into the kübelwagen they fled.

* * *

The kübelwagen approached at speed and, as it came level with the rear of the Commandant's truck, that vehicle's primary occupant was puzzled the other vehicle only contained Martin.

Slowing his pace to that of the truck, Martin held the Commandant's anxious gaze, his intense loathing for the Todt functionary finally fully revealed on his face. All the Commandant's doubts about Martin crystallised into raw dread. Keeping a firm grip of the steering wheel with his right hand, Martin used his left to lob a grenade into the back of the truck.

As it twirled on the floor, the Commandant looked down at it in bewildered fascination. On finally computing what it was, he made a leap for survival - just as it exploded. Buttocks and thighs peppered with hot shrapnel, the Commandant fell with an agonised scream into the roadside ditch. The horses panicked and despite its weight the burning truck's smoking carcass was hauled away, a Todt guard on fire from head to toe - yet issuing no scream, no sound at all - toppling from it onto the road where the flames consumed him. Martin span the kübelwagen around, stopped it and climbed out.

At the side of the road a couple of stunned Todt men were gawping open-mouthed and such was their shock they did nothing to stop the prisoners scattering to either side. Martin raised the MP40 and sprayed bullets, which ripped ragged, bloody holes across their chests.

Another guard took a pot shot at him but missed by a wide margin. Martin identified the tree behind which the man lurked. Calmly taking aim he squeezed the trigger and a burst of four shots sent tree bark and bits of skull flying. The remaining Todt guards and the Arrow Cross thugs ran away and Martin let them disappear but then he heard a click and a curse behind him, spinning around to find the Aide struggling with a pistol whose mechanism had jammed. The Aide had not forgotten Martin's promise to kill him if he failed to look after Lorelei and so had tried a pre-emptive attack.

Martin strode over, ripped the weapon from the man's grasp and hurled it away. Feeling ecstatic at unleashing the hatred he felt for the Todt swine, Martin laughed and shoved the man in the chest.

The Aide tripped over his feet and sprawled on the road.

'What did I tell you about keeping your weapon clean?'

Holding his arms up to shield himself the Aide cried out:

'Have you gone insane?'

'A long time ago,' Martin sighed.

Meanwhile, the Commandant was crawling away down the ditch, Martin spotting the movement out the corner of his eye. Escorting the Aide over to the kübelwagen, Martin shoved him into the passenger seat, reached into the back, found a length of rope and used it to bind the terrified man's hands. 'Stay there!' he ordered.

Martin strode over to the ditch where the Commandant lay very still, trying to pretend he was dead. Jumping down, Martin prodded him in the back with the muzzle of the MP40.

'Sit up,' he ordered, the Commandant meekly complying.

Martin sat down beside him.

'What did you do before the war?'

'What!?'

'Answer the question.'

'I was an accountant.'

Martin snorted derisively: 'How suitable.'

Martin got to his feet, staring down at the Commandant with murder in his eyes. 'If the maggots and gangrene don't get you the Red Army will make short work of you. Or maybe some of the people you lorded it over will come and string you up?'

Martin glanced back down the road where prisoners taking cover to either side watched in stunned silence, uncertain what to do next.

With a whimper, the Commandant began crawling again.

Martin climbed out of the ditch and went over to the Kübelwagen. Climbing in beside the somewhat distressed Aide he did a three-point turn and drove away to the east. Those prisoners who had been lying on the road rose to their feet and parted as he passed slowly through them.

'Scatter you fools!' Martin shouted. 'Go home!' A woman cried out: 'Our homes and lives are gone!'

'Well, don't hang around here!'

As he accelerated away down the road, Martin noticed in the wing mirror some of the younger prisoners had picked up rifles and clubs abandoned by the guards. There was a high-pitched scream as blows rained down on the Commandant. It was cut off by gunshots.

8

The Huntsman's Lodge

After finishing his story, the German seemed relieved of a great burden, as if Eric had been his priest in the confessional.

Martin was resigned to his fate. A life of solitude, wandering the woods, cleansing them of human vermin, as he saw it, was not an end in itself. He had, without comprehending it until now, merely been in limbo - waiting for the Englander to come calling.

The German took the stopper out of the schnapps bottle and filled a glass, shoving it across to Eric.

'Let us have a final toast to lost comrades and lost love,' Martin suggested with a wistful smile, drinking from the bottle.

'Tell me something,' Eric asked, not touching the schnapps, 'what did you do with the Commandant's lackey? Did he get away?'

'I let him go, after discovering he knew nothing about Lorelei's fate,' Martin replied, then paused to turn something over in his mind before nodding and adding: 'For my part, I wish to surrender into your custody.'

Eric wondered if the German was mocking him, but, from the

serious look on Martin's face, clearly this was not the case. Standing up, letting the Walther lie on the table, Eric put on his beret.

Martin picked up the G43 semi-automatic rifle, pulled out the magazine, and ejected the chambered round, standing it on the table. He offered both rifle and magazine.

'Please accept my formal surrender.'

Half tempted to salute, but resisting the impulse, Eric took them from Martin, slinging the rifle over his shoulder, pocketing the bullet and magazine. Eric instructed Martin to put the rifle's remaining ammunition and a few things he may need by way of personal effects in the knapsack, which would be looked after by himself. Martin also fetched the K98k bolt-action rifle and handed it over to Eric.

The idea of weapons and bullets just being left around for someone else to find and use for nefarious activities offended Eric, even if an unrealistic ambition due to the garbage of war still scattered across almost an entire continent.

'I must say Captain Wise, the news that Lorelei did survive after all has brought me peace,' Martin confessed happily as he gathered the stuff together. Eric realised this was the decisive factor in the German giving himself up. He wondered if he should tell Martin that, in fact, there was no hard evidence who the Bad Gastein girl was – just because she was fascinated with the *Lorelei* poem did not make her Martin's lost love. Lorelei could well have died in the woods, though the aviator's jacket she wore was perhaps a shred of corroboration, even if circumstantial.

What if another girl from the camp had taken Martin's coat off the dead Lorelei and then later swapped it for the aviator jacket?

Eric decided not to puncture Martin's bubble of hope, particularly if it meant the German would come quietly.

* * *

Going around to the front of the lodge they found waiting none other than Major Dostoyevsky and Sergeant Ivanov, standing either side of their GAZ, weapons raised in a most unfriendly fashion.

'This seems to be the day for people pointing guns at each other,' thought Eric. There was Martin's rifles and the Walther pistol – *God knows how many people those weapons had killed* - then there was his own Browning, a weapon not useful in his hands at anything but close range. Now here was Dostoyevsky's Tokarev TT-30 pistol and Ivanov's PPSh submachine gun joining the party. The cold steel of the Tokarev's snout had no doubt been pressed at the base of many victims' skulls before their brains were blown out.

'How very nice to see you Captain Wise,' Dostoyevsky said with a sardonic smile. 'I am here to relieve you of the fascist so he can face justice.'

This served only to arouse Eric's indignant outrage:

'Fuck off!'

That elicited a laugh from the Russian officer and a puzzled look from his sidekick whose English did not extend to Anglo-Saxon profanities.

'I'm not handing over my prisoner,' Eric said between gritted teeth, just so his position was crystal clear.

Dostoyevsky kept his pistol squarely on Eric, while Ivanov made sure the PPSh was covering the German, whose demeanour had become extremely tense, eyes filled with hostility. Yet, even Martin realised this was not a situation that favoured himself and the Englander, so he stayed still.

The unloaded rifles were slung over Eric's shoulders, along with the knapsack. Any attempt by the British officer to pull the Browning from its holster or Martin's Walther from his trouser pocket, would need some kind of gymnastics and surely see them both killed. The Russians had the drop on them.

'You should bow to our demand captain,' Dostoyevsky suggested, utterly confident he had the upper hand. Digging in a tunic breast pocket for a packet of smokes, the Russian officer pulled a cigarette from it with his teeth. Putting the packet away and, again using his left hand, Dostoyevsky retrieved a lighter from the same pocket and lit the cigarette, took a puff on it and revealed:.

'We have done our own investigations after taking into custody several of the Hungarians who were with the death march and also the pond scum who was Aide to the Commandant.'

Dostoyevsky, took another draw on the cigarette, exhaled a cloud of self-satisfied smoke and added: 'They all signed confessions, providing certain useful information before they were, unfortunately, killed while trying to escape.'

Colouring with anger, Eric countered self-righteously: 'Someone who surrendered in the British zone to a British officer would be dealt with by us, so that justice is seen to be properly done.'

Out of the corner of his eye, Eric saw that Martin was shifting from foot to foot, clenching and unclenching his fists.

'Don't,' Eric hissed out the side of his mouth.

'Yes, don't try it,' Dostoyevsky purred, 'or we will have the pleasure of imposing your suitable sentence now. I have to thank you by the way, Captain Wise for running this fascist to ground, for we did not know of him until after we had withdrawn from this sector and handed it over. Now you should assist by surrendering him and we can go our separate ways in peace.'

Martin's anger at the Russian's smug arrogance boiled over and he roared: 'Bolshevik animal!' To which Dostoyevsky replied: 'Nazi scum!'

To defuse the situation, Eric asked a leading question that had been bothering him but which he felt Martin was not qualified to answer.

Only the Russians could.

'And who gave the order for the aircraft to slaughter the slave workers on the march?'

Dostoyevsky's cocky smile disappeared and he dismissed it angrily: 'That is an irrelevance.'

'You killed quite a few,' Martin suggested.

Dostoyevsky flicked the cigarette away, telling Martin with a venomous glare: 'Shut up.'

'Come on major,' Eric kept on, 'it's only fair that you tell us all you know, especially Russia's part in slaughtering those civilians.'

Dostoyevsky was outraged at the Westerner's audacity.

'Look in the mirror Captain Wise! We could not have sent out aircraft to try and stop the Nazis moving the prisoners back to the Reich without information from the British.'

Eric's blood ran cold, as he instantly realised his own complicity in the matter – this could even be the information he had been given by the Dutchman about the German plan to march the slave workers back to the Reich. 'The idea was to save them,' Eric gasped, feeling sick to his core.

Dostoyevsky laughed derisively.

'Now it is my time to say fuck off,' the Russian sneered. 'The Germans raped and murdered many in my country all in the cause of total war, including my own family. You truly expect us to weep over the destruction of their human raw materials, that they could have used to make more guns and more rockets to kill us. We Russians are not snivelling, sentimental idiots.'

'Why burn the corpses?'

'Not because we were ashamed!' Dostoyevsky spat, then insisted: 'I told you before, they were diseased, so rather than just put them back in the grave we cleansed them with fire…Mother of God, you British burned down the Belsen camp to stop a typhus outbreak, so who the fuck are you to call us to account? We all do what we must! They were already dead!'

Eric's head was spinning from the realisation that his mission across the river in Holland had, far from saving lives, possibly enabled the Russians to eradicate them.

Dostoyevsky and Ivanov roared with contemptuous laughter, while Martin looked on in utter dismay, realising that he was about to fall into the hands of the Soviets, the most hated of all enemies.

The Russians' laughter was suddenly cut off by a Devonian voice bellowing: 'Lay down your weapons!'

Straightening up, Eric found Ted Bodman and two of the military policemen from the investigation team had trumped Dostoyevsky. Having crept stealthily through the trees, their Thompsons and Sten guns were cocked and ready to mow down the Russians if they did not do as ordered.

Realising the tables had been turned and they stood no chance against such firepower, Dostoyevsky and Ivanov sullenly complied.

Recovering enough to assume command of the situation, Eric took great pleasure in telling the Russians: 'Leave your weapons behind, get in your vehicle and go east, not stopping until you are out of the British sector.'

Dostoyevsky had no comeback on that one, and both he and Ivanov obediently climbed into the GAZ. Utterly depressed at his failure to take Martin into custody, from the passenger seat of the vehicle Dostoyevsky, remarked loudly and petulantly: 'My superiors will be making representations on this matter – of that you can be assured.'

The GAZ engine roared into life, Ivanov having trouble getting it into gear, before shooting away down the track through the trees to the main road, leaving behind a cloud of blue exhaust fumes. 'Good riddance to that bastard,' Ted said by way of an unfond farewell.

'He must have been following us at a distance all along,' Eric said with a grimace, his temples throbbing with pain.

'You should never go off alone into the woods,' Ted chided Eric. 'Never know who you are going to bump into.'

9

THE CONVOY of trucks and jeeps motored west, the road snaking around the contours of thickly wooded lower slopes. As it approached another tight bend the sound of gunfire echoed off the valley sides and Eric ordered Ted to pull over, the other vehicles following suit. Up ahead there was a loud explosion followed by several bursts of machine gun fire.

'Bandits,' Martin observed, almost casually.

Eric nodded, got out and cocked his Thompson submachine gun. Martin leaned forward from his seat in the rear of the vehicle and suggested: 'Let me help.' The MP corporal sitting beside him put his arm across Martin's chest, pushing hard to make him sit back.

'Lay off mate,' the corporal warned.

Eric looked Martin in the eye, warning sternly: 'No funny business, you'll be on your honour.'

Martin, smiled, holding Eric's eyes and promised: 'On my honour - bandit scum are our mutual enemy.'

Eric believed Martin was sincere, and it was worth the risk to have his help. 'It's alright,' he told the corporal, 'let him have his gun.'

The NCO looked very dubious.

'Are you sure, Sir?'

Eric nodded. 'He has certain skills we may need.'

Martin climbed out, retrieving the rucksack and pulling out a box of bullets, laying it on the bonnet of the jeep. He opened it and stuffed rounds in the pockets of his hunting jacket. Eric ordered the corporal to fetch Martin's K98k rifle from the back of a truck and bring it around to him. Martin wasted no time in loading it.

Three MPs, including the corporal, all fully armed and eager for a fight, clustered by Eric's vehicle to join himself, Ted Bodman and Martin. The rest of the convoy's military personnel would stay with the vehicles to protect the medics.

Eric fixed his fighting group with a fierce look and shouted:

'Come on then!'

Coming around the bend, sparks flying from hobnailed boots, they found a scene of utter disarray – lorries on fire; dead bodies in ditches or hanging from vehicles; smoke pouring into the sky; puddles of blood on the road.

The vehicles had their tyres punctured by caltrops, which had been scattered in their path, and explained why they hadn't simply accelerated away and driven through the ambush.

The assault group split into two – two of the MPs plus Ted jumping down into the left-hand ditch at the foot of the slope, moving fast; Eric, the corporal and Martin running down the road, guns at the ready, trigger fingers curled. As they approached the rearmost lorry – which had a small Union flag painted on its tailgate – one of the bandits, a skinny figure dressed in a patchwork waistcoat and open necked shirt, emerged from the back, dropping down onto the road, British occupation currency notes fluttering around him. Eric squeezed the trigger of his weapon, which jumped hotly in his hands. Several bullets punched the bandit in the chest, throwing him against the lorry, a look of utter surprise frozen on his dead face.

There was no time to stop, Eric leading his group up the right-hand side of the lorry, seeing two more bandits ahead. On hearing the burst of fire they had stopped carrying off booty to look back down the road.

The MP corporal let rip with his Sten gun, three 9mm bullets spraying one bandit's blood and brains all over the side of a truck - the other vanished around the front of the vehicle.

There was gunfire now from the other side and, as Eric's assault force reached the end of the convoy, they found bandits climbing into their own lorries and racing off down the road, disappearing around the next bend. A few bursts of fire chased them on their way.

'Look!' Martin cried out, pointing down the slope. Some other bandits were scrambling down it, struggling to make off with a beer keg.

Martin ran to the side of the road, dropped into the kneeling position and calmly framed one of the keg carriers in his rifle's ZF39 telescopic sight. He squeezed off a round, aiming for the man's upper torso.

It hit the bandit in the back of the head, sending him tumbling down the slope, dead before he even touched the ground. His friend tried to hang onto the keg, but a deflected bullet from a burst of Thompson fire squeezed off by Eric persuaded him to let it go.

The beer keg rolled into the trees at the bottom of the slope, the bandit sprinting for cover in the woods. Martin had already sent death his way, the high velocity round piercing his back and passing through the bandit's heart, instantly dropping him.

'Nice shooting,' Eric remarked, impressed but also a little horrified at witnessing Martin's cold-blooded efficiency. The German stood up, not acknowledging he had even heard what Eric said.

'Maybe there's more down there, hiding in the woods,' Martin remarked, as if suggesting they go in and hunt them. Eric shook his head, not only worried about a bandit ambush but that Martin might disappear.

'We've got our own convoy to protect and a mess to clear up.'

With a loud clang a bullet hit the bonnet of the vehicle behind them.

'That came from above!' Eric shouted, the two men taking cover by the truck. Martin raised his rifle, scanned the trees through the telescopic sight, catching sight of a muzzle flash from someone shooting down the slope from between two trees. He returned fire.

'Hit him?' Eric asked, sneaking a look around the bonnet.

'Possibly.'

Eric grinned at Martin, adrenalin pumping and keen to make sure.

'Come on then.'

And so up they went, weaving between the trees, one going forward while the other covered him - lying down or kneeling behind a tree to cover the other man as he ascended. It was hard going and really made them sweat, with Eric's old leg wound aching more the steeper the slope got.

Another bullet came their way, which buried itself in a tree, Eric and Martin returning fire. Eric got up, exhausted but determined to make one last effort and catch the bandit. Telescopic sight fixed on something up ahead, Martin shouted: 'Wait!'

Eric got back down, cautiously took a look around the tree, spotting a figure close to the ground, crawling, then getting up to stumble forward. He must be as tired as they were. Martin kept his sight on the man, clear and sharp enough for a kill.

'I have him.'

'Don't,' Eric gasped, 'the bastard deserves an introduction to Mr Pierrepoint.'

Martin turned his head and gave Eric a puzzled frown.

'Who!?'

Eric got up and ran forward; so Martin settled down to cover him, keeping the telescopic sight on the bandit, finger ready to pull the trigger if the target made a wrong move.

Pulling his eye away from the sight for a moment, Martin saw Eric reach the man, the Thompson submachine gun pointed straight at the bandit's head. Then the gun dropped, Eric lurching forward, grabbing the man by the collar and dragging him out of sight behind the tree.

* * *

The most extraordinary thing had happened.

Who should Eric find smiling up at him - dazzling white grin in a dirty sun-tanned face under a flat cap - but his own brother.

'Bert!?' Eric cried in shocked disbelief.

Looking equally amazed, his brother shot back: 'Well, I never!'

Eric slung his Thompson, lunged forward, grabbing Bert by the scruff of the neck.

Bert was by then unarmed, for the Lee Enfield rifle he had used to shoot at his own brother had jammed and lay discarded further down the slope. 'You tried to kill me!' Eric protested, shaking with fury as he stood over Bert. 'I didn't know it was you!' Bert exclaimed, starting to get up, but Eric shoved him down again. A much worse prospect had replaced the shocking realization that his little brother was a bandit; he knew that at any second one of Martin's bullets could blow Bert's brains out, so he dragged him out of the line of fire.

* * *

Bert was gabbling an explanation about how he didn't die after HMS *Aztec* was sunk – *that was pretty self-evident, thought Eric* - and how he got mixed up in the black market in Spain – *yes, he always did have a talent for ducking and diving didn't he?* – then he came into northern Italy when the Germans surrendered. In recent times he'd moved to Austria.

Conscious all the while that Martin was down slope with his sniper rifle ready to kill, Eric moved to try and mask any part of Bert's body that was showing. *What would his mother say if he allowed Bert to have his brains blown out?*

* * *

Martin kept his eye pressed against the sight. *What the hell was the Englander doing? Surely, he had to realize it was always better to wipe these swine off the face of the earth?* His muscles were getting sore holding the rifle in the same position, but he was determined to take the shot if he could but while he could see Eric, he got no clear view of the bandit.

* * *

Eric demanded to know why his brother didn't just make his way to the nearest British embassy or consulate in Spain and hand himself in?

Bert admitted he'd thought of that, once he'd recovered from the ordeal, but he was so well looked after by the family of the fisherman who found him washed up on the beach.

He earned his keep, going out in the boats - one time he even saw a British battleship go past - but as time went on he got used to his new life. Bert felt too many questions would be asked if he handed himself in, that he'd be blamed for desertion or something. Well, anyway, then there was some trouble after he struck up a relationship with the fisherman's rather lovely daughter.

Eric gave a dismayed groan.

Bert looked a little sheepish.

Anyway, he had to get out and his friend Pepe from the village knew some people and that's how he came to make a living from a bit of harmless black market trading. Then, of course, he moved on and here he was today, after falling in with this villainous lot.

'And it's all gone terribly wrong hasn't it brother?' Bert shrugged apologetically, shifting his weight against the tree trunk as his bottom was getting wet and numb.

* * *

Was that something? An elbow? A leg? Just visible through the Englander's own legs? Martin stroked the trigger. *What he needed was a headshot, but maybe if he clipped the man, then they would be obliged to finish him off. But, no, he might hit Eric – and that would be no good. Martin smiled, thinking it strange that just a year ago the whole point of his existence was to kill the Allied enemy. And that meant all Englanders.* Martin shifted his elbows, trying to get some more circulation into his arms. He tucked the rifle stock tighter in to his cheek, waiting for the clean shot chance.

Now there was some movement.

Martin inhaled, the barrel went down.

He exhaled, it came up, level with where the target should appear.

Through the sight he saw a blur of khaki.

Pulling his eye away from the sight again. Martin squinted up the hill. *It was the Englander, coming down alone.*

* * *

Standing up, cradling the sniper rifle in his arms, Martin watched Eric finish his descent, calling out: 'What happened up there?'

'Got away,' came the subdued reply.

On getting closer, Eric avoided eye contact and went on by while Martin lingered, staring up the hill, to see if he could spot movement, maybe still see a chance to kill the bandit.

Eric called out sharply: 'You are on parole!'

Martin reluctantly turned away, following Eric back down to the road. Something very strange had just happened, of that he was sure.

Eric paused by a lorry, finding a grim-faced Katherine talking to one of the Field Security squad, and with several anxious nurses staring down from the interior of the vehicle. They had taken cover in a ditch as ordered by Katherine but were now back aboard.

'Everything alright here?' Eric snapped, irritated at the soldier possibly talking out of turn and scaring people.

'Yes, Sir,' the man said, wisely making himself absent.

'Can we help with anything?' Katherine asked tentatively.

'All dead,' Eric revealed with a heavy sigh, seemingly studying something on the still-warm Thompson in his hands while above, in the lorry, nurses exchanged the news in shocked whispers.

When Eric raised his eyes, he found Katherine pale-faced and visibly shocked.

'No survivors *at all*?'

'Sorry, nothing you can do,' he confirmed, wanting to comfort her somehow, but this was not the time or place.

Looking up at the back of the lorry, he told the nurses with an attempt at a reassuring smile: 'No danger now, so we'll be resuming the journey back to Graz.'

Climbing up into the vehicle, Katherine ordered her charges: 'Settle down now!'

Once she was sat down by the tailgate, Eric nodded and smiled at her, which she returned. He was grateful they were all alright, but especially her.

By the jeep, Martin opened the breech of the rifle, extracted the bullet and handed it over with others from his pockets to the corporal, who shoved them inside the knapsack. Next, he yielded the rifle. He and the corporal climbed back into the jeep and watched while two of the wrecked lorries were eased off the road, careering spectacularly down the slope to crash into trees at the bottom.

Geddes the naval surgeon volunteered to stay behind with some of the military policemen and a jeep, to take care of the dead. They had already put in a radio call to the nearest infantry unit, requesting the immediate despatch of some troops.

Eric climbed back into the jeep, the driver started the engine up again and the convoy moved off. 'The German did some amazing shooting didn't he Sir?' the corporal in the back remarked admiringly.

Eric made no comment, so the corporal added:

'Sir, to get them at that range, what with them running down the hill?'

'Yes, corporal, I bloody well heard you.'

Martin, who had been watching the exchange with interest, leaned forward and tapped Eric on the upper right arm.

'What do you think Captain Wise?'

Without looking back, Eric told him: 'You must have incredible vision to kill those men at that distance, that's what I think.'

Martin smiled at the corporal and remarked: 'My vision gets better and better, but sometimes I think my eyes deceive me.' The bemused corporal glared at him: 'What do you mean by that?'

'Lay off corporal,' Eric snapped.

The jeep pulled out and passed down the remaining lorries. The lead one, which he and Martin had sheltered behind when Bert was firing at them, was now tight against the left-hand side of the road, half in the ditch. Eric glanced at a bullet hole in its open bonnet and then up the slope into the trees. He wondered if his brother was watching.

Martin looked the other way, across the valley and in the far distance spotted a white-tailed eagle circling, riding a thermal and looking for prey on the forest floor.

10

THROUGH THE BARS of his cell at Karlau Prison, Martin could see far-off snow-topped mountains. He kept vigil at the unglazed window each morning as the sun climbed higher into the sky, its rays revealing the shining peaks in their pristine glory. Martin also watched at dusk as it dropped below the horizon in the west, giving the distant summits a golden halo.

Shorn of his beard and with his hair trimmed, some of the old Martin had emerged, but, somehow, he was not the same - not so hard around the edges. Late one evening Eric visited him to confirm he would have to stand trial for his part in running the labour camp, even if he had subsequently saved many lives. This news provoked no discernible reaction, but Martin decided it was time to unburden himself of his darkest secret.

As Eric rose from the cell's single chair to leave, Martin told him from where he sat on the bed: 'Lorelei never knew.'

'Knew what?' Eric asked.

'That I'm as guilty, as rotten as any.'

Eric sat down again.

'How, Martin? In what sense?'

Closing his eyes and throwing his head back, Martin inhaled deeply, before exhaling one word: 'Russia.'

Looking up at the cell window as the light faded, Martin told Eric the story of what happened when his troops came across a village on the march to Moscow.

* * *

The approaches to Smolensk, July 1941

A sea of golden wheat beneath a vaulted cobalt sky seemed to last an eternity, falling off the edge of the world; four black figures pushed their way through it, swimmers struggling to shore.

Behind pilot's goggles under a steel helmet, Martin's pale blue eyes were deadened by the sheer vastness of Russia and his mind numbed to any potential danger lurking within the rippling cereal crop.

The swish as they parted the stalks mingled with the jingle-jangle of webbing and equipment but otherwise there was a hot, oppressive silence.

In their path lay a village, not much more than a squalid collection of ramshackle huts, but possessing a single redeeming feature – a dazzling white, wooden-built church, with two blue onion-domes, adorned with gold stars – promising Heaven to the misbegotten residents of the district.

The village was accustomed to the depredations of armies. In 1812, Napoleon's soldiers plundered what little it offered by way of sustenance. Later Cossacks burned it to the ground, in order to leave no shelter for the French during the retreat from Moscow. In the anarchy of 1919 the Poles murdered the menfolk and had their wicked way with the women, stripping the church bare of all its pathetic gold.

Now there was war again and in the yard of a hovel on the edge of the village a one-year-old in ragged clothes crawled in the dirt among feverishly pecking chickens. His mother, clad in threadbare peasant rags, came to the door to smile at her offspring, who grinned and gurgled back.

Something drew her gaze to the horizon, so she shielded her eyes to get a better view. On seeing the four dark figures, the mother gathered up her child, amid frantically clucking poultry and rushed indoors.

With the crying child clamped to her hip, she shook her dozing husband out of his slumber on the ornate wrought iron-framed bed that dominated the main room. Cursing her, he pulled himself off it and, going to a window, stared out, suddenly full of dread when he saw strangers pushing through the wheat.

* * *

The peasant mother poured kvass from a stoneware jug into crude wooden beakers for Martin and the other visitors. Still wearing his pilot's goggles – the bile of distaste at this pantomime rising in his throat - Martin refused the sour, fermented rye drink, pushing the beaker away. He got up and left.

Behind him Bruno made a ribald remark about the peasant woman's large breasts, which were straining heavily against her blouse, the other Waffen SS soldiers laughing heartily, gulping down their kvass.

Her husband grinned, trying to ingratiate himself with them.

Outside, Martin found the rest of his well-drilled platoon had swept in from other directions and was now distributed in guard positions.

He ordered a squad to follow him and they stalked through the village, wary of snipers while all around them peasants hiding in their homes watched fearfully from the shadows.

At the far end stood the church, its dome surmounted by a golden cross - the only outward sign of wealth in the whole damned place. Martin posted two soldiers at the front door and went in, momentarily blind as he crossed from a bright summer's day into a dark interior where candles burned and incense filled the air – a heady mix that made him nauseous.

Martin's eyes behind the glass of the pilot's goggles grew accustomed to the gloom and, accompanied by six of his men, he strode across the nave towards the iconostasis before which he found a priest on his knees in silent prayer, determined to carry on with his invocation, despite the Germans standing over him.

Martin stepped forward and shoved him hard, the priest sprawling on the floor. 'Get up old man,' Martin ordered.

The priest did as instructed, adjusting his robe and staring Martin calmly in the face. Regarding the priest with contempt - Martin turned away and walked over to inspect the display on the iconostasis.

'We'll take some of these,' he said.

The priest rushed forward as Martin reached up to prise an icon depicting Mary and Baby Jesus free of its mounting.

'No!' the cleric exclaimed in German.

Martin smashed him with an elbow, the priest going flying, blood streaming from a broken nose. Martin and one of his men dragged the priest out of the church, hurling him into the dust. As he went back in Martin shouted: 'Shoot him if he tries to follow!' A few minutes later, Martin and the other Waffen SS soldiers came out, the latter carrying looted icons under their arms while the priest was on his knees, hair and beard matted with blood.

He fixed Martin with a penetrating, accusatory stare.

Coldly furious, Martin ordered:

'Burn the church.'

Two of the Waffen SS troops opened the doors, while a third hurled grenades in. After several explosions the tinder dry church started to burn.

Martin levelled his pistol at the priest's forehead. Drawing on incredible inner peace – summoning the full power of his Faith - the priest stared calmly at Martin and moved only to cross himself. With a growl of disgust Martin lowered his gun and holstered it, waving his men to follow him back across the village.

The priest stayed on his knees, bowing his head in prayer while roaring flames greedily consumed his church.

On reaching the hovel on the outskirts of the village, Martin found König not looking out for approaching Russians but watching something going on inside it. He was even taking photographs with his Leica camera.

Angry at König neglecting his duty, Martin screamed: 'What are you doing!?' Jumping as if lightning had hit him, König turned around, colour draining from his face. Martin pushed him out of the way to discover a disgusting tableau - Bruno had the wife on a tottering dining table, with her skirt down and was thrusting away inside her.

She was mute, tears streaming down her cheeks, but otherwise offering no resistance; the husband was being held down in a chair by two other SS soldiers.

He was weeping silently. The baby wailed, forsaken in a soiled cot.

The faces of the Waffen SS men were contorted into hideous gargoyles while Martin's face reddened with rage, the woman's pain-filled eyes burning into his soul. He went outside and, for what seemed like an age, stood silently staring out across the sea of wheat, haunted by the woman's stare, though the child had at least soon stopped crying. Martin turned around as Bruno emerged, buttoning his fly up. 'Burn it down!' Martin screamed, ablaze with shame.

'Burn them all!'

* * *

White and brown smoke polluted the sky, making an ochre disk of the sun.

A half-track armoured personnel carrier rolled up, squealing and grinding to a halt, with laughing SS troops climbing aboard.

Martin pulled his goggles down, his face dirty except for the area around the eyes, which was a startling white. He stared, with eyes narrowed, into the flames of the burning church and houses, allowing a flicker of doubt to enter the clear blue Aryan certainty of his gaze. 'Time to go, Sir!' Bruno cried out from the half-track. Martin pulled his goggles back up to cover his eyes and then also climbed aboard.

Once the vehicle was gone, the air was filled with the evil crackle of flames along with the groan, crash and hiss of walls collapsing into the inferno.

This was nothing exceptional of course in the annals of Hitler's armies as they raped and pillaged their way from Poland to the Caucasus and almost to Red Square.

Martin's report on the incident would claim there were partisans in the village who had fired on his patrol and so a righteous retribution had been visited upon it. The entire village was burned down for harbouring partisans and its 30 inhabitants killed as an example to others. Yet, there was something different about this episode that would burrow deep into Martin's being. He was haunted by the accusatory, pain-filled eyes of the woman as Bruno raped her and felt his soul was indelibly stained. And then there was the silent, unwavering accusation in the priest's eyes.

* * *

On finishing his terrible tale, Martin enquired miserably: 'Do you think Lorelei could have heard that confession and found it in herself to love me?'

Shocked by the brutality of the deed, the squalid horror of the scene sketched for him, Eric had no wisdom to offer. *But, should any of it surprise him after what he had seen on the death march route?*

Martin seemed a lost soul, forged of steel in the fires of rage against the world stoked by the Nazis – and only held partially in check by some kind of warrior code and forlorn, malformed love for Lorelei.

His was a confession that would ensure a death sentence and Eric could not ignore it. He wanted to ask Martin if he might feel ashamed in the eyes of the world, not just Lorelei, but one look at the German's wretched face provided the answer. As for the young woman at Bad Gastein, she had disappeared not long after Eric's visit, so nobody got to the bottom of who she really was.

11

A MONTH later Eric was required to visit the British Headquarters in Vienna to meet someone from the Judge Advocate General's office who had important new information connected to the death march case.

There would be trials of several former Todt and Nazi Party officials and, of course, Martin - that much was certain - but Eric had no idea what this new development could be.

Under a lightweight khaki raincoat Eric made sure to wear his best uniform for the trip, the Sam Browne belt highly polished, and with the Browning 9mm pistol in the holster.

He was relieved trains were running on time again and, thankfully, had been able to book himself a seat in a quiet first-class carriage.

Eric barely glanced out of the window during the three-hour journey and uppermost in his thoughts, as he did some background reading courtesy of intelligence files, was what to do with Martin Walder?

While justice had to be delivered, Eric hoped to see off a bid by the Soviets to have Martin taken away for a show trial in Moscow.

This was not out of leniency, but more a reflection of his enmity towards Major Dostoyevsky and feeling that justice must not be carried out in some cellar at the Lubyanka. The British and Americans had in the past handed over thousands of Russians, Ukrainians and others who had fought for the Nazi cause, in addition to Austrians and Germans.

The Russians were, for example, fiercely intent on bringing the hardcore Nazis of the Waffen SS *Totenkopf* Division to justice for their actions in the Soviet Union. As a special favour, in summer 1945 – during the warm afterglow of victory and amity between East-West allies - the Yanks gave them up to the Russians. As the intelligence summary of this episode in the files explained, 'very few of the *Totenkopf* men expected to survive being taken into captivity by the Soviets.' It also noted: 'That duly proved to be the case, with the senior officers executed and the rest of the troops sent to Siberia to die a miserable death.'

But then there was the case of the *Wiking* division of the Waffen SS, which had mounted a fighting retreat all the way from Balaton into Austria, offering its surrender to American forces. 'No German unit wanted to surrender to the Soviets,' observed a report, 'least of all the *Wiking*.'

Eric read that it had been mainly composed of volunteers from the Baltic States, Scandinavia, Belgium and Holland, though it included Germans too. In its 'brutal career' the *Wiking*, so the report revealed, 'had committed numerous killings of civilians and hundreds of captured Soviet soldiers.'

It added: 'Its harvest of death also included slaughtering Jewish prisoners on forced matches through Austria, not least dozens executed near Graz. In the Soviet Union the *Wiking* was implicated in killing thousands of Jews,' but, so the report revealed, 'its men were not handed over to the Soviets.' Clearly, such co-operation between the Russians and Americans in 1945 was short-lived - the Western allies were no longer interested in crimes the Waffen SS had committed in the East.

When he turned to the report on Martin's own unit, the *Das Reich* division, Eric learned that it had not only played a role in massacring 920 Jews near Minsk in 1941, but also murdered hundreds of men women and children in France during 1944. 'It was some consolation that it lost thousands of its own men to Allied attacks in Normandy,' the anonymous author of that report remarked. Nowhere was the burning down of a village near Smolensk and killing of its inhabitants mentioned.

Small beer compared to other crimes on the Eastern front, perhaps, but while others of his kind had disappeared in the chaos of war's end, Martin had been found and confronted. To his credit he had accepted that he must now pay, for while Martin Walder's crime was different in scale to others by the troops of the Waffen SS, its nature was the same. Eric felt a man who had been responsible for such a repugnant act had to receive appropriate punishment and no judge would pardon him.

Especially as he had confessed to it.

Even so, aside from trying to prevent Martin from being presented to the Soviets, Eric was determined to make sure Pierrepoint didn't get him. Hang other Nazis by all means, but not this one – he'd get a soldier's death with no hood over his head. It was strange kind of world that saw Eric exerting himself to give Martin the bullet rather than the noose. Lifting his eyes from the file resting on his knees, Eric stared out the window at the passing landscape and pondered the strangeness of his work. 'What has my life come to?' he thought. 'Getting ready to argue about the style of execution for a Nazi war criminal?' It was a very long way from being a beat copper in Plymouth.

* * *

At Vienna's main railway station Eric rang the Judge Advocate General's office for a ride to the British Army HQ. It was located within the famed Sacher Hotel, where Pierrepoint had recently stayed and which had been one of the world's great establishments of its kind but was somewhat elegantly dilapidated these days. It at least retained an excellent restaurant - resplendent in all its ostentatious Austro-Hungarian finery - where much of the key business in the city was conducted.

Passing into the hubbub of the reception area, which was packed with soldiers and civilians milling about, Eric tucked his briefcase under his right arm, and folded his raincoat over his left forearm. The military clerks behind the desk all seemed very busy, affecting the rather impressive skill of avoiding eye contact without actually appearing to ignore Eric deliberately. He banged the desk bell, its ding drawing a hot, darting glance of annoyance from one of the clerks, a tall beanpole in khaki, who stilled its entreaty with a palm.

'Yes, sir?' he enquired stiffly.

'Captain Wise, here to see Major Forbes in the Judge Advocate General's office.'

The clerk ran his finger down an appointments book.

'It says here that he'll see you in the restaurant at Noon, Sir.'

Eric glanced at his watch; 15 minutes away.

'You can have a coffee at your table, Sir,' said the clerk, adding something Eric could not make out due to the din.

'I'm sorry?' Eric enquired.

'I said, Sir, that the Sachertorte is recommended - even these days they seem to be able to get the chocolate and apricot filling just right - and goodness knows how!'

Eric was quite amazed at how animated the man had become.

'Thanks.'

'My pleasure, Sir.'

* * *

Eric did as suggested and ordered a black coffee and Sachertorte, scanning his surroundings from a corner booth.

Flanked by a potted palm on one side and a large humidor on the other it was well situated for a private meeting, which was probably why Forbes had reserved it.

Shoving his raincoat and briefcase around the seat a little, Eric took off his cap and placed it next to them. The place was very busy, with waiters dashing here and there. Two MPs stood at ease by the main entrance, but otherwise you wouldn't know it was anything but a hotel restaurant, rather than the heart of British rule in Vienna.

The waiter returned with the coffee and a large slice of Sachertorte, bidding him 'bon appetit' before withdrawing to loiter watchfully nearby.

Eric looked at the cake, with its heavy dark chocolate icing complemented with a huge dollop of whipped cream. He'd not seen anything remotely like it since before the war and so was afraid to cut into it.

His mind was transported back to a day in the summer of 1936 when he was a baby copper. While waiting to give evidence at the nearby crown court, he and his sergeant had gone to Goodbody's Café in Bedford Street – a rather grand place with a high, vaulted ceiling. They had a pot of tea and some chocolate gateaux – like a cut-price version of the Sachertorte.

It was all a bit too refined for humble beat coppers, but they couldn't exactly go for a pint when they were in court. Goodbody's was long gone now, wiped out by the blitz of '41 while the Hotel Sacher endured.

As Eric's fork hovered tentatively over the Sachertorte something strange happened. Piercing the cacophony in the restaurant came a distinctive laugh – loud and mocking – and a voice that Eric was sure he knew due to its familiar timbre. While Eric was absorbed in trying to place it, a waiter came to the humidor and extracted a huge, fat cigar.

On impulse, deciding to find out exactly who the voice belonged to, Eric got up and walked across the restaurant, following on the heels on the waiter with the cigar, who stopped at a large circular table.

Arrayed around it was a group of raucous men and women – civilians, smartly dressed, five of them in all. Holding court was none other than Bert with a blonde and a brunette female in garish plumage on either side. Eric's brother was somewhat different in appearance from how he'd been in the woods. Here he was resplendent in a suit and tie, hair slicked back, looking prosperous and polished. He puffed the cigar into life as the waiter touched a match to it, his eyes momentarily bulging in shock when he saw his brother standing before him.

Bert swiftly recovered his composure, taking the cigar out of his mouth and through a cloud of smoke called out: 'Well bugger me, if it isn't my big brother!'

The women looked the smartly-dressed British officer up and down, not understanding what Bert had said, but from the tone of voice realising this was someone he knew. Bert dismissed them from his presence with the wave of a hand, ordering:

'Go and powder your noses, girls.'

They sullenly withdrew from the scene.

The two other men at the table were swarthy, rough-looking types - almost indistinguishable - barely contained by straining double-breasted suits and one of them pulled a chair out for Eric before he and his colleague went over and sat at an adjacent table, their Sachertorte going with them.

Their watchful eyes took in everything, especially Bert's expression and tone of voice. They were guard dogs doing their master's bidding and ready to strike. One of them had his cold, coal black eyes fixed on the British officer's holster. Still shocked, Eric sat down under Bert's amused and insolent gaze.

'Fancy a cigar?' Bert asked, blowing smoke.

Eric shook his head.

Bert leaned forward and poured black coffee into a dainty little cup on a saucer.

'Sugar?' Bert asked, lifting up and putting down a bowl of sugar lumps with tiny silver tongs precariously balanced on it. 'No thanks,' Eric responded, mind racing, trying to figure out how to handle this bizarre situation.

Bert pushed the coffee cup and saucer across to Eric.

His brother was clearly not just a country bandit on the run, 'or he wouldn't be holding court with hoodlums and floozies in the restaurant of the British headquarters,' thought Eric, rather ungenerously.

Yet, he was secretly impressed - who'd have thought his little brother could be top dog in any gang?

'So?' Bert enquired, leaning forward to tap the end of his cigar on the edge of a crystal ashtray.

'You look better than last time we met,' Eric responded sarcastically.

Laughing, Bert stuck the cigar back in his mouth and made a show of flicking lint off his lapels. 'Not bad Eric, not bad – I'm doing alright.'

Eric sipped his coffee, sneaking a sideways glance at Bert's hoods. Their jackets bulged in just the right places for pistols in shoulder holsters and Eric wondered *what kind of idiot let in criminals with firearms?*

'You look pretty smart yourself Eric,' Bert remarked, balancing the cigar on the rim of the crystal ashtray so he could sip his own coffee. 'But, what brings you up from the sticks? No more Nazis to hang in the South?'

Eric smiled, but his eyes were hard as marbles.

Smoothing the tablecloth with a thumb to remove a wrinkle, Eric observed with false levity: 'We don't care who we hang or shoot – petty criminals skulking in the woods will do us just as well.'

Bert chuckled mirthlessly, picking his cigar up, sucking on it, blowing more smoke his brother's way as sign of defiance.

'Maybe I should have let a sniper do his business,' Eric suggested. Bert frowned and asked: 'What do you mean?'

'All the time we had our little chat in the woods,' Eric told him, 'someone had their crosshairs on you ready to put a hole in your skull, but I made sure he couldn't a clear shot by dragging you into cover.'

This knocked Bert off balance and he looked a little pale at the thought of it. One of the thugs at the other table, didn't like it one bit, shifting in his chair and glaring. His hand slid up the inside of his jacket. Spotting this, Eric warned: 'Tell your attack dog to mind out.'

Eric unbuttoned his holster, a movement spotted out the corner of his eye by the other hood, who stiffened and stopped shovelling Sachertorte into his mouth. Bert laughed nervously and waved a hand.

'Calm down Eric, nobody wants a gunfight – this isn't the woods,' adding with special emphasis, 'is it, brother?' then carrying on: 'No snipers here – things work different, and your bosses wouldn't like it, trust me. Anyway, you wouldn't shoot your baby brother, would you?'

Eric moved his hand away from the holster, and smoothed the tablecloth out, wanting badly to reach across and throttle all the bravado out of the smug little git.

'Anyway Eric, it's been nice to see you again, but I have to go.'

Bert lifted his right arm and clicked his fingers.

The waiter who earlier brought Eric his cake and coffee appeared, smiling ingratiatingly. Noticing Eric was there, he frowned, perturbed at a guest changing tables.

'Do you wish to have the bill Herr Falke?'

'Yes please, Friedrich and that was an excellent lunch. Pass on my regards to Chef.'

'I will Herr Falke.'

The waiter darted away, leaving Eric feeling as if the earth had opened up below him.

Falke?

Hawk.

Eric's right hand began to quiver with a surge of adrenalin-fuelled fury and he grabbed the tablecloth, the force of his grip disturbing china cups, spilling their contents into saucers.

His brother was The Hawk!? *The black market bandit king?*

'You look a little pale,' Bert remarked, getting up, buttoning his double-breasted jacket with his right hand and then stubbing the cigar out in the ashtray. The two hoodlums also got to their feet, neither of them buttoning their jackets, Eric catching sight of the pistol butts.

The waiter returned, Bert handing him a wad of Occupation currency.

'Oh, thank you, Sir! '

On sensing the tension, the waiter backed away swiftly.

Bert flashed Eric a cheeky grin and held out a hand.

'Shake on it, brother - let bygones be bygones?'

Eric stood up, reached out and gave his brother's hand a crushing squeeze, pulling Bert half across the table, and putting his mouth to an ear. 'Next time we meet, I *will* fucking kill you first and ask questions later,' Eric whispered.

Grimacing and jerking his hand away, falling back into his chair all a fluster, Bert looked scared. The hoods leapt forward to grab Eric by his arms, one either side, a pistol sticking in his ribs.

'It's alright boys,' Bert told them, regaining his composure. 'Our dear old mum doesn't deserve to lose both her sons, does she Eric?'

With that Bert passed a hand over his slicked-back hair – *a nervous tell if ever Eric saw one* - tugged his jacket down, flashed an insolent grin and made his exit - a fast-moving figure dodging between tables flanked by enormous henchmen glaring menacingly at anyone who even dared look their way. Regaining his own composure, Eric realized everyone's eyes had switched to him. 'I say old chap, you better tidy away your sidearm,' a silky, urbane voice remarked. Whipping around, Eric found a major standing behind him. 'It's not really the done thing in here.'

Eric nodded, right hand buttoning up the holster, his left reflexively pushing his tie up tight against his shirt collar.

The other officer held out his right hand:

'Giles Forbes, Judge Advocate General's office.'

Still trembling with adrenaline, Eric shook his hand.

'Captain Eric Wise, S.G.2. from Graz.'

'Let's go, I'm starving,' suggested Forbes smoothly, leading Eric back to the corner booth, sliding a slim briefcase under the table by his feet.

'How is old Spendlove?' Forbes enquired warmly, gesturing for the waiter to come over. 'He's a rogue, isn't he? But a bloody good chap.'

Still in turmoil, Eric made no response. Before sitting down he took off the Sam Browne and pistol holster, laying them gently on top of his raincoat and briefcase, covering them with his cap.

The waiter, who'd regained his courage and so came across, asked Forbes: 'Sirs, what may be your pleasure?'

'Can you bring us the menus, the wine list and also a couple of Asbach brandies. Doubles, I think.'

The waiter nodded and backed away.

Lowering his voice, Forbes enquired: 'Do you actually know who that little fellow was?' Eric didn't seem to hear, apparently immersed in studying his untouched Sachertorte. In his mind he saw Bert as a bandit in the woods – then in his shiny Vienna guise – finally, as a sailor dancing around the kitchen with his mum at home in Turnchapel.

'Captain Wise?'

How could he ever tell his mother about any of this, never mind his superiors? His brother was The Hawk.

The bastard.

'Do you know that little fellow in the loud suit?'

Eric shook his head and smiled sadly. 'No, Sir, I don't know him. It was a case of mistaken identity. I thought he was somebody I'd had dealings with in the past, but I was wrong.'

Forbes was not convinced, advising Eric frostily: 'We can't have any of your Spendlove Group rough house stuff here in our Headquarters you know.' The brandies arrived and Eric downed his even before the waiter had finished handing out the menus and wine list. Bert's grinning face, as he chomped on a cigar, flashed into Eric's mind.

Forbes asked the waiter: 'Can you bring my friend another brandy?' Friedrich nodded and withdrew.

Carrying on in a conspiratorial tone, Forbes told Eric: 'If that was the little chap I think it was, then you really ought not to upset his applecart. I believe he's been very useful in sorting out some tricky situations with the Russians.' Eric's mind began racing again – trying to figure out exactly how his brother could be involved in such business.

'You see up here in Vienna, where we live cheek by jowl with the Reds, things are very complex,' explained Forbes, 'and punch ups and gunfights are to be avoided.'

A fresh glass of brandy arrived and this time Eric savoured it, finally calming down. 'So,' suggested Forbes, as he scrutinized the menu, 'what shall we have while we discuss how to have your Nazi stormtrooper dealt with by us rather than by the Russians. I fancy a steak. Rare. Bloody.'

And then, almost as an afterthought, Forbes remarked: 'You do realise, there is no question at all that he will face the severest penalty, your German?'

'He's not *my* German.'

With a grunt, Forbes pulled the briefcase from under the table. Putting it on his lap, he snapped open the clasp to pull out a slim file. 'Take a look at this,' he suggested. Eric opened it to find a single sheet of foolscap paper, at the top of which was typed:

Walder, Case File 03

Received from Soviet Authority,

via Maj M. Dostoyevsky, Budapest.

Subject: Photographs, ref Smolensk village massacre.

July 1941.

Note: Prints of images found on film in camera of Waffen SS Unterscharführer, or corporal, captured and killed while trying to escape, August 1941.

This appeared to be Dostoyevsky's desperate riposte for failing to take Martin prisoner in the woods? The Russian's bid to ensure Martin's execution was to be signed, sealed and delivered, even if he wasn't handed over.

Eric flipped the sheet over, revealing an envelope containing the snaps glued to the reverse side. It was difficult to understand the subject of the rather blurry first photograph, but from the caption written on the back, apparently the indistinct black and white shapes were a man's buttocks between a woman's legs.

'It's truly astonishing that the Huns kept paperwork *and* took photographs of everything,' Forbes pointed out in an amazed voice, 'even the most obscene crimes – like they were on some bloody holiday outing around Europe and Russia to record their hi-jinks for the family album.'

The next shot revealed hideously contorted faces, as a group of bareheaded soldiers with SS flashes on their collars grinned fiendishly. Filled with foreboding, Eric turned over the photograph, laying it on the table next to the first – the caption suggested it was 'Walder's men, Smolensk village.'

'Of course, it's an absolute gift to prosecutors,' Forbes observed with some satisfaction.

The third picture showed a domed, white-painted wooden church on fire, smoke pouring into the sky. Finally, there was a shot of Waffen SS soldiers clustered around a bearded man with a battered face who looked like a priest. The Germans were gurning for the camera, except for one. There, with aviator's goggles slipped down around his neck, standing off to one side slightly, was an unsmiling Martin Walder his eyes full of hatred.

For who?

The photographer?

The priest?

Russia?

The whole world?

A phrase suddenly leapt into Eric's head:

'Give death, and take Death.'

Wasn't that the SS motto?

Well, Eric thought bitterly, Martin had given death... All that remained now was for him to collect on the other half of the bargain.

Eric tidied the photographs away into the envelope and handed the file back to Forbes. They were merely confirmation of what Martin had confessed to already.

There was another matter that Eric thought the well-connected Forbes could now help him with. 'I wonder if you could tell me,' he asked hesitantly, 'about how much we truly know about the Russians using their aircraft to kill death march prisoners?'

Forbes gave him a chilly smile, weighing up his response carefully.

'As I explained about our little friend in the cheap suit, sometimes we have to do deals with bad people to get things done.'

This wasn't good enough for Eric.

'The thing is, Sir, people died to give us intelligence of those death marches and I am sure they didn't want it to be used to murder civilians, but rather to save them.'

A career lawyer in uniform, Forbes had a precise response for that.'I can tell you that we gave intelligence to the Russians in good faith – what they did with it was their business…'

Forbes paused, giving Eric what he hoped appeared to be a sympathetic smile, though his eyes were not smiling.

'Nobody working on our side of the fence, or Iron Curtain if you take the Churchillian point of view, should think that any blame is attached to them. And, in the scheme of things, the Russians killing those poor wretches stopped them from being either executed later on during the march, or in the final weeks of the war expiring in some underground weapons factory. It was but a very small tragedy in the scheme of things. For those who survived, the Soviet strafing actually *saved* their lives.'

But Eric still felt the shame of it and thought that maybe somebody ought to expose the Russians, to let the world know what they did.

'But did you know,' he informed Forbes, 'that the Soviets actually dug up the corpses of those that they had slaughtered with the cannons of their aircraft, smashed the bones and then burned them, to obscure the evidence? Seems they felt guilty about what they did, or feared exposure.'

Forbes had visibly tensed and gave another cautious, measured response: 'I wasn't aware of that and I do not believe it was in your report of proceedings for the investigation.'

Forbes was clearly a master of his brief, but his disapproval would not deter Eric. 'No, Sir I didn't actually collect any of *that* evidence, and especially with the Russians present at the time but we found one of the pits where they burned the bones. Major Dostoyevsky gave me some cobblers about them burning the bones to stop the spread of disease. I thought that I might go back and investigate further. What do you think to that, Sir?'

Forbes' sympathy seemed to have evaporated, for with a hard

edge to his voice he told Eric: 'I don't think you need to do that Captain Wise – maybe Dostoyevsky was telling the truth about the ashes? Did that occur to you?'

He went on, seeking to apply a pragmatic, sympathetic veneer while definitely warning Eric off.

'It would, and you'll have to pardon the punning, be most unwise of you to start digging around in it Eric. Some things are way above your pay grade, and beyond Colonel McFaul's, possibly even beyond Spendlove's orbit – despite his low connections in high places. You know that this war has given birth to some pretty dreadful weapons, which the greater good of humanity demanded we stop people like the Nazis perfecting. That was the bigger picture. My advice would be to forget about it and have another brandy, some steak and wine too, so you can enjoy a good, restorative kip on the train home.'

Forbes caught Friedrich's eye and the waiter rushed over, as eager to serve the British as he had been to look after the Nazis when they ruled Vienna.

12

The pfennig on a fragile silver chain around his neck had been his talisman. When the Russian artillery pounded, and he crushed himself against the juddering earth, Martin's gritted teeth had bitten hard onto it, and, like him, the pfennig did not yield.

Turning it over, the dim light filtering down from the barred window of the cell revealed the relief of an Imperial Eagle on its dirty, dull face. On its reverse the '1' had been filed off and instead engraved on it was: *Meine liebe wacht.*

His mother had given it to Martin on the day he left for war in 1939, defying the furious disapproval of his father to see him off at the railway station. Tears streaming down her crumpled, careworn face, she had pulled him into a last embrace, closing one of his hands around the lucky pfennig.

'It kept your father safe in the old war.'

Choking back his own tears, he had nodded, unbuttoning a tunic pocket and slipping it inside.

Now here he was, more than half a dozen years later, with much blood spilled and dark deeds committed, so many people gone whose names he could barely recall. And how many of the enemy had he killed?

At least a dozen. Then there was the village and its occupants.

Also Lorelei. Gone. But he had *it* still.

His lucky pfennig.

Luck, though was a matter of degree, and, as he whiled away his final hours in his cell, Martin felt that, in basic terms, it had failed him utterly.

Yet, Martin felt it was better to face his fate at the hands of the British than be handed over to the Soviets. In that sense he had been lucky, or luckier than perhaps might otherwise have been the case. Though, on any objective basis, being sentenced to death for war crimes was not the most fortunate outcome. Still, it was better to receive a soldier's end – at the hands of a firing squad than be hung.

When he wasn't contemplating strange twists of fate, Martin read poetry. For one day, when Eric visited him for a game of chess, the Englander had presented him with the book of Heinrich Heine verse. Martin thanked him, suggesting that soon Eric would get it back.

He thought that, when the time came, he would also give the British officer his lucky pfennig. Eric didn't ask if the book meant anything special to Martin. While by now he was well aware the German had been sent to Bad Gastein to recover from his wounds, he decided to let it lie.

Martin did not admit it was his writing on the inside front cover and neither man mentioned that the book contained 'The Lorelei'.

* * *

And then the fateful day arrived, keys rasping in the lock, the cell door swinging open to reveal Eric visiting unusually early.

Martin - who was freshly shaved and shorn, altogether more like a warrior in Eric's eyes - gestured towards the chair while he sat forward on the bed. Eric took his cap off and placed it on the floor, running a hand through his own hair. 'How are you Martin?' Eric enquired, offering a cigarette, which the German declined.

'I have something to tell you,' Eric revealed.

'Oh, yes?'

The British officer seemed rather more solemn than usual.

'It's tomorrow.'

Long prepared though Martin was, it was still a blow to hear tonight would see his last sunset and tomorrow his final sunrise. He had grown accustomed to the rhythm of his strange little existence – the food wasn't too bad either and there was daily exercise. He got to think through a lot of things he had never bothered about before and read whatever books could be found for him – even in English.

'Thank you for coming to tell me Eric.'

'Is there anything you need?' the British officer enquired in German, which made Martin smile. He responded in turn with false would-be English jocularity. 'No thanks old boy.' An awkward silence fell, Eric picking up his cap and examining its peak. He had no words of comfort to offer in this situation – he had brought a war criminal to justice who was about to receive the penalty that even Martin felt he deserved. Still, Eric had come to know Martin a little and recognised that even a villain could possess a measure of humanity.

'Eric?'

'Yes, Martin.'

'One last thing, before you leave...'

'Of course.'

Martin reached forward, grabbed the other man's forearm and looked into his eyes. 'I don't know what happened to my mother and father – but you recall the story of how that Gestapo investigator took me back to Berlin to try and make them give up a Jewish boy they were hiding?'

'I remember.'

Martin squeezed his arm.

'Can you find out what happened to them?'

'I'll do my best – and the boy, too?'

Martin let go of Eric's arm and sprawled back on his bed.

'To ensure they are safe,' Martin emphasised while staring up at the cell window and reflecting: 'There's a certain justice in that don't you think?'

Eric nodded. 'Yes. I'll try my best – my unit is very resourceful - although it won't be easy. I may fail.' Martin sat up again, fixing him with an earnest look. 'I understand, but you will surely try?' Martin offered his hand and they shook on it.

* * *

Lorelei came to him in the cell that night – *reunited at last, by some miracle* - on the eve of his execution; the last wish of a condemned man, her luminescent, alabaster beauty dazzling him. Smoothing her skirt behind her thighs, she sat down on his bed.

'I didn't think you would come,' he whispered. She smiled, but her eyes were full of sadness. Leaning forward, Lorelei took one of his hands in hers. He thought he would explain about his crimes – how a different Martin, not the one she knew, committed them.

She placed a finger on his lips.

'Shush.'

Lorelei enveloped him, the overpowering scent of soap and perfume inflaming his nostrils, the crispness of her blouse on his cheek making him swoon. Stroking his hair, she began to rock him in her arms, singing softly; soothing him into unconsciousness.

* * *

It was a mirage and, as he lay there, the hours dragging by, other ghosts and memories inevitably crowded in – lost comrades in arms; a Russian sniper bleeding to death in the Kharkov tenement; poor Azzura lying on a stretcher under a white sheet after being killed by Yugoslav partisans; the raped woman's pain-filled and accusing eyes in that Belarus hovel; a priest's stubborn defiance and an ochre disk of the sun behind smoke from the burning village.

All washed over by shame at the rape and pillage he and the rest of Hitler's willing accomplices had inflicted across Europe.

Then there was his own father's fury and mother's sorrow - his miserable regret at the manner of their last parting - and who could forget the doomed Waffen SS recruit at the bridge in Simontornya, brains scattered by a Russian bullet, his death part of the futile last stand as the 1,000 year Reich collapsed.

It was good to let it rise up, for Martin felt that if he didn't it would not be possible to greet the morning with strength and purpose - a determination to pay the debt and retrieve a shred of honour.

Though, in the eyes of the world even his death would not redeem him or what he fought for, except in the irredeemable hearts of Nazi fanatics who would cleave to the cult of Hitler until the fires of hell froze over. Martin had, at least discovered that he was not one of them before he died, thanks in part due to his poor, pathetic doomed love for Lorelei.

* * *

The night ended and, grabbing the iron bars and pulling himself up to the window, Martin watched the sun's beams slowly reveal the world beyond, drinking in his last dawn and enjoying the warmth on his face. Now, after the darkness, his heart's horizon was visible.

A few minutes later a key turned in the cell door to end his reverie. Martin dropped down and sat on the bed, the guard finding the condemned man looking at him expectantly – not afraid – but utterly calm. Ready to meet his fate.

In the middle of a courtyard stood a bullet-riddled wooden stake, to which a Royal Military Police corporal led Martin. Beyond the stake was a high deep bank of sand thrown against one of the walls, which served to absorb any bullets that missed their target.

The SS officer still appeared to be calm, his bearing upright and unafraid inside the loose-fitting prison uniform. The corporal gently shoved him against the stake, making to tie Martin's hands behind it but the condemned man said in English:

'I do not need that or a hood.'

Hesitating, the corporal looked worried.

With a reassuring smile, Martin told him:

'I won't run away or weep.'

* * *

To prepare for this moment - to harden his heart - Eric had pondered the many innocent people those like Martin had, one way or another, eradicated. And to stiffen his resolve knocked back some whisky. He'd also recalled what Pierrepoint the executioner said when explaining his own rationale: 'Y'see Captain Wise, it's all about speed and humanity…'

In a guard room just off the courtyard, six British soldiers stood rigidly to attention as Eric Wise gave them final instructions in a flat voice, deliberately devoid of emotion.

'Two of of you have blank rounds, to ensure sensitive souls need not feel guilty about delivering the fatal shot,' Eric explained, noticing a young private whose hands gently trembled, causing the rifle, held at port arms, to waver.

'I will be watching closely to make sure nobody tries to sneak a look and find out who has it. Keep your bolts rammed home.' The shaky private gritted his teeth. Eric coughed to dispel his own tension, and then, sweeping his eyes along the line of men, added: 'All of you should make sure your aim is true.'

* * *

As the execution squad filed into the courtyard, the corporal again came over to Martin who had his hands clasped behind his back, as if waiting patiently at a bus stop.

'Any last requests?'

Martin shook his head.

Smiling apologetically, the NCO pinned a white paper disc on Martin's chest, over his heart, and then took up a position behind the execution squad alongside Eric.

Martin looked down the line. They were all so young, not unlike the lads he had led in Russia, except of course for Eric. Martin smiled and Eric nodded imperceptibly, his face expressionless. Off to one side stood an equally impassive medical officer, there to sedate him if needs be, and to later check that he was dead.

Hands still behind his back Martin looked up, beyond the walls of the courtyard, calmly reciting his favourite fragment of *The Lorelei.*

He does not look below…

Eric passed along behind the execution squad.

'Present arms!' he ordered.

…to the rocky shoals.

Six rifles pointed at Martin.

He only looks up at the heights.

Martin stared into the endless blue late summer sky, full of hope that he would find her soon. His heart swelled with happiness and soul lifted up, soaring into a bright nothingness of beyond.

In his head he was standing at the door of a lodge in the high pastures above Bad Gastein, the last rays of the sun falling across the mountains, while Lorelei sat at an open window watching the sunset. The warm orange light made her face glow. She looked at him and smiled, her eyes brimming with love.

Martin smiled, head thrown back - his own leaking tears of joy...of love…

'Fire!'

The rifles crashed.

Hit squarely in the chest by four bullets, their impact threw Martin against the stake, his body glancing off it to land with a heavy thud.

The only sound then was an exhaling of air from his lungs – a last breath, as Martin's spirit departed. Eric went over, carrying the Browning for the final act. Ordinarily the presiding officer would administer a *coup de grace* with a bullet in the brain but he could see Martin was dead without need of confirmation of the medical officer waiting to come forward and examine the executed German.

Blood soaked the white paper disc and his jacket - *shot right through the heart.* Eric put the pistol in its holster and knelt down. He appeared empty of emotion as he gently closed Martin's eyes.

* * *

Leaving a NCO to supervise the disposal of Martin's body, which would be buried, along with his lucky pfennig, in an unmarked grave at a nearby cemetery, Eric escaped the courtyard, desperate to get away from its suffocating confines.

Heart thumping and head spinning, he wandered the city centre aimlessly. Letting his mind go blank - in a zombie-like state – and he found himself scaling the Schlossberg via a zigzag of steps, until he came to an empty bench just below the clock tower.

Sitting down, he stared out over the city and across the plain to the mountains in the far distance. Eric couldn't explain the lump in his throat or the upwelling in his eyes – *why on earth would he feel so shattered over the death of a German war criminal? It was just the bloody war - still haunting him.* Now, in his head he saw his father - dressed in his number one naval uniform - on a summer's afternoon in 1939, with a waltz playing on the radio and twirling Mother around in the kitchen while Bert – *the future black marketeer most foul* - whistled and clapped along.

Even war's aftermath was full of folly, waste and cruelty, Eric thought, although sometimes justice was done and mercy delivered. In this case, simultaneously.

He was pulled into wondering about a Martin without sin - the boy and then man he could have been, blue eyes laughing with joy rather than burning with rage.

And tears leaked from his own eyes - for Martin the lost boy and for his own losses - and Eric tried to push them back inside with the palms of his hands, for fear of passers-by finding him sitting, shuddering on the bench – nakedly exposed as his own internal suppressed pain welled up and over flowed. He got to his feet and tried to make his mind blank but, no matter how much he paced up and down beside the bench, it did not happen.

Please, God.

He inhaled and exhaled deeply and it didn't work, so he gave in to another shudder of grief, hoping this would end it. Sitting down, holding a hand up to his forehead, more tears came amid a flood of memories, a jumble of scenes and sounds, even smells - screaming bombs and raging fires eating the heart out of Plymouth; the dank stink and choking dust as buildings collapsed....

Other random scenes from his life crowded in...the Dutchman showing him the well-thumbed photo of his family; the girl on the Cornish beach with the top of her head sliced off; the German officer letting go of life as they struggled in the window at Monte Cassino railway station.

Then, his father again – this time ecstatic at a bullseye while playing darts in a Turnchapel pub...his mother polishing the silverware - as if her life depended on it after hearing the old man had gone down with the *Courageous*...weeping and sniffling, but nobody could prise her away from that task...and his impish brother - not the bastard in the Vienna hotel but rather the cheeky sailor chatting up a barmaid...

They still haunted him, so it seemed, which was a shock when he thought – hoped - war had cleaned the slate.

...and then, finally, there was his love for Katherine, which he'd tried to kill when he thought he wouldn't make it...but here she was, in his head and heart again - his beautiful comforting angel at Stonehouse naval hospital.

He bitterly regretted his spurning of her, especially as now it seemed he would survive after all. And he laughed at the irony of that, wiping the last of his tears away, resolving to do something to make amends - to win her back. If she crushed him, then he'd deserve it and would bother her no more.

* * *

As he walked back through the city to the prison Eric's mind cast back to an incident just a few days earlier when he had received a large, bulky package from Doc Darrow at Bad Gastein.

On opening it, he discovered a newsreel, of the kind British Pathé distributed to military camps across Europe.

A note from Darrow explained that he'd been to a film show in the same hall where he and Eric had seen the horrors of the death camps. There was a short piece in the newsreel on the exodus of European Jews to Palestine. He suggested Eric should watch it.

Setting up a projector and screening it for himself on the white wall of an office in the barracks, Eric was duly astonished.

There, on the deck of a vessel bound for the Holy Land was group of young people, laughing and at the centre a young woman with light coloured hair. It certainly looked like the girl from the hospital at Bad Gastein, but she was so different - full of hope, happiness and joy - except wearing a summer dress rather than wrapped in an aviator's jacket.

Ordering Martin brought across from the Karlau Prison, Eric watched the German's face as he screened the newsreel. On reaching the sequence featuring the girl on the ship, Martin got up and walked over to the wall, fingers touching her face for the few seconds she was there.

Eric switched the projector off and opened up the wooden shutters on the office window. 'Was that Lorelei?' Eric asked Martin, who was still standing over by the wall.

Using a cupped hand to shield his eyes from the bright light flooding in, Martin responded in a voice choked with emotion: 'Not the Lorelei I knew.' Eric felt that now Martin, too, was in a better place.

PART V

1

April 1947

ERIC WAS NOT SENT home to be demobbed as he wished. During an afternoon meeting in the Berlin office of Spendlove at the Olympic Stadium, he was informed there was still plenty of work for the 'S.G. boys' in countering 'the pesky Red Menace.'

While Eric felt like telling his boss to sod off and resigning his commission - pointing out, not for the first time, that he was supposed to be *Hostilities Only* - Spendlove raised his pay and promised a nice long leave in England. Revealing the steel in his silken tones, as they sipped stewed tea and chewed burned crumpets, Spendlove added: 'Besides, if I say you can't quit my unit right now then you thunder-fucking well can't.'

Softening he then implored:

'Please do bear with us a little longer my good fellow.'

Sighing, and pouring the tea while Spendlove buttered crumpets, Eric enquired resentfully:

'So, having been pals with the Russians to beat the Fritzes are we now going toe-to-toe with the commies?'

'Well, things change Eric, and sometimes best buddies find their friendship chills,' Spendlove observed, 'but there's another detail of that whole death march affair, about which you must not breathe a word to anyone.' Spendlove gave Eric a very stern look over the top of his steaming hot cuppa, adding: 'Do you swear to keep it zipped, as the Yanks say, if I tell you Eric?'

'Scout's honour - shan't tell a soul,' Eric promised, so Spendlove proceeded to enlighten him.

'Well, while you are deeply acquainted with how those poor souls were marched from Balaton and into Austria, you do not know the whole story. The project on which they would have been worked to death in the caves of St. Georgen an der Gusen was connected to the pursuit of an atom bomb of some kind.'

Eric's mouth dropped open.

'What!?' he exclaimed, rather too loudly for Spendlove, who frowned and put a finger to his lips. 'Keep it down Eric,' he urged, continuing in a hushed voice, as if walls might actually have ears. 'It was most fortunate our American friends got to Gusen first, as it was not the sort of weapon we could risk Stalin getting his hands on.'

'Yes, but how far had the Nazis got with it?' Eric wondered.

'It remains uncertain,' Spendlove revealed, 'as the Nazis blew in all the cave entrances in when they ran away, but massive levels of radiation were discovered using those counter things. There have been several efforts to get inside and see what secrets can be found – not a healthy pursuit in my humble opinion. Nothing as yet to confirm one way or the other how close Adolf was to having his ultimate doomsday weapon to hand.'

Eric sighed, glowering at the pile of glistening, burned crumpets on the plate in the middle of the desk.

'When did you find out about The Bomb angle, Sir?' he enquired, not bothering to hide his irritation. 'Was it the real reason poor souls killed on the death march were of such little importance?'

'I can assure you that I only got to know recently,' replied Spendlove, slightly affronted.

'Of course,' Eric observed cynically.

'Scout's honour,' Spendlove added, looking shocked Eric might disbelieve him.

Spendlove put his cup down, spooned in more sugar and stirred thoughtfully.

'But at that time it was, of course, in our common interest to prevent the Nazis developing any kind of weapon of mass destruction – and by whatever means possible.'

Eric rose from his chair, picked the leather gloves out of his cap, which he'd placed on top of Spendlove's empty 'In' tray.

'I suppose, Sir, the end justifies the means?' Eric observed acidly, putting his cap on and saluting.

The rather insolent tone annoyed Spendlove, but he could not disagree with Eric's deep dismay at the twists and turns of the case. Not even bothering to return the salute, Spendlove waved Eric out of the office with a crumpet held daintily between thumb and finger.

* * *

The Berlin visit provided Eric with an opportunity to go on his quest to find Martin's parents and the boy.

A few days earlier, he'd contacted Major Forbes for advice, who suggested he went to see a Commander in the Naval Intelligence Directorate. By happy coincidence this man was located in the same building by the Olympic Stadium as the Spendlove Group headquarters. The Commander's office turned out to be a flight of stairs down and boasted on its door a name plate that announced 'Cdr Henry Glashirfryn, Records and Research O.C.'

There was a notice underneath it that advised:

ON KNOCKING

AWAIT GREEN LIGHT

BEFORE ENTERING!

There were two light bulbs in bakelite fittings directly over the door, one of them dimly glowing red. When Eric knocked, it went out altogether and the other flashed green, but only for a few seconds.

Eric didn't know what to do, so knocked again.

This time the door was torn violently open, revealing a fair-haired naval officer with a closely trimmed ginger beard in full blue suit rig - white shirt and black tie, three gold rings on his jacket cuffs. His good eye surveyed whoever was disturbing him; a pink scar down the left-hand side of his face below a black eye patch seemingly pulsated with fury. This shocking, piratical vision made Eric blurt out: 'Sorry, Sir – I was confused by the lights.'

Craning his head back to stare at them, the naval officer lifted up his walking stick as he leaned against the door frame, using it to gently poke the fitting. 'Bloody thing is more bother than it's worth,' he observed with sigh, the heat of his anger dissipating. Flashing Eric a sheepish grin he apologised. 'Apologies for the reception – but it does *so* infuriate me.'

Putting his weight on the walking stick, he offered his right hand, which Eric shook. 'I'm Harry Glashirfryn - you must be Captain Wise of Spendlove's mob?'

'I am, Sir.'

'Come in then.'

Lowering himself into a swivel chair behind a large dark wood, highly polished desk – its surface bare except for a phone and a spotless blotter - Cdr Glashirfryn gestured towards a refectory chair on the other side. Laying his cap on the desk, taking a quick look around as he sat, Eric noticed three large filing cabinets on the left-hand side of the office. They were impressively garlanded with locking systems, while a large window on the right-hand side of the office offered a good view down a tree-lined avenue.

Eric turned his attention back to the naval officer who was explaining how 'the lights thing is so I can lock secret papers away and all that nonsense – it puts me on edge to be honest, a right old fuss.'

'I understand, Sir.'

Glashirfryn shook his head and smiled graciously.

'No need for the Sir thing,' he said with an embarrassed grin, adding: 'But what is it exactly that I can do for you?'

'Major Forbes in Vienna said you could help me track down the parents of a Waffen SS officer I had dealings with in Graz.'

Glashirfryn span his chair around and, using his legs, scooted across the office to the filing cabinets with a speed that quite astonished Eric, almost making him laugh out loud.

Pulling a set of keys on a chain from his right-hand trouser pocket, Glashifryn opened the bottom drawer in the middle cabinet. He pulled out a fat file, placing it in his lap while he closed and locked the drawer again.

Shooting back across to his desk, the naval officer placed the file on the blotter, grinning a little self-consciously, out of breath and admitting: 'I know that looked a little ridiculous but with my leg it's the easiest thing – the strength is returning but getting the thing to straighten out is a bugger.'

'War wound?' Eric enquired, reflexively caressing the scar of his own leg wound through his trousers. Spotting this, Glashirfryn smiled and nodded as if acknowledging a fellow wounded warrior.

Opening the file he scanned its top sheet.

'On the Atlantic convoys?'

Looking up, as if not quite sure what Eric's question had been about, Glashirfryn enquired: 'Convoys?'

'Yes, in action – the Atlantic?'

Eric had noticed an absence of campaign medal ribbons on Glashirfryn's jacket, which was puzzling, bearing in mind the man's injuries, but there was one for a DSO. Glashifryn smiled enigmatically, shook his head.

'Not exactly.'

The naval officer closed the file and sat back in the chair, loosening his tie and undoing the top button of his shirt. Eric waited for him to speak, but instead Glashirfryn turned his head to stare out the window, lost in thought for a moment.

'It all seems like it's a dream, or rather a nightmare,' Glashirfryn mused and then switched his attention back to Eric, adding: 'The bloody war, I mean – don't you agree?'

Eric nodded. 'Yes, one long nightmare.'

Steepling his hands in front of his face and tapping his lips with them, Glashirfryn then revealed: 'We helped Forbes out with your Martin Walder case, you know, because, as luck would have it, we were gifted a whole mass of records – Gestapo investigation reports, eye witness testimony, every spit and cough of numerous episodes. The documents were removed by someone friendly to our cause and hidden away to stop the Soviets getting them.'

Eric nodded towards the file on the desk.

'Including *that* one?'

Glashirfryn smiled enigmatically.

'When Forbes rang me up and said this military policeman in Graz was trying to prevent an SS officer from being handed over to the Soviets for their brand of justice, my curiosity was acutely aroused. He asked me what we might have on Martin Walder, so I gave him a summary of what we understood to have happened. That was all.'

'Does the material you have say where his mother and father, and the boy they hid, went?'

Glashirfryn responded by opening a desk drawer, pulling out a bottle of whisky and two glass tumblers, which made Eric smile.

Puzzled, Glashirfryn enquired: 'Something amusing?'

Eric shook his head, thinking of Martin and his offer of schnapps in the Austrian lodge after karate chopping him. 'No, not at all Commander, just remembering an interesting time that I had chatting with someone over a few drinks.'

'It's a single malt,' Glashirfryn explained, pushing the glass across the desk, its golden liquid glowing alluringly in the still warm spring sunlight coming in through the window.

'The real thing,' he explained with a smile, 'not to be sniffed at, although it does have a lovely nose on it.'

Eric reached for the glass of Scotch.

'It's just the other time someone offered me some hard stuff across a table I feared they were soon going to kill me.'

Glashirfryn raised his eyebrows.

'Nothing so melodramatic today, I assure you.'

Eric sipped the whisky, its complexity and peaty mountain stream taste confirming it wasn't rotgut conjured up by black marketeers in a Berlin garage. 'I can't let you take the files away unfortunately,' Glashirfryn explained, 'but if you're settled and you have the time, I can brief you properly on the details?'

'Please do, Commander.'

Glashirfryn nodded, taking a sip of Scotch.

'Alright then – and it's a yarn worth hearing in my humble opinion.'

The naval officer swivelled his chair and, looking out the widow down the tree-lined street - with the late afternoon shadows beginning to soften - told the story.

2

Berlin, 1944

In his office at Gestapo Headquarters, Kriminalinspektor Alois Hecht sat with his feet up on a desk, reading an English language edition of F. Scott Fitzgerald's *The Great Gatsby*. The telephone ringing interrupted his reading, but rather than place the book face down and risk damaging its spine, he took a mental note of the page number and closed it.

The impatient phone trilled angrily and, on picking it up, Hecht found his boss barking down the receiver that he wanted to see him *immediately!*

Hecht gingerly placed the handset back in its cradle, slid the book into a desk drawer, stretched and yawned.

Rising, he took his suit jacket off a hook on the inside of the office door. Standing in front of a full-length mirror, beside a chair on which rested a black fedora, he pulled the double-breasted jacket on and buttoned it up. After making sure his tie knot was firmly at the top, with a triangle of cologne-scented handkerchief peeking out of the breast pocket nicely symmetrical – and blonde hair firmly slicked back - he finally made his exit.

* * *

The skeletal individual sitting in a ludicrously huge leather scroll wing chair behind the massive oak desk wore the full uniform and regalia of an SS Brigadeführer. Despite the sun not having reached its midpoint in the sky, Siegfried Breslau had a frayed napkin at his throat and was tucking into a plate of pork Eisbein and sauerkraut as he talked, also swigging from a bier stein brimming with Berliner Weisse beer.

Hecht was inwardly repulsed, but outwardly impassive, giving a stiff-armed Nazi greeting to a portrait of a smug-looking Führer on the wall behind Breslau's bald, shiny head.

'Heil Hitler!'

Breslau nodded and carried on munching, waving his fork to indicate Hecht should sit in the mahogany desk chair on the other side of the desk. Thus ensconced, looking up at his boss from the inferior angle the latter conferred, Hecht enquired:

'What's the problem, Sir?'

Breslau cut savagely into the meat.

'A bicycle,' he snorted, raising a piece of pork for close inspection before tearing it from the prongs with his crooked, yellow teeth. Hecht raised his eyebrows, partly in disgust at Breslau's actions, but also in surprise at the root cause of trouble.

'A bicycle, Sir?'

Breslau forked a steaming pile of sauerkraut into his mouth.

'In a ditch,' he slobbered.

The Brigadeführer gulped down more beer, wiping his mouth on the back of a hand before continuing. 'The commander of one of our Special Treatment Trains - during a halt to take on boiler water - had to teach some troublesome Jews a mortal lesson and left them in the ditch for one of our cleansing units to clear up.'

Hecht nodded. *This was all very well, but…*

'The bike, Sir?'

Picking up a whole piece of pork, which had many bristles on its crinkly skin and was dripping with juices, Breslau looked it over.

'It isn't the bicycle in isolation,' he told Hecht.

Breslau bolted the pork down, skin and all. Hecht almost threw up, but swallowed the urge.

'Our cleansing men found the bicycle close to the corpses in a ditch by the railway and there is a boy missing from the body count.'

Breslau's thin, glistening lips curled into a death's head grin, again revealing his decaying pegs as he emitted a pungent belch. Grimacing, the Brigadeführer observed: 'It is most odd, Hecht.'

Retrieving the cologne-scented handkerchief from his jacket breast pocket, Hecht coughed into it to mask his disgust.

The Brigadeführer dabbed at his lips with a napkin, suggesting:

'…and we don't like loose ends, do we?' But, he wasn't finished: 'And, as you must know, the Führer is not keen on bicycles, due to their subversive nature, never mind missing Jews.'

Breslau's unblinking aqueous eyes held fast those of Hecht, who was reminded of an albino goldfish he had kept in a glass bowl as a child. It wasn't keen on bland diet of flakes or pellets, got constipated and soon expired.

But, anyway, the bikes…

'Subversive nature, Sir?'

'Yes, subversive!' snapped Breslau impatiently, 'possibly enabling covert activities!'

While Breslau distractedly picked over his food with a fork Hecht waited in silence - having not yet been dismissed - and recalled reading some memo or other a while ago. It detailed measures to coral cyclists into their own lanes and even an SS-led effort to invent bicycle pedal light reflectors, so two-wheeled menaces couldn't whoosh around hither and thither invisibly, with some undoubtedly up to no good. Of course total bicycle control was an impossible task to enforce, a bit like the smoking restrictions.

Breslau sighed, having found nothing more that took his fancy on the plate and laid his fork down. Surprised to discover Hecht still sitting there in front of his desk, he barked: 'Jews and bicycles cannot be permitted!'

'No, Sir!'

'Tidy things up, Hecht. You may go.'

'Yes, Sir!'

* * *

Joachim Endrass perched on a tall stool, staring out over railway junction levers and through a window, at nothing in particular. In the background a radio played music from Wagner's *Die Meistersinger*.

Climbing down, Joachim picked up a knapsack from over by the door, digging inside to pull out his supper of cheese and bread, all wrapped in a red and white gingham linen napkin. He spread it on a tall side table by the stool, and clambered back onto it.

Unseen by Joachim, a car pulled up outside the signal box, Hecht climbing out the passenger side, while Kruger, wearing a long black leather overcoat and a dark blue trilby, went around to the boot.

Hecht sprinted up steps on the outside of the building, suit jacket flapping, melodramatically throwing open the door, almost causing Joachim to fall off his perch.

'Good afternoon!' boomed the Gestapo man, displaying his best shit-eating grin from ear-to-ear, and doffing his hat – more like an ostentatious magician than to show respect. There was an awkward silence as Joachim chewed and swallowed a rather dry piece of bread, Hecht maintaining the grin. 'My name is Hecht, Alois Hecht. You can call me Kriminalinspektor Hecht.'

Joachim wrapped up his remaining bread and cheese in the napkin and enquired nervously: 'Kriminalinspektor?'

Stepping forward, Hecht pulled open the lunch bundle, choosing a piece of cheese, which he popped into his mouth.

'Yes,' he acknowledged, as he chewed. 'Geheime Staatspolizei.'

Hecht tore off a piece of the bread.

'Nice,' he mumbled as he consumed it.

'My wife made it.'

'Really? Where on earth did she get real flour?'

Joachim looked even more worried, so Hecht gave him a reassuring smile. 'Don't look so anxious. The Gestapo isn't concerned about illicit bakery. No, we are interested in bicycles.'

Hecht took Joachim by the arm, leading him out of the signal box, down the steps and around the back to a large shed.

The Gestapo man knocked on one of its double doors. As Hecht held the right-hand door open for him, Kruger emerged, wheeling two bicycles - a black one and a blue one.

The latter, found in the ditch next to the dead Jews, had been brought across from Gestapo HQ by Hecht and Kruger by car. Placed in the shed by Kruger, the blue bicycle was now to be used as a ploy to catch Joachim in a lie - to gain psychological dominance - and, hopefully, reveal more conspirators in the mystery of the missing Jewish boy.

Hecht asked Joachim: 'Which one of these is yours?'

The signalman pointed at the blue bicycle, the one on Kruger's right.

Hecht pursed his lips in doubt.

'Really?'

Joachim nodded.

'And which bicycle did you ride to work on?'

'Mine.'

'That's extraordinary.'

Joachim realized that he'd fallen right into a trap. In all the turmoil the previous night he'd mistakenly ridden home on the Herr Doctor Walder's bike - the black one - and then rode it in for his shift today, stupidly deciding to have supper before he went off to look for his own bike in the ditch.

His bowels loosened.

Hecht decided to have a bit of sport with him.

'But, are you sure it wasn't stolen last night?'

'Stolen?'

Hecht put an arm around Joachim's shoulders.

'Please don't answer all my questions with a question. Was your bike stolen last night Joachim?'

The railway worker acted as if he suddenly remembered.

'Yes…Yes it was…how foolish of me not to recall. I must have ridden the other one, the blue one, to work last night. I borrowed the black one to get here today.'

Hecht squeezed his shoulder a little too hard.

'There, you see. I knew there would be a good explanation for why *your* blue bike was found in a ditch just over there early this morning and this other one – the black one – was in the shed. No wonder you are confused, I am too, my dear fellow, and I am an investigator for the Gestapo!'

Hecht span him around to look down the road towards where the bike had been found in the ditch.

'The thieves chickened out, when they realized that theft is a very serious business in a country at war. Left it in the ditch. People have been shot for less than stealing a bike you know. Fortunately, we knew we could swiftly return it to you, as there is a name plate with your address on the frame. As luck would have it, our enquiries told us you would be found here today.'

Joachim grinned nervously.

Hecht let him go, declaring: 'We are glad to be of service!'

That railwayman nodded, avoiding Hecht's eyes, which seemed to penetrate deep into his soul.

'Never say the Gestapo doesn't put its full energy into solving a case, no matter how modest.' Joachim blinked, frowned, suddenly very, very scared.

Hecht took the black bike off Kruger, who leaned the blue one against one of the shed's open doors.

'So, who did you borrow this black bike from? And how did you get home after your shift last night if your blue bike was stolen?'

Joachim froze, mind going blank. Hecht gave him the shit-eating grin again and raised his eyebrows as a prompt for the railwayman to provide an answer.

'Well…I borrowed it from the pastor this morning.'

'The pastor?'

'Jonathan Walder.'

Hecht looked at Kruger, who took that as his cue to take out a small notebook and write something down.

'It's a vintage classic,' said Hecht, adding: 'Don't look so worried!'

Hecht gave Joachim a nudge with the black bike, who grimaced as its front wheel pressed into his groin. 'Once again my dear fellow, how did you get home last night?' Joachim stepped back to disengage, seized the handlebars of the blue bike and wheeled it inside the shed, trying to think what to say. He had used the pastor's's bicycle the previous evening, not realising he'd left his own blue bike in the ditch. Pastor Walder headed back into Berlin in a car belonging to someone else - the reason for which Joachim was terrified of giving away. Hecht followed him into the shed. After leaning his bicycle against a wall, Joachim turned around. In a sudden moment of barely suppressed panic he tried to work out if he could break out by the Gestapo investigator, but Kruger barred the shed door using the black bike.

Caught in the full beam headlights of a big fat lie, Joachim's large bovine eyes blinked fast,.

'I walked home,' he ventured, rather pathetically, hoping that would do. Hecht nodded and said with a reassuring smile: 'Alright then.'

The Kriminalinspektor decided it would be pointless to take Joachim in just yet and get Kruger to beat the truth out of him. It would be worth watching the railwayman run, to see where he ended up.

* * *

They waited in their car for Joachim's shift to end. Kruger had secured the black bicycle to a carry rack attached to the boot of the big, chunky Mercedes 260D, which was from the motor pool at Gestapo headquarters. It was now parked on a broad track that ran into nearby woods, with a good view of the road to Berlin.

Hecht savoured a cigarillo, which Kruger felt was a little hypocritical considering how hardline his boss was with his own smoking habits, but dared not say anything.

'Thick as elephant dung,' Hecht remarked, blowing smoke out the side of his mouth, winding the passenger side window down.

Kruger chuckled.

'You had some sport with him.'

Hecht did not laugh, reaching forward to pull out the ashtray in the dashboard, tapping his cigar ash off. 'My dear Kruger, it has only just begun.' Joachim swept past them on the blue bicycle, pedalling furiously. After a few seconds Kruger started the car and they followed on, Hecht sucking on his cigar. He expected the railway signalman would reliably lead them straight to wherever Pastor Walder of the black bicycle resided.

3

Elsa Walder scrubbed and scrubbed, but no matter how much elbow grease she used on the steel pot, a dark fleck of cabbage would not come off.

She rinsed it again under the tap, laid it on the draining board and seized a copper kettle that sat on the worktop next to the sink, pouring its contents in. The hot water, not far off boiling, seared her skin as it splashed onto her forearm.

Elsa cried out in pain, slammed the kettle back down on the worktop and gave the pot a shove of disgust, dropping the scrubbing pad into the water. The conversation around the kitchen table fell away as she glanced around, smiling apologetically at Jonathan and Joachim.

The two men, who were huddled over cups of acorn coffee - brows furrowed with anxiety - stared at her only for a moment before resuming their intense discussion. Elsa leaned momentarily against the sink for support in suppressing fear that coursed through her body.

Picking up the scrubber, she gently scoured the bottom of the pot again, her body distracted and calmed by the motion, but she couldn't help listening to what the men were saying.

Jonathan sighed, exasperated by the railwayman's determined resistance to his words of reassurance, hopeless though they might be in reality. 'I'm so scared - for my family,' responded Joachim, fearful eyes meeting the pastor's deceptively calm gaze.

'Just stick to the story about it being stolen Joachim and I'll tell them I loaned you my bicycle this morning.'

Elsa dropped her scrubber again, turned around, her unease boiling over into an outburst: 'But, Jonathan, the Gestapo are like dogs with a bone!' Jonathan glared at her for stoking the fires of anxiety. 'Elsa, are you mad?' he hissed between clenched teeth.

Elsa shook her head angrily, wiping her hands on the apron.

Jonathan was exasperated – *there was no hiding their mortal peril from Joachim now* - and gave her a furious look.

Elsa put a hand over her mouth and turned back to the sink, then resumed her work but it seemed to take all her strength just to gently scour. Joachim had watched the earlier exchange with mounting horror - rather opposite to Jonathan's objective when he invited him in for a coffee to try and calm things down.

Big meaty fingers nervously stroking the fragile handle of the cup, Joachim asked: 'You think they'd do *that*? Kill us too, like the poor souls in the ditch? Would they, pastor?'

Jonathan suppressed his own fear, shaking his head, endeavouring to present a façade of pragmatic calm.

'I am sure they wouldn't go that far. Look, go home, keep calm, go to work as normal.' Joachim nodded, staring blindly into the coffee cup, in his head seeing only the faces of his poor wife and children, whom he had now put at such risk due to helping a Jewish lad. What a fool he had been. He should have thought of his own family.

* * *

Parked outside the pastor's house - in the shade of trees that lined the broad street - the diesel engine of the Mercedes ticked as it cooled down. Two figures could be dimly made out, slumped low in the front seats.

Joachim didn't notice them as he came out of the front door, bent over to put on his bicycle clips, then pedalled down the short driveway and onto the road. Inside the car Hecht was lighting and sucking on another cigarillo. Prising the cigarillo from his lips, the Gestapo investigator told Kruger, still staring intently at the pastor's house: 'Start up and follow on.' The four-cylinder motor coughed noisily into life, Kruger hauling the wheel around, a glance over his shoulder, and then pulling away from the kerb.

* * *

Elsa reached into the cupboard below the sink, pulling out a bottle of schnapps. After retrieving a shot glass, she sat down at the kitchen table to pour herself a steadying shot.

When Joachim left, her husband had gone upstairs to a bedroom at the front of the house, peering cautiously around the edge of the nets. He saw the Mercedes pull away from the kerb opposite. It could have been a coincidence but somehow he felt not. Something told Jonathan there was a darker significance - especially as it had what looked like a black bicycle attached to a rack on its boot. *Like his.*

Going back downstairs and into the kitchen - dreading the Gestapo confronting him with the black bicycle - Jonathan was not surprised to find Elsa sipping schnapps. He looked reproachfully at her, but his wife's eyes blazed defiantly.

'Do you really think they'd do *that* Jonathan? Kill us? I mean we're not undesirables, are we?'

Going over to the cupboard where they kept the cups and glassware he found himself a shot glass and sat down opposite her. Unstoppering the bottle, he remarked with a sigh: 'I'm beginning to think they're capable of anything.'

'I can't believe it...'

'You would if you'd seen those dead people in that ditch.'

Hands shaking, she knocked the alcohol back in one and poured herself another while her husband, sipping his own, shook his head.

'Elsa, is that wise?'

She looked down at the table, shoulders heaving as she wept silently. Outside an air raid warning siren began to wail. Jonathan leapt to his feet, startling Elsa. 'What is it?' she asked, her eyes still full of tears.

'The siren, didn't you hear it?'

She shook her head, reaching for the bottle.

Hands on her shoulders, Jonathan whispered gently in her ear.

'Leave it.'

She released it and let him guide her from the kitchen and out into the hallway, heading for the understairs shelter. As he opened the door, she looked up, suddenly snapping out of her self-pitying misery.

'What about the boy?'

'Just settle in and I'll get him.'

'He'll be scared.'

'Don't worry.'

Elsa descended.

Jonathan headed upstairs, the explosions as the bombs dropped, rattling the windows. As he pushed down the bedroom door handle, a deep rumble made the house shudder. Without switching the overhead light on, Jonathan went over to the bed to find the bedsheet and blankets thrown back.

Empty.

'Where are you boy?' he enquired softly.

Jonathan heard a whimper coming from under the bed and, getting down on his hands and knees, peered in, the boy's moon face with its huge eyes staring back at him. 'Come on,' Jonathan said gently, offering a hand, 'I'll take you downstairs to our shelter.' The boy crawled out from under the bed, yelping with pain from his bandaged left upper arm – the wound caused by a graze from a German bullet the night before.

* * *

In the Mercedes, as they made their way across the city in the wake of Joachim on his bicycle, Hecht sucked on his cigar - nerves ice-calm and taking in a spectacle on the horizon like a massive public holiday fireworks display. Occasionally a gun would crash nearby or a stick of bombs fall a little too close for comfort, Kruger flinching involuntarily at the wheel.

'For fuck's sake drive straight would you,' Hecht remarked pulling the cigarillo out to exhale some smoke and glare at his driver.

Kruger grimaced apologetically, hunching even more over the steering wheel and gazing fearfully through the windscreen.

The Kriminalinspektor returned to his spectator sport, puffing calmly on the cigarillo, occasionally catching a fleeting glimpse of a ghostly British bomber high above frozen in a searchlight beam. Hecht thought it looked like a glittering valkyrie, its tumbling bombs chasing them all to hell and damnation. That made him smile grimly. Catching sight of this out the corner of his eye Kruger did not feel inspired by the defiance of his boss. He knew that smile. It seemed to manifest itself on Hecht's face whenever death was close at hand, usually for some poor soul arrested for crimes against the State. Except, amid the hellfire of this Berlin night, it seemed to Kruger more likely to foretell their own demise. 'Sir,' he suggested with great trepidation, 'shouldn't we stop and find a shelter?'

Hecht shot him a contemptuous glare.

'Keep following him.'

A horse pulling a cart bolted between the Mercedes and Joachim on his bike. Kruger slammed the brakes on, Hecht reaching out for the dashboard to stop himself from going through the windscreen.

Spitting his cigar out, he yelled: 'You idiot!'

'Sorry, sir, the horse….'

Hecht said nothing more, gesturing for Kruger to drive on, picking up Joachim on his bike again. A building they had just passed was hit, its facade crashing into the street. Furniture and ornaments tumbled into the street amid a cascade of bricks, plaster and timber. A great white cloud of dust enveloped the car. 'Christ!'

Kruger exclaimed, swerving to the side of the road, bringing the car to a halt. Face betraying no emotion at all, Hecht patted the arm of his driver and in a quiet, steady voice suggested: 'It's better if you don't blaspheme, or God will not look out for us.'

Nodding, gathering his composure, Kruger turned the wheel and the car pulled away. 'I'm sorry, Sir, but I think we might have lost him,' he admitted apologetically.

'No matter,' Hecht remarked, reaching inside his jacket pocket for the cigar tin. 'I know where he lives, so just keep straight on.'

The Mercedes pulled in to the side of the road just as Joachim was abandoning the bicycle on the pavement, wheels still spinning, to bound up the steps and into a shabby apartment block. The thickset railwayman emerged a few minutes later, ushering his wife and two young children down the steps and off up the street.

The Gestapo car, still unnoticed by Joachim, crept slowly along behind them, lights out. It drew to a halt by the entrance to a small park into which a shelter had been dug, beneath an old bandstand. There was a brief flash of light as a blackout curtain covering the entrance was drawn aside then pulled across again, with Joachim and family swallowed up.

'Shouldn't we follow them down there, Sir?' Kruger asked, trying his best not to sound too shaken up by running the air raid gauntlet. 'For our own protection?'

Hecht stared at Kruger as if he was mad.

'Don't be stupid. We don't mix with the plebs. I know a much better one down the block, under a flak tower with booze, dancing girls…the lot.'

Kruger was delighted at the prospect.

'You mean the one by the Zoo, sir?'

Hecht gave an apologetic smile.

'But you'll have to stay outside in the car.'

Kruger started as a nearby flak battery suddenly roared into life signifying another wave of British bombers.

'And leave me out in this!?'

Hecht laughed and punched him on the arm, exhaling cigar smoke as he did so. 'Of course, you can come!' he roared, 'but keep your bloody gob shut and don't embarrass me if we meet any pretty young ladies or party officials.' A bomb hit a building behind them, creating a massive cloud of dust and debris coming fast down the street. The Mercedes lunged away from the kerb, accelerating hard and swerving to avoid a corpse in the middle of the road.

4

Hecht had always admired Berlin's many varied parks, even though he was not a natural lover of cities. And in Germany's capital, every park told an amazing story. There was the Peacock Island garden, created in the English style during the 1790s for Friedrich Wilhelm II as a playground for the lusty Prussian king and his mistresses. The massively famous Tiergarten was once a hunting ground for the blue bloods to kill beasts for their dining tables.

The small park laid out in front of Hecht right now had no such illustrious pedigree. It was constructed merely to give workers crammed into the dreary tenement blocks somewhere to expose their pale selves to the sun. Some well-heeled patron had provided the bandstand – a simple platform with a concrete base and a wrought iron balustrade. Topping it off, and sitting on six posts, was an ostentatious oriental pagoda roof. Before the war, Bavarian oompah bands were more likely to occupy it than highly trained military musicians or bow-tied string quartets pumping out the likes of Mozart, Wagner or Saint-Saëns.

No matter, as nobody would ever play music in the park again.

A stick of bombs had churned up its badly laid out flowerbeds, ripped across its thinly gravelled paths, rent asunder its tufted turf and tore apart the bandstand's crude ironwork. The concrete base had collapsed inwards when a direct hit burrowed into the air raid shelter beneath it.

Having finished his survey of the ruined park in the cold morning light, a drizzle forcing him to turn his coat collar up and pull his black fedora down over his brow, Hecht strolled over to a pair of middle-aged firemen atop the bandstand rubble.

One of them was standing very still, like a statue, his weight on a pickaxe, a black coal scuttle helmet with shiny aluminium comb pushed back from his forehead. His eyes were closed.

The other fireman was bareheaded and bent low, his big arse in the air, dark blue trousers straining as he used a stethoscope to listen. He glanced up with an angry frown as Hecht scrambled up beside him, making noise by dislodging debris. Crouching down, Hecht mouthed 'sorry', and waited until the man finished. The fireman straightened up, slumped onto his backside, his walrus moustache drooping disconsolately.

'Nothing,' he revealed mournfully and squirted some spittle into the dust to show his disgust. Hecht offered him a cigarillo, asking: 'They all bought it?

The fireman accepted the cigarillo but didn't light up, putting it in a breast pocket of his tunic.

'Thanks, I'll save it for when the rain holds off.'

Glancing up at the overcast sky, Hecht nodded.

'Yes, probably wise.'

He slipped the cigarillo tin back inside his jacket pocket. The fireman with the walrus moustache handed the stethoscope to his helmeted colleague, grabbed the pickaxe and used it to lever himself up onto his feet. Hecht stood up, too, the helmeted fireman scrambling away across the rubble to listen elsewhere. 'Did you have friends who might be in here?' the bareheaded fireman asked.

'Not really,' Hecht replied. 'A man I knew through work. I called by his apartment to pick him up, just now, but an old lady said he and his family had not returned from the shelter.'

The walrus moustache twitched, the fireman shifted in his boots and coughed. 'Well if they're in here, I doubt we will find any of them alive. Or any significant part of them.' Hecht nodded, wearing a resigned, regretful look. Looking down at the rubble of the bandstand, he wondered how he could best approach Pastor Walder now.

'You have a car?' the fireman's suspicious question interrupting his musings. Hecht nodded, still a little distracted, adding casually:

'Essential war work.'

The fireman stroked his walrus moustache, gave Hecht a knowing look - not fearful, but not friendly either - which showed he had twigged the stranger's area of employment. He picked his own helmet up, put it on and pulled the chinstrap down, offering his hand: 'Thanks for the cigar and good luck.' Hecht gave him a tight smile and returned the firm handshake, adding with genuine feeling: 'Thanks for trying.'

The fireman turned and unsteadily lumbered across to his comrade and, with a groan lowered himself onto his haunches. Hecht took one last look around the ruined park and sighed. He conceded that while it wasn't the Tiergarten, it must have been a welcome little patch of green for the working classes. Now it was their grave.

* * *

Hecht sank into the passenger seat of the Mercedes with a groan. Kruger, took his nose out of the *Berliner Morgenpost* - one of the few newspapers still printing despite paper shortages - folded it up and put it away in the glove compartment.

'Bad news, boss?'

Hecht wiped the misted-up passenger door window with the handkerchief from his suit breast pocket. The hole in the condensation revealed the two firemen marching across the road, tools over their shoulders and looking tired but perfectly in step. 'A slight setback,' Hecht admitted.

'What?'

'A British bomb took out the entire shelter.'

'That's it then?'

Hecht sighed, weighing up the worth of pursuing the Walder lead.

Sweating a pastor, accusing him of being a traitor with no solid evidence, all over a missing Jewish kid, who might well have crawled away and died in the woods…well, it all seemed hardly worth the effort. Yet, it could make good sport to call on the pastor, depending on what Brigadeführer Breslau felt.

Hecht tapped the dashboard.

'We'll see what the boss says. Let's head home.'

* * *

Breslau teased a glistening black morsel from a little stoneware pot, smearing the caviar on a piece of toast and popping it into his maw. His yellow tombstones crunched it, lizard-tongue chasing its mush around inside his mouth before going down.

The process of consumption began again, but with a tiny bit of caviar dropping from the corner of Breslau's mouth. It hit the sheet of paper he was reading. He flicked it off, leaving a dark smear on the tightly-typed paragraphs that offered Hecht's report on proceedings so far. With his left hand, Breslau lifted a dripping bottle of champagne from an ice bucket that sat next to his chair. He let the sheet of paper flutter from his right claw onto a food-stained desk blotter.

'It's no good Hecht.'

Having topped up his glass, Breslau slurped down some champagne and observed grumpily: 'More loose ends.'

He stuffed another piece of caviar on toast into his mouth.

'*Bigger* loose ends,' he blurted, a spray of mashed toast and sturgeon eggs filling the air, making Hecht press himself back into the chair.

'Yes, Sir,' the investigator said, faced screwed up with distaste, though Breslau was too busy poking his jar of caviar with the tip of the knife to notice. Gobbling again, Breslau ordered: 'Find out what this pastor is up to. Look into it.' Wiping his fingers on the grubby napkin around his throat, Breslau fixed Hecht with his enormous, penetrating orbs. 'A Jewish fugitive, a bicycle in a ditch…a signalman killed in a bombing raid without full interrogation. A pastor he saw just hours before he died and who may, or may not, have loaned him a bicycle. Most untidy. Very messy.'

Hecht thought it was incredible how this cadaverous eating machine managed to keep his black uniform, with its white piping around the collar and silver oak leaves rank badges, so pristine. There was no sign of a caviar speck, soup stain or fragments of pork garlanded about his emaciated person. His person was immaculate. Breslau slurped more champagne, waving a hand at Hecht to signal he was dismissed.

Hecht rose to go.

'Thankyou, Sir.'

'We don't like loose ends. Tidy them up.'

* * *

'According to Dr Goebbels "the enemy's destructive desires make us even harder and more determined to fight", or so it says here…'

Kruger nodded, not sure what he was meant to say, if anything to what Hecht was reading out. Hecht glanced at him over the top of the newspaper, eyebrows raised. 'Don't you agree Kruger?'

Hecht's loyal assistant was more interested in pouring out exceedingly hot coffee from a stainless-steel flask. It wasn't easy reaching from the driver's side across to the open glove compartment lid where two small Polizei issue porcelain cups sat. Mission accomplished, Kruger put the top of the flask back on and slipped it behind his seat. Hecht screwed up the newspaper and tossed it over his shoulder into the back of the car.

'Thanks,' said Hecht, picking up a coffee cup between thumb and forefinger and sipping, a thoughtful look on his face. 'I think the Führer's spokesman has it just about right,' he told Kruger, 'the more the foes of the State try to destroy the fabric of the Reich the harder we have to work to stop them.' He glanced at Kruger, again with the enquiring raised eyebrows.

Kruger, slurping noisily, looked sideways at Hecht, wondering if that was a mocking gleam in the other's man's eye. Or was it total dedication to the Nazi cause? One day Hecht would meet a piss-taker just like himself, but for now Kruger felt it was wise not to lean either way with his opinion.

'Yes, Sir, you are right - and so is Dr Goebbels.'

Hecht smiled inscrutably and took another sip, the steam from the coffee making the tip of his nose gleam.

Across the road from where they were parked, the kitchen door of the pastor's house opened and a middle-aged woman emerged, in a lightweight coat buttoned up to the chin, wicker shopping basket in hand. Kruger reached over to the glove compartment and put down his cup.

Glancing at his wristwatch, he retrieved the notebook from inside his jacket. Pulling a pencil from a sleeve down its spine, he licked its tip, flipping open the cover and recording: '8.00am. Woman, believed to be Frau Elsa Walder, exits pastor's house. Going shopping.'

Kruger asked: 'Should we follow her, Sir?' Hecht shook his head. 'I have no desire to watch a hausfrau on her hunt for turnips, potatoes and acorn coffee.'

* * *

The weather turned as evening approached, with rain tipping down, huge splashes erupting in a rapidly spreading puddle that covered one side of the road. The large wooden front door of the pastor's house swung open and, after pulling it shut behind him, Jonathan Walder hurried along the short path to the church itself. Meanwhile, Hecht snoozed, hat pulled down over his eyes as Kruger looked at his watch, retrieved his notebook and wrote: 'Herr Pastor Walder exits house to take evening service.' So it continued for the rest of that week, with Frau Walder shopping, the pastor taking his services; the few parishioners who attended hastening home to avoid being caught out by the air raids and their hail of death.

No sign of any Jewish boys.

'What now?' Kruger asked on the Friday.

'Take him in for questioning?'

'No. I want to play with the mice a little longer. But we can call it a night.'

Dropping his boss off outside Zoo bunker nightclub where he seemed to live, Kruger leaned over and stopped Hecht from shutting the door completely. 'Sir, please don't forget it's late,' Kruger told him through the gap, 'and the bombers will soon be here.'

Hecht nodded, giving his assistant a wolfish grin.

'I'll be fine,' he said, pointing upwards, 'It's in the stars.'

The door slammed shut, Kruger shaking his head as he drove away, heading for the peaceful suburb where he lived with his wife, and which was, so far, largely untouched by the bombing.

* * *

On the following Monday evening - back in the office after another futile day of watching the pastor's house - Hecht's attention was entirely given to the Waffen SS personnel record of Martin Walder. It contained a portrait photograph, showing the Knight's Cross of the Iron Cross at Martin's neck. Martin's firm jawline, steely gaze and perfect Aryan bone structure were also impressive. Hecht admired Martin's varied service, including the French campaign of 1940, Yugoslavia in 1941, the thrust through Byelorussia and the Ukraine to Moscow of 1941, then the battles for Kharkov and Kursk in 1943.

'What a supreme warrior,' Hecht remarked, failing to distract Kruger from his *Signal* magazine, regardless of which he continued to marvel aloud.

'Martin Walder is to be the only Waffen SS officer in the rank of hauptsturmfüfrer to receive the award of the Knight's Cross with Oak Leaves and Swords. He already has the Knight's Cross of the Iron Cross for heroism in Yugoslavia in '41. Now he's getting another salute for his courageous holding of the line near Kharkov and later destruction of a Russian tank battalion. He truly is a hero of the Reich.'

'What?' asked Kruger, finally taking notice.

'The pastor's son. A superb example of our master race. Maybe we can close this case with his help? Perhaps we can get the Führer to invite him to Berlin, to personally present him with the new medal for his exploits. It says here in this report that he is currently convalescing in Austria after being shot in the head.'

Kruger hauled himself out of the battered old armchair and came around to lean over Hecht's shoulder and take a look. 'I bet he doesn't look like that anymore!' he exclaimed.

Hecht pushed his chair back suddenly, making Kruger leap away and knock over a waste basket. Balls of screwed up paper tumbled out all over the floor. 'Mind my filing system.' Hecht laughed, reaching for the suit jacket hanging on its peg behind the door.

'Let's go.'

Kruger retrieved the last ball of paper and popped it in the bin.

'To Austria? Tonight!?'

Hecht looked at himself in the mirror, straightened his jacket, smoothed his hair and made sure his pocket handkerchief was perfectly arranged. 'No, Kruger.'

He turned around, scooped the file on Martin Walder into a desk drawer and locked it using a small key on a chain attached to the inside of his right-hand trouser pocket.

'You're going to drive me to the Zoo flak tower nightclub and then bugger off home. I'll see you here sharpish, at 7.00am in the morning.'

Looking in the mirror on the back of the office door - at his sparse, close-cropped hair and shiny suit - Kruger recognised that he was not made for the sophisticated kind of Berlin nightlife his boss enjoyed.

Hecht, meanwhile, was eager to get away.

'Come on, man - stop admiring yourself,' he remarked.

'I'm on a promise.'

After gently shoving Kruger out Hecht turned off the light, closed and locked the door. As they marched off down the dimly lit corridor, their heels clicking on the linoleum, they seemed to be the only people working in the entire building. Except, of course, there would be interrogators hard at it in the basement cells.

'On a promise with who, Sir?' Kruger dared ask.

'Hanna Reitsch. You know, Hitler's favourite flyer.'

'Pardon me, Sir, but fuck off!'

'I can get you a bunk up with her mother sometime,' Hecht chortled.

'Again, Sir, fuck off!'

'You are such a brute Kruger!'

The two men roared with laughter, which echoed down the dead corridors. Deep below, in the cellars – well insulated against sound leakage - fingernails were being torn out, prisoners beaten to a pulp and hot wires applied to genitals.

It was all in a night's work for the men and women of the Gestapo, but with British bombers doing their work after dark and the Americans during daylight, while Russian hordes got ever closer, they were all living on borrowed time. Surely a reckoning would come, but for now Hecht, Kruger and their comrades were cruel puppet-masters who played their perverse games with impunity.

5

Berlin, April 1947

GLASHIFRYN'S OFFICE was now shrouded in darkness, relieved only by the street lights flickering into life along the avenue down below.

Head a little fuzzy from the whisky - and also spinning from the incredible level of detail Glashirfryn had reeled off - Eric rose from the chair and walked stiffly over to the window.

'Those Gestapo files were certainly comprehensive,' he observed, stifling a yawn. With a groan Glashirfryn climbed out of his chair, leaning on the desk for a few moments to let the blood return to his legs, before grabbing his walking stick and coming over to stand by Eric.

'Of course, and we have other sources too,' Glashirfryn revealed.

'But, still – it's a lot to take in and to recall.'

'I have a photographic memory.'

'Useful in your line of work I suppose?'

Glashirfryn gave dry laugh and remarked: 'Sometimes too useful. There are some details one would rather forget.'

Eric nodded.

'Martin told me only a few – the medal presentation from the battle-scarred Führer; some sort of confrontation with his parents; keeping his lips sealed when it came to the slimy Gestapo investigator; then back to Austria before being sent to Hungary. So, did this Hecht character have a fit of humanity and give up? And if so what happened to Martin's parents and the boy?' Glashirfryn turned away from the window, went over to the desk and refilled the whisky glasses, observing: 'Goodness, that's a lot of questions. No, the Gestapo man did not give up, but sit down and I'll finish the tale.'

Berlin, July 1944

'Time to pay some house calls,' Hecht had suggested to Kruger as the car pulled out of the Friedrichstrasse station after dropping off Martin for his train back to Bad Gastein.

The Mercedes headed for Dahlem, Kruger grumpily peeping the horn at a group of cycling munitions factory workers dawdling along. He groused: 'It said in my horoscope that I should avoid unnecessary journeys.'

Hecht observed sourly: 'I don't believe in that occult bullshit Kruger, even if our dear Führer does.'

Taking his left hand off the wheel for a few seconds, Kruger felt inside his jacket for the butt of the pistol in its holster under his left armpit. He rubbed it three times, a habit of his before every arrest.

Kruger tried to defend Hitler by reminding his boss: 'But, Sir, remember the Führer's astrologer who correctly predicted British bombs would turn the Propaganda Ministry to rubble - he also said Montgomery would beat Rommel.'

Hecht gave a warning frown.

'Really Kruger, you do know that he was arrested as a traitor and sent to a special camp?'

'So, why does the Führer *believe*?'

'I would suggest the Führer only acknowledges positive astrology. Anyway, you are staying in the car when we get there. Read your horoscope by all means. There is no need to utilize your muscular talents just yet.'

They fell into silence, with Hecht staring out the window lost in thought, pondering his tactics for the forthcoming interview. Pulling up outside the church, as Hecht climbed out, Kruger warned: 'Sir, please don't forget the bombers will soon be here.' Irritated, Hecht paused to put his fedora on, remarking brusquely: 'Yes, I am well aware of that, you old woman - no need to remind me each time I get out of the car.'

* * *

'Frau Elsa Walder?' the man enquired politely, taking his hat off.

'Yes.'

'I wonder if I might see Pastor Walder?'

Elsa's senses had been numbed by some schnapps sneaked while cooking, but the fog cleared instantly with the chilling realization that the blonde-haired young man on the doorstep was likely the caller she had feared since Jonathan gave the boy refuge and Martin's alarming visit. *Gestapo.*

She tried to hide her fear with a sickly smile.

'If you go into the church, I will send my husband across.'

The Gestapo man put his hat back on and smiled.

'Of course, I'll await him there.'

Closing the door Elsa collapsed momentarily against it.

Emerging from the shadows on the landing – from where he had observed the doorstep exchange - Jonathan came swiftly down the stairs, took Elsa in his arms and held her tight.

She sobbed into his shoulder.

They couldn't lose another boy – first poor little Manfred to the influenza, then Martin to the Führer and now young David, whose family were probably already murdered by the Nazis.

'Be strong,' he murmured, 'it won't take a moment to put David somewhere safe.'

* * *

Jonathan entered via the vestry, coming around behind the pulpit so he could, hopefully, get eyes on the man before he was noticed.

The visitor was sitting in a pew at the front of the church, by the main doors - head back, arms splayed along the back of it. He was seemingly lost in profound contemplation but straightened up on hearing footsteps on the aisle's flagstones.

'Pastor Walder?' the man enquired, getting to his feet, right hand outstretched. 'Yes,' affirmed Jonathan, taking up the offer of a handshake, 'and you are?' The visitor smiled disarmingly, revealing: 'Kriminalinspektor Hecht, Geheime Staatspolizei.'

Not batting an eyelid at this revelation, Jonathan enquired:

'What can I do for you Herr Hecht?'

'Well, pastor, it's more a case of what I can do for you.' They sat down side by side in the pew, Jonathan leaning back into a corner while Hecht sat forward, playing with his hat as he looked around.

'This is a lovely church.'

Jonathan gave a tight-lipped smile but said nothing.

Hecht waved a hand towards the main entrance.

'The rose window is very beautiful.'

Jonathan looked up too.

'Especially on a sunny day like this,' said Hecht with a beatific smile.

Suddenly turning serious, Hecht's face clouded over as he looked down and ran a finger around the brim of his hat. Returning his eyes to Jonathan, he asked: 'Funded by grateful parishioners – the window?'

'Yes, some time ago.'

'Has the war hit your congregation numbers hard?'

'A little. People don't seem to have the time or the inclination during such difficult days.' Hecht straightened up, hands and hat in his lap, and frowned, apparently applying his mind to the fall in attendance.

'You'd think it would make them *more* inclined to come.'

Jonathan shrugged.

'There again,' acknowledged Hecht, 'I am a living example of laxity. Raised a good Catholic, but hadn't seen the inside of a church for years, until today.' Churning up inside despite his calm exterior, Jonathan grew impatient and asked, somewhat irritated: 'What is it you want to know Herr Hecht?'

'Ah yes, the reason for my intrusion… I won't insult you by prevaricating any longer. Well-placed sources have alleged that you are hiding an enemy of the State somewhere in your house or, God forbid, if you'll pardon the expression, in this very church.'

The pastor was the picture of a man aggrieved that his reputation had been unjustly impugned. 'An enemy of the State…who on earth can have said this?' he asked, but thinking 'so this is the person who sent Martin to try and get us to give the boy up.'

'I know - a ridiculous allegation,' agreed Hecht disingenuously, 'particularly when laid against a man of God and father of a hero of the Reich.'

Jonathan tensed at the mention of his son.

'Indeed,' he remarked, his mouth turning dry.

Hecht enjoyed the reaction, decided to push his advantage.

Looking back up at the Rose Window, he innocently enquired:

'How is your son?'

'Well, we hope,' Jonathan replied. 'His mother hasn't had a letter for several months.' That last bit was not a lie of course.

Visit, yes. Letter, no.

Hecht nodded, an ersatz expression of pained sympathy etched on his face. Inside he was shocked that a man of God would lie so stupidly.

'But, Herr Hecht, I must insist you tell me, who has told you we are hiding an "enemy of the State"?' Jonathan experienced a twist of fear in his gut.

Hecht looked down at the floor, smiling while a stone-faced Jonathan waited for him to reply. The Gestapo man eventually looked up, this time with steely eyes. 'To satisfy myself and put these ridiculous allegations to rest, do you mind if I have a look around the church?'

'Not at all,' replied Jonathan, heart racing with fear.

As they began their inspection tour, Jonathan realized that an old friend was also likely in peril. *Had the Gestapo already arrested him?*

Jonathan felt sick, his mind racing, filled with guilt about involving Brandt in the whole affair.

* * *

Slowly the boy became aware of the fact that he was not alone in the ditch. Sitting up, he was terrified of Jonathan's pale moon face staring down at him.

David was not sure if it was a corpse, a ghost or live human being.

He retreated, legs pushing him away on his backside. Sharp, hot pains shot up his left arm, sticky with blood due to the graze from a SS bullet. His progress along the ditch was blocked and, feeling behind with frantic, fearful hands, the boy found the warm corpse of an old lady.

Realising he was grasping dead flesh, David let out a yelp in fright. Jonathan and Joachim lunged, arms flailing, aiming to grab a hold of him.

The boy fainted and, pulling his limp form off the old lady, the two men stared down, not knowing what to do next.

Joachim had phoned his pastor for help, blethering about bodies lying in a ditch, so Jonathan cycled out there. Now, Jonathan stooped down, patting his hands over the boy's body, holding a glistening hand up to his face and sniffing.

'Blood…He's been shot.'

'What can we do?'

'Call a doctor.'

'But, who?'

'The phone is in a cupboard on the outside of the signal box?'

Joachim nodded.

'Alright, stay with him, I'll be back in a minute."

Jonathan hurried over to the signal box, swiftly finding and opening the little cupboard containing the telephone, its rusty hinges protesting. He was put through and Brandt himself answered, Jonathan keeping it sparse in detail and hoping the operator did not pass on notes to the Gestapo.

'Hans, it's Jonathan.'

'I was just going to bed…what's wrong? Why are you whispering?'

'I need your help.'

In this cursed world there was only one person that Hans Brandt would risk his life for on a dark night - Jonathan Walder. They had been comrades-in-arms in the trenches during the last war, dining on rats and mouldy bread while dodging the singing bullets of Tommy snipers. More than twenty years on, Brandt took his precious car out after dark, using up his meagre petrol allowance, to hunt for Jonathan by the road at some godforsaken railway junction. Brandt peered over the steering wheel, squinting owlishly through his spectacles as the car's feeble narrow-slitted lights were just about picking out the surface of the road.

* * *

Waiting for Brandt to arrive, Jonathan and Joachim lifted the boy onto the road to take a look at his injury. Jonathan folded his jacket to make a cushion for the boy's head, Joachim giving up his jacket to cover the lad against the cold. They stood there side-by-side in silence, listening to owls screeching eerily in the woods. Their exhalations hung in the air with Jonathan kneeling down every now and then to make sure the boy was still breathing. After half-an-hour a car could be heard approaching.

'What if it's not Doktor Brandt?' Joachim asked, voice full of foreboding.

'Good point,' said Jonathan.

They gently lifted the boy down into the ditch again.

The car slid by at a walking pace, coming to a halt a few yards away. The driver climbed out and they heard Brandt sigh and mutter:

'This is a fool's errand.'

'It's him,' Jonathan whispered to Joachim.

Before they could attract his attention, Brandt climbed back into the car and started the engine. Jonathan scrambled out of the ditch, running as fast as he could after the slowly rolling vehicle. Catching up, he hammered on the roof. It lurched to a halt. Winding the window down, an alarmed Brandt exclaimed: 'Dear Lord almighty! I almost had a heart attack!'

Brandt climbed out but told them to bring the boy to the car, so they could use its internal light for him to take a look at the wound.

'Hang on a minute,' he hissed, reaching into the boot. 'I'll put a rug on the back seat. I don't want my leather covered in blood.'

Satisfied his car's upholstery would not suffer, Brandt gestured for them to slide the boy in one side while he pulled him gently from the other.

Jonathan and Joachim looked in as the doctor gave the boy - who stirred and moaned a little but did not open his eyes - a cursory inspection. 'It's a bullet graze,' he declared and added heatedly: 'I hope you don't mind me asking, but what the bloody hell are you doing out here with this boy!?'

'He came off a train,' explained Joachim. 'I think he's a Jew. They shot some others and left their bodies in the ditch also.'

Brandt felt scared, ashamed and angry all at once. Shaking his head, he reached into his bag, pulled out a bandage - to replace the makeshift thing Jonathan and Joachim had put on the boy's left arm.

He exhaled angrily - a precursor to an explosion. 'Jonathan, what are you doing!? Risking all our lives for someone like this.'

'But, if he was your son?'

'My son died in Poland,' Brandt responded, sighing heavily and adding: 'What on earth do we do with him?'

'Drive him back to my house.'

Brandt nodded resignedly.

'Alright then.'

Jonathan told Joachim to ride home and, relieved beyond belief to be released, the railwayman cycled swiftly off into the night without a backward glance.

As he came around to the driver's side of the car, Brandt noticed something in the ditch. Jonathan watched the doctor crouch down to get a closer look, hearing Brandt made a sharp intake of breath on discovering the corpse of an old man. There was a massive exit wound in his face from a bullet in the back of the head.

They climbed into the car, Brandt letting the engine run, staring though the windscreen, turning over the discovery in his mind. Jonathan watched his friend's face intently, waiting for him to drive on and asked what he'd seen.

'An old man,' Brandt sighed, looking at his friend, 'with his brains blown out and discarded in a ditch.' Jonathan nodded, giving the doctor's shoulder a comforting squeeze.

* * *

The boy looked deathly pale, propped up against some pillows in Martin's old bed. Brandt tended to him with a look of grave concern on his face while Elsa and Jonathan hovered apprehensively in the background. Elsa came forward to mop the boy's brow with a damp cloth, remarking.

'Poor soul.'

When they turned up at the kitchen door with the boy she had been very angry – especially fearful for her husband, who was prone to doing stupid, impulsive things. She often warned he could not save the world - particularly in its current state - and he must stick to salving souls. Jonathan told her he would explain later, but right now they needed to do what they could for the lad.

So, after carefully stripping him, putting him into crisp pyjamas trousers their son had worn when he was also 12-years-old, they settled the boy into the bed. He was surrounded by Martin's old things: a scruffy teddy bear nestled by the wall above the pillows; the sporting pennants on the bedroom ceiling; a pile of motorcycle racing magazines on the bedside table.

They left the boy for a while and would check on him shortly.

Downstairs, in the kitchen, Jonathan related to Elsa the story of the train and the executions as told to him by Joachim. As she put the boy's stinking rags into the fire of a stove, Elsa shook her head in disbelief. If the story had come from any other man, she would have screamed at him to get out of her kitchen. But her husband would not lie and was not prone to exaggeration.

'Who would do such a thing?' she asked, pouring black, steaming liquid into fine Dresden china cups. As Dr Brandt lifted the cup to his lips, she saw his hand shake. Jonathan's hands, though, were steady and he gave her a cheerless smile: 'He's Jewish Elsa. It's no secret they are being got rid of – we just choose to ignore it.' She felt very frightened and looked down at the brightly polished coffee pot and its distorted reflection of her face, all ugly and stretched out of shape.

* * *

With the study's roaring fire crackling, the orange reflection of the flames washed across the polished surface of the drinks cabinet and was refracted by crystal decanters to dance on the wall. It seemed to suggest Götterdämmerung and Jonathan shook his head, to throw off that pagan thought. He and Brandt had retreated to the study for a further discussion while Elsa watched over the boy. Brandt entered, closing the door behind him, leaning against it, taking a deep, calming breath. Jonathan poured brandy into a pair of balloon glasses, stepping forward to supply sedative for the doctor's frayed nerves.

They settled into comfortable winged armchairs by the fire.

'It's spring and the fire is going,' muttered Brandt, all hot and bothered, tugging at his tie, spreading open his collar.

'I was cold…I can put it out if you like,' suggested his host.

Brandt waved his left hand to indicate it was alright, raising the glass to his lips and taking a very big sip of brandy.

'You and I are so different,' said Brandt, cleaning the grit out of his tear ducts with a thumb. 'I'm surprised we've remained friends. The last war made you turn to Him, while I turned away.'

'You still know what's right and wrong – better than many of the clergy who think that "Him" stands for the Führer.'

Brandt shrugged, his nose in the brandy glass.

Lifting his snout, he snorted: 'We don't decide what is right or wrong. The State does. In that context I'm not sure what we did tonight was correct. Hitler's right about the evil of communism. They're no friends of God either. Maybe we should forgive his dislike of certain elements, so we can win the bigger battle against Bolshevism?'

'You blind yourself Hans.'

'I think, Jonathan, that ministering to all those blasted English, French and American diplomats before the war softened your head to the very great injuries they did to us at Versailles, with their reparations – our nation bled dry. Such villains.'

This was an old argument, but it had been given an edge by the evening's events and so Brandt's eyes blazed. But there was fire in Jonathan's eyes too and he scoffed at his own foolishness.

'Until tonight, I must admit that I was merely deeply troubled by aspects of Nazi social policy. You remember when Galen was speaking out in his pulpit against the forced euthanasia of the insane, the disabled and the promiscuous youth I just wrote a letter of mild protest about Reich laws being broken?'

'Yes, and you were lucky not to be carted off by the Gestapo for that,' Brandt observed. 'Even Galen blessed the crusade against the godless Bolsheviks.'

Jonathan sighed heavily.

'Yes, yes, there were elements that Hitler promised us – an end to economic chaos, return to prosperity, all that….and action against "foreign invaders" who were parasites. And so he suggested that workers of the world of all classes should recognise a common enemy – and he was explicit in whom he meant.'

Brandt nodded, but dared not say it, so Jonathan said it for him: 'He meant the Jews, Hans…and tonight including the boy and the others we found some slaughtered by the railway tracks…I'm not so sure I can live with it, if this is how they "resettle" people or "re-educate" them. I'm asking myself where it's all going to end…and maybe - if we can save one desperate soul, this boy - then it's worth it. Don't you think?'

Brandt nodded reluctantly, acknowledging what ailed the German patient.

'But, it was the genius of their approach was it not Jonathan?'

He pressed on without waiting for a response.

'Offering some hard truths and simple solutions, apparently - and they were democratically elected after all - but they introduced a new cancer of autocracy… worse than that – it spread through the body politic, into the vital organs, the bones, the brain of the nation, infecting our young – a mind virus - step by step destroying our fragile liberty, removing the safeguards against dictatorship.'

Brandt winced at his own words.

'Anyway, I have said too much in this confessional, Jonathan.'

'We are left, to place our hopes in the better angels,' suggested his confessor.

Brandt shrugged and downed the rest of his brandy, holding out the glass.

'Pour me another, so I can forget what we did tonight,' he asked, clearly also not entirely impressed with Jonathan's suggestion of how to obtain salvation.

'You have to drive home later Hans.'

This depressed Brandt even more and, groaning, levered himself up and out of the armchair. 'You're right...I should go.'

He sighed heavily, shook his head, putting his empty glass on the mantelpiece next to a photograph of Martin as a choirboy, looking angelic in his white surplice and red cassock. 'Have you heard from your son lately?' Brandt asked as he contemplated the framed image.

Jonathan shook his head, wearing an expression of seeming indifference. Then, suddenly, with a sickening tug in his gut, it occurred to him that he'd left his bicycle in the ditch by the railway line. Suppressing a sudden panic, Jonathan decided not to mention it as, all things considered, there were surely more important things to worry about than a lost bike?

* * *

It was after one of Dr Brandt's visits to check on the boy – who was making an excellent recovery – that Hecht and Kruger, still watching from the Mercedes, spotted him.

'Could be a friend, possibly a church elder,' suggested Kruger.

Who else would visit a house of an evening in a car?

Hecht shrugged, suggesting: 'An essential war worker, getting on in years, in a suit - but did you see the bag he carried? He's a doctor. Call me Sherlock, but I think if we check lists of patients and doctors we can link Walder with someone. Also check the number plate of the car.'

* * *

Having identified Brandt and his link to the Walders, Hecht decided to save picking up the doctor until the afternoon when Martin was safely tucked up back at the Hotel Adlon, sleeping off his post-medal ceremony drinking session. The receptionist at Dr Brandt's surgery was some years older than the century and had seen all sorts of visitors to her employer's practice in her time, but never as dangerous as this one. He was clearly not good news, and yet devilishly charming.

Although the gentleman reassured her it was nothing to worry about, as she took the few steps from her desk to the doctor's consulting room, she feared for the future and her prospects of gainful employment.

Dr Brandt turned pale when she announced the visitor from Gestapo, Hecht sweeping past her all smiles and with an extended hand.

'It is excellent to meet you Her Doktor Brandt!' he boomed, seizing the doctor's hand in a strong grip, so different to that which he used when first meeting Martin Walder. 'Please do not get up.'

Released from the handshake, Brandt gestured for Hecht to sit down in a chair on the other side of the desk. Coughing nervously, the doctor took his spectacles off and laid them on the desk, enquiring:

'How may I help you?'

The man from the Gestapo gave a reassuring smile and held up a beseeching hand.

'On the contrary, it's more a case of how we might help you.'

'I see,' Brandt replied deciding brevity was best - aware he was now walking a razor's edge.

'No, I don't think you do Herr Doktor. Sometimes misguided sentiment blinds us. Being a good Christian, or a good samaritan, is not always compatible with being a good German. Do you agree?'

Brandt kept his eyes locked on Hecht's - desperate not to show any fear - but picked up his glasses and fiddled with them nervously.

'I'm not sure I get your meaning. I'm not terribly religious.'

Hecht went for the jugular.

'I'll get straight to the point. We believe that yourself and the pastor Walder, together with a railway worker called Joachim Endrass, who is sadly no longer with us, may have helped an enemy of the State to escape justice.'

A tense silence fell, broken only by a lorry changing up through gears as it passed by in the street. Brandt coughed, at a loss for something to say in response to such grave accusations. He stopped fiddling with the spectacles and let them lie in his limp hands.

'Is your silence a confession of guilt?' Hecht asked with a sinister smile. Brandt shook his head and mumbled: 'Not, I mean… er...no…it's…'

Keen to whisk the doctor away for a proper interrogation at Prinz-Albrecht-Strasse, Hecht broke in: 'I think Herr Doktor you best come with me for a chat in private.'

Having lodged Brandt in a cell at the Gestapo HQ, they left him to stew in his own juice overnight, while Martin was taken to the Zoo flak tower nightclub to properly celebrate his Knight's Cross. Hecht would interrogate the doctor properly later.

6

AFTER THEIR FIRST encounter in the church, where Elsa told him to wait – and when Jonathan feared Brandt might had already have been questioned by the Gestapo – the pastor felt compelled to invite Hecht into house.

This was a bid to discover exactly how much trouble they were in. *Also, how can one refuse hospitality to such a visitor without appearing guilty of an accusation?*

On hearing the front door open, Elsa emerged from the kitchen, wiping her hands on a flour-covered apron. She wore a brave smile but Jonathan could tell she had been drinking more schnapps to deaden her fear.

Fixing her with a cautionary look, Jonathan explained: 'Elsa, Kriminalinspektor Hecht of the Gestapo would like to make sure there are no enemies of the State lurking in our house.'

Elsa's smile became a rictus grin, Hecht scrutinising her with a poker player's faint smile painted on his face. Her hands grasped the apron even more tightly. 'That's fine, isn't it, Frau Walder?' Hecht enquired brightly, slipping his raincoat off.

'Of course,' said Jonathan, placing it over the newel post at the bottom of the stairs. Hecht popped his hat on top of it. This all seemed to give Elsa time to recover and she enquired: 'A cup of tea or coffee first, Herr Hecht?'

'That is kind, but no thanks.'

The air raid sirens started to wail, indicating the imminent arrival of American bombers. Hecht opened his arms wide, glanced up at the ceiling.

'No time to lose anyway…Where is your shelter?'

Jonathan took Elsa by the hand and led her to the door under the stairs. 'In here,' he revealed to Hecht, ushering his wife inside.

'Why don't you both take cover and I'll just do a quick search.'

Hecht put his head around the door and watched them settle hesitantly onto a pair of old oak dining chairs. Smiling reassuringly he called out: 'I'm sure we'll be fine!'

He closed the door, smile vanishing instantly. Spotting a chair in the hallway, Hecht wedged it under the handle so they could not get out.

He made a swift survey downstairs, checking all the cupboards and cabinets, but finding no Jewish boy. *The smell of baking in the kitchen was, however, delightful.* Hecht thought Pastor and Frau Walder would never get through all those cakes *unless they had the help of a hungry little mouth?*

Next it was upstairs and, soft as he could, Hecht took two steps at a time, moving lithely - the only sounds his breathing, the creak of leather shoes and groan of wooden joists.

There was nobody hiding in the wardrobes of the bedrooms. And yet, in what was clearly Martin Walder's old room, while the bed *appeared* undisturbed, Hecht did find it curious that a pile of motorcycle magazines from before the war looked a little untidy.

Frau Walder would keep them very neat for her absent son, surely?

Hecht spotted the most telling clue of all behind the door, *shoved there in a panic* – a tray with a plate upon which was a piece of half-eaten black bread and an almost empty soup bowl, with spoon beside it. Kneeling down he lifted the bowl up to sniff. *Turnip, with a pinch of pepper.* Lifting the black bread up to the ceiling light, he saw that whoever chomped on it had a child's teeth.

Hecht wondered aloud to himself: 'Where can you be?'

He got down to look under the bed.

Nothing.

Opening the wardrobe, Hecht pushed his arms in through some clothes to check for a false back. *Solid.* Going over to switch off the light, Hecht paused to scrutinize a framed photograph of Martin with his parents, taken when he was, say, 12-years-old – *an open-faced, pleasant looking lad, and yet a hint of defiance in his eyes.*

Hecht next drew up the blackout roller blind – which was down even though it was late afternoon - and opened a side window, leaning out to look up the roof. There was nobody clinging to the slates. Closing the window, Hecht carefully put the blackout arrangements back in place

Going onto the landing, Hecht heard the first bombs fall some distance away – an American heavy bomber raid presenting its credentials. The anti-aircraft batteries in a nearby park opened fire with a jolting crash. The whole house rattled.

That's when he noticed the loft hatch over the landing. Certainly, no small boy could get up there on his own.

As more bombs fell, making the house rattle, Hecht took another quick look around the rooms upstairs, but could find no ladder.

Back on the landing, he smiled grimly and - on tiptoes and stretching his right arm - poked the hatch with his fingertips to see if it would move easily. To gain more reach Hecht drew his Mauser HSc pistol from its holster.

On the other side of the locked hatch David had an ear against it, right hand resting lightly on it too. Behind him was a makeshift bed on some boards, but he couldn't bear just lying there when he heard someone coming up the stairs.

It took him back to his family hiding in the loft of a tenement in Prague while search teams of Nazi troops stomped around below, bellowing and screaming - trying to ferret out Jews in hiding.

Now, in Berlin, closing his eyes, heart beating in his chest fit to burst, David in his mind's eye saw his mother holding his sister in a tight embrace below a

dormer window of the Prague loft, their ghostly-white faces and saucer-eyed fear revealed by the dim light leaking 'round the edges of the shutters. He screwed his own eyes even tighter shut to erase that vision.

Separated from David's head by the thin plywood - the muzzle of Hecht's pistol pushed insistently, the hatch giving against its hinges slightly, lifting a few millimetres.

Resisting an urge to cry out in terror, David gently pushed down with both hands, the bandaged arm extremely painful.

Hecht lowered the Mauser, put it away in the holster, his face wearing a self-satisfied smile – *he had his answer.* He had wanted to growl something about huffing and puffing and blowing the house down but contented himself with making a pistol of the thumb and forefinger of his right hand, pointing upwards and pretending to shoot.

In the loft, tears ran hotly down David's cheek. When he felt the pressure below released he dragged himself over to the bed and buried his head in the pillow, whimpering.

Hecht decided to go back downstairs and take his leave - for now.

A stick of bombs fell nearby, making the bannisters judder. There was a salvo of anti-aircraft fire and then an eerie silence settled, broken only by a chiming grandfather clock in the hallway.

4.00pm.

It was another salvo of gunfire that dislodged one of the marbles David had been playing with earlier on the landing.

The boy had been told several times by the pastor and Frau Walder not to play up there, for fear of someone slipping on them and breaking their neck by falling down the stairs. *But, what could he do?* The landing was a nice open space and David was frequently bored with just reading.

After teetering at the top, the marble tipped over the edge and went *clickety-clack, clickety-clack, clickety-clack* on bare wooden steps, all the way to the bottom. Huddled together on their chairs below, the Walders stared up in horror as the marble made its progress down the stairs above.

Following its sound with their eyes, they recoiled as it hit each step – for they both knew what it meant and hardly dared breathe. Elsa suppressed an urge to scream, closing her hands over her mouth and burying her head in her husband's chest.

Hecht clattered down the stairs after the marble, looked around carefully, but could not spot it. He crept over to remove the chair from under the door handle. Having done so, and with the neighbourhood all-clear siren sounding, Hecht rapped loudly on the door with his knuckles, making Jonathan and Elsa jump apart.

'All safe now!' he shouted.

Jonathan opened the door, finding Hecht waiting by the bottom of the stairs, lifting his hat from the newel post.

Smiling as he put it on and tweaking the peak of the fedora between thumb and forefinger by way of salute, he announced: 'Everything seems in order.'

As Elsa made her way to the kitchen, Jonathan saw their unwelcome visitor out.

'You mean no "enemies of the State"?' Jonathan enquired in a deliberately flat voice, despite his wildly beating heart.

Hecht made light of the situation.

'I'm sincerely sorry for the intrusion. I don't know how people can make such unfounded allegations and I hope it was no bother.'

Jonathan lifted the raincoat off the post and handed it to Hecht, enabling something to escape from the folds at the bottom, which rolled across the floorboards to stop by the toe cap of the Kriminalinspektor's right shoe. He stooped down, picking it up between thumb and forefinger.

He held it up to the light, admiring the way the translucent blue iris and a tiny black pupil were held in suspension at the core of the small glass ball.

'A marble,' he remarked, seemingly surprised.

Jonathan killed any reaction on his face. *Damn that boy and his games.* Taking his coat from the pastor, Hecht handed the marble to Jonathan, who pretended he was bemused by it.

'How curious Herr Kriminalinspektor.'

As he opened the door to make his exit Hecht remarked with a smirk: 'I would hate you to lose your marbles.'

The door closed, leaving Jonathan to tighten his fist around the hard, unyielding traitor in his palm.

7

Kruger looked expectantly at his boss as he climbed into the car.

'I didn't imagine I'd find you still here,' Hecht remarked, 'thought you might have made a run for the nearest shelter.'

Kruger shook his head and put a brave face on it. 'I've spent too much time with you, Sir. Bloody fearless I am these days.'

Hecht settled into the passenger seat, extracting a cigarillo, and, as he lit it, Kruger wound his window down to let the smoke out.

'Well?' he asked.

Hecht took a couple of dramatic sucks and puffs before responding. 'There is a likely hiding place.'

'So, now we send a team in to rip it apart?'

Hecht shook his head.

'No.'

Kruger was most surprised.

'No?'

Again, Hecht was amazed at his assistant's lack of finesse.

'You really don't understand the subtleties of this do you? This misguided man of God who has given shelter to an enemy of the State is the father of a hero of the Reich, who is also a member of our Führer's praetorian guard - one of our most decorated crusaders against the Bolsheviks on the Eastern Front. To simply execute his parents would be very bad public relations. We've got to make them hand the boy over and then devise an exquisite means of sending them to their fate, at Dachau or Sachsenhausen, or some other holiday camp.'

Kruger remained none the wiser but enquired: 'What about the doctor, in the cells?' Hecht nodded. 'Good point, we'll have a chat with him when we get back to base.'

'One more thing, though Sir,' Kruger ventured as he started the car engine.

'Yes?' his boss asked mildly.

'What about the black bicycle stuck on the back of the car?'

Hecht nodded, giving an inscrutable smile while pondering the bike's fate for a moment. 'You know, I'd quite forgotten about it.'

'So, Sir?'

'Ditch it, for now' Hecht decided, with an evil little chuckle adding: 'Somewhere in the evidence store, so we can present it for shock value to the the pastor Walder after I've worked on him a bit more.'

* * *

At Gestapo HQ, Kruger parked the car and took the bike away for storage, while Hecht climbed the stairs to make a report to Breslau whom he found reading paperwork while sipping a glass of milk. Hecht chose to remain standing, Breslau listening impassively to his report with his unsettling eyes wandering around the room. Hecht tried not to stare at the other man's prominent Adam's apple as he detailed the latest happenings.

Report concluded, the Brigadeführer fixed his gaze on the Kriminalinspektor.

'Without a confession – or the boy in the flesh - we can hardly execute the father of a hero of the Reich,' Breslau rasped. 'It's a pity we have nothing to connect him to the bomb plot against the

Führer.' He sighed heavily, before going on: 'Which would be very convenient. The ultimate loose end tied up.'

Breslau made that strange death's head grin that passed for amusement on his part.

'Still,' Hecht ventured, 'there is my gut instinct about that railway worker who was killed and the good doctor who we may yet squeeze into some form of confession, Sir.'

Breslau pursed his lips and shook his head: 'Regretfully, before you could interrogate him properly, the good doctor took himself off to the next world.'

Hecht was stunned.

'What!?'

Breslau noted in exasperation: 'Some fool let him keep his spectacles in his cell, so the doctor improvised a tool with which to puncture his jugular - made an extraordinary mess, apparently.'

Hecht grunted in disgust. 'Idiots.'

'It is all very unfortunate,' Breslau conceded, 'but your gut instinct has never failed me Hecht. Deal with it how you see fit. There can be no public trial, no public execution without solid proof.' Breslau finished his drink, dabbed his lips with a white handkerchief, mopped up some spilled milk on the desk top and remarked: 'I must say, though, that you have taken a long time on what is a very minor case, Hecht.'

'Just being careful, Sir,' responded the investigator, 'especially with the pastor's son being decorated by the Führer for bravery.'

'Yes, but more efficiency is required,' suggested Breslau, 'even on such small matters.' Breslau lifted the paperwork up with a boney hand and deposited it in the 'Out' basket on his desk, then gave Hecht an intense look.

'You realize that every task we give you, no matter how minor, is fraught with danger, due to your own background?'

The hairs on the back of Hecht's neck prickled with alarm.

'I am aware that I must prove myself more than others.'

'Yes, indeed,' the Brigadeführer agreed, 'it must be hard to live with that flaw but you did well when you went to Kiev and rounded up those army traitors.'

Hecht shrugged as if it was nothing, making an effort at a nonchalant smile. 'Actually, Sir, it all makes me double determined to prove myself.'

'Of course, but it renders you always to be a little suspect.'

'I chose to be German, sir. I loathe my father, or rather loathed him.'

Breslau nodded, looking down at his lapel and flicking off a crumb.

'Killed in an air raid I think you said?'

Hecht suspected Breslau was trying to catch him out in some fashion. It was very tiresome. 'Yes, while bedding one of his whores in a London hotel.'

'No other family in England?'

Breslau knew all this already.

'A half-brother.'

'Is he fighting?'

Breslau fixed his underling with those unsettling orbs.

Hecht felt very uneasy, but again tried to shrug it off.

'I have no idea, Sir.'

Breslau laced the fingers of his hands and cracked the joints, leaning forward in his chair, then pushed himself back into it and gave the death's head grin. 'You can go now and show how loyal you are by fully resolving the loose ends of this piss arse case.' Hecht's arm shot up and he exclaimed: 'Heil Hitler!' Breslau waved it away, nodding impatiently and observed: 'And we must make a clean sweep – the Walders and the little Jewish rat they are hiding.'

* * *

Back downstairs in his own office Hecht enjoyed a nip of potato vodka with a small cup of acorn coffee as he leafed through his notes on the case, assessing his options. On the radio the Führer was storming through another speech, to which Hecht momentarily cocked an ear.

'I may not be a light of the church, a pulpiteer, but deep down I am a pious man,' proposed Hitler. Hecht reflected that it was an entirely appropriate allusion with regard to the Walder case.

Perhaps there was more from the Leader?

'I believe that whoever fights bravely in defence of the natural laws framed by God and never capitulates will never be deserted by the Lawgiver,' suggested Hitler, 'but will, in the end, receive the blessings of Providence.'

It was almost as if the Führer was speaking directly to him, though the Walders would likely receive the wrath of the Reich rather than Providence.

On the other side of the office, Kruger was oblivious, lounging in the battered armchair, once again reading *Signal.* There was an interesting article on Hanna Reitsch, the Führer's darling test pilot Hecht had pretended he was screwing. The piece featured, among other things, a heart-warming photograph of the aviatrix. The Iron Cross nestled proudly in her cleavage - she was wearing a dress rather than aviator gear - as Reitsch cuddled up to her elderly Austrian aristocrat mother. 'Do you think the Tommies have women bomber pilots?' asked Kruger, showing the magazine spread to Hecht, who glanced up momentarily from his studies. 'What?'

'You know, like we have Hanna Reitsch?'

'I have no idea, but if they did, perhaps you and I would have been hit by a bomb by now. The Russians even have women snipers, but please don't distract me with more of your literature.'

Hecht returned to his own, much more relevant, reading.

Kruger didn't like the idea of female combatants at all. 'It's fucking horrible, Sir, women killing people in war, not right - against nature.' Turning his attention back to *Signal*, Kruger snorted: 'Bloody animals.' Hecht put the files away in a drawer of his desk and locked it.

'Come on, Kruger, time for the threat of your fists to do the talking with pastor Walder.'

As they headed across the city in the Mercedes, blackout conditions ensured it was a painful affair. Kruger was hunched over the wheel blinking hard as he tried to make out obstacles in their way – assorted rubble, dead horses and even lumps of deceased humans, all were scattered along the route by the beast of war. With a violent lurch they ran over something, after which the car didn't steer right. Pulling in to the right-hand side of the road, Kruger got out to inspect the front underside.

Hecht climbed out also, for a breath of fresh air while he thought about tactics in his forthcoming encounter with Pastor Walder - and how to ensure nobody else died before the facts of the case had attained clarity. He leaned against the car bonnet, holding his hands out - they were trembling, making him smile.

Must be the Catholic upbringing?

Looking down the street, Hecht found the lights of a nearby bar blazing forth in blatant defiance of the blackout. Such disregard of rules actually made him feel much calmer. *Almost like normal times.*

Kruger, having found nothing stuck under the car - and no visible damage - was climbing behind the wheel when Hecht told him:

'Stay here. I'll be back in a minute.'

As he walked down the street to the bar, air raid sirens started to wail and anti-aircraft guns bashed away. Bombs were exploding in the distance, but getting nearer. Kruger was scared and climbed out of the car to shout after his boss: 'Sir! Shouldn't we press on to make the arrests!?'

Hecht ignored him.

The bar was empty except for a stout, balding fellow in a white open-necked shirt and black apron, with a butcher's ruddy-cheeked complexion and a dark, bushy monobrow. With a welcoming grin the barman waved Hecht in, having instantly recognised who, or rather what, his customer was.

The barman poured out a shot of peach schnapps, pushed it across the bar. Knocking it back, Hecht asked: 'Don't you close during an air raid?' With a defiant grin the barman replied: 'The Tommy artillery on the Somme didn't bother me the last time around, so I'm hardly going to let them see me running now, am I?

Hecht nodded, tapping his empty glass on the bar.

'I'll have another then.'

As it was poured, a stick of bombs fell close by, jiggling the bottles and glasses with a hellish tinkling.

Hecht knocked the schnapps back then flexed his hand in front of his face. *Steady as a rock.* An anxious-looking Kruger walked in and, judging by his sweaty brow, was not finding it easy to hold his nerve.

Hecht waved him over. 'Let's have one for the road Kruger.'

They sat down at a small table on the far side of the bar, with two more glasses of schnapps between them, Kruger twitching to each bomb thud. The barman brought over cups of black coffee, the surface of which trembled as another bomb exploded nearby.

Hecht reached into a pocket for some money.

The barman smiled and shook his head.

Hecht smiled back.

'Most generous.'

Kruger cast a nervous glance up at the ceiling. To calm him Hecht enquired: 'Where do you come from Kruger? You know, I don't think I've ever asked.'

Knocking his schnapps back, Kruger replied hoarsely: 'Leipzig, Sir.'

'Ah, a Saxon.'

'You're from er Munich?'

'Sort of…'

Hecht took a nip of his schnapps and then a sip of coffee.

'The real stuff - amazing.'

Kruger gulped his coffee down with no comment.

'How do you mean, "sort of", Sir?'

'Well, and don't shout out when I tell you, but I was born in England.'

Kruger looked genuinely amazed.

'Bloody hell…do the top brass know?'

Hecht laughed.

'Of course. I'm half German – my mother came from Munich. When I was ten my parents were divorced, due to my father's philandering and I came home to the Reich. I attended Freiburg and then, as you know became a lawyer, and a pretty shit one at that, rather too fond of wine, women and song.'

Kruger remained shocked, couldn't quite take it all in.

Hecht chuckled at the surprised look on his face.

'Why did *you* join the Gestapo, Kruger?'

The Kriminalassistent shrugged.

'Being a copper was good work, regular and steady and I have always enjoyed hunting down criminals – it's just sort of satisfying.'

Hecht tried to attract the attention of the barman to indicate more schnapps but the man was busy wiping down the bar at the far end.

'Forgive me for asking, but why did *you* join the Gestapo, Sir?'

Hecht drained the last of his coffee before replying.

'To prove myself I suppose – to make sure people realised I was a loyal German. I also like the work – poking my nose into peoples' business.'

A bomb went off a few blocks down, making their chairs vibrate. Kruger coughed nervously and ran a finger around the top of his shirt collar, as it if was suddenly much too tight.

Hecht waved Kruger in closer, so he could confide something. Kruger anxiously looked up at the ceiling when another explosion made the glass tulip light shades sing, but leaned in as ordered. 'This may shock you Kruger, but I have a half-brother who flies Lancaster bombers, and could be bombing us right now…'

Hecht had a talent for making Kruger forget his immediate worries and this revelation was like an electric shock, making him sit up with a stunned look. 'Surely not, Sir,' he suggested in a whisper.

Hecht chuckled again and nodded.

'Did you ever meet him?'

'No. I know what he does because, well…'

Hecht paused to see if he could catch the barman's eye again, but no luck, and so added rather too casually: 'We all have our sources, don't we?'

Kruger frowned and weighed up his next question very carefully before asking: 'You've *truly* never suffered from split loyalties, Sir?'

Hecht smiled and shook his head at the apparent stupidity of the question. 'On the contrary – an *excess* of zeal.'

Kruger had to admit he had never seen any doubt in Hecht's actions when they were hunting down undesirables.

'I do wonder, though, Kruger, if zeal sometimes leads us into rather over-elaborate solutions.'

Kruger frowned, asking: 'How do you mean, Sir?'

'You recall I went to the Ukraine without you in September 1941.'

'To arrest those Wehrmacht traitors who tried to blow up the Fuhrer's plane?'

'That's it. I was perfect for the job as I was acquainted with one of the conspirators and so we could get a lot more out of him during interrogation. Knew the swine at university. Well, after we'd rounded them up, the local Gestapo boys took me out to lunch where we drank too much alcohol. One of them said that we should go and take a look at some "essential war work" that was being carried out. He telephones the military governor, Brigadeführer Kurt Eberhard - who was truly showing excessive zeal - for permission. Anyway, we all climbed into a couple of cars, then headed for these woods. So out we get and trudge up this path – and by now we can hear gunfire…'

Hecht stopped, on finally catching the barman's eye, and held up two fingers. The bombing seemed to have paused, allowing Kruger to feel a little more at ease and he was curious to hear the rest of the story.

'A battle, Sir? Did you find a battle?'

Hecht shook his head and resumed the tale.

'No, but we came to this ravine…'

Kruger grinned.

'Your guns at the ready?' Kruger enquired eagerly.

'How many partisans did you kill?'

'I didn't kill any Kruger.'

The other man frowned.

The drinks came over.

Hecht smiled at the barman and handed him too many Reichsmarks.

'Keep the change.'

The barman grinned and went away.

Kruger, was most anxious to hear the punchline.

'Sir, the ravine, the partisans?'

Hecht corrected him.

'Not partisans as such. Jews…'

Kruger sat back in his chair eyebrows raised.

'Jewish terrorists!?'

Hecht took a sip of schnapps and shook his head.

'I don't think you understand.'

Kruger knocked his drink back and sat forward again, suggesting:

'They were hiding in the woods and it was a big round-up?'

Hecht shook his head again, took another sip before continuing.

'No, they had gone there voluntarily, or rather come out of hiding to be taken there...under certain duress I suppose. '

'Did they try to escape?'

'We Germans – so cunning and fucking clever – thought we would get around 6,000 or so when they saw posters promising them a better life than in the city, in the country. We got a lot more than that. The warning on the notices that failing to turn up as punishable by death might have been an added inducement. They had no idea what awaited them anyway.'

'That's a lot of Jews to process isn't it, Sir?'

'Yes, and too many in fact for the capabilities at hand.'

Hecht stopped, looked Kruger in the eye and, after downing the rest of his drink, leaned forward until their heads were almost touching. 'They required elimination,' he whispered, 'instant. On the spot.'

Kruger whistled.

'How?'

'A bullet in the head each.'

'That's a lot of fucking bullets.'

Hecht sighed deeply, sat back and continued, in a low voice, so only he and Kruger could hear. 'Yes, more than 33,000 Jews cleansed in two days, and time consuming, wasteful of resources. Very upsetting for some of those pulling the triggers who got blood and brains all over their uniforms.'

Kruger's eyes widened at the image of spoiled uniforms in his head.

'That's not good.'

Hecht gave a resigned sigh and carried on.

'They made the Jews undress – I was astonished by how meekly they complied – and led them down into the bottom of the ravine and grabbed, pushed down to lie on top of the already dead…and shot.' Kruger's face took on a strange aspect – Hecht couldn't tell if he was grinning with delight or horror. His crude features were sometimes hard to read.

'How many did *you* kill, Sir?'

Hecht looked down, studying how his empty shot glass refracted the light as he turned it in his hand – magnifying his fingers, reminding him of that time in the Prague mirror maze with Martin.

He smiled sadly, studying his assistant's expectant face, but without seeing him, and lost in thought.

Hitler's Germany was a gigantic mirror maze.

Frowning, Kruger pressed Hecht for a reply.

'How many did you kill?'

'None.'

Kruger nodded, unsure what to make of *that* lack of zeal, again nervously running a finger around his collar. He ventured hesitantly:

'Didn't they suspect you of lacking courage?

'No, not really,' said Hecht, meeting Kruger's gaze steadily, pondering the question in silence for a few seconds before going on. 'I think lots of people thought it was distasteful. I was outraged by the stupidity of it. And the English half of me - my sense of fair play - was appalled by how mean it was.'

'Mean?'

'Yes, taking their suitcases, making them take off their spectacles and shoes and coats, stripped naked and led to their doom…'

Hecht fell silent, again turning the shot glass over in his hand, staring at the viscous film of residual schnapps glistening on its interior. Even Kruger was lost for words, but, before he could make some crude comment to hide his discomfort, Hecht carried on.

'And you know what, Kruger, in some cases – with some of the corpses on the top layer - those fuckers in the cleansing teams were pulling out the gold teeth using plyers. All for recycling, for use elsewhere, you know…but still, a bit mean. Kill them, but really? Steal their possessions…even their teeth?'

'Sir, be careful,' Kruger hissed, looking around to make sure they were not being watched from a dark corner of the bar.

Hecht laughed harshly and gave him a hard stare.

Was Kruger taking the piss or being serious?

Hecht gave an exasperated sigh.

'I realize that they were just rats who had to be eliminated.

It was just the way it was done so inefficiently.'

Kruger nodded, knocked the dregs of his drink back.

'That was just the start of it,' Hecht went on, 'and soon our old friends the gypsies and assorted other civilian renegades were added to the pile, or so I hear. Himmler later agreed with my analysis that it was most poorly done.'

Kruger flinched at a bomb dropping nearby but he was still awestruck by Hecht's namedropping.

'*You met* Himmler?'

Hecht nodded.

'I made an oral report to him. It's not the sort of thing for which he has the stomach. After all, he chucked his guts up on going to see some of our other early attempts at special treatment. So, now we handle everything so much better, though I can't help thinking the drive for efficiency will hang us all.'

Kruger's eyes flickered in fear as the shock wave from a stick of bombs made the whole bar sway and lights flicker on and off.

'One day maybe I'll make sure of it,' Hecht sighed.

This utterance befuddled Kruger even further.

'Sir? How do you mean?'

'Never mind, come on let's go.'

They got up and weaved their way between the tables, Hecht

waving farewell to the barman. As they walked back to the Mercedes, bombs clumped down the street behind them, like a great big clumsy giant's footsteps – shattering buildings left, then right as they came on. Hecht didn't seem to notice, but Kruger glanced over his shoulder and his courage shrivelled.

They reached the car, Kruger digging frantically in his pockets for the keys. Hecht, meanwhile, pulled his cigarillo tin out, flipping it open to find a solitary cigar, which he hesitated to smoke, but shrugged and decided 'it's now or never.'

A bomb hit the bar, demolishing it in a huge eruption of smoke, dust and leaping flames - splintered wood, bricks and glass hurled in all directions, the hammer blow presumably also obliterating the bartender. Dust swept over the Gestapo men and their car. Kruger dropped the keys, yelping as he kneeled down to retrieve them from under the Mercedes – cursing, retching and swearing like a trooper as he reached blindly in, fingertips scrabbling, not quite touching them.

Coughing from the dust – *which, so he reflected, presumably contained tiny fragments of the bartender?* – Hecht spat out the cigar, laughing and shaking his head. 'The Tommies got you this time my friend,' he observed with a cackle.

A bomb hit the rear of the apartment building that loomed over the car and detonated with a deep, throaty rumble, yet seemed not to have harmed it.

Hecht leaned against the Mercedes, apparently lost in thought, staring down at his filthy shoes.

Finally getting the keys, Kruger got to his feet. Grinning, he jangled them triumphantly. Relief turned to speechless horror as, looking up, he saw the building beginning to topple over. He realised that it was one of the Judenhäuser – squalid over-populated buildings specially assigned to house Jews created after the Nazis came to power. He had raided it a few times to take them away, though they were all surely gone a long time ago.

On hearing the gathering thunder of the collapsing façade as it swooped down to smite them, Hecht lifted his tired, red-rimmed eyes to confront his demise without fear. The Kriminalinspektor's last words came in a hoarse, emotional whisper: 'Fee-fi-fo-fum.'

Martin Walder's parents and the boy would, after all, receive the blessings of Providence.

* * *

Glashirfryn fell silent for a moment and, through the office window, the glow from the streetlights below starkly lit up his pale face, its brow furrowed and with the black satin eye patch shining.

'Of all the creatures that breathe and move upon the earth, nothing is bred that is weaker than man,' Glashirfryn remarked with a regretful smile.

Mystified, Eric enquired: 'Pardon, Sir?'

Glashirfryn shook his head, dismissing whatever he was pondering.

'Nothing, captain…just something from Pope's translation of *The Odyssey*.'

'Never read it.'

The naval intelligence officer swivelled his chair back to the desk, switched on the lamp and reached into the long drawer under its lip, pulling out a blank sheet of paper.

He scrawled something on it, adding his signature at the bottom, then held it out to Eric, explaining: 'Get your boss to write to the military intelligence registry in London with my authority and ask for the current address of Frau Walder and the boy – sadly I can't release it direct… in fact I don't know it – but they will yield it if I order it to be so.'

Eric took it, nodding, folding the sheet in half and, with a deep frown on his face, asking Glashirfryn: 'You just said, Frau Walder and the boy, Sir.'

Looking perplexed, Glasirfryn enquired: 'Did I?'

'Yes. No mention of the pastor.'

'Didn't I?'

'Because?' Eric enquired.

'I am afraid the pastor Walder was killed, mid-sermon in his pulpit, when a Russian Katyusha rocket came right through the rose window of the church. Or so I've been told.'

Feeling upset, as he'd come to admire Jonathan as the tale unfolded, Eric nodded but said nothing. 'Anyway,' said Glashirfryn, 'I hope you succeed in finding Elsa and David.'

Using the walking stick to rise, Glashirfryn held out his right hand. As he got to his feet and put his cap on Eric observed with a smile: 'Recalling even half the details would be entirely beyond me.'

Glashirfryn gave a humourless smile, the scar under his eye patch seeming to glow a little with embarrassment.

'Goodnight Captain Wise.'

8

SPENDLOVE SUBMITTED a request for the address of Martin's mother and the boy to London, but warned Eric such things took time.

In the meantime, he should return to Graz and shut down that end of the S.G operation before heading back to Blighty for some long overdue leave.

Therefore, finally, Eric headed back to Plymouth, finding himself living at Raglan Barracks; still unable to be at home with his mother in Turnchapel, though she was overjoyed to see him occasionally for afternoon tea.

It tore Eric apart when he left her all teary-eyed at the garden gate, yet he simply couldn't go back there. He dare not tell her about meeting the undead Bert, even though Eric was often tempted to burst his mum's bubble when she lamented *her poor lost boy*.

As for Katherine, spending time with her was a different matter – every minute was wonderful, though even with her influence taking the edge off him, Eric recognised he was generally less easy-going and more restless.

She had gone back home earlier and he wrote regularly to her from Austria. Once Eric also returned they took things slowly and steadily, this time romance blossoming without Eric getting in a brawl and ending up in jail, which had to be an improvement.

One day Katherine suggested they celebrate the onset of spring by taking the train to Totnes for a walk out of town. She put on one of his Army shirts, her shorts and walking boots.

'Mighty fine' she looked, as his potato picking American friend Cyrus might have said. Eric donned his field uniform and army boots.

There was, of course, the obligatory picnic basket containing a flask of tea and enamel mugs, corned beef sandwiches wrapped in greaseproof paper and a couple of apples, along with a small tartan rug to sit on.

They also stuffed some light raincoats – along with a headscarf for her and beret for him – into a backpack. You never could trust the English weather, particularly in April.

The path she had in mind ran parallel to the railway line, starting just outside the station, deviating into a field at the foot of a steep hill topped with a clump of trees.

They started to scramble up the slope, Eric taking the wicker picnic basket, but he slipped and fell. Cursing, divesting himself of the backpack, he left her halfway up and went off to retrieve the basket from where it had rolled to, scattering its contents after the buckle snapped.

Slipping again at the bottom, he fell onto his backside. Katherine hid her mouth behind her hands to repress her hilarity, as she felt it might serve only to enrage him further.

Eric shook his fist at the heavens as a rain shower came piling in. He gathered up the picnic bits – muddy, mangled sandwiches, bruised apples, the flask with its silvered glass inner sleeve shattered, and besmirched white enamel army mugs - put them in the basket and climbed back up the hill. She dug into the backpack for her headscarf, laughing openly now but he did not find it at all funny. They helped each other up to the summit, him still grumbling and her giggling.

Finally, they made it to the trees, where Katherine encouraged him to give her a cuddle to warm up as raindrops dripped on them from the branches. Eric, dumped the soiled basket, calmed down and laughed - just a little - at his own stupidity, then kissed the rain off her cheeks. She closed her eyes in bliss. 'A fine picnic this has been,' he observed with a sigh.

'Never mind,' she beamed, 'it's been fun!'

He paused, drinking in her lovely face and then kissed her on the lips.

His heart exploded with joy. Katherine was overwhelmed, too, after all they had come through, *with the war and all that.*

They kissed again.

The rain stopped, he picked the flaming picnic basket up, while she took the backpack and they began to walk back down the hill, assisting each other and going very carefully, mindful of the slippery grass.

Two swans flew over, carving a graceful arc, stark white against a patch of blue amid the fluffy clouds. Katherine pointed and cried out: 'They mate for life, swans do!'

'Do they now?' he enquired with a teasing smile.

She blushed, laughed and they ran down the rest of the hill, slipping and sliding but, somehow, holding each other up.

* * *

Waiting on the Totnes station platform for the train back to Plymouth, Eric studied the Milk Marketing Board depot opposite. Stainless steel blue-liveried tank wagons were pulled in, emblazoned with 'EXPRESS DAIRY – MILK FOR LONDON'. A lorry was parked alongside one of the wagons, with a chain of men offloading churns and pouring their contents into the top of a tank. 'Penny for them,' Katherine asked, putting a hand on his knee, bringing his attention back to her on the bench beside him.

'Not much to report – except a fascination for the milk train opposite.'

'Wondered if you were thinking about the war? Sometimes you drift off elsewhere and into enigmatic silence.'

The turn of phrase made him smile.

'Ah, well…sorry'.

She touched his cheek, kissed him lightly on the lips.

He turned his head away, suddenly emotional, not wanting her to see his eyes filling up.

'It's funny, at the time you think that it will never end,' he observed, 'but then it does and once you are out of it – back here in England – it's almost as if it never happened…you end up wondering if you dreamed it all.'

He looked around at her and she nodded.

'One long nightmare,' Katherine acknowledged, 'but thankfully now over.'

He pulled her into an embrace and then they settled back on the bench, both staring at the milk wagon, but their minds occupied by the recent past. 'The worst time was your rejection of me,' she observed, not bitterly, more matter of fact, but he felt terribly guilty.

'It was wrong of me.'

She squeezed his hand.

'But I came to understand. You were trying to avoid breaking my heart.' Katherine gave a little laugh, laced with a reproach.

'But did it anyway,' he conceded sheepishly.

Eric sighed, took his hand out of hers, crinkled his brow and stared down at his boots, feeling irritated at being reminded.

'It was cruel,' he sighed, 'but intended to be kind. I couldn't cope with being a twisted fool like Martin Walder – holding onto the crazy dream of love when I could be killed.'

Katherine suddenly looked very sombre.

'Eric, you could *never* be like that war criminal.''

She turned to him, put a hand on his forearm and he looked at her, finding she was a bit teary, so reached into a pocket and gave her his handkerchief. 'You're always ready with a hankie,' she sniffed. 'But Eric I do understand - even though I had my share of things to deal with.'

'Yes, and I was stupidly forgetting that, while what you did on that death march investigation was…'

'And my girls too.'

'Of course – all of you were heroic and it took real guts.'

'I never doubted you'd do the right thing, by those poor people the Nazis killed,' she said, 'while there was no debt of honour owed to Martin Walder - not somebody who was every bit as vile as the bandits he killed in the woods. Yet trying to save his mother and the boy from the beastly Russians is a good thing.' As she said this a station guard was coming across the bridge from the main ticket office on the other side of the tracks - a sign their train was imminent.

Appreciating Katherine's faith in him, Eric gave her a hug as it puffed into view from the direction of Newton Abbot.

'Alright me 'andsomes - all aboard for Plymouth!' the station guard yelled, in a broad Devonian burr, grinning at the couple who were the sole occupants of the platform. With a wink and an even broader grin, he added: 'No time for cozzyin' up moi luvvers!' They stood up, exchanging slightly embarrassed smiles and boarded the train home.

9

ERIC REVEALED via a telephone call to Spendlove in Berlin that Commander Glashifryn's note giving authority for the address of Martin's mother and the boy to be released had done the trick.

If there was something decent to be extracted from the whole affair, then it was ensuring they were safe - even bringing them to England, and Eric suggested he would give them a home, at least temporarily.

He even offered to help out in Berlin, but Spendlove said not to worry – this was, after all, a mission well matched to a man of his resources and cheek. *It would all be done in two shakes of a lamb's tail. Just send him the address where Frau Walder and lad were and he'd pop over and pick them up.*

And so, a few days later Spendlove grabbed a general-purpose S.G. brute named Sgt Brendan O'Higgins, a former Army boxing champ – useful in case things did cut up rough with the Soviets - who drove them in Spendlove's Humber Super Snipe staff car into the East.

By then the Spendlove Group were based in a half-ruined, but rather grand building on the Eberstrasse, not far from the bedraggled and battered Brandenburg Gate, which retained a downtrodden majesty though in places whole chunks had been chewed out of it. The horses pulling the chariot atop the gate had been decapitated, while the goddess Victoria was similarly violated.

Spendlove took all this in from the back seat as the Humber waited in a line of traffic passing into the Soviet sector - held up by 'the usual checkpoint nonsense,' he thought.

With the Russians satisfied by appropriate British Control Commission authorisation papers, O'Higgins swung the Humber around the side of the Gate, for nobody was allowed to actually pass through it.

With O'Higgins stepping up the speed, the Humber swept past the now burned out Hotel Adlon. A red hammer and sickle flag – tattered and with ragged holes in it – still hung from the window where triumphant Russian soldiers had fixed it as the city fell. 'About time they took down that stuff,' mused Spendlove, 'or would the Russians bang on about their so-called "Great Patriotic War" forever?'

The hotel had survived the battle almost intact, without major damage from artillery, with its ornate and luxurious rooms serving as a German military field hospital in the final days of the struggle. Unfortunately, after its surrender, a group of drunken Russian soldiers – taking a break from pillaging and raping to plunder the Adlon's wine cellars – started a fire, which soon ran out of control. Now the majority of the once palatial hotel was a blackened shell, which suited the Soviets as it was a suitable monument to the defeat of the fascists.

As the Humber skirted around the Adlon, O'Higgins had to turn the wheel smartly to avoid colliding with a huge portrait of Stalin in his Marshal of the Soviet Union uniform. This all-seeing monstrosity was mounted in the middle of the road, within a gigantic frame flanked by Doric columns, which Spendlove felt was 'not exactly proletarian.'

O'Higgins accelerated away down the broad Unter den Linden, between massive mounds of rubble. Human chains were passing buckets of bricks down from their summits and at the bottom others were cleaning them up, in order to rebuild the shattered city. The

Soviets were now trying to create a new communist state out of occupied eastern Germany, including their sector of Berlin; so raping the local women was no longer permitted and anything worth looting was long gone. Bored Russian sentries dreaming of sweethearts back home stood idly by while the German women worked, their menfolk dead, captured and starved or frozen to death when being marched to Siberian prison camps. Or, if they were lucky, still held by the Western allies.

Some men were simply missing. Either way it was women such as these - whom Spendlove glimpsed through his car window as it sped by - who now picked up the pieces of a shattered Germany.

* * *

The Humber followed a more or less direct route to Immanuelkirchstrasse, making no effort to shake off a Soviet shadowing team in a GAZ trailing close behind.

Via contacts in the Soviet sector of Berlin, Spendlove had sent word for Elsa and the boy David, now a gangly 15-year-old, to be ready, with the minimum baggage for travel. It had been easy to persuade them to leave their current digs, and indeed the misery of a divided Germany, where they were barely existing under oppressive communist rule that added insult to horrors inflicted by fascism.

Spendlove explained that they had been selected by the Allied authorities for resettlement in England.

The widow Walder and David were living in a grim four storey tenement, whose frontage had bare brick work showing through here and there where the plaster had been torn off by heavy calibre machine gun bullets. They were in an apartment on the ground floor, to the left of the main entrance and Spendlove went a-knocking on a window, the one with 'Kaffee' painted on the frontage above.

O'Higgins followed on behind to carry the luggage, such as it might be. After a curtain twitch and the pale flash of someone taking a quick look, out Frau Walder and the boy came, carrying a couple of small, carboard suitcases that had seen better days.

As they all went across the road, the GAZ pulled up and three burly Russians in green uniforms - with blue piped MGB collars and epaulettes along with distinctive blue-topped peaked caps - clambered out. Spendlove told O'Higgins: 'Escort the VIPs to the Humber while I have a word with these fellows.'

Watching from the back seat of the Humber, David saw the British officer go straight up to the Russians and start talking. As they gathered around - all towering over him – Spendlove showed them some papers. These were scrutinised by the tallest Russian, who suddenly stiffened and saluted the British officer, yelling at his comrades to return to their vehicle. The GAZ pulled away at speed, the soldier in the passenger seat leaning out the side, gesturing for the Humber to follow on.

Spendlove tumbled into the front passenger seat of the staff car, chortling as he stuffed the paperwork inside his battle dress blouse.

'That was fun!' he declared.

The Humber received an escort all the way to the Brandenburg Gate where the occupants of the GAZ climbed out, lined up and delivered a perfect set of salutes as the British staff car sped by. Spendlove couldn't stop guffawing, much to the consternation of the others in the Humber who feared he might explode.

* * *

Elsa and David were taken to Templehof airfield, to board a US Air Force aircraft for a flight to Paris. From there they took a train to Brest and would board a passenger-cargo ship sailing from Brittany to Plymouth. Spendlove, meanwhile, put a telephone call through to Raglan Barracks to let Eric know they were on their way.

'How on earth did you manage it so quickly?' Eric enquired during the chat.

'Just drove over in me staff car,' Spendlove explained light-heartedly, 'and picked them up. Some Ivans tailed us and asked what the hell we were doing. I showed them my special authorization from Marshal Stalin to take the woman and the boy away to exile in the West.'

'Where did you get that from!?'

'Well, I just typed it up myself,' Spendlove revealed, his voice dripping with his own cleverness, 'using a special Cyrillic typewriter we have here – and made up Stalin's signature.'

'I didn't even know you knew Russian.'

'Tell a Tovarish what to do and he's happy – tell him Stalin has ordered it, he poohs his long johns and can't do enough to help you. It was absolutely thunder-fucking wonderful – they gave us an escort all the way to the Brandenburg Gate.'

Eric observed that Spendlove had surpassed himself.

Spendlove thought so too, adding: 'They've been told your name, and given all the right paperwork, but not the exact reason why you are their host. You can deal with that in your own sweet way.'

* * *

Three days later Eric parked a Ford Anglia borrowed from the Raglan motor pool on the Hoe foreshore road to await the ship's arrival from France. It would soon make its way through the deep channel and around to Millbay Docks.

Eric was enchanted by the scene – the hot sun making the gently undulating surface of the Sound shimmer; fishing boats with seagulls dipping in their wake and yachts criss-crossing; the occasional warship carving through them, its klaxon blaring and provoking sudden darts to port and starboard by the smaller craft to get out of His Majesty's Ship's way.

Eric even went and bought himself an ice cream cone from a van parked nearby, making him later than he should have been but it was only a short drive around to Millbay.

By the time he got there people were streaming off the ship and through passport control. Leaving the Anglia by the rebuilt Millbay railway station - smiling at the memory of how he'd told the two air raid wardens off outside it during the blitz - Eric walked over to the terminal building. Scanning over the heads of the throng, he could not at first see Elsa and David. And then he spotted what had to be them going by a description Spendlove provided during the phone discussion.

They stood out in their drab clothes and starved appearance amid all the jolly returning English holidaymakers in their Sunday bests. They were hanging on tightly - both to each other and a pair of small cardboard suitcases. Buffeted by the sea of people around them, Elsa looked anxious and the boy wary.

Taking his beret off – Eric had decided to wear uniform to stand out – he waved it and shouted their names, battling his way towards them.

Then they spotted him and both grinned in relief.

Eric introduced himself in German while Elsa and David said hello and gave him their names in perfect English – the boy had proved to have a flair for linguistics and she had enjoyed teaching him a second language. *It would perhaps one day become his first.* Eric took the cases and told them to follow him over to the car so they could head for the cottage that, with Katherine's help, he'd rented on the edge of Dartmoor.

* * *

Eric drove them through the city centre and for Elsa and David, it was a shocking and familiar sight. On all sides they were confronted with a wasteland. Here and there one or two buildings still stood, but otherwise Plymouth's historic heart had been flattened.

Elsa was appalled.

'It's as terrible as Berlin.'

'Perhaps not,' Eric observed, 'but we did get it bad.'

Elsa was suddenly very anxious.

'Everyone will hate us.'

'No, they won't,' he reassured her, 'what's done is done.'

David, with his face pressed against a back seat window asked:

'Will we be living in the ruins again?'

'No,' laughed Eric. 'Where you are to live is in the countryside. There was no bombing there.'

'Is it green?' the boy enquired.

'Yes.'

'And pleasant?'

'We think so.'

David smiled broadly, something Elsa had seldom, if ever, seen the boy do. She beamed with joy and knew that, at last, their long nightmare was over. As the car paused at a road junction by the ruined church of Charles Cross, David asked: 'Is this still like the song says "a land of hope and glory"?' Looking back from the front passenger seat, Elsa laughed and told him off: 'You and your questions David!'

Eric smiled, putting the car into gear and moving off again.

'Hope, yes,' he decided to tell David. 'Glory? No. Just glad it's all over.'

EPILOGUE

A FEW WEEKS after Elsa and David arrived in England, a special Army courier delivered a buff envelope, marked 'CLASSIFIED' to the Dartmoor cottage. A clerk working in the Berlin office rang on the new phone Spendlove had ordered installed so Eric could be contacted any time day or night. Eric was advised of an imminent arrival by motorbike that morning.

Shutting himself in the front parlour, tearing the envelope open, Eric found four sheets of A4 paper clipped together – a carbon copy of a closely typed report marked 'MOST SECRET' and from the London secret service archives, or so it seemed.

FROM: COLONEL CHARLES MORGAN, RM,
HEAD OF COUNTER-INTELLIGENCE DIVISION, ADMIRALTY.

TO: ADMIRAL SIR GEORGE FITZGIBBONS, SECURITY SERVICES DIRECTORATE GENERAL.

22 July 1946

This is a briefing note to advise you on the status of 'Agent Heinrich', the deep cover operative we placed within the Gestapo during the recent conflict with Germany.

As you were previously advised he initially had some success. He joined the British security service in the early 1930s, while on an extended holiday from Freiburg University to visit his father in Wales, the late steel magnet Sir Henry Pike.

'Heinrich' was given an accelerated course of instruction at the Naval College in Dartmouth, under an assumed identity, to ensure he was of appropriate character and physical fitness as well as personal discipline. This was followed by requisite training during subsequent leave in Britain, in the appropriate crafts necessary for espionage work.

He was an ideal recruit. The rise of the Nazis had outraged his sensibilities of fair play and justice, and he always had an inclination to favour his father's side of the family, despite being sent to live with his mother in Germany.

'Heinrich's' chosen German name of Alois was merely the use of his given forename, Louis, with a translation of his Pike surname into 'Hecht'.

There was no need for him to assume a new name or back story as it would have been easily rumbled anyway, so best keep to a measure of truth, the best cover all.

He continued to feed us excellent intelligence on the activities of the German secret services and Gestapo after joining the organization, having deliberately failed in his civilian law practice.

As you are aware, sometimes our agents have to maintain their covers by indulging in activities that would never be permitted otherwise, certainly veering into the criminal by our standards. The strain on 'Heinrich' was considerable, but through nearly six years of war he was able to walk the tightrope of doing just enough to convince his superiors that he was a faithful servant of the Third Reich.

He was under suspicion more than once, but successfully threw off his accusers. After early 1942, Heinrich was consigned to second tier work and not given any investigations of a high-level nature. On the pretence of working late in the Gestapo Headquarters he was still able to retrieve much useful intelligence for us.

A crucial reason for him being consigned to the second tier was that after a trip to Kiev in September 1941 Heinrich showed signs of squeamishness, having been witness to the Babi Yar massacre, which he wisely did not participate in, not even for the benefit of his cover. His reluctance to take part was noted in Berlin. You will be aware that 'Heinrich' reported back to us both on the Babi Yar event and also other details on trains to Poland he suspected were carrying people for liquidation at special camps. You will also be aware that, at the time, it was felt among the higher echelons on our side that it was far better to win the war and then address that particular problem. Besides we had no definitive documentary proof – or at least any that we could share without destroying our intelligence networks in enemy occupied territory.

'Heinrich' considered that we should have made a greater effort to expose what the Nazis were doing. He took considerable risks to get this information to us. I believe it was the strain of working deep inside the regime - maintaining his cover by carrying out work he found deeply distasteful - combined with his disillusion at our failure to take serious action on the point of the liquidation camps, that more or less meant he was a spent agent by July 1944 (around the time of the failed attempt to kill Hitler with a bomb).

Having given no direct or even indirect assistance to the plotters, 'Heinrich' was not likely to be arrested. However, the strain reached new levels and he found the case of the pastor Jonathan Walder, who saved a young Jewish boy from execution by hiding him, to be a significant burden. As he later told debriefers, he played out the investigation for as long as possible, to see if it would resolve itself without a need for him to become involved in drastic action on behalf of his Nazi superiors. Arguably this was an error, raising the risk of him being exposed for tardiness in the investigation, and the fate of a single Jewish boy and his saviours was such a minor affair.

'Heinrich' lost sight of the fact that sometimes there have to be small sacrifices for the greater good. He allowed his concern for the pastor and the boy, indeed the entire Walder family to endanger his cover – he even arranged for their son, the war criminal Martin Walder to be sent to work at a labour camp in Hungary rather than to a penal battalion. This was further proof that he, 'Heinrich', was spent – too emotionally engaged.

In the end events caught up with 'Heinrich', and he was almost killed when a stick of bombs from an RAF bomber demolished a street he was in. His assistant in the Gestapo was killed, but, showing amazing resilience, despite losing the sight of an eye and a seriously injured leg, 'Heinrich' managed to extract himself from the rubble. This was mainly due to the fact that his crushed car saved him from more serious injury and he was able to crawl away, and to make contact with one of our Berlin organisations.

> Patched up enough to make it out of the country, we smuggled him to Sweden, where, after recovering sufficiently, he was brought to England via covert means. 'Heinrich' spent the rest of the war recovering physically and mentally.
>
> He is at the moment on a long leave of absence, we believe sailing a yacht somewhere in waters of the Outer Hebrides. He has not checked in for some time and there is some doubt that he may return to the Service. I firmly believe that with appropriate persuasion, and proper training the former 'Agent Heinrich', may yet prove useful to his country, possibly running our own agents under Admiralty cover in Berlin?
>
> This would have to be subject to passing the usual tests to ensure he is mentally and physically robust enough, as well as sound in his political views. With the former Prime Minister's recent speech about an Iron Curtain descending from the Baltic to the Adriatic, I would suggest we may need men like Lieutenant Commander Louis Pike, to use his actual rank and name. I therefore earnestly propose that we seek him out at the appropriate time, in the right fashion, and bring him back into the fold. Though, in times such as these, I feel we are more in need of wolves than sheep.

Spendlove had scrawled in a space at the bottom of the last sheet: 'Agent "Heinrich" did come back to the fold – and you met him in

Berlin, under his new cover as an Allied powers administration officer. How about that?'

Commander Henry Glashirfryn!?

Eric was so stunned he had to sit down on the arm of a chair, his head spinning. This was how the naval intelligence officer knew so much about the Walders! He was 'Heinrich'? Aka Hecht the Gestapo investigator?

Photographic memory be damned. The man had lived it.

Spendlove had also written:

'I thought you had a right to know - don't tell anyone else!
BURN AFTER READING.'

Eric kneeled down by the fireplace, placing the envelope and the sheets of paper in the grate, striking a match to set them alight. After watching the flames consume and turn the papers into ashes. Eric used a poker to ensure every last trace was gone.

* * *

— Martin's Eyes —

AUTHOR'S NOTE

In the late 1990s I co-devised a show called *Wine Hunt* that was eventually broadcast by Channel 4 on UK television.

At around the same time I was writing a prospective movie script after spending a train journey from Plymouth to Hemel Hempstead seeing if I could plot it in a notebook.

Once I was happy with a draft of *Martin's Eyes*, the movie, I showed it to a young agent at the London talent agency representing me for *Wine Hunt*. He loved it. However, he suggested that a narrative entirely revolving around a German warrior, who had himself committed war crimes, and was trying to save his parents from the Gestapo, might not be an easy sell.

He was right of course but that was the point. A few years earlier, in 1995, I had for a newspaper interviewed at length a retired senior police detective who in the late 1940s hunted down Nazi war criminals in Austria. The same year I interviewed other WW2 veterans who suffered terribly due to the war crimes of their captors while prisoners of the Japanese.

Aside from questioning those men and writing about their experiences, I asked them: what kind of people committed such foul deeds?

It was their insights that inspired me to construct a narrative via the eyes of a war criminal as a means to study the human condition. A cautionary tale, if you like, of how ordinary people sometimes did very bad things and how others found courage against the odds when confronted with evil, or were its victims.

So that's how we got the German side. I had already started to novelise the script when, in about 2012, I suggested to my literary agent Tim Bates that I had a work of fiction on the go. But it had a German problem, so to speak. He suggested putting a British protagonist in the story. And so, Eric Wise was born, opening up many new possibilities for the story, and increasing the players in the drama.

It is of course historical fiction, set within a WW2 world of my creation peopled mainly by characters and events I made up - not only inspired by my long chats with war veterans, but also places I have visited, and things I learned or absorbed in those locales.

I have also learned a great deal from various military experts I consulted not least about the Battle for Monte Cassino and the art of sniping. This was allied with my own deep research, and things I did as a young cadet - range shooting and drilling with WW2 British rifles and acquiring field skills. Some things you never forget!

I would like to thank all of those who helped me during the long journey from scribbling notes during a train ride home to Hemel to beta reading my evolving epic yarn. I very much remain in your debt.

And I would like to also thank those who shared my research trips. Even if we did not at the time realise those adventures would provide material for this story - usually they were journalistic assignments unrelated to WW2 history.

I cannot conclude without expressing my eternal gratitude to Stuart Leasor for seeing the potential in *Martin's Eyes* and publishing it.

Last, but very much not least, I must express my love and admiration for my wife Lindsey and sons Robert and James, for lasting the distance and being so incredibly supportive.

Iain Ballantyne,
March 2026.